THE SECRET LIFE OF MARY WHITE

Darkness Into Light

THE SECRET LIFE OF MARY WHITE

Darkness Into Light

A novel by

LENAYE MARSTEN

For Mary's family and descendants
and to all those with the courage to speak their truth

For my father,
the poet and novelist Robert Siegel

And for Lewis,
always a faithful protector

Contents

An April Evening

The Counting House Museum sits on the bank of the Salmon Falls River in South Berwick, Maine. A quaint brick relic mourning its early days—or so I imagined as I followed the Historical Society volunteer out of the damp twilight, into the building's main hall. The smell of musty artifacts and furniture polish greeted me. The library lights flickered on overhead, revealing metal shelves lined with an assortment of mismatched books. At one end of the room, an exhibit of artifacts from a local seventeenth-century archaeological dig was on display.

I'd recently moved back to southern Maine, where I'd lived briefly in the years before my marriage and two children. It is a region close to both mountains and sea, and home to a number of my early New England ancestors. My plan was to research and write about one of them, William Thompson, as interesting information about his origins had recently come to light. I felt inexplicably drawn to learn more about his life, even though he was by no means the most illustrious of my forebears.

I stood paging through records and taking notes. Rain poured down against the windows, but inside the small brick building it felt cozy and intimate.

Until the volunteer handed me another open book.

"Here, I've found something unusual on the family."

As I read and reread the passage she handed me, my stomach pushed my heart into my throat. My viscera contracted with intense emotion that my conscious mind could not at all understand.

Breathe, I told myself, trying to keep a calm exterior.

The record was not particularly earthshaking by modern-day standards. It looked like my ancestor's wife had birthed a child out of wedlock—certainly not the end of the world for us. Why, then, did this affect me so strongly? The strangest thing about my reaction, as incomprehensible as it seemed, was that I somehow *knew* the record was a lie.

From that moment on, I had to learn the truth about Mary White, my great-grandmother ten times removed.

My suspicions were confirmed during a metaphysical reading several months later.

"The record is a lie," the psychic told me, "and there is more than one lie written in the records about the family."

Shivers ran through my body.

"You have set it up perfectly to heal Mary's experience," she explained. "Mary needs a voice, and you are here to give her one."

Dreams began to come back to me. Dreams that I had dreamt years earlier, seen through the eyes of a seventeenth-century girl and woman. A memory of another life—last consciously recalled at the age of four—and a disturbing nightmare I'd had when I was six, both made perfect sense to me now.

Mary White. The name felt like a coat of paint, beneath other coats of differing colors and thicknesses, chips and cracks exposing it to view once again.

I began to research Mary. Where the records fell short, unconventional modes of discovery filled in the missing pieces. To write Mary's story became my passion and was nothing short of an adventure as I watched it all fall into place like a living jigsaw puzzle. A story that has waited lifetimes to be told. One that expanded my mind and heart and, in the end, astounded me with a special gift.

PART I

-- 1 --

Devon, England, 1637

Mary stood apart from the crowd, a transfixed expression upon her small eight-year-old face. The parishioners were all gathered in the churchyard after the morning service while the other children played their games. Mary's interest lay elsewhere. Like a silky seed wafting on a gentle breeze, she disappeared around the corner of St. Peter's. Behind the ancient stone church where things grew wild, and the scent of earth and daffodils hung thick and intoxicating. Many townsfolk were afraid of the back-garden graves.

Mary pushed through an overgrown hedge that surrounded a mausoleum. A stone cistern rose up out of its center. Sitting upon the edge of its flat smooth surface, she relaxed, her fingers absently tracing the remains of an inscription long worn away. She could hear the distant laughter of the other children. Folding back her lace cap she tilted her face to the sun, squinting her eyes to watch her eyelashes sparkle blue. It felt good to be alone. Then she spread out her taffeta petticoat like a fan; its color matched the mossy undergrowth almost exactly. She was, after all, the queen of the garden.

A flock of wrens flew to the cistern, and Mary reached out her hand. One of the birds hopped onto her finger.

"You're beautiful, little one," she said, bringing the creature closer. Its shiny black eyes looked back at her fearlessly. "Do you know who I am?"

The bird flew up and hovered over her head.

A giggle escaped her lips. She jumped to her feet with delight, dancing until, with a sharp note of alarm, the entire flock took refuge in the evergreens. To her consternation, part of the hedge began to move, and a woman's head appeared over the top. Mary's stomach tensed.

"Ye all alone?" the miller's wife asked, her eyes narrowing. "I heard ye pratin' with some 'n." The woman looked around and, seeing no one else present, fixed Mary with an accusing gaze.

"'Twas just a bird," Mary replied, regretting her words immediately as the woman's expression hardened.

"*Not* on God's consecrated ground ye do!" the miller's wife spat. "I've got me *eye* on you, Mary White—know that all o' us do, the *good* Christian people of this town, and we'll have none of *your* business. Come here now—out w'ye, or I'll box thy ears!"

A man's voice sounded behind her. "What th' devil ye got there, Moll? Not the wench wi' the eyes? That 'un needs a sound thrashing. Better yet, the ducking stool."

Mary didn't wait to hear more. She was off in a heartbeat, and she could run when necessary. Out of St. Peter's gardens, past the castle to Frog Street she flew, her skirt flying behind her.

Oh, that her mother wouldn't hear! Maybe her grandmother could temper it. After all, the townsfolk could see birds. If it had been the little people she sometimes saw, it would be much, much worse. She pressed on to Water Lane, then uphill along Town's End, where the cobbles grew scanty and the leat gurgled in its trench nearby.

From a young age Mary had learned to keep to herself, mostly because others found her different. This was partly because of her eyes. In the looking glass, they appeared ordinary to her, large and brown, flecked with green and gold.

"What uncanny eyes she has. It's as though the child can see right through me," she heard time and again.

"The godly maiden keeps her eyes demurely lowered," her mother always told her. Or, "For St. Peter's sake, pull your cap down lower."

Mary knew she had to be careful and keep quiet about many things. However, there was one thing she found difficult to silence. Something that flowed through her as naturally as breathing and left her no peace until imparted.

Her mother had asked when she was only four years old, "Mary, how did you know what remedy Goody Field needed? Did your grandmother tell you?"

"No, madam. I just knew to use the hyssop."

She couldn't forget how her mother's eyes had blazed.

"Maybe the bees whispered it in my ear?" she'd ventured.

"Child, we don't talk such!" Her mother had washed Mary's mouth out with lye soap—which her tongue still burned to remember.

Mary stopped at the top of the lane, out of breath. Looking back down at the town, she was relieved to see that no one had followed her. The townsfolk had never gone out of their way to spy on her before. This she found troubling. She unlatched her family's gate.

Then she heard a noise. In a cloud of dust around the corner at Town's End, the gaol cart came into view and began the upward climb alongside the leat.

Mary ran for her life now. Out of the town and into the surrounding hillsides, tearing through wild entanglement of gorse and meadow. She did not stop until she was far from the clutches of the gaoler, the eyes and ears of the town, and her mother's anticipated wrath.

The natural world was Mary's refuge. She felt a love and oneness that fed her soul while listening to the stillness of an ancient beech or the heart-expanding notes of birds among the gorse. From this place, she could feel the essence of everything, whether it be man, beast, rock, or plant. Everything had a resonance, a voice.

Only Mary's grandmother understood. Her beloved Nama had watched over her carefully ever since she could remember. Nama would know where to find her: in the high meadow above the town, one of their secret places where they were unlikely to encounter another human being. Hidden here amongst the gorse, Mary watched wild rabbits play. The sun journeyed imperceptibly over the valley until the clouds in the west shone golden. Nama would be there soon. Mary could sense her approach, catching a glimpse in her mind's eye of where the country lane and the overgrown stile by its side rose steeply upward.

Indeed before long, Mary heard a soft birdlike whistle and her grandmother made her way across the meadow carrying a basket, her long silver hair tied back loosely under her hood.

She smiled and hugged Mary tight. "My darling child . . . what happened?"

Threats of the ducking stool were not to be taken lightly. The stool angled out over the River Exe on a long plank. Many drowned after being left under the water too long or caught dampness in the lungs and died soon afterward. Mary recounted her time behind St. Peter's with the birds.

"Fools. They should know better." Her grandmother shook her head. "In fine shape this town would be without my physick or your mother's midwifery. Your mother is furious, of course, though let's not fret. Relieved we are to have you away from it all. Come, you must be hungry."

Nama took a wool blanket from her basket and spread it out for them to sit upon. Mary ate the bread, butter, and cold pullet hungrily, and drank from an earthen jug of small beer. The food tasted wonderful. Nama reached out to tuck a strand of Mary's chestnut-colored hair gently back under her cap. The sun blazed orange on the spires of St. Peter's below, the only sound a distant bleating of sheep.

"I'm sorry for it all, child. You did not deserve this. When you're older, your clever works will keep many folk from the jaws of death. Mark my words—once they realize how indispensable you are, it will change. They will know that you are blameless. So 'twas for me."

"Nama, how do you know 'twill be so for me?"

"You, as ye well know, carry a gift that has been passed down our family for time out of mind, one that your great-grandmother had."

Mary wiped her hands carefully on her napkin. "Mother has never thought it very special."

"Nonsense! She just wants to keep you safe. She's teaching you prudence, child—as she should." Her grandmother moved to the edge of the blanket to harvest a lush patch of nettle leaves. "Someday you will do great things with your gift."

Mary hoped so. This always felt true in her grandmother's presence. A wild rabbit nibbled wildflowers close by. She held a clover blossom to its mouth, which disappeared rapidly with a wiggle of its nose.

"How are your studies with the reverend?" Nama asked. Mary's quiet perceptiveness had not gone unnoticed by their parish priest. Being a family friend he had offered to teach her to read and write, her grandmother instrumental in this, of course.

"He says I'm almost finished."

"Finished? But what about Latin?"

Mary hadn't wanted to tell her. "He said he won't teach me Latin."

"Whyever not?" Her grandmother's voice sounded sharp.

"He says Latin isn't a proper course of study for a maiden," Mary said slowly, "that even the boys at Chilcott's school don't learn Latin." The rabbit kicked up its heels and dashed away, and the shadow of a goshawk swept across the meadow.

"Hmm! Well, I disagree." Her grandmother frowned. "I will have a word with him. 'Twould help our alchemy, Latin. Quite disheartening . . ."

Mary didn't want her grandmother to be disheartened. Their experiments were very exciting. Clandestine by necessity, they held them in the smokehouse at the back of the garden. Not another soul knew—not even her mother.

"Nama tell me again about God's wisdom."

"Ah—yes, my love. God's wisdom is not only in the hearts and minds of mankind. 'Tis right here in this very stalk, in this very leaf! In everything God has created He abounds. He has gifted this wondrous bountiful earth to us, so full of mystery, so full of beauty and natural magick." Nama winked at her, a sparkle in her clear gray eyes. "As you know, 'tis our job to unlock its secrets."

To hear this always left Mary with an inspired, magical feeling. "How do you know it's God who tells me what remedies to use?"

"Only God would desire His children to be healthy and well, wouldn't He?"

❧

The town of Tiverton had grown with the wool trade. It lay surrounded by sheep-covered hills at the junction of two rivers whose waterpower enabled plentiful fulling mills. Mary's father, a draper by trade, dealt in the various cloths manufactured there, and her family had prospered with the town. Her father would make the journey downriver to Topsham, where the River Exe rose and fell with the tide. From there, shallops would load his wool serge to sail down to Exmouth and its awaiting merchant ships. Sometimes he took Mary along as he'd discovered her gift for himself when she was very small and would tell him what he needed for his ailments. Mary always knew whom he should sell his cloth to and, in this way, she helped her father develop very lucrative business connections. His competitors marveled as his fortune grew.

"I have an announcement," her father said upon arriving home from Topsham on his own one evening, a fortnight after the incident at the church.

The excitement in his voice made Mary's mother turn from the hearth, her grandmother raise her eyebrows, and her younger sister Sarah hold her poppet perfectly still. They all stared at him.

"I've been offered an opportunity, one that many men desire and yet never realize." He fairly shook with enthusiasm. "'Tis a dream come true, Britania!"

Mary's mother said nothing. She wiped her hands on a dishcloth and sat at the table.

"I'm accepting this offer because I cannot bear the thought of missing the opportunity to farm my own plantation and have lucrative employ while I do so. I will be sailing to New England come autumn, and I will have my family join me," he said.

It was Mary who had pointed out a certain young man to her father a few months before.

"That young fellow, are you sure now?" he had questioned.

She was sure. Nicolas Shapleigh was the young man's name, and his father Alexander, as luck would have it, a Dartmouth merchant of some repute. Alexander Shapleigh had now hired her father to oversee his importation business in the colonies.

Mary had always counted herself as safe from a watery death upon the sea, living in the landlocked town of Tiverton in the center of

Devon. Indeed, the only ships she had ever seen adorned the parapets of St. Peter's, up high and carved in stone, ships that conjured up such a tempest of wind and wave to her young imagination that she dared not stare for long.

But her fears of the impending voyage seemed trivial under the gravity of what she learned next: Nama would not be coming with them.

"My life is here," her grandmother explained, alone with Mary in the garden. "What would the people of Tiverton do without me?" She took Mary's face in her hands. "Your mother feels it best to start a new life where no one knows the family history. It's not my place to stand in her way." She gently dried Mary's tears with a corner of her apron. "Oh, my darling child—though there be an ocean between us, know that I will always be with you."

As summer ripened to autumn, Mary's heart grew heavier each passing day. Standing alone in her family's hall, her gaze wandered over the familiar furnishings that filled the room sparsely but neatly—all the things that would be staying behind. Baskets, pots, and foodstuffs hung from the ceiling, the smell of drying herbs, sweet and pungent. At least her father's great chair was coming with them. She often sat upon it in the late afternoons, reading her family's Bible as she waited for him to come home, the casement window rattling whenever a cart passed outside.

Mary could still remember crawling across the rush-strewn flagstones with the cat as her companion, the churn and earthen crocks towering above her, the dark interior lit by sunlight spilling across the floor through the diamond-paned window casement. Her fingertips stroked a scar on her palm, the raised welt of a burn from grabbing a cast-iron cooking pot. Children learned early. Her burn wasn't so bad—she'd seen much worse.

She sighed, took up a handbasket, and walked out the door.

Outside lay a walled courtyard baked by the sun and ripe with the smells of animals. Here she'd first made friends with the hens while her mother milked the cow or washed the laundry nearby. In the garden, Mary filled her basket with the golden buttons of tansy as other memories flashed before her eyes. She wanted never to forget and had spent the last few days memorizing the look of everything that was home.

A cloud drifted across the sun, and Mary realized she must be going. Basket in hand, she stepped into the narrow lane that sloped downhill toward the town and spires of St. Peter's. The leat gurgled softly in its trench alongside, as if it could feel her sadness.

Dressed plainly in earth tones and a crisp white collar and cap, she made her way discreetly around the edge of the market crowd and arrived at her family's stall. The last Saturday market at which Mary would ever help her beloved Nama. Crooked gables lined the square where the sweet smell of baked goods mingled with the sour smell of the street cobbles. She breathed it all in, her senses wide open to the unseen vibration of this country town. In two days, her family would be leaving to sail across the sea to a new life.

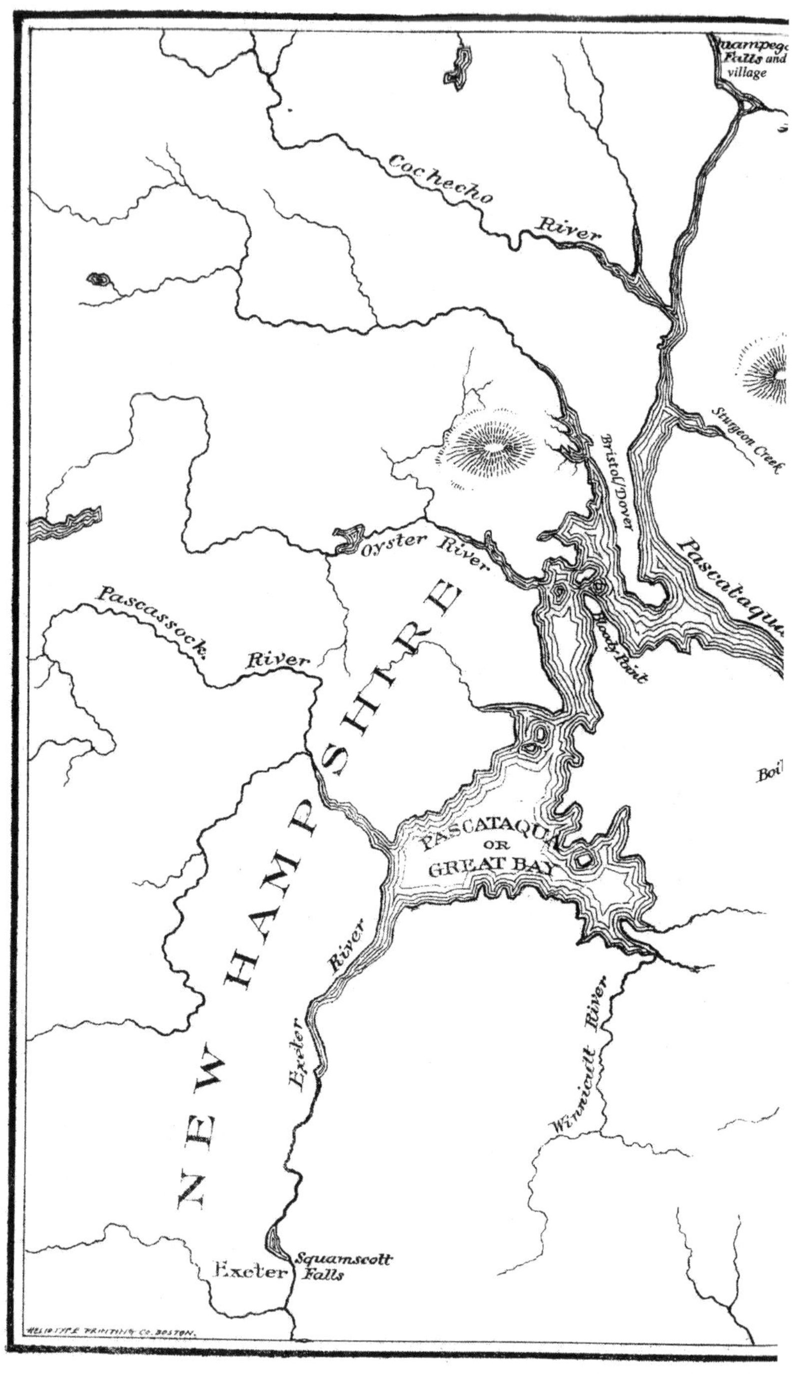

Falls and village
Cochecho River
Bristol/Dover
Sturgeon Creek
Pascataqua
Oyster River
Pascassock River
NEW HAMPSHIRE
PASCATAQUA OR GREAT BAY
Exeter River
Winnicutt River
Squamscott Falls
Exeter
HELIOTYPE PRINTING CO. BOSTON.

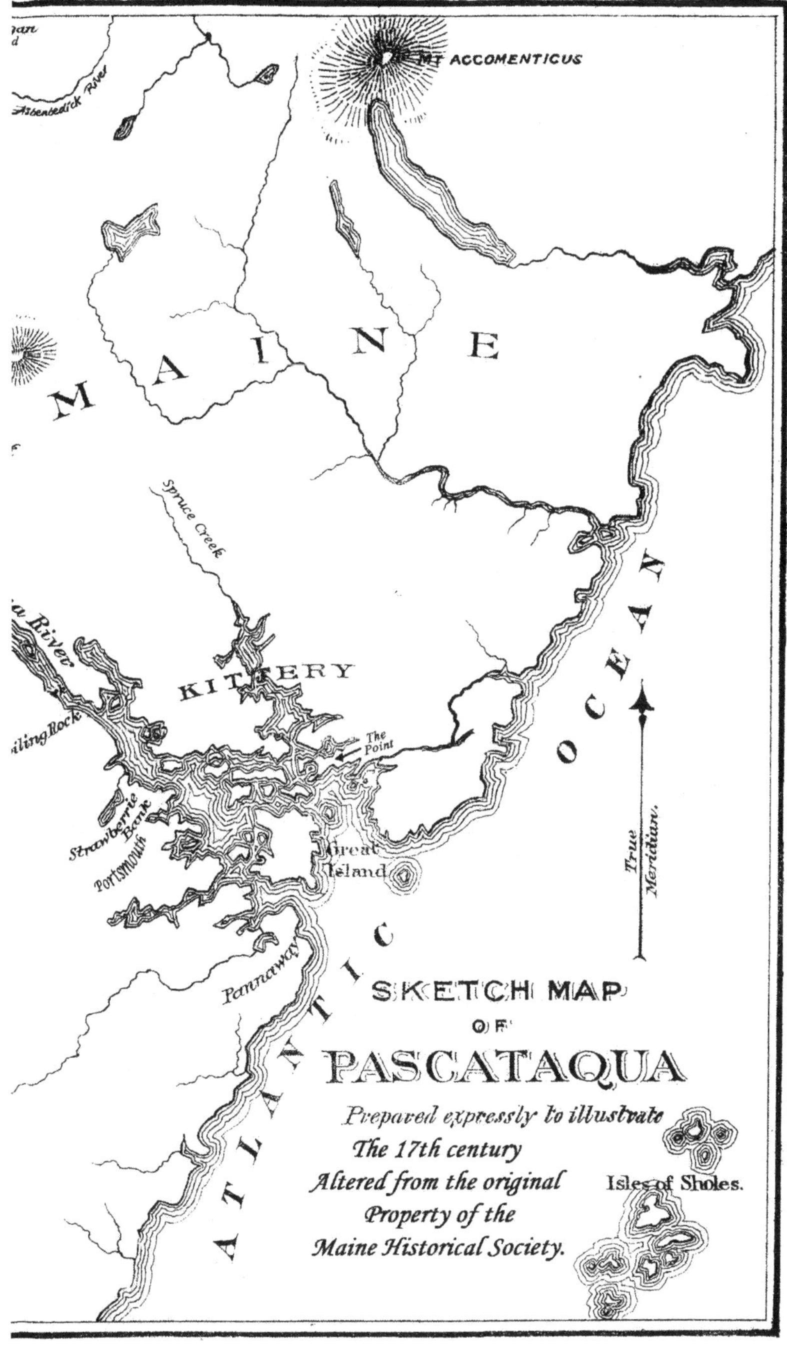

MT ACCOMENTICUS
Agamenticus River
MAINE
Spruce Creek
KITTERY
The Point
Strawberrie Bank
Portsmouth
Great Island
Pannaway
ATLANTIC OCEAN
True Meridian.
SKETCH MAP
OF
PASCATAQUA
Prepared expressly to illustrate
The 17th century
Altered from the original
Property of the
Maine Historical Society.
Isles of Sholes.

-- 2 --

Strawbery Banke

Mary lay in the half-light, footsteps pounding the deck above her. *It won't be long now.* She sat up slowly, slid her feet to the narrow floor, and peered into the hood of her sister's cradle. A task she'd begun to dread and for good reason. Her breath caught at the sight of the thin dark tail beside Hannah's cheek.

She snatched off the coverlet and leapt back. Two mice flew out, one of them streaking onto her sister Sarah's pallet. Sarah woke and jumped to her feet with a sleepy gasp, and the mouse dropped to the floor and disappeared. Mary shook out her skirt with a shudder. She should have warned Sarah; it was uncanny how the creatures went exactly where you hoped they wouldn't.

"Sorry . . . go back to sleep," she said.

Sarah's pale face sank back down, the wool blanket pulled tightly up to her chin.

Hannah's flesh looked sound. Mary tucked the coverlet back tightly around the still-sleeping babe. She never used to mind mice. In fact, she used to feed them back in England when her mother wasn't looking.

Stepping between the boxes and sacks, she steadied herself as the ship rolled, then perched on the bottom of the companionway ladder. From here she could see down the length of the "gully," everything in hues of brown: dark, dingy sepias and hanging rows of sullied bedsheets. The sheets afforded families some privacy, but everyone still knew everyone else's business.

She stared with increasing revulsion. All the women and children were crowded on top of their belongings. The cloying stench of unemptied chamber pots, sickness, and sweat permeated everything. The sailors hadn't bothered to refresh the jakes that morning, the sawed-off barrel half filled with seawater. Goody Foster's brassy voice usually demanded they change it, but now she and her six children were ill with throats that burned like fire.

Mary and her mother had come to their aid.

"Seawater," Mary blurted before she could stop herself. "They need to gargle warmed seawater." She alone noticed the sharp look her mother gave her—certainly the Fosters did not, reduced as they were to a pallid heap of human suffering.

But as Mary left to fetch the seawater, one of the Shapleigh servants stood staring back at her from the other side of the hanging sheet. Rebekah, a girl of fourteen who had taken an avid dislike to Mary for no apparent reason. Rebekah must have been listening. There was not much Mary could do about it now other than pretend it had never happened.

Ears were everywhere. Boredom, like illness, was a daily affair onboard ship. At least the seawater had helped the Fosters—there was little complaint from them now. Few comforts eased the rise and fall of wave or broke the monotony of the long days and nights aboard their little ship that had set sail from London Town.

Earlier that morning, they'd reached the Isles of Shoals—the first good look at the land that would be their new home. All who could had clambered up to gawk at the cluster of islands lying stark and gray upon the sea, inhabited by seabirds and empty fishing huts. Stages crowded the shoreline, befitting a large seaside town more than a strange deserted island.

On deck, her father had told her the fishing season would begin in a few months. He also said they would have been within sight of their new home if a bank of fog wasn't concealing the horizon.

They must be very close now.

Against the shipmaster's orders—as only when he said so were the women and children allowed up on deck—Mary climbed up the ladder. No one seemed to be watching. She just couldn't stay below.

On deck, brightness greeted her, and she gulped lungsful of the fresh cold air. Unseen by the crew, she tucked herself behind the fishing baskets nearby and pulled on her hood. The sea looked gray.

A vaporous white mist hung suspended over the water in a ghostly fashion.

The passage had been rough, but only a sailor had died. She was thankful they hadn't met with any great storms. Mary squinted upward past the weathered sails at the chalk-colored sky. God would help them here too. She prayed silently to ease the anxiety in the pit of her stomach. Anxiety that had been building for days.

The mist began to thin. When the way was clear on the middle deck, Mary dashed over to the gunnel. She scarcely noticed its salty burn under her chin as she stared wide-eyed at the vista opening before her. They were in what looked to be a large bay; a vast forested shoreline surrounded the ship on either side while the dark water took on a shallower greener color. The land smelled sweet—fresher and more pungent than the land they had left behind six and a half weeks earlier. On a point of land ahead sat a small fortress, with gun and portals and the king's colors flying above.

Mary closed her eyes for a moment, half believing that when she opened them the land would be gone, replaced by the endless horizon of ocean she had been staring at for weeks; but there it was—what she'd been waiting for and dreaming of ever since the voyage began. She looked back the way they'd come. Behind them lay a solid wall of gray. A wave of sadness washed through her as she thought about her grandmother. *There may be an ocean between us, but I will always be with you*, she heard her dear Nama say for the hundredth time.

Then her arm was roughly seized. "Injuns gotchu!" Anthony Nutter hissed in her ear. "You're not supposed to be out o' the gully."

Mary tried to pull away. "Let me be!"

The boy only laughed and began to wring her arm, his knuckles turning a gruesome white in contrast to the black oily crescents under his fingernails. Her arm on fire, Mary turned her face toward his. Anthony Nutter's grin began to fade. Then the strong arm of a sailor grabbed the nape of his neck and sent him sprawling face-first across the deck into a windlass. Anthony sat up glaring and sputtering, blood running from his nose.

"Ho there, my young Mary White!" Another pair of hands laid hold of her shoulders, gently this time. The voice was an instant comfort, for it belonged to Nicolas Shapleigh.

"Are you hurt?" He frowned.

Mary shook her head. She hated to have caused such a scene, but Nicolas didn't seem angry. She glanced up again shyly, his face softening as he caught her eye. Anthony Nutter had been nothing but trouble on the voyage, traveling with his mother and siblings to join his father in the colonies.

"Good thing that lad'll be up in Bristol. Ye'll be spared him soon enow." Nicolas ushered her back to the hatchway.

As they reached it, the other women and children began to emerge. Rebekah scowled, catching sight of Mary with Nicolas before he left to join the men up on the stern deck. Up next was Lizzie. The Shapleigh housekeeper was as friendly as Rebekah was not and as round and plump as Rebekah was thin and pinched. Everyone liked Lizzie.

Mary waited by the hatchway, hoping her absence had gone unnoticed. Last on deck came her mother and Sarah, wrapped up together in a woolen blanket. Her mother raised an arm, and Mary ducked underneath, cringing at the pointed look she was given.

Mary's mother, if on the petite side, was a fair woman of round maternal stature. She took in the shoreline soberly, holding Mary and her sister close.

Mary looked up, reassured to see the white plume of her father's hat above the crowd of men on the stern deck. She could see the men pointing to landmarks and wished she could hear what was being said.

Raindrops began to fall—the weather was so funny and mixed! On the nearest shore, she could make out a stone house surrounded by a palisade, smoke drifting from its chimney. Up ahead inside a cove appeared another dwelling whose shingles and clapboard were made of fresh-cut wood. There were few other signs of settlement. The landscape looked wild and desolate. Dense woods rose above the rocky shoreline as far as the eye could see.

The Pascataqua River was a pristine and primitive frontier, dividing the province of Maine from other settlements to the south. The forest along its shores held remnants of autumn color, and there were strange dark pines that towered hundreds of feet into the sky, branches arcing upward as if to beseech God in the heavens for their existence here. Mary had heard tales of the moose, bear, and wildcat which roamed the land; of the beaver and muskrat that filled the marshes; and the waters teeming with salmon, sturgeon, cod, and mackerel—the shallows paved with lobster and shellfish. She had heard too of the packs of yellow-eyed wolves and, of course, of the Indians—half-naked savages who were not happy with the English settling their lands.

The wind blew freezing tears back across Mary's temples into her hair. She suddenly felt bitterly cold. The wind blew again—gusting fiercely, tearing at the blanket, and threatening to carry them away.

"Come, children, let's wait below." Mary's mother nudged them toward the hatchway, then back down the ladder into the reeking gloom of the gully. Once below, her mother busied herself with the contents of a chest, pulling out the last clean smocks and pressed collars saved to look presentable upon their arrival.

"Madam . . ." Mary placed her fingers on the soiled lace of her mother's sleeve cuff.

Her mother stopped rummaging and turned toward her, unable to hide the disappointment in her face. "Trees—just trees everywhere . . ."

Mary clasped her mother's hand.

They sat—Mary, her mother, and Sarah in the dim light, quietly listening to the creaking ship move through the water in that anxious space between endings and beginnings. No longer pitching and rolling, they could feel the shallowness of the water by the change in its rhythm and tempo. Baby Hannah slept on soundly in her cradle, a peaceful smile upon her face.

The ship came up the river through the Great Island gut to the south, anchoring where the water remained deep at low tide next to the settlement of Strawbery Banke. Here, the shoreline sloped gradually upward from the water, and twenty or thirty dwellings lay scattered, most little more than tiny shuttered cottages. Only one of the houses looked somewhat large and inviting, with windows of diamond-paned glass. Someone said it was the local governor's. A fishing stage marked the mouth of a small tidal cove at the foot of the settlement. Beyond, animal hovels and planting fields stretched back to the edges of the forest.

Waiting on deck with the other women and children, Mary felt less keen to get off the ship than she'd thought she would be. "Fools to be comin' here," she heard a sailor laugh before the bosun's whistle scattered them to their duties. She looked around, but no one else seemed to have heard him.

The river current proved powerfully strong. The oarsmen pulled hard while the gully passengers sat squeezed together in the longboat, clinging for dear life. Only when they managed to clear the main flow and head for a stretch of shingle near the fishing dock did Mary relax somewhat. It felt odd to see their ship shrink behind in the distance and unnerving to see a crowd of strangers on the shore to greet them. She had the distinct, if uneasy, impression that the crowd was as glad to see them as they were to get off the ship.

But as the landing place grew close, her fear turned into an excited, giddy feeling. They were about to step foot on solid land again! Mary hardly cared that a drenching rain shower was now driving in sideways, soaking them all to the bone. Hannah began to cry, Mary's mother sheltering the babe with her cloak as best she could.

As the keel came to rest upon the shore, the oarsmen began helping everyone out. Mary leapt out on her own. Her feet met with the land, and as she took her first steps up the gravelly beach, she burst into laughter. The ground swayed beneath her as though she were still at sea. She grabbed Sarah's hand, and together, they managed to get up onto the turf. Their fellow passengers, looking worse for wear, tottered up to the waiting crowd behind them.

"Mary and Sarah, stay with me," commanded their mother.

The place became chaotic in all the excitement. Smaller children ran about joyfully or clung to their mothers' skirts, the hems of which were soiling with mud. Standing on solid ground was growing easier, and Mary let her feet slide off the funny round hillocks of grass that sprouted everywhere. Everything looked different and felt strange but smelled so good.

The villagers were very friendly and forward, given they were strangers, all wanting news of England. One woman complained loudly about her dropsy, inquiring as to medicine. Catching Mary's eye, her mother discreetly shook her head. Another woman with a swollen pasty-looking face asked if they needed lodging. Mary's mother declined.

Then an old woman stepped up, one who looked ancient, though her movements were quick and wiry. She smiled boldly, showing a set of gold-painted wooden teeth.

"I have a place fur ye, a warm hearth an' more space 'n most!"

The widow Gyles was her name. Her accent was coarse, but her clothes were clean and of good fabric, if of a cut no longer fashionable. Mary's mother didn't turn her away. Lizzie and Rebekah were declining offers nearby as their master would provide for them.

Mary's father landed in the next boat, tall and imposing in his French velvet doublet and plumed hat. Mary felt proud he was her father. "Let's have a look at the place—I have much to tend to," he said brusquely, but he smiled at Mary as she skipped along beside him. Seeing Rebekah's sour expression staring after them hardly troubled Mary as her family left the crowd.

The widow Gyles's home did prove roomier than most, being made from the hull of an old Dutch pinnace turtled above the tidal cove, its timbers worm eaten and patched. A large stone fireplace rose up out of its stern end, and inside, the earthen floor was strewn thickly with rushes.

"Me 'usband, God rest 'is soul, was more 'n pleased with such a ready-made 'ouse," the widow said, proud of his obvious cleverness. "Leaked more at sea than it do now!" She laughed a throaty cackle that finished as a wheezing cough, taking a drink from a battered tin cup to squelch it. "Fisherman 'e was. Thought we'd make it rich here in Pascataway. But then 'e left one morning and never came back.

’Twas nine days afore ’e was discovered in the weeds, just off them rocks o’er yonder island. The lobsters ’ad got to ’im . . .’Twas ’is teeth that gave ’im away.”

The pinnace was made up of two rooms, divided into stern and prow. In the stern end, a plank table stretched lengthwise from the hearth, and an oilskin window brightened the place, which resembled a tavern with its score of mismatched drinking pots hanging from the old bilge beams. The widow used the smaller prow end for storage, yet it too had a small oilskin window and looked roomy enough to sleep Mary’s family. Almost everything else that might be needed hung from the various rafters and walls, including drying foodstuffs.

A servant girl sat on a settle by the hearth, shelling multicolored beans from a shuttle-like cob. She stared at them unabashedly until the widow rebuked her.

“Mahgret, don’t just sit tha gawking. Fetch some drink fer our guests!”

Setting her work aside, Margaret quickly obeyed her mistress.

The widow Gyles’s lodgings satisfactory, Mary’s father went off to see to the landing of their goods and chattels. Mary, her mother, and Sarah stripped off their rain-soaked outer layers and draped them over the back of the settle to dry. It felt so good to Mary to feel the damp from all those weeks at sea drawing out of her flesh and bones.

That afternoon, their sturdy little ship weighed anchor, her sails unfurling, catching the breeze. The ship’s master was anxious to make a settlement farther east that had ready supplies to restock her with. A one-piece salute was fired off, and as the puff of bluish smoke settled out over the water, the ship turned slowly and fell downriver with the tide. The smell of gunpowder stinging her nostrils, Mary thought of the sailor calling them fools as the ship’s sails disappeared behind the Great Isle.

“Ye’ll be fine here,” Margaret said. “Everyone feels a bit o’ regret t’ see ’em go.”

A short while later, Mary sat with Margaret outdoors on a felled tree trunk, pulling quills from the bounty of her father’s musket. He’d fired on a whim at a large flock of ducks raised by the ship's salute. The skies were alive with migrating birds.

"There's not much of anything 'ere but food, if ye know where ta look for it," Margaret said. "We 'ave plentiful food except at starving time in the late winter. We eat cockles out of tide pools then."

The maidservant spoke in a softer dialect than the widow, having come over two years before with another master and mistress.

"They rest o'er yonder now." She gestured with a nod.

Across the cove on a knoll above the river lay a scattering of small wooden crosses.

"Mistress Gyles took me in. She's got 'er wits about her, though the devil might take 'er."

Margaret liked to talk. Mary's eyes wandered over the Point of Graves as they worked. So sad to have crossed the sea, only to die.

The quills and feathers plucked and saved in a sack, they went over to a nearby stump hollowed out like a shallow dish. Here Margaret gutted and cleaned the birds, careful to scrape the bloody innards onto a coarse old cloth. "For the fishermen or Dr. Reynolds's hogs—got to be mindful ta keep the bears and wolves away." She kicked at a tabby mouser lurking nearby.

Mary tossed the cat a few pieces from the cloth when Margaret wasn't looking. Scanning the edges of the forest, she thought about the bears. She'd heard of one that did tricks on a lead at fairs back in England. She'd also heard they could tear a man's head off with one swipe of their claws.

That evening, the delicious smell of roast duck filled the pinnace. Mary's stomach growled emptily; she couldn't remember ever wanting to eat something as badly as this. The fowl spun from their hangings inside the hearth, the pan beneath hissing as it caught the fatty drippings. She and Sarah sat on the settle, holding baby Hannah on their laps. It was their job to keep the ducks winding so they cooked evenly. At the table, the widow prated on to her mother about life in New England.

"An' if that isn't enough to send a body packing, in winter, tha's so much snow, ye've never seen the like—why, it covers whole 'ouses!

Folk dig out like moles, and some so starved they're like to boil their shoes. Poor broth that makes."

Mary listened in fascination, swaying Hannah on her knees to keep her quiet. Her mother didn't look so happy; but they had plenty of foodstuffs with them—enough, her father said, to get them through the winter and then some.

"An' if ye survive," the widow continued, "as mere skin 'n bones, there're hordes of bloodthirsty flies that eats the rest of ye alive in spring 'n summer, given the chance. An' o' course, the woods are swarming with wild beasts wanting to do the same."

This was not the New England Mary's father had talked about.

The widow paused, looking somehow satisfied.

Hannah fussed to get down, so Mary sang her a little ditty. Singing had helped them weather the voyage—it always made Mary feel better. Sarah took it up in roundelay, their voices clear and sweet. Hannah sat still, her eyes wide to listen:

I had a little nut tree,
Nothing would it bear,
But a silver nutmeg
And a golden pear;
The King of Spain's daughter
Came to visit me,
And all for the sake
Of my little nut tree.

"Don't ye stop, maids. 'Tis a delight on me ears!" the widow encouraged.

Margaret listened too, her work forgotten.

Mary smiled and looked toward her mother, who nodded permission.

She and her sister sang until they tired, and the widow's hall transformed into a more familiar, cheery place.

A gust of wind rattled the pinnace, whistling its way through cracks in the planking and brightening the firelight. A sudden downpour drummed overhead, drowning out the sound of approaching voices. Someone pounded on the door, and the widow Gyles sprang to lift the latch.

In from the weather came two men smelling of fish and wet wool. The widow welcomed them cheerily, hanging their cloaks. Margaret served the fellows tankards of beer and trenchers of pottage, taking the cleaned fish one had brought and promptly planking and propping it in the hearth to roast. It became clear that the widow's house functioned in part as a kind of ordinary, and these were two of her regulars.

"Wot, sarvin' us pottage and savin' the birds for yourselves?" one of them complained, his hat worn so low that Mary could only see the end of his nose.

"Thomas Crawley keep yer greedy hands on your own lot, or ye'll be trussed up next to them ducks!" rebuked the widow, shaking a pothook at him. "They belong to my lodgers."

The man's nose swung toward Mary's mother and back, and with a peevish disgruntled air he began to spoon in his pottage. His collarless shirt was a filthy gray, its untied throat exposing a tarnished half groat on a chain nestled on his hairy chest.

Mary liked the widow's home better without her patrons.

"Goody White, why don't you 'ave a seat, and Mahgret will sarve your supper now too?" said the widow in a much more civil tone.

"No, thank you. We shall wait for my husband." Mary's mother then turned to Thomas Crawley. "I'm sure there will be plenty for all of us to share."

Thomas Crawley's lipless mouth spread wide, reminding Mary of the shark the sailors had caught at sea. She hoped her father would be back soon.

Another fisherman arrived, an older man, bearing a large silvery haddock that Margaret hung from a hook along the wall. Its big glassy eye was so fresh and staring that Mary was unsure it was really dead. What did the fish think of a warm, cozy house after living in such cold, deep waters? She was growing very tired.

When Mary's father returned, they all feasted heartily. Mary and Sarah stood at one end of the table, with a wooden trencher, spoon, and mug to share between them. They ate fresh fish, the succulent fowl, and Indian corn pottage until they were full. The food tasted heavenly after the barreled fare onboard ship, and there was plenty to go around. Mary found the Indian corn delicious.

In the back room for the night, where their bed sacks lay heaped with coverlets and rugs, it felt terribly cold and damp away from the cheery fire. The thick layer of rushes did little to break the chill of the earthen floor as she and her sister stripped down to their smocks. After their bedtime prayer, her mother let the wool hanging drape back across the doorway, sealing them in the unfamiliar blackness.

Sarah soon fell asleep, but Mary lay quietly, taking comfort from the voices in the next room. She let her awareness move outside the pinnace into the dark beyond, where the wild beasts roamed. Feeling the secure warmth of her bed, she pulled the blankets up over her head. It would be impossible for anything large to come in through the little oilskin window in the hull, she reassured herself.

The prick of tears began at the corners of her eyes. She did not know why exactly, but she cried about everything: her grandmother, the voyage, this strange, unfamiliar place . . .

After she was finished, she turned her cheek away from the cold, wet spot on her pillow and fell fast asleep.

-- 3 --

The Devil's Work

"Mary, would you look at this?" her mother asked when they awoke the next morning. In the diffuse light of the oilskin, Mary peered at a strange swelling on her mother's neck. It didn't look good. She wished her father hadn't already left for the day.

Margaret took one look and went all funny and apologetic, searching their bedding with a stick like a crazy person until the culprit was found halfway up the wall: an enormous brown spider. Margaret whacked it with the sole of her shoe and it fell, crumpled up like a small dark mushroom. A poisonous biting spider. Spiders back in England weren't known to be venomous or bite.

"My sincerest apologies, Goody White," the widow said. "Such things happen here, I'm afraid. I tell ye, these colonies aren't for the faint of heart. Maybe ye'd like a wee bit o' rum?"

Mary's mother declined the rum, but she did lie down to rest on a pallet by the hearth. The bite continued to swell and began to itch. Mary dug through the medicine box with shaking hands to find the pot of clay, hoping to draw out the poison.

The widow sat smoking her clay pipe, apple-pip eyes glimmering. "No one's died from such yet, child."

Mary felt heat rise in her chest. *That should have been told first thing!* She poulticed the bite with clay. Not an auspicious beginning for their first morning.

"I will survive, Mary, God willing," her mother said and patted her arm. "You'd best get started with our laundry."

"Mahgret would be happy ta help," the widow offered.

Margaret helped Mary lug the family's bag of laundry and brass kettle up the gentle slope behind the pinnace to the spring. The day had broken sunny and cool, and the freshness of the air lifted Mary's spirits despite herself. She did love the smell of this new land and its wide tidal river that welled and swirled past the settlement. The forest, having shed much of its color in the wind and rain, looked naked surrounding the tall scattered groves of pine.

They found the Shapleigh servants Lizzie and Rebekah at the spring, busy with their master's laundry. "Good morrow, Mary. How d' ye fare?" Lizzie called out, her round face flushed from exertion.

"Morrow, Lizzie. A spider bit my mother's neck. She's got an awful swelling from it."

The housekeeper's forehead wrinkled in horror. "Oh . . ."

"'Tis bad luck to be bit by one of those," remarked a woman who was drawing water nearby. "Not a good thing a'tall. I have some simples if your mother's in need."

"Thank you," Mary replied. "But we have lots of simples. My mother's a practitioner of physick."

"As am I," the woman said, gazing intently at Mary from beneath her felt hat. "Jane Walford is my name. I'm here tending a sick neighbor, but I live on the Great Island across the way." She gestured back toward the mouth of the river. As she walked away, Mary noticed her gait listed curiously to one side.

"Don't listen ta Goody Walford about bad luck," Margaret said. "Everybody gets bit by those nasty things 'ere."

"*Everybody*?" Lizzie repeated. "Er . . . are they very large spiders?"

Margaret nodded. "They come inta houses when it gets cold, some as big as your hand."

She sounded like the widow Gyles, Mary thought. Leaving Lizzie searching the ground fearfully with every step, she and Margaret got to work filling the kettle with spring water.

Margaret continued to prattle on about the time her first mistress was bit to Rebekah, who just rolled her eyes and pushed past them rudely, ignoring Margaret. "What's got inta her? And what happened to her 'ere?" Margaret wondered out loud, touching the side of her own face where the slash of a livid burn disfigured Rebekah's jaw.

Mary shrugged. Lizzie had told them aboard ship that Nicolas had hired Rebekah because he felt sorry for her but had never mentioned why.

Mary and Lizzie gathered kindling and lit a fire beneath the kettle. They folded in the garments along with some soft gray lye soap, stirring with a stick. When Mary's mother and Sarah finally joined them, the laundry was boiling away, whitening. The swelling on her mother's neck looked smaller.

"You and Sarah can join the other children so long as you stay close by," her mother said.

Mary started off joyfully with Sarah. They could see some village children over by the landing. One of the older boys had fashioned a game that all the other children had to abide by. He stopped and stared at Mary and her sister as they approached, sizing them up.

"Ye have to go over to the gaol." He pointed to a scraggly tree where a few smaller children waited glumly.

Mary looked around at the other children hiding under the fish flakes or throwing rocks at nearby gulls.

She grabbed Sarah's hand and turned on her heel. They would leave them to their silly game. She could make better fun on her own in this new and wild place that dazzled with possibilities.

A rock sped by her ear as they walked away.

She and Sarah wandered back around the edge of the cove, passing the widow's pinnace and other simple dwellings. They picked bouquets of the remaining meadow flowers, a hound dog from the village accompanying them.

On the opposite shore of the cove, the Point of Graves lay above the river, solemn with its small wooden crosses. Mary wound some of the flowers she carried around the wooden circlet of the nearest cross. It marked a grave so new that weeds hadn't even started to reclaim the soil, and the hound sniffed about it. She and Sarah made a game of decorating the wooden crosses, not willing to leave one unadorned no matter how old or rotted. They gathered the dried leaves, flowers, and berries from the surrounds, creating lavish laurels until the other children at the fish flakes on the opposite side of the cove spotted them. Shouting, the children began to run around the edge of the cove toward the girls, the older boy in the lead.

"Quick, before they get here." Mary grabbed Sarah's hand again; this time, they ran down the far side of the knoll, following an overgrown path farther along the shore. The hound bounded into the lead, happy to scout. Briars snagged at their clothing, but they did not slacken their pace until they were sure they were not being followed. Here, there were several dwellings near the shore, so they chose a path that ran behind them up an incline to a grove of towering pines that felt cathedral-like to walk under. From this vantage, they spied on the other children now milling about the Point of Graves.

"I hope they don't ruin our flowers," Sarah said.

"I don't think they'd dare to with the ghosts about. Look," Mary laughed, "they don't know where we've gone." She could see the older boy looking this way and that, scratching his head.

Behind the girls, a meadow opened out on the far side of the pines. It sloped down to a much larger tidal estuary than the cove, its water sparkling in the sunlight. An interesting plant grew in the meadow, tall with large pods bursting forth a white cottony fluff. Mary pulled one of them apart. Its stem oozed a bitter white sap while the silky fluff floated lightly away on the breeze.

"Sarah, this could be a new kind of cotton. We should take some to show Mother."

Sarah's face brightened at the idea, and the girls fell to work, filling their aprons with dozens of the pods until the hound, scratching in the sun nearby, growled ominously. Mary and her sister stopped what they were doing. The hound pointed toward a thicket at the far end of the meadow. There was something there that he didn't like.

Mary's mouth went dry. With hardly a moment's hesitation, she and Sarah fled back toward the river, hearts pounding as they clutched their pod-filled aprons, the dog trailing behind them.

Back down along the side of the cove, they stumbled upon the crowd of children who had followed them to the graves. One small child was scarlet-faced and howling, and the others were all gathered around.

"'Twas a bee that stung him," someone said.

"No, 'twas a hornet. I saw it fly away. It had a big black tail," said another child.

"It looked like a bat to me," someone else said.

Mary tucked the corners of her apron into her sash to hold the pods. "Let me see," she said, making her way through the ring of gaping children.

The little boy's hand was beginning to swell. She knew exactly what he needed; she'd already seen it here, similar to what grew back in England. Mary walked up from the rim of the cove until she spied the plantain with its characteristic paddle-shaped stringed leaves. She picked a leaf and began to chew it. Once back with the child, she poulticed its green pulp onto the boy's hand while the other children watched.

"Now give it a minute or two, and it will stop hurting."

The boy snuffled, blowing bubbles through the snot running down his face. His wailing quickly reduced to a whimper and then subsided completely.

Mary held a plantain leaf to his lips. "Chew more of this, 'twill clear the poison. It doesn't taste very good, but 'twill help."

The boy's quick recovery made Mary and her sister the children's new best friends, and the little crowd happily escorted them back to the settlement, the older boy swinging a stick at invisible beasts as he led the way.

Back at the widow's, Mary and Sarah deposited their pods on a rock shelf behind the pinnace. Inside, Mary's mother examined some of the silken fluff.

"Looks indeed to be a promising filling, Mary."

"Some call it milkweed," the widow said. "Ye can try an' use it—no good for spinning on its own."

That afternoon, when their laundered linen smocks had dried to a crisp white stiffness on the surrounding bushes, Mary's mother heated the kettle in the widow's hearth so they could bathe. Pouring the heated water into a shallow basin, she helped Mary and Sarah scrub with a cloth until their skin grew red and tingly, then washed their hair with meadow rue to discourage any vermin.

It felt good to be clean from the salt and grime of the voyage. Mary and Sarah sat by the hearth while their hair dried, and their mother retired to the back chamber to bathe.

The widow cackled, amused. "Soon, it'll be so cold, you won't want to change your shift 'til spring! Though goodness, your cheeks be rosy now."

"Mary," her mother said when she rejoined them at the hearth, "Lizzie has asked for you to tend her master's livestock on the morrow as she and Rebekah are still washing. I told her you would. She said the pail and yoke would be by the pen, as would the sickle."

"Yes, madam," Mary answered, surprised to have been given such a task.

"You'll have to cut fodder from the salt grass a ways upriver at the marsh," the widow informed her. "But there'll be others there still puttin' store away."

Early the next morning, Mary made her way to the newly built hovel of woven saplings where the Shapleigh livestock were penned. Silver frost covered everything, still and silent. The air felt bracingly cold compared to the day before. She stamped hard on the animals' frozen water barrel with her foot, which only sent a splitting pain up her shin. Spying the yoke nearby, Mary pounded its end against the surface until it broke through with a crack, splashing icily.

She was glad for the wool stockings that covered her hands. Margaret had told her to wear them. But her toes felt the burn ofthe frozen ground right through the leather soles of her shoes.

The animals crowded around, pushing their steaming noses toward her. Her friend the goat who'd weathered the voyage on deck, tied to the foremast, began to chew at her apron. She'd helped milk her twice a day for the young children on board.

"No!" Mary cried, pushing her away. "You'll have your breakfast soon enough."

First, they needed fresh water; then she'd be about the milking. She hooked up the empty buckets and shouldered the yoke, which was much too big for her, and made her way up the hill. It helped to keep her feet moving. Cocks resounded in the morning stillness and sounds of the settlement stirring reached her ears.

Then another sound caught her attention. It came from farther off, faint but magnified across the frozen landscape—the sound of verse being chanted. The sort of thing the cunning did in private to ward off evil spirits. Curious, Mary set down the yoke and followed the sound past the farthest dwelling, where the brush grew thicker. She peered through a leafless thicket to see the huddled figures of three women. One of them raised a witch's bottle skyward by its rounded bottom, where it caught the glow of the sunrise.

"*This is our will, so mote it be!*" they intoned in unison like a psalm.

Mary watched in fascination. Her grandmother had helped someone with a witch bottle once. Then one of the women saw her. In a flash, the bottle recoiled and disappeared inside the cloak. Mary sank down lower behind the thicket, trying to hide. The women sidled off like crows, staring in her direction. Mary recognized one of them as Goody Walford by the tilt of her body—the herbwoman who had warned of bad luck.

Once they'd gone, Mary hurriedly retraced her path to the spring, praying they hadn't seen who she was. It was embarrassing enough to be caught spying, but to witness such a ritual was far worse, even if they were blameless. Clever or cunning folk were considered either blameless for anything unexplainable, or in league with the devil. The latter was deadly.

Mary brought the animals their water, uneasy despite the company of others at the spring. Once the goat had been milked and the bucket handed off to Lizzie, she started up the path, sickle in hand, to cut the animals' fodder. The sun had completely risen now, and that made her feel a little better. The women certainly could not have seen her very clearly, she assured herself.

At the highest point of the Banke, an oak tree spread its branches in all directions. From this vantage, the river lay open to the northward, a dazzling azure blue. Mary could see acres of marsh ahead and the stooped figures of those already hard at work.

Continuing down the back side of the hill, she followed the footpath along the dipping curve of shoreline past a short strip of sandy beach with several large interesting rocks and tidal pools.

At the marsh, she found a spot to herself and began to twist handfuls of the sharp salt grass together, cutting them off close to the roots until she had as much as she could carry.

Later that day, on a return trip from the marsh, her feet led her down to that alluring strip of sandy beach. To be caught idle from her work would be frowned upon, but no one could be seen coming in either direction. Leaving her sheaf of salt grass hidden by the embankment, she crouched down beside the largest rock with a tidal pool at its base. The surrounding landscape was dead and dying but not so beneath the water's surface. A crab scuttled back to hide in the greenish-gold seaweed as soon as it knew she saw him. Above the crab's hiding place, two pinkish-orange starfish clung to the submerged rock, which was covered in barnacles. It was a very beautiful world, full of color. Mary decided she loved the sea and never wanted to live far away from it again—its vast mysterious waters connected her to her grandmother. The thought made a lump form in her throat.

Seeing several women approach loaded down with sheaves, Mary hid behind the largest rock. She waited until they had gone up over the hill and out of sight before retrieving her sheaf and scrambling back to the narrow footpath. She wondered at this path beneath her feet, worn so smooth and perfect as though it had been used for time out of mind. When she looked up again, a lone figure was coming toward her—a figure that leaned a little to the left.

Mary's heart beat faster.

As they drew abreast, Mary stepped well to the side, and Goody Walford passed her by with nary a word but a long icy stare.

It was near suppertime when Mary noticed something was wrong. The pigs stood before her, devouring their scraps; but where were the goat, the cow, and the sheep? She couldn't believe her eyes when she saw the gap in the fencing, its branches scattered on the ground. An opening rent just big enough for the taller animals to step through.

Mary looked desperately about for them. It was beginning to grow dark. *Oh, please be close by so I can herd you back in!* She had taken such good care of the animals all day, and now she would be to blame.

After a few minutes of searching to no avail, she ran to the widow's to summon help.

Darkness had fallen by the time the animals were found and returned to their pen. The sheep had stayed together, grazing behind the widow's pinnace. The goat was found in the act of consuming a neighbor's bedsheet, causing a scene until Lizzie offered to replace the sheet with one of a much finer fabric. And the cow was discovered in the patch of salt grass at the far end of the cove.

Mary breathed a sigh of relief; it looked like no real harm had been done. She stood by the pen after everyone else had left, reluctant to leave the animals despite how cold and dark it had grown. She would have been in such awful trouble if they hadn't been found. Someone had said they wouldn't have survived the night without proper enclosure.

"You sneaky beasts. How did you get out?" she said, thinking she was alone until a figure materialized by her side.

"Who were you talking to?" It was Rebekah.

"Myself," Mary answered.

"Mr. Shapleigh will be outraged. I'd hate to be in your shoes," the maidservant said. Nightfall obscured her face but not the malice in her voice. "Poor caretaking if I've ever seen it." She sniffed and spun on her heel, her figure dissolving back from whence it came.

Stung by Rebekah's words, Mary made her way back to the widow's. The Shapleighs would likely blame her, and her father would be very angry. The animals couldn't have done it themselves. The other children wouldn't have done it either, she thought. They were her friends now. Had Goody Walford and her consorts broken the fence? The thought made her afraid. A high resonant howl rose behind her in the direction of the marsh, echoed by another one louder and closer from the woods nearby.

Mary ran blindly in the dark until she was safe inside the pinnace. She'd never heard the howl of a real wolf before. It was a truly wild and unmistakable sound that set her hair on end.

At supper that night, her father reported that one of the carpenters had narrowly missed getting struck and killed by a tree across the river that day, and a servant boy had almost drowned. Those on shore had pulled him in with a long branch. A day of mishaps, all told. She was surprised her father wasn't angry with her when he heard about the broken fence.

As Mary's family settled down for the night in the prow of the pinnace, she overheard her parents talking in low tones.

"The task at hand is daunting," her father said. "What all of us really need is a day of rest, which we're not going to get at this point."

"I trust you'll be granted some relief soon?" her mother whispered.

"Unlikely, at the speed we're making. And then some scoundrel has the gall to destroy our handiwork here."

"Why is what I'd like to know," her mother said. "And our daughter put such care into her work—she's in no way to blame. Who would wish us harm?"

But Mary knew who might. She also knew that to say something might make it much worse.

The next morning, Rebekah came to the widow's door.

"Master's sheep are in fits. Lizzie asked me to fetch you, Goody White."

Mary rushed to the pen with her mother. To her great distress, the two sheep were lying on their sides, breathing with difficulty.

"There's naught that can be done," her mother said.

Word spread quickly throughout the settlement that the sheep were bewitched, and a crowd soon gathered.

"'Tis a sin they weren't cared for properly," Rebekah rebuked loudly enough so that everyone present could hear.

The crowd of children were all there. Most of the village was, except Goody Walford and her friends. The goat and the rest of the animals seemed well and fine, but the sheep died within hours. No marks of any kind could be found on their bodies. Mary petted the goat sorrowfully at the pen. Everything felt depressed and gloomy as though the sun had gone permanently behind the clouds.

That afternoon the widow went out, leaving Mary, her mother, and sisters to themselves.

Margaret stayed unusually quiet, busying herself outside, crushing shelled Indian corn into meal with a log pestle. Then a man in a shabby military coat stopped in for a visit. The widow, returning over the threshold just as their visitor stood looking disdainfully about, slid past him to grab her iron tongs before he knew she was there.

"I see, Captain Wannerton, that ye have welcomed yourself into my abode!" He gave a start and spun to face her. "What be thy business?" she asked gruffly.

Mary hadn't seen the governor up close. A stout man with a large face, he cleared his throat in an authoritative manner. "It has been brought to my attention, Widow Gyles, that you've been selling drink to some of the fishermen."

"Yes, I have, and *good* drink it is too!" said the widow. "Couldn't blame 'em for wanting somethin' more 'n watered down tummy rot, could I?"

Mary watched, amazed by the widow's audacity. Margaret, her mother, and Sarah appeared to be shrinking into the walls, terrified of the confrontation.

"Look here you old gammer," the governor snarled, his massive jowl flushing crimson.

The widow advanced on him with her tongs.

He backed away. On the threshold of the pinnace, he stopped. "They spend their coin on *my* drink and no one else's!" He shook his finger at her threateningly. "Ye watch yourself, if you know what's good for ye!" With that, he turned and was gone.

Everyone sat silent for a minute, afraid he might come back.

"Rogue," said the widow quietly, slamming shut the door and pulling in the latchstring. She turned back to the hearth and hung up the tongs. Then she brushed off her hands in a satisfied sort of way and helped herself to a dram of her rum as though nothing out of the ordinary had happened.

"Goody White," she said, sitting down upon the settle. "The gov'nor might only be concerned with his own pocket, but the death o' the sheep has upset most here. Some say your whole party be jinxed."

Margaret looked down at her lap.

Mary's mother sat up tall and stared the widow straight in the eye. "I challenge that, Widow Gyles. We are God's people who obey His Word!"

The widow stared back, obviously not afraid to look the lion in its mouth. "Well, that jinxed business just be more fodder for the gossips to champ on, I suppose." She drained her cup. "A few years back, a milk cow died the same."

Later that day, sent out to empty a pot in the middens behind the pinnace, Mary stopped to watch a flake of snow drift softly down. She caught it on her open palm. Her eye followed another flake as it eddied and looped, landing on the rock shelf where they had cached their milkweed pods. Mary stared at the lichen-covered rock. Where had their pods gone? Bits and pieces of silky white fluff clung to the ground, and there was fresh sheep dung nearby. A thought stopped her cold: *Could the pods be poisonous?* She already knew the answer.

"'Tis best to say nothing about it," her mother said sadly when they were together later in private.

Mary felt terrible. Her mood grew even more depressed the next day when the rest of the families with whom they'd crossed the sea left upriver. She helped Margaret knead bread dough, trying to keep busy. Margaret prattled on about her old mistress' baking until the sound of shouting outside in the settlement caught their attention.

The girls peered out the door. Dark, leaden clouds scudded by, matching Mary's mood, the wind ravishing the remaining leaves on the bushes and trees. A boy ran past them, out of breath. "Somebody's been shot in the fowling party. Don't know who 'tis!" he cried. "But they're bringing him back now!"

Mary's father had gone out fowling with the Shapleighs. Heart in her throat, she ran over to where a crowd had gathered. *What if it's Father?* In the distance, she could see a small procession carrying somebody on a bier of branches. Fear stopped her in her tracks until she saw that her father carried the back end. An enormous relief, yet a bittersweet one, for it was Nicolas Shapleigh who lay upon the bier, still and pale, his face and gold satin doublet blackened with gunpowder and dried blood. His father, Alexander Shapleigh carried the front of the bier, looking grim and gray as a stone.

"He's gone," Nicolas's manservant, Tom said to Mary's mother.

"But . . . how?" her mother asked in disbelief.

"Musket exploded back on 'im." The man snuffled, wiping tears from his eyes.

No, Mary thought, *it can't be*. Not Nicolas. He had been so nice to watch over them.

Weak in the knees, she followed the procession into the governor's house, out of the pressing crowd. Once inside, Alexander slumped into a chair and covered his face with his hands. Somewhere outside, a drum began to beat slowly.

By lantern light, Mary's mother washed bloody, grimy soot from Nicolas's face and hands. Lizzie sobbed, an absolute wreck; she'd been a household servant for many years. Rebekah stood off to one side, her face inscrutable in the shadow.

Laying out the dead was a ritual most women were accustomed to, though it was never easy. In a dark windowless back chamber, they were left alone to do the work. Within an hour, her mother had washed, dressed, and shrouded Nicolas's body upon a makeshift table of board. Captain Wannerton sent a messenger upriver to call down the reverend from Bristol.

"The blast must have knocked his soul loose," Mary's mother said. "Nicolas's wounds are shallow, from what I can tell."

Mary sat with her mother and the others that night, blankets wrapped around them in the unheated chamber, keeping watch to protect the dead from evil spirits.

Near midnight, while she and her mother were alone in the room, the widow Gyles appeared, covered in a woolen shawl. She sat down next to Mary's mother. Mary guessed that Captain Wannerton must have been sound asleep for her to do so.

"Folk be afeared," the widow said quietly. "They say ye most certainly carry a jinx of bad luck and death." The old woman turned her gaze to rest upon the dead, wound in a linen shroud from his father's stores.

"Infidels and ignorants!" Mary's mother breathed out. Her eyes fastened on the lantern flame burning next to Nicolas's body, the side of her jaw tightening.

Mary shivered. The chamber grew colder, its deepening shadows playing tricks on her eyes. Muskets and swords of various lengths glinted from the darkened walls. There were bandoliers, pieces of armor, and a row of shiny pikes and halberds. Budge barrels of black gunpowder lined the far wall. A frightening place, one suited to violence and death.

She stood, wrapping her blanket more firmly around her shoulders, and lifted the shroud to see Nicolas's face one more time. She never wanted to forget it; he had been so kind.

"The young man's lucky to 'ave one of those," the widow said, eyeing the shroud. "Many 'ere are buried e'en without, like a dog—like a common cur." She clicked her tongue.

Mary placed her hand on top of the shroud, over Nicolas's folded hands. A dead body felt cold to touch, even on a summer's day, but the hands she felt were not cold and lifeless. They actually seemed warmer than hers. "Nicolas," she cried close to his face, pulling at his folded hands. "Nicolas!"

Everything moved in slow motion. Mary saw her mother coming for her, her expression sad, her arms outstretched. At the same time, the dead man struggled to sit up and began thrashing around like a snake, wound so tightly in his shroud.

The widow fell backward off her stool with a howl.

Rebekah, entering right at the fateful moment, screamed shrilly and clung to Lizzie behind her. Lizzie screamed too and shook like a jelly. Then the lantern crashed to the ground, leaving them all in darkness.

Nothing seemed real, only confusing and dreamlike. Through the dim doorway, sleepy heads roused from all around the next room.

In the red light of the hall embers, Nicolas—looking not unlike Christ himself risen from the dead, albeit a bit unsteady—entered the hall, his shroud unraveling behind him.

"God bless us!" gasped his father.

"Nicolas?" croaked his servant, Tom.

"What ar-art thou?" quavered another voice, and the man drew a knife.

"A shroud?" Nicolas mumbled in bewilderment. "In God's name, why am I sleeping in a *shroud?*" he demanded, growing more indignant. "And what the devil's wrong with all o' ye?"

❧

Margaret entered the widow's pinnace, stamping her feet and blowing upon her hands.

"What be brewing out 'n about this mornin'?" the widow asked from her bedstead.

"Folk are stirred up," she answered her mistress.

"Huh! I don't doubt that a'tall," the widow snorted.

Mary sat at the table eating a breakfast of Indian pudding, bleary-eyed after only a few hours' sleep. The events from the night before seemed a strange, nightmarish dream. Margaret seemed rather stirred up too, Mary thought, noticing the maidservant's attention oddly riveted upon her.

Mary's mother appeared from their chamber with Hannah in her arms. "Nicolas Shapleigh is certainly blessed by heaven. Such a miracle we've witnessed!" She laid the sleeping babe in her cradle.

Margaret continued to stare at Mary. "Is it true what they're saying? That Mary brought Nicolas back to life with the touch of 'er hands?"

Mary stopped chewing.

Mary's mother looked sharply at Margaret. "Who has propagated such nonsense?"

"I dunno, m'dam, but one from your party, Rebekah says she saw it with her very own eyes."

"Oh, the prating ninny," Mary's mother scoffed. "Nicolas was only knocked into such a torpor that even *I* mistook him for dead. What else did Rebekah say?"

Margaret hung her head. "Madam, it's what t'others are saying . . ."

"Go on, Margaret. We're bound to hear sooner or later," ordered the widow from her bedstead.

Dread fluttered Mary's innards.

"They say," the servant began, half swallowing her words, "that Mary must be p-party to the devil, and th-the . . . goat is her familiar."

Mary felt the room kilter on its side until a rap on the door righted it again.

Lizzie stuck her head inside the pinnace. "The Reverend Burdett from Bristol has arrived. He's asking to see you, Goody White. You and Mary." She stared at Mary too, her chest heaving.

"Oh," said Mary's mother, her face gone pale as her smock. "Please inform him, Lizzie, that we'll be honored to oblige." But when Lizzie had gone, her mother changed her mind. "You're to stay here Mary," she said firmly. "I will go see the reverend alone."

Mary set down her spoon, unable to eat another bite.

That Sabbath morning, the entire village gathered beneath the oak on the hilltop for psalms and prayers. Mary stood in the circle of congregants with her parents and the Shapleigh party, including Nicolas, who seemed to be fully recovered despite scabs and bruises.

"You needn't worry, Mary," her mother had reassured after her meeting with the reverend. "I explained everything to him. He seems a reasonable man." The reverend had since returned upriver to tend his own flock.

Even so, Mary noticed that no one from the village would meet their eyes or stand too near their party, except for the other children, who stared at her like she had the plague. Walking back down to the pinnace after the service, she could feel eyes on her back.

She kept inside the next day, spending time with her quill and parchment, glad she could read and write. She smiled to remember how astounded their parish priest had been with how fast she had learned and how proud it had made her grandmother.

In the afternoon, Mary found herself alone with the widow.

"We'll be gettin' a nor'easter soon," the old woman said. "I be feelin' it in me bones." From her seat on the settle, the widow filled her pipe and reached for the pipe tongs. "Here child, be so kind to stoop for me. Me side's painin' to split."

Mary put down her quill and captured a live coal from the hearth. The old woman's apple-pip eyes followed her every move.

"Thank 'ee, deary." The widow lit her pipe and puffed away slyly.

Mary ignored her as best she could, trying to focus on her impressions of Strawbery Banke, its people, and all that had occurred since their arrival. Her small hand scratched the sepia-colored ink slowly across the paper, forming neat cursive letters. A letter to her grandmother.

"Tell me, child," the widow said presently. "I know what happened to that young man weren't no accident. I ken ye are more than just herbwomen . . . you and your mother?" The widow leaned toward her, a hungry expression on her face.

"No, 'tis as my mother has said: Nicolas was never dead, just unconscious."

"Come now, child, I can't say that I'm an expert on such things. But I know what I seen."

"Nicolas was never dead," Mary repeated. The widow's stubbornness was exasperating.

"Looked cert'nly dead enough to me. 'Tis a miraculous happenin'—I never seen the like." The widow stood. "Ack, me back," she groaned.

"It's your kidneys. You need to eat barley," Mary snapped.

The widow's eyes narrowed.

"I mean . . . *if* it's your kidneys," Mary corrected herself.

Over the next few days, Mary spent most of her time hiding in the pinnace, venturing out only to help with necessary household chores. She avoided the village children, who had taken to throwing stones again while their parents pretended to look the other way. She wondered if Goody Walford was satisfied. Had the herbwoman and her friends orchestrated their bad luck? Nicolas Shapleigh had gone across the river to the Point to escape from it all. Mary wished she could go there too.

-- 4 --

Twist of Fate

Mary's feet did not want to move. Her mother's hand pushed her firmly up the slope to the top of the hill. The gathering of villagers looked much larger than usual. The closer they got, the dizzier she felt.

"Aye, here she comes," a voice rang from the crowd. The pressure on Mary's back faltered. Her knees began to shake as necks bristled all around. Mary's father strode on ahead to the inner circle of villagers, where he stopped abreast of Alexander Shapleigh and crossed his arms over his chest. Her mother pushed her up behind him, holding Mary firmly between the two of them.

"All o'ye be jinxed!" someone yelled. Angry voices rose around them. Mary's legs felt like the tall brittle weeds still holding out rakishly on the hillside, ready to collapse at any moment.

How a Sabbath worship could possibly be held remained to be seen, when Captain Wannerton approached, flanked by his close associates and bellowing a long, drawn-out "*Silence*!" The governor strode to the top of the circle, where he stood twisting the hilt of his sword and glowering furiously about. "What are ye *thinking*?" he spat.

The crowd shrank backward.

"Are ye plum-headed *daft*? A merchant with all manner of goods comes to live amongst ye, and ye *coxcombs* bite the hand that feeds? Turn thy backs on Providence because *our Lord God spared* a man's life?"

Mary felt her mother's grip relax a little.

A man stepped forward from the crowd, his hat in his hands. "Christ Himself rose from the dead. 'Tis a good omen, I say."

The crowd murmured.

Captain Wannerton stared about vexedly. "Enough, I say!" he ranted. "What *fortune* for us—think again or think at all, *ye prating fools*!"

"The Lord has watched over us. 'Tis fortunate indeed the governor has taken our side," Mary's mother said later that day when she and Mary were alone in the prow of the pinnace. "Still, we must take great care. The irony is that you've done nothing—nothing a'tall. Woe be it if you had done *something*." A look of fear clouded her mother's face. "Mary, you didn't do anything to wake Nicolas, did you?"

Mary swallowed. "No, madam, it's as you say—I did nothing."

Her mother's expression cleared. "Good . . . I pray that folk here have short memories."

Mary didn't have the heart to tell her mother that she wasn't so entirely innocent, at least in the death of the sheep: Goody Walford probably wouldn't think so.

As welcome a relief the governor's intervention was, it did little to allay the villagers' suspicion. Mary found they continued to whisper and stare.

"Aren't much likely to stop neither," the widow remarked. She still treated Mary differently. Even Margaret looked afraid of Mary now.

That night, Mary overheard her parents again in their confined family sleeping quarters. "Wannerton," said her father, "perfidious knave, has us between the millstones. He's set a steep price with Alexander Shapleigh to keep the peace. A disgusting shame."

Winter set in within days. It snowed furiously one afternoon, the sky low and gray, and continued all night long, the wind howling from the northeast. It snowed most of the following two days as well, as though it would never stop. Mary and her family watched with amazement as the widow's tale came true: the snow piling higher and higher, burying them inside the pinnace.

Mary's father kept the doorway cleared with a wooden spade whenever he went out to fetch firewood. The path to the woodpile soon became a trench whose sides rose almost above his head.

When they were seated around the table, he told them stories of Old England and read to them from his Bible. Inside the pinnace, it became remarkably snug and quiet as the snow fell deeper all around. Mary welcomed the relative isolation, spending the time writing in her journal. Her ability to write fascinated Margaret, which got the upper hand on the maidservant's fear, especially when Mary wrote out Margaret's name for her on a scrap of paper.

The morning after the storm blazed a blinding white. Strawbery Banke lay barely recognizable under its new mantle, and life slowed to a simpler rhythm. Shoveled pathways of good intent soon gave out to trails made by folk just pushing through the snow as best they could. Men ventured into the woods to cut masts and spars for export while women visited from house to house, easing their cabin fever by knitting or sewing in company. All conserved and reused what they could. Merchant ships weren't likely to arrive until spring.

That day, Mary's father left on a hunting expedition. Deer would be easy to track in the snow, and fresh venison would be a toothsome addition to fish and salt pork. Her father, Nicolas, and a small party of others rowed across the icy river to Spruce Creek, whose head lay back in the remote countryside of hemlock ravines and wintering deer.

Something about the hunt left Mary feeling uneasy, but then most things did lately. But by the time she went to bed that night, her father still hadn't returned.

"He'll be home soon. Don't you worry," her mother told her.

Mary awoke. She sensed it wasn't close enough to dawn to rise, but a rosy glow emanated through a crack in the hanging and she could hear the sound of low, whispered voices from the hall. Thirsty, she extracted her legs from the warmth of her bed and sought out her latchet shoes with her toes. *Father must be home.* Shivering in her smock, she crept to the door.

The widow and Margaret were asleep in their bed next to the dividing wall. She could hear the widow's whistling snore. Her mother sat by the hearth, talking with Nicolas. Mary stood sleepily in the doorframe, unnoticed.

Something was wrong. Her mother's hands were twisting her apron and her head was bent forward. Mary suddenly found herself wide awake. Nicolas, silhouetted by the glow from the embers, was speaking to her mother.

"Which will lend you some peace of mind, Goody White."

"We mustn't let the village learn of this," her mother said. "'Tis one more thing to condemn." She bowed her forehead down to her clasped hands.

Mary's heart froze. *Where was Father?* "Mother?" she said.

Her mother and Nicolas looked up.

Mary walked over to where they sat. "Where's Father?"

"We don't know," her mother whispered miserably. The hollow tone to her voice made Mary's skin prickle.

"He's off on an adventure, we believe. We should know more tomorrow," Nicolas said in an unconvincing cheery voice.

Word of Mary's father did not arrive that morning. Everyone went about their business, but no one said much. Sarah, who did not know their father to be missing, began to sing.

"Sarah, today the rest of us would like silence," Mary's mother said.

The minutes dragged on slowly.

It was close to midday, judging by the sun's zenith, when the click of the door latch made everyone look up. With bated breath, they watched the door swing inward. Mary's mother hadn't moved from the settle all morning, intent upon the warm woolen waistcoat she was sewing for Mary's father. She stood up when she saw Nicolas at the door, clutching the waistcoat to her midriff. Nicolas did not look happy.

The hair stood on end under Mary's cap.

"Goody White, I must inform you that the drifting snow has concealed the tracks, and our search party has turned back. We're sending inquiry upriver to the sagamore of Quamphegan—Rowls, the local sachem."

Mary's mother gave a gasp and sank back down.

"But if I may say so, madam," Nicolas said attempting to comfort, "the local Indians are not known to be unreasonably hostile."

"What? The savages 'ave got 'im? What's this?" cried the widow.

"He seems to have had a run-in with them, judging by the empirical evidence," Nicolas answered.

Sarah began to cry. Mary didn't know what to think until the door opened again a minute later. In came her father, not only alive and well but in high spirits to top it off.

Mary's mother screamed and rushed to his side, laughing and crying simultaneously. Mary had never seen her mother so emotional with her father, but her attention quickly shifted to the men who stood behind him in the doorway, dressed in feathers and furs. One was tall, his long hair worn up in a topknot. The other man was older, his iron-gray hair held back by a quilled band, his tattooed face serene and calm. His dark eyes caught hers for a moment in their sweep of the room. She felt no fear, only curiosity. The two Indians wore fur mantles and carried on their backs the corded pelts of animals—rich browns, blacks, tans, grays, whites, and reds.

Her mother, with Sarah pressing shyly into her skirts and Hannah in her arms, beckoned Mary toward the back chamber. Reluctantly, Mary began to follow until her father handed her the big key from his belt.

"Britania," he called out, "bring a bundle of the trucking cloth to the table."

In the prow, Mary's mother laid Hannah on a pallet and sat down herself in a swoon.

"Madam!" Mary cried.

"No, child . . . just need . . . to catch my breath."

Mary watched her uncertainly. Her mother had fits like these upon occasion. They were always worrisome. Her mother took a deep breath, and Mary could tell it was more the excitement than anything.

"Madam, I can take the trucking to Father."

"No, Mary, I shall do that," her mother said firmly, gesturing for the key, but she swooned again.

"Madam . . . methinks—"

Her mother was already nodding. Mary unlocked her father's chest as she had seen him do many times. She lifted out a canvas-wrapped bundle. It was heavy, but she managed.

The men were seated at the table, smoking. Taking the bundle from her, Mary's father slid his dagger from its sheath and cut away the twine, unwrapping the woolen cloth. Blue, red, and brown measures of it, clean and new and lovely to look at. The Indian men stroked it with their hands, the way her father and Nicolas stroked and examined the pelts that lay on the other half of the table. Mary knew her mother expected her to return to the back room, but she stood watching quietly, her feet rooted to the spot. The widow and Margaret watched as well from the settle, their tongues strangely silent.

The Native men had slid their fur mantles underneath them when they sat, and Mary couldn't help but notice the quills, bones, and shells that adorned their brown-skinned bodies. She found it fascinating to hear them speak, but their presence alone spoke so much more. They had a dignity and directness about them that she liked very much.

Mary's father demanded the widow serve drink and victuals. Margaret served the men. The natives refused the drink and asked for water instead.

When the trading finished, all the men seemed happy. Nicolas too had traded his hunting knife for some pelts.

"Mary, *shame on you.* You shouldn't have stayed out here with the men," her mother scolded once their guests had departed.

"No, Britania, she was acceptable where she was," her father said. "She brings me luck." He winked at Mary. He was in fine spirits, knowing what he could earn for his fur on the next ship bound to England.

Mary stroked the fur pelts. They were cold and soft to the touch, the silky stoat her favorite. The life force that emanated from each was still palpable. She shuddered to imagine all the animals suddenly coming back to life—teeth bared and sharp claws surrounding them, angry for having their lives taken. Their lives cut short, but a wild ferocity still lingered . . . a terrible, beautiful, beastly pile.

"A word of warning," the widow piped up. "The cap'n's going to be none too pleased if he gets word ye 'ave traded right under his nose. Got a territorial bent, he does."

"Oh?" Nicolas said. "I'm sure my father can soothe his ruffled feathers."

"Ye can hope." The widow blew a stream of smoke out one side of her mouth. "But said cap'n's got a penchant for the gallows like I ne'er see."

Before long, it was Christmas Eve and, inside the pinnace, celebration was afoot. Mary and Sarah helped Margaret hang garlands of pine over the hearth and entryway, and the table was laden for a feast. Her mother and Margaret, with the help of Mary and Sarah, had baked, stewed, and roasted tirelessly for two days; singing carols and preparing the feast in the best of spirits, the widow Gyles cheering them on from her bedstead. The pinnace felt warmer and cozier than usual, but the widow kept to her bed and bolsters. Mary thought the old woman looked like a hermit crab with her boney fingers extending out from her cap, clutching her drink on the counterpane, her attention riveted on the wassail bowl.

Grinding away with mortar and pestle, Mary breathed in the heady scent of fresh nutmeg, cinnamon, cardamon, and cloves. Spices were among her favorite things and combined with the smells of fresh pine and delicious food, they made the joy of Christmases past rise up in her breast.

"Methinks it will do your father good to be the lord of misrule," her mother said from the hearth, stirring small dried plums from their Devon garden into the pudding.

Mary didn't think her father well suited for the role at all. Back in England, the master of festivities had always been a fun-loving uncle. Well, her father had cut an enormous Yule log, which was a good sign. Traditionally, the celebration could continue for as long as the Yule log burned.

Just then, the pinnace door flew open, and the hall filled with a frigid blast of air. A boy entered, his cheeks bright red from the cold.

"Mind the door!" Margaret cried. Dish in her arms, she hastily pushed it shut with her backside while the widow moaned pitifully. Mary's mother stood up out of the hearth.

Upon seeing her, the boy remembered his manners and removed his hat. "Madam, my mother needs your help!" he pleaded, his eyes wide and fearful. He looked a little younger than Mary.

Her mother took him by the shoulders. "What's the matter, boy?"

"Her time has come. My father's gone to fetch the doctor!"

Midwife as she was, Mary's mother did not hesitate. She quickly placed herbs from her medicine chest into her handbasket. She didn't know who was in labor or where, but go she would. Dr. Reynolds lived out on the Great Island in the river. The channel, half iced over, would be treacherous to cross once it grew dark.

"What's your name, and where's your mother?" her mother asked the boy, tying on her cloak.

"Charles Frost, madam. My mother's at home upriver. The servants at Captain Wannerton's said to come fetch you."

"Mary, tell your father where I've gone. There's plenty to feed him with," she added dryly.

Yes, it was Christmas, but labor was labor. When it was a woman's time, all else went by the wayside.

"I shall take care of everything, madam," Margaret reassured her.

Mary's mother nodded, pulling on her hood. Then the door opened again, and Mary's father nearly collided into them.

"A woman's time has come," her mother told him, following the boy Charles out over the threshold. "I will be upriver at the Frosts'."

Childbirth was where a man stood back: it was women's business. Mary's father stood in the doorway and watched them go.

On impulse, Mary did a bold thing. Grabbing her cloak, she looked up at her father. "Sir? I must go too. Mother will need my help." She could hardly believe the words she heard coming out of her mouth; it was not her place to demand anything. And after all, the plum pudding smelled tantalizing, and the feasting would soon begin . . .

To her complete amazement, her father nodded. "Yes, go with her, Mary. Help your mother."

She found herself half running, half sliding along the frozen path to the dock. Tiny crystals of snow stung her face. The wind blew in swirls and gusts, the western sky streaked a purple orange. Not the best of days for a journey by water, but her excitement goaded her on. She needed to prove her worth; then things would get better. *If Strawbery Banke only knew what good she could do.*

"Madam!" Mary cried, catching up with her mother and Charles at the dock. "Father said that I should come with you."

Her mother raised an eyebrow. "You know what is expected?"

"Yes, madam," Mary answered, relieved her mother did not turn her away. This would be her first birth. She would be careful. She cradled the wrapped heated stone a Wannerton servant handed her and pressed against her mother for warmth. Surprisingly it was the governor's shallop that was transporting them. A sturdy, safe craft. Still, she looked at the dark blue water whipped by the icy wind and whispered a quick prayer.

Night had fallen by the time they arrived at the Frost homestead. Half-frozen, Mary followed her mother and Charles across the threshold of a dwelling set back from the river. Inside, she had little time to assess her own condition as a gut-wrenching cry greeted them from the next room.

"Bring me a basin of hot water with what clean linen you can find," her mother instructed, dashing to the woman's aid.

Two small children sat huddled inside the hearth. A frightened-looking maidservant emerged from the next room and pointed to a decoratively painted cupboard. "The cloth's in there."

Mary blinked the ice crystals from her lashes and reached for the linen with sticklike arms, trying to look competent. The children watched her, their eyes round and terrified.

"Mother will be fine now that she has help," their brother Charles said, but he did not sound convinced of this himself.

The Frosts' maidservant helped Mary heat the water, and they brought the items into the birthing chamber, cold and dimly lit despite the fire in its hearth. Goody Frost lay on her side upon a bedstead while Mary's mother pressed her hands into the woman's laboring back.

"Steep the comfrey in the basin, Mary," her mother instructed calmly, a soft, almost-happy tone to her voice. "And then we'll need some raspberry leaf and shepherd's purse." Her mother was a good midwife; everything would be all right now Mary hoped.

Once back in the hall, she looked around curiously as the blood painfully returned to her fingers and toes. A Christmas feast lay upon the table here too, untouched. The furniture had been brought from England: a great chair, the cupboard, and a chest. A tapestry of a hunting scene hung on one wall, as did a shelf with some books upon it—books held between two beautifully carved book ends.

Charles saw her looking at them. "My father cut those off the ship we came on to have as a keepsake," he told her.

Charles's younger sister's name was Anna. She watched Mary steep raspberry leaf and shepherd's purse. Once Mary had delivered the second infusion to the birth chamber, two-year-old Anna climbed into Mary's lap and curled up against her. They all sat in the relative warmth of the hearth corner to wait, listening to the bitter wind whistling down the chimney.

"My father should be back soon with the doctor," Charles said, chewing on his nails.

In the warmth of the hearth, Mary dozed off with the youngest Frost children huddled against her. It must have been the wee hours of the morning when they were all startled awake by a hair-raising cry.

"Mary!" her mother called.

Extracting herself from the little ones in a panic, Mary dashed to the next room.

"Hold the lantern just above," her mother instructed the Frost's maidservant.

Mary watched in amazement as her mother eased a tiny head into the world, followed by the smallest human body she'd ever seen.

"Ooh, wee one, thou has a good pair of lungs!" her mother crooned. She wrapped the newborn babe in the linen cloth and handed her to Mary.

Holding the infant frightened Mary. The babe's umbilical cord coiled out of the swaddling, a glistening, living entrail. Then the crying stopped, and the newborn's eyes moved from Mary's face to look calmly about the chamber and Mary's fear vanished. She thought about her grandmother, who had midwifed her birth and had been the first loving touch she'd ever felt, the first one to look in her eyes. A lump tightened her throat.

"Give her to her mother," Mary's mother said gently. Goody Frost snuggled her newborn while Mary, her mother, and the servant girl wiped tears from their eyes.

Once the placenta followed, Mary's mother began to press down on Goody Frost's stomach in a kneading, gathering manner. "This will help shrink the womb and stop her from bleeding so much."

But the bleeding didn't stop.

"Madam," Mary whispered, "she needs snow."

"*Snow*? What would she need snow for, Mary?" her mother snapped.

"'Tis the cold she needs," Mary said, glancing uncomfortably at the maidservant kneeling beside the bedstead, holding her mistress's hand. The girl looked terrified.

"Fetch some then," her mother said through clenched teeth, the cloth blooming dark crimson under her hands.

The icy-cold snow did staunch Goody Frost's bleeding.

"I say," Goody Frost said, smiling weakly, "I've not known the cold to ever feel so good."

Mary's mother gave Mary's arm a warm squeeze. She smiled back at her mother. Her mother certainly would have to appreciate her gift now.

When Charles and his siblings were welcomed in to meet their new sister, Mary braved the frigid cold outside for another bucketful of snow. The night sky was clear, and the stars sparkled brilliantly. She caught sight of two dark figures moving up from the river against the snow and hurried back inside. Almost on her heels, the frozen specters of Goody Frost's husband and Dr. Reynolds strode into the birth chamber, radiating cold.

Mary's mother greeted them merrily. "Goodman Frost, congratulations—you have a Christmas baby!"

"A boy?"

"No, a beautiful baby girl."

At daybreak, Mary followed the two men down to the river. Goody Frost and child were doing well, but her mother would stay a little longer to help with their lying-in. Her mother also wanted to be sure that Goody Frost and her maidservant understood Mary to be blameless.

Mary's first sight of the craft that was to transport her back to Strawbery Banke terrified her. It looked impossibly narrow and so low to the water that she was afraid it would sink right under.

"A canoe doesn't look a'tall like a sturdy craft," Dr. Reynolds said. "But if it'll hold me, it'll hold you, lassie and Nicolas here is a good navigator." The doctor was a large man. Mary didn't doubt him.

"Just don't stand up," Nicolas Frost instructed.

She held her breath and stepped inside, crouching down. So far, so good. Her knuckles clenched reflexively on the gunnels while the doctor got in, but they remained buoyant. Nicolas took his place last and pushed them off. They glided over the surface with only a paddle, following the current and pull of the tide. Gently, like a floating leaf.

The men were tired, and no one said much. Mary began to relax and enjoy the ride. She removed her frozen hands from the gunnel and tucked them under her cloak. In the stillness of the Christmas dawn, she watched her breath steam and a beautiful rosy sunrise glow from the east over the wintry landscape.

Back at the Banke, Yule logs had survived the night, judging by some shouts and merry laughter. As the canoe made for the dock, a lone figure stood upon the crest of the hill beneath the oak tree and sang at the top of his voice,

I saw three ships come sailing in on Christmas Day,
on Christmas Day.
I saw three ships come sailing in on Christmas Day
in the morning!

A week after the caroler's heartfelt serenade, Mary stood with her family on that very spot along with the entire village yet again. Her feet were frozen and sunk deep in the snow, and the sky threatened to unleash more any minute. She didn't want to be there. It made her nervous with the villagers staring at her the way they did. But this time, the gathering had nothing to do with her or their party, and it was not a Sabbath service. Perhaps it was her they'd really like to hang. The nauseous memory of a blackened fly-covered corpse dangling from a gibbet came to mind. They'd sailed past the execution dock while leaving London Town. Mary shuddered.

Captain Wannerton looked mean as the devil standing next to a young man whose hands were bound behind him. A noose hung from a branch of the great oak tree, where a ladder was propped. The expectant crowd grew still.

"O that Thou wouldst slay the wicked, O God," the governor began with a psalm, *"depart from me, therefore, men of bloodshed. For they speak against Thee wickedly, and Thine enemies take Thy name in vain. Do I not hate those who hate Thee, O Lord? And do I not loathe those who rise up against Thee? I hate them with the utmost hatred. They have become my enemies . . ."*

Wannerton's prisoner stood hatless and unshaven. He wore no cloak to protect himself from the cold, and his doublet was rent in places. He looked like some unfortunate servant mistakenly accused, whose body and mind had been beaten to a bruised and bewildered blankness. The more Mary stared at him, the more certain she was he did not deserve this—whatever it was that he'd done. She looked around in a panic, but no one else seemed to think anything was amiss.

"Stop!" Mary screeched.

Her mother clapped a hand firmly over Mary's mouth. Her father cleared his throat and shifted his weight.

The crowd shuffled nervously and heads turned their way, but only for a moment, as first a sack and then the noose were placed over the prisoner's head. Then a halberd prodded him up the ladder. "Caught trading with the Indians on the Sabbath," someone said nearby.

Mary stared miserably down at her skirt. She couldn't watch. She heard a loud snap and then a creak as the rope stretched taut. The crowd cheered. Mary looked up to see the young man's body swinging lifelessly.

Mary, her mother, and sister hurried away, back down to the shore of the cove and into the widow's pinnace to warm by the fire. But the heat of the hearth did little to alleviate the chill that burned inwardly.

-- 5 --

The Point at Spruce Creek

On a midwinter afternoon, with the Whites' remaining goods and chattels loaded into a seaworthy shallop, Mary and her family bid the widow and Margaret farewell.

"Ye come back to visit now, ye hear, dearies?" the widow called after them, her face a skull-like specter from the door. Margaret stood near the frozen step, wiping her eyes with her apron.

Her father rowed them through the ice floes to a small cove hidden behind several islands in the river. To that peninsula of land on the opposite shore known as the Point. Here, a newly built cottage lay blanketed in snow and nestled against a backdrop of trees, a stone chimney rising up out of one end.

In the deepening twilight, Mary's father carried her mother in over the threshold. Inside were the joyful surprises of Mary's mother's dowry chest and cupboard, as well as her father's great chair. They lit a fire of sweet-burning birch logs in the hearth. Everything smelled fresh and new. It felt wonderful to have a home of their own again.

Mary helped her mother unpack their crates and boxes. Even the family crockery and pewter seemed new again. Their mahogany clock had survived the journey too. It was a gift from a nobleman to Mary's grandfather for saving the man's son from drowning. Now it sat on top of the cupboard, the crowning grace above Mary's mother's pewter plates, redware, and little green-stem Venetian glasses with encased bubbles that reminded Mary of the sea. The clock's rhythmic ticktock filled their new home with the soul of their old.

The Point was a small and isolated settlement bordering the mouth of Spruce Creek, a tidal tributary that flowed into the Pascataqua. The storage house where the family's belongings had been kept since their arrival lay only a short way through the woods. The fishermen who wintered there were now out at the Isles of Shoals for the start of their season, and the place was quiet.

A trader named Phillip Swadden lived along the creek and was known for driving people off with his halberd if the mood struck him. He'd taken an Indian woman for a wife, and she'd then left him, taking their child with her. The cottage of two fishermen named Billings and Landers lay next door to theirs, but they had no wives nor family and were usually out to sea. The only other dwelling, through the woods along the shore in the opposite direction, was Alexander Shapleigh's new house, which had been finished the month prior. Here, their only female neighbors lived, the Shapleigh servants Lizzie and Rebekah.

The morning after their arrival, Lizzie came to call. She was weeping and snuffling, her eyes all puffy and red. Mary's mother sat her down in the great chair. "Lizzie dear, whatever's the matter?"

The Shapleigh housekeeper recovered herself momentarily, but as she began to explain, her tears started anew. "I d-didn't do it!" she wailed. "I . . . I would *never.*" She dabbed at her eyes, her pocket handkerchief twisted up like a seashell.

"There, there." Mary's mother patted Lizzie's ample shoulder. "Perhaps you need a little something? Mary, fetch her a draught of brandy, please."

Mary poured the gurgling liquid into one of her mother's Venetian glasses. It was fun to have a visitor, even one that was unhappy.

Lizzie drank the brandy down and soon had calmed enough to tell them her story. "Master boxed me ears and was lief to kill me," she began.

Mr. Shapleigh was a shrewd and wealthy man, but not exactly known to be violent. Lizzie had served the Shapleigh household since she was twelve years old and was much liked by them. "Alexander boxed your ears?" Mary's mother exclaimed. "Whatever for?"

The housekeeper sat silent a moment, her face flushing to the edges of her cap. "Goat's dung," she said hoarsely. "He found goat's dung in his pudding."

Mary's mother drew her breath in sharply. "Fie, Lizzie! For goodness' sake, how did that happen?"

Mary bit down hard on her hand to stifle a giggle, but one escaped all the same. A glare from her mother silenced it.

"I don't know," Lizzie answered. "I would *n-never* do such a thing. He said I was a filthy housekeeper and that he might as well put someone more competent, like Rebekah, in charge."

"Oh?" Mary's mother said. "We all know what a tidy housekeeper you are, Lizzie. I wonder what hand your fellow servants may have played in this."

A frown passed over Lizzie's round face.

Other unexplainable things had happened in the Shapleigh household. Recently, a stew had turned out to be saltier than the sea; and prior to that, Alexander had found sand in his bed after Lizzie had warmed his sheets with the bedpan.

"Lizzie," Mary's mother warned, "if I were you, I would keep a careful eye on Rebekah and the young menservants. Sand and salt don't just appear on their own, to say nothing about goat's dung."

Outside of the drama unfolding in their neighbor's household, the Point proved a suitable place. Surrounded by water on three sides, it was relatively safe from wild beasts; and Mary took to exploring when she could, feeding the small winter birds breadcrumbs from her pocket. The silence of the woods after a deep snowfall fed her soul, and her spirit soared to connect to God in the way she did best. She often stayed out until her feet were wet and frozen, gathering dried branches for kindling, a worn pair of her father's gloves on her hands.

The month of March brought more snow than Mary's parents thought possible. In the month that planting began in earnest back in England, they were still surrounded by deep, impenetrable winter. Depressing, to say the least. Then worrisome to find that their very last barrel of salted meat had gone bad, and hunting was next to impossible in the heavy, wet snow. Fortunately, their fishermen neighbors were catching fish, and this sustained them, along with a small ration of peas daily—all that was left of their supplies. Haddock for breakfast, cod for dinner, haddock for supper, or some such variance for days on end. Pine needles began to look appealing.

A mouthful of them did not taste so nice, but Mary discovered they made a palatable and energizing tisane when steeped in hot water.

One morning, after a week of fish, Mary's mother opened the cottage door to find a haunch of venison on the doorstep. "Who would be so kind?" she remarked.

Mary knew who would be, though she dared not say anything. The possibility of Indians still made her mother nervous when Mary's father left for the day, leaving them alone.

As the month began to wane, warmer, thawing days followed, and the sun shone more brightly. Mary and Sarah began to venture out again. A large rock in the woods above their dooryard became their castle, the snow melting from it before anything else. Around the rock grew a forest of large gray beech, through which the path to the community sawpit led. The sound of wood being sawed and chopped became something they heard almost every day. But soon, the budding undergrowth and forest became alive with other sounds: the songs of birds, thousands of them, passing through on their migration, the likes of which Mary had never heard before. March 24 came and went and with it 1637, as it was the last day of the year under the Julian calendar. The patches of bare earth grew larger until they transformed into patches of snow melting away.

On a day with the sky threatening rain, Mary's father paddled her across the mouth of Spruce creek in his new Indian-built canoe. "What do you think about this spot here?" he asked, pointing to a place with few trees on the opposite shore.

"'Twould be a good place, sir."

He tied off the canoe, and Mary climbed up the viney entanglement after him to the edge of a brush-choked clearing. Her father sank his knife down into the earth. Ah—the soil's rich and dark—and it smells sweet. 'Twill make a good planting ground once I clean out that large briar patch in the center."

With the further discovery of a spring nearby, Mary's father fetched his scythe from the canoe and fell to the briar patch. Mary helped by piling his cuttings nearby. The task proved difficult, and though the day was damp and cold, her father soon peeled down to his shirt. "We might have to burn the site. There's just too much here," he said.

He continued to slash away at the worst of the thicket until a swipe of his scythe exposed the unimaginable: caught up in the brambles was a human skull. It stared back at them in macabre fashion, its jaw twisted in an agonizing grimace. Vines grew out of its eye sockets and into its grinning mouth. "Merciful Father!" her father gasped.

Mary stared in disbelief.

Other sweeps of her father's scythe uncovered more: the rib cage, pelvis, and femur bones were there as well. Mary's father continued clearing, only to discover two other skeletons in various postures of death. Vines had lifted some of the bones skyward.

"Dead from plague, likely," her father said. "This must have been the site of an Indian village."

Mary sat a distance away, feeling queasy. One of the remains was that of a child. *Maybe this isn't such a good place for Father to grow his corn after all.* But her father still seemed to think so.

He dug a grave in the soil at the edge of the clearing. Perhaps another man would have raked the remains carelessly into a midden or thrown the bones away like pieces of rotten wood into the trees. But not Mary's father. He buried them properly on the edge of the field, reading the passage from Job 19 commonly read at Anglican funerals from the little Bible he carried on his person. None of the other verses seemed to apply.

"*I know that my Redeemer liveth and that I shall rise out of the earth in the last day, and shall be covered again with my skin, and shall see God in my flesh: Yea, and I myself shall behold him, not with other but with these same eyes.*"

This moved Mary to tears. Her father had just finished rolling a good-sized stone atop the grave when an eagle's feather drifted to the ground by her side. She left it next to the marker in silence.

That week, her father burned his new field to prepare it for planting and helped her mother rock in a raised border for the kitchen garden so she could get the peas and spring greens into the ground. H
a fence of cut saplings and branches around the dooryard, fer

a small paddock with split rails for the milk cow he planned to buy, and built a henhouse. The promise of abundance after months of deprivation raised everyone's spirits. Out on the river, their neighbors Billings and Landers were dipnetting the early spring herring run; giant schools of fish turning the river silver as they leapt from the water.

On a blustery mild day that smelled of damp earth, Mary's mother began the task of washing all the household linen. She strung twine between the trees above the cottage, and soon their little house lay surrounded by a dozen flapping white sails as though it were a ship at sea.

The wind felt warm coming out of the south. Mary marveled at a flock of red-breasted birds, much larger than the English robins she knew. The birds landed hungry, looking for worms, as the buds on the undergrowth and trees were swelling.

When Mary returned to the house to fetch another spool of twine, a pile of corded pelts on the form outside the door caught her attention. *Had that been there before?* She had scarcely finished the thought before she discovered two Indians seated inside at the table. They stared back at her quietly, untroubled.

One of them was the older man her father traded with named Migwah. She didn't recognize the other. Alarmed, Mary turned to go find her mother, but the men followed her out to where her mother was hanging laundry.

Her mother looked terrified. She tried to explain to the Indians that Mary's father would not be back until midday for dinner. Whether or not they understood, Mary couldn't tell. They moved over to some tree stumps on the edge of the clearing. They sat together, talking little. Mary could feel her mother's fear and agitation as she held Hannah on her hip with one arm and tried to wring out stockings. After a while, when nothing untoward had come from their Indian company, her mother set Hannah down. Peeking out from behind the drying sheets at their visitors, little Hannah smiled. Soon, the men were drawn into her game, pretending surprise to see her when Hannah moved her hands off her eyes.

It didn't take long for Mary and Sarah to lose their shyness and for the natives to loosen their reserve. Migwah unfastened a little birchbark pouch from his waist. Gesturing to his mouth, he handed Mary a light brown piece of something. She bit into it cautiously, not knowing what to expect. A most incredible sweet taste greeted her tongue. The substance melted like sugar but changed in complexity as it dissolved. Mary thought it absolutely the most delicious thing she'd ever tasted. Her surprise and pleasure must have shown, for Migwah grinned. Then he handed her sisters pieces of the same.

"Senomozi'i," Migwah said, and then in English, he explained, "Blood of a tree." He pointed to the maple and birch trees from whence it came. Then he cut out a strip of the inner bark from a birch for Mary to try. It tasted surprisingly tender and good.

Later that day, after their Indian visitors had left, Mary stood at her father's side as he inspected his newest stack of pelts.

"Five fox," he mused aloud, "the last of the winter pelts."

"Sir, can I ask you a question?"

"Yes, my wild rose?" He liked to call her this when he was happy.

"Is Migwah a sachem?"

"Migwah is a medicine keeper, what the Abenakis call a *medeoulin*. Not a sachem, but he holds high respect and esteem in his tribe.'"

A medicine keeper! Mary pulled at her sleeve cuffs excitedly. "He taught us how to make a syrup from trees today before you came home."

Her father looked down at her. "Migwah is a good man—for a heathen." He looked around to see if they were alone in the house and lowered his voice. "He's been helping us out more than you're aware of."

"I know he has. It makes good pottage."

Her father smiled.

Mary smiled back.

"Let's keep it our secret, my little seer," he said with a wink.

❧

In a clearing up behind the Whites' cottage, Migwah crouched down. He dug at a plant with a sharpened stick, pointing out the rosette of leaves close to the ground that identified it.

Ever since laundry day, Mary considered him her special friend. She'd been looking forward to his next visit with her father, hoping he'd show her more edible and medicinal plants. She was not disappointed.

With a click of his tongue, the *medeoulin* pulled up a long reddish taproot.

"For eating?" Mary asked. She still felt a little shy standing next to him, but comfortable enough to be close to his fierce-looking presence. What he showed her was fascinating. So much was right here underfoot. She fairly shook with excitement.

"Unh-honh," he answered. "Yes, very good for eating."

With Migwah as her mentor, she could help so many people, and her knowledge would make her that much more indispensable.

As Migwah cleaned the root with his knife, Mary looked up to see Rebekah watching them from a short distance away over a wild tangle of bittersweet vines. Rebekah, realizing she'd been seen, turned abruptly away. So renowned, Mary thought with irritation, that even Rebekah would mind her own business.

Migwah had seen Rebekah too. Mary noticed his gaze lingered over the place she'd been.

A few days later, Mary sat quietly in a clearing near Spruce Creek while two fox cubs played with their mother. The vixen didn't seem to mind Mary's presence at all, and the cubs crept up to her curiously. Mary sat perfectly still while the little ones sniffed at her hand. Nearby, their mother gave a toothy yawn and began to preen her coat. Mary played tug-of-war with the cubs with a stick. They made her laugh with their posturing and growls until their mother suddenly barked and scolded them away. Wondering why, Mary looked around. Again, she caught sight of Rebekah, this time trying to hide behind a tree.

"Good day, Rebekah!" she called out.

The girl said nothing but just stared at Mary before she walked away. What Mary had first attributed to loneliness or curiosity on the maidservant's part now seemed to have a different motive altogether, and it worried her.

But she was not without defense. Up past the beech trees that grew behind her father's cottage stood a stand of young white pines whose boughs grew low to the ground. Mary loved to climb to the highest branches of one that offered a nice bird's-eye view of the surrounds. Without leaves on the other trees, she could look down on their cottage roof and the cove, as well as see clear over to the Shapleigh house and out over the river to the Great Island.

One day shortly after the incident with the fox cubs, Mary sat comfortably secured between two branches, enjoying the view, until she saw Rebekah approach. The maidservant came to a stop below in the clearing and looked around, staring at Mary's family's cottage as though she were listening or expecting something. Mary's fingertips discovered the tiny beach stones and shells she had collected inside her pocket. Taking a handful, she tossed them down at Rebekah.

Through the pine branches, Mary glimpsed Rebekah start and look around. Mary launched a second handful. Rebekah gave a surprised cry and looked wildly about, but Mary was well hidden by the boughs.

"Who's there?" Rebekah called out, obviously frightened.

Mary could hardly keep from laughing. She threw a third handful, forcefully and straight down. The girl screamed and ran back in the direction of her master's house. Mary made her way down from the tree, giggling in amusement. *Maybe now Rebekah will mind her own business.*

❧

Mary's father had spent weeks clearing, turning soil, and planting when an unforeseen disaster struck. His seedlings were nary two inches high when the ground froze white with frost one night and wilted them all to the ground. Seasoned settlers said the spring was unusually cold. With determination, he planted again. Without homegrown food, they would have little to eat; and with New England's short growing season, every day counted. Then on the twenty-fifth of April, snowflakes as big as shillings fell for two hours, covering the ground a foot deep and destroying her father's second planting. All along the Pascataqua, settlers lost their plantings. Spirits sank very low. Some from Pascataway went out to the Isles of Shoals to trade what they could for foodstuffs with the fishermen who had come in from England for the season.

Several days after this snowfall, which melted away almost overnight, the first merchant ship since the previous fall arrived. Excitement ran paramount as the ship slipped upriver, its sails fully spread like an angel of mercy.

Anchoring first at Strawbery Banke and then upriver at Bristol, the ship brought much-needed goods and supplies as well as newcomers to the plantations. Practically in its wake followed a ship of Alexander Shapleigh's. Mary's father barely got his field planted for a third time before he found himself at his employer's beck and call. Goods of all sorts needed to be accounted for and transferred from the ship to Shapleigh's newly built warehouse at the Point.

When Mary's father's work at the Point was finally complete, he set off in his canoe to Strawbery Banke, taking Mary with him. He was anxious to sell his furs at the best possible price and expected her guidance, as he was used to back in England.

From the bow of the canoe, Mary watched Strawbery Banke appear from behind a channel island, its familiar landscape filling in with green, a weak sun burning overhead. New warehouses and docks were sprouting along the shore, and with three large ships now anchored, the place fairly swarmed with sailors and traders. She pulled the hood of her cloak over her cap, hoping no one would recognize her.

Her father guided his craft across the fast-moving current to calmer water under the stern of one of the anchored ships. They looked up at the weathered transom, *The Fairwind of Bristol* just legible on its scrolled stern. The ship's gigantic rudder plunged down into the water, its dark surface streaked orange with rust. At the waterline barnacles clung visibly while emerald-green seaweed ruffled softly just beneath.

There were two other ships anchored nearby, and her father looked at her questioningly, resting his paddle. "So which one is it to be, Mary?"

"This one," she said. It felt right.

From the *Fairwind*'s small casements above, the sounds of laughter and the ring of glassware spilled. Hearkening, her father called up, "Ho there, gentlemen! Anybody in need of beaver pelt?"

The laughter quieted, and the face of a man leaned out above. "Might be . . . I daresay!" boomed his voice, catching sight of her father's enormous piles of fur.

On the ship's deck, Mary looked around while her father bartered. This ship was much larger than theirs had been. A cat peered out at her from the sill of a companionway. It scampered over, and she picked it up. A young thing, it began to purr and knead the air with its paws. What a sweet creature. Mary wished she could have her. The cat was solid black except for a white mark on its chest—a mark that had no doubt saved its life. The officers on board were tippling a ceremonial round. One of them offered Mary a confection from a decorated tin. It dissolved on her tongue and tasted of rose water. He smiled at the cat resting regally upon her shoulder.

"I think she's found a mistress, she has. Take her with you, if you like. She's the last of the litter," he told her.

Mary looked at her father, who was in such good spirits that he could hardly refuse. They had certainly picked the right ship: the men had bought every single one of his pelts—and for coin. His purse hung heavy with gold crowns.

"We'll take the cat into the bargain," he said, laughing. He washed down the last of his glass and winked at her. He was over the moon— in fact, she'd never seen her father so happy. He'd just become a rich man.

As her father had other Shapleigh business to attend to, he next paddled over to one of the newly built warehouses that lay below the hill where the oak tree stood. The shore rose steeply here, and Mary followed him up the wooden dock, her cat and their dinner basket in her arms. She was not welcome inside while the men talked business, so she contented herself to wait on some stacked boards and barrels in the yard nearby.

The spot proved to be a good hideaway, the leafing bushes concealing any view of her from either the village or the water. The sun shone warmly, and the smell of the spring air was sweet. A meadowlark sang from the top of a nearby bush.

The cat amused her by exploring the newness of solid land and the natural world until a dog arrived. Picking up the cat's scent, the hound snuffled about despite Mary's scolding. She was glad when at last it trotted off, lured by other things.

"You can come out now," Mary told the glowing round eyes hidden between the boards.

A company of sailors pulled up to the dock below, their longboat riding low, piled with casks and goods. The crew sat, waiting to unload.

"So, mates, did ye hear about the crew in the shallop laden w' powder?" A strong West Country accent spoke up. Mary couldn't help but listen. "Them was under way from Winter Island ta Boston, wi' two on watch," the sailor drawled. "One o' them pulled oot 'is pipe, sayin' 'e was goin' ta 'ave a smoke—he couldn't take it no more. T'other told 'im to wait on it, but 'e got awful antsy an' said pox on't. 'e was going to 'ave a smoke if it blew 'im to kingdom come, an' 'e didn't care neither. So he lit 'is pipe, and the shallop blew into pieces and sank right down. All hands were rescued, but for the pipe smoker. Never found e'en a finger of 'im!"

Crude laughter followed. Mary could smell pipe smoke. She hoped the cargo in the longboat wasn't gunpowder. More laughter. What were they up to now?

She peered through the leaves to see a sailor parodying Alexander Shapleigh walking along the dock, waving his hands for ears.

"What's taking ole sail ears all this time?" someone said.

The laughter continued. Mary was glad they didn't know she was there.

"Master's going to 'ave it in for us, I'll tell ye," said another man, "seein' us twiddling our thumbs on this dock while Mr. Shapleigh's up there, drammin' with that dandy in French clothes."

Mary felt the blood rush to her face; they were making fun of her father now. She knew her father was seen as arrogant by some, especially the cruder sort.

The door to the warehouse opened, and the dockside prattle came to an abrupt stop. Her father emerged to give the sailors their work orders. Then as she feared, he called her name.

She skipped around the yard away from the waterside, hoping to keep her proximity a secret from the sailors now bent under the weight of their burdens.

"There you are, Mary. Go ahead and eat your dinner. I have to head out to a ship for a short while. I'll eat when I get back."

"Yes, sir," she replied, unable to look him in the eye.

The sailors finished unloading and left with her father. She and the cat both ate some of her mother's newly made cheese.

Shortly, another craft approached the dock. Mary peered through the leaves again to see Captain Wannerton and Nicolas Frost tie off a canoe loaded with trucking cloth.

"Any spirits you might spare us, thirsty traders?" the captain called out to Mr. Shapleigh as he appeared.

Mary's father had discovered that Nicolas Frost also hailed from Tiverton. She wondered how his wife, Bertha; little Anna; and his baby daughter were faring and then turned her attention back to her cat, who was now springing out of hiding to ambush her shoe.

A loud guffaw came from the dock below. "No, no—I must decline," she heard Mr. Shapleigh say. "Enjoy yourselves, my goodmen. There's much I must get done as I'm leaving for England with my ship."

"Poppycock, you know your man White'll see to it. Speaking of White, you're lucky I don't break both his legs or worse!" growled Captain Wannerton.

Mary froze, suddenly afraid for her father. She neither liked nor trusted the captain, even if he was the reason the village had left her alone. To think of the young man swinging from the oak still made her ill.

Shapleigh's voice turned in her direction. "Would ye care for a stave or two cross-side the head? I've got quite a stash."

Mary panicked, not wanting her proximity to be discovered, but Mr. Shapleigh stopped short.

"Wannerton, you're a rogue and a knave," he huffed. "And the spirits will cost you a double crown in beaver, payable to my son."

"We'll see to it, Alex," Nicolas Frost laughed. Casting off, the two men set out upriver.

Mary watched their canoe move across the water until it became a dark speck in the distance.

They were off to trade with the Indians, but something about their mission did not feel good to her at all—it made her feel sad.

-- 6 --

The Mice Will Play

It was May Day, the traditional day to celebrate spring, and Strawbery Banke looked to have the resources for a merry celebration, with half a dozen ships anchored off her shores. A festive mood flourished up and down the river, and torches had burned long into the night for days.

Mary and Sarah swung little Hannah between them, laughing at her shrieks of delight. Everyone at the Point acted much more relaxed with Alexander Shapleigh gone. He'd departed for England only the day before. Now Mary's parents, Nicolas, and his manservant, Tom, had left for Strawbery Banke for the day and the Point felt almost deserted.

Misty sunlight filtered through the unfurling leaves, and Mary's heart leapt with all the newness and possibilities. She imagined the fun they'd have spending the day with Lizzie.

Inside the Shapleigh house however, she found a rather melancholy Lizzie sighing wistfully as she prepared a supper for the return of her master. Rebekah was mending stockings in the light of an open casement, her face sharp enough to cut. "Methinks we shouldn't have to miss May Day altogether," the girl grumbled, ignoring Mary and her sisters. "No woods gathering last night, not a wreath or a nosegay to be had. It's just not fair. It's not even *English*, I say!"

Lizzie sighed again. "Pascataway is no Merry Mount, Rebekah."

Rebekah rolled her eyes. "What kind of land is this, anyway? It's May Day, and the leaves have *barely* come out! And flowers . . . well." She sniffed. "There aren't any."

Mary wondered how Rebekah could be so mistaken. There were many flowers. She had found mayflower blossoms, trilliums, and lady slippers—dozens of them—and sweet-smelling crab apple blossoms, and others whose names she didn't know.

"Finish the darning. Then you may take a rest," Lizzie answered, plainly sick of the other's discontent.

This did little to appease Rebekah, who continued, her voice taking on an exaggerated tone of longing. "Not even a *whitepot* to be had—pity. Though we *have* the cream for it *and* the rose water *and* the sugar . . ."

Rebekah, the sharp-toothed shepherd, lured Lizzie, the docile cow, to the gate. Everyone knew Lizzie was fond of sweets. "Well, I s'pose we could make whitepots," Lizzie said. "We'd have to fire the bake oven."

Mary's mouth watered. The thought of the sweet, creamy pudding was intoxicating after such scant winter fare.

"Oh yes!" Sarah cried. "Please let's, Lizzie. We can help!"

Directing the girls, Lizzie prepared some embers. She had just tipped live coals into the oven with the iron peel when two other household servants, Eddy and Samuel, strode in the doorway. The lads looked a sight, having twisted wreaths of ferns, vines, and flowers in their hair and about their persons like mummers. Eddy began to morris dance wildly across the room.

Lizzie turned and screamed at the sight of them, dropping the peel onto the hearthstones with a ringing crash.

"Dear maidens," Eddy, a strapping nineteen-year-old, shouted in the din, "stop your toils and drudgeries, for the Lord of the May Games is here!"

Samuel stood by laughing, carrying a brimming pitcher. He was younger than Eddy, a skinny and rather awkward fellow, his complexion covered with spots.

Eddy set a flowery wreath over Lizzie's head with a flourish.

"Leave me be!" Lizzie screeched, throwing the wreath off with a wave of her hand. "I'll have none such sport. *Shoo*!" She beat him off with her apron, her size alone a force to reckon with.

"And why not, my maiden?" Eddy queried, standing safely out of apron range. "'Tis May Day, and Nicolas is not back 'til late—*if at all* t'day. Why not have a little celebration of our own?"

Samuel set the pitcher on the table while Rebekah scurried to get drinking pots off the cupboard shelves.

Lizzie looked aghast. "For *shame*, tippling our Master's stores!"

"Oh, Goody Two-shoes," Eddy teased her, flashing Lizzie his most comely look and wink of his eye. "There's more sack than'll be missed w' such a large cask in the storehouse." He grinned. "Why shouldn't we partake in a little festivity too?"

Lizzie stood with her hands on her hips, shaking her head and wagging her finger until the lads, in desperation, each grabbed an arm and jigged madly about the room with her. Only after Lizzie accepted a cup from Rebekah and took a rather thirsty swallow to the cheers of the other three did she concede to a bit of celebration.

"But I daresay ye look as fair as savages!" she puffed, patting her brow with her pocket hanky.

"What about the whitepots?" Sarah's very concerned little voice piped up.

"Those 'uns can make 'em," Rebekah said to Lizzie, tossing her head in Sarah's direction.

"We can make them, Lizzie," Mary agreed, looking to see if Rebekah looked pleased, but there was no indication Rebekah had even heard her. Funny how Rebekah spied on her in private but ignored her in public.

"Hmm, a taste o' them would be good for the stomach," Eddy said, draining his drinking pot.

"Aye." Lizzie nodded, still recovering her breath, and waved her approval at Mary.

Mary and Sarah set the rice to boil while Hannah tottered about, chewing Sarah's poppet. The girls began a game of cat's cradle, but it was the servants' game of goose—a board game played with dice and stones or whatever was handy for pieces—that really held their attention. The first to land on the final square would win the pot—in this case, a penny, an embroidered handkerchief, a tin snuffbox, and a small glass vial of lavender water.

Rebekah won the first round, the corner of her mouth lifting into a sly smile. While Samuel went off to the warehouse to refill the pitcher, Eddy commenced to singing a rather bawdy song Mary and her sisters had never heard before about a handmaid and her bonnie lover.

Remembering Mary and her sisters, Lizzie sprang up from the bench, her eyes glassy and unfocused. "How about draughts? Ye must like draughts."

Mary and Sarah nodded from their seat on the settle.

Lizzie rummaged clumsily through a chest and pulled out a wooden checkerboard with its leather pouch of pieces, paint peeling off the red and black squares.

The girls began a game of draughts but still watched in innocent fascination as the winning pot at the table began to be composed of such things as "a kiss" or "my share of pudding for a week," the servants' few possessions already gambled away. Lizzie, face as pink as a posy, scandalously lifted her skirts so that Eddy could kiss her plump ankle.

As the Shapleigh servants grew more inebriated, Mary found herself feeling uneasy.

"A double huff!" Sarah cried, snatching Mary's pieces from the board. "King me."

But Mary was no longer paying attention to either game, her gaze gone to the open window casement. Sarah shrugged and kinged herself.

The servants' game had come to a standstill. Samuel stretched himself out on the bench, a silly grin on his face, and put his head on Lizzie's lap beneath her ample bosom. Lizzie caressed his spotty cheek like she would an infant's. Rebekah sat herself on Eddy's lap, though she soon hopped off and pulled Eddy to his feet. They began to dance around the room, which quickly became a game of cat and mouse, Rebekah fending off her stalker with a broom.

"Mind Hannah," Mary said to Sarah and slipped out the door.

"But our game!" Sarah wailed after her.

The air outside felt damp and chill, smelling of the sea and fresh manure. Mary drew a deep breath. All was so quiet—too quiet. A mist had rolled in, blocking out the sun. She walked past the warehouse and through the woods to her family's cottage, feeling something was wrong.

But the cottage looked sound. The cow grazed at shrubbery contentedly, the chickens were undisturbed, and the hearth was banked properly.

Mary walked down to the cove below and stood near the bottom of the long flat rock that ran up its middle. The sea was almost completely concealed by a thick bank of fog, and the tide was near high. As she watched, even the shoreline began to disappear, the gray mist swallowing everything in its path. Countless tiny beads of water swirled in the air in front of her.

Presently, she heard the hollow scraping sound of a boat beaching on shingle and what sounded like the shipping of an oar. Had the fog brought her parents home early? The sound had come from the direction of the Shapleigh landing. On the edge of one of the neighbors' fish flakes stood her cat, Inky, fur and tail puffed out, staring in the direction of the sound. Why was her cat afraid?

Mary cautiously made her way back toward the Shapleighs' until a sudden fearfulness made her hide in a thicket. None too soon, for out of the mist ahead of her, the shape of a man appeared, his face kerchiefed and his hat pulled low. Two others followed on his heels, also masked, hands sprouting with knives and axes. Mary's blood ran cold—were they going to be attacked?

The bandits trod stealthily past her in the direction of the warehouse, the mist closing in behind them. When they were gone, she ran as fast as she could around the inland way to the back side of the Shapleigh house.

The celebration came quickly to an end.

"*What!* How many?" Eddy cried, Rebekah falling to the floor as he jumped to his feet. He grabbed a musket from the wall while Samuel, weaving unsteadily, grabbed a pike propped in a corner. Rebekah got to her feet and brushed herself off with a scowl.

Emboldened by the drink, the two boys set off despite the wails and protests of Lizzie.

When they had gone, Lizzie and Rebekah wasted no time pulling in the latchstring and barring the door. Lizzie swung the window casement shut, locked it, and drew the curtains. Then she readied herself with the heaviest iron skillet she could find. She looked like a madwoman with sack spilled down the front of her bodice and her hair frizzing out around the edges of her cap.

Mary sat next to wide-eyed Sarah and pulled little Hannah close against her thumping chest. Everything had happened so fast.

Rebekah minced over to the table, poker in hand. She topped off her glass with the remains of the pitcher and took a long swallow. Then she sat down, facing the door, alert and staring.

"Shame on us, carrying on like so. We deserve this," Lizzie moaned. "Something bad's going to come of this. I just know it!" Hiccupping, she wiped her mouth with the back of her hand and peered between the curtains on tiptoe.

Rebekah gave her a haughty look.

Presently, the sound of a musket shot shattered the air. Then shouting. They all sat still, hardly breathing, ears straining in the ensuing silence. Minutes came and went.

Finally, when they had begun to think the worst, the sound of footsteps approached. Lizzie and Rebekah, weapons in hand, readied themselves on either side of the door.

"Lizzie, 'tis us," came Eddy's voice. "Open the door."

"And how am I to know it really is you?"

It took Lizzie a minute to comply, slow as she was to be convinced it was really them. When Eddy and Samuel came into the hall, they looked shaken, but unharmed.

"What happened?" asked Rebekah, lowering the poker.

"There was a good handful of 'em. We don't rightly know how many. They were robbing the warehouse."

"*How?*" Lizzie wanted to know. They all knew the warehouse had a heavy nail-studded door and a large padlock.

Eddy looked at Samuel, who sheepishly held up a ring of keys. "I left them in the door," he explained, looking down at his feet.

"They would've gotten in anyway w' the axes they had," Eddy espoused. "They meant business. Must've thought we were all gone to the Banke."

"Did you ken any of them?" Rebekah asked.

"Nay, couldn't get close enough. They sure made off fast when I shot the musket!" Eddy said, obviously pleased with himself. "Don't think they got away w' anything. We rolled two kegs o' rum back inside."

"Oh, rogues and thieves, what's next?" Lizzie sat down, one hand on her chest in a swoon. "You are both such brave lads!"

Eddy's chest rose a little higher, and he postured one of his looks in Rebekah's direction. Rebekah looked away.

"Master will be well pleased with us, I think," Samuel said proudly.

"*Pleased*? He should cartwhip us all!" Lizzie retorted.

"Nicolas wouldn't ever," Samuel said with a shake of his head.

"Aye, 'tis a good thing for us Alexander's a'ready left," Eddy said. "Look what I found on the warehouse floor." He held up a broken chain from which dangled a tarnished coin.

"Let me 'ave a look!" Samuel grabbed for it.

"Finders keepers!" Eddy held it high up over his head.

Something about it looked familiar to Mary. Where had she seen such a thing before?

Then Rebekah spoke up. "What's to stop the thieves from coming back? What if they've gone to fetch muskets themselves?"

The lads looked dumbfounded for a moment, before Eddy turned on his heel and strode straight back outside with the musket, running smack into their neighbor Phillip Swadden in the dooryard. Swadden had recently returned from the Banke, judging from the garland that hung unraveling from his hat. Mary peered around the doorframe at him.

"What in God's name's the hubbub about?" the man barked. Swadden, a short whiskery fellow, was as strong as a bull with purportedly a temper to match. He stood swaying in the dooryard, shouldering his musket.

“We just rid ourselves of a bunch of thieves breakin’ into the warehouse,” Eddy explained. “’Bout a dozen of ’em, armed w’ knifes and pickaxes. They came in by boat through the fog.”

“The sneaking devilish rogues!” Swadden growled and spit over his shoulder. “I was thinkin’ somethin’ of the like was bound ta happen when I saw this piece o’ fog rollin’ in. Could’a been the Frenchies, if you ask me. I hear they’ve been ogling the merchants. Well, lad, let’s see if we can’t part their hair s’more!”

Eddy and Phillip Swadden disappeared in the direction of the warehouse, and before long the sound of dual volleys cracked the air.

Mary felt her tension begin to melt away. No one in their right mind would tangle with Swadden, she’d heard her father say more than once.

The news of the attempted robbery hung heavily on the residents of the Point. It proved just how vulnerable they all really were. The small band of local soldiers who initially offered the region some protection had left for points east. Captain Wannerton was the only one left, but he and his henchmen held no one’s great confidence.

Mary heard her mother suggesting to her father that perhaps they’d be safer if they moved farther away from the open sea. After all, the Indians were friendly enough, and Bristol had begun to organize a militia.

Please, please stay at the Point, Mary hoped. After all, they had Phillip Swadden and Eddy the brave. The Shapleigh servants, knowing their behavior to be well deserving of punishment, had begged Mary and Sarah to keep mum. Rather, Lizzie had on the others’ behalf. It was an interesting turn of events, and Mary delighted that she now had the upper hand when it came to Rebekah. The maidservant would hardly dare prate or spy on her now, Mary thought with satisfaction.

But her father evidently agreed with her mother, for within a few days he announced he’d bought a tract of land upriver in the province of Maine. A tract he’d helped negotiate with the Indians, just north of land owned by Alexander Shapleigh. They would be moving as soon as he could get his plantation built.

❧

Overnight the cool spring weather disappeared. A plethora of blossom and leaf, sweet and euphoric, hung in the air. Pollen dusted the surface of still water a yellowish green. Planted fields grew quickly now to make up for lost time, and the fish flakes along the river were covered with drying herring, mackerel, and salmon.

As each season seemed to have its bane, mosquitoes now were quite noisome to hands and faces. But in the evenings, as the twilight deepened, thousands of tiny winged lights replaced them, hovering and drifting like sparks above the meadows and among the trees. Fireflies—a magical sight to behold and the likes of which Old England knew not.

The afternoon of the fifth of June, Mary sat with Sarah at her family's table at the Point, teaching her sister to write words with quill and parchment.

"*Hand*, *head*, and *heart*. That's it, the *e* sound really comes bef— stop kicking the table!" she snapped at Sarah. The table was rattling in an irritating manner.

Sarah looked at her strangely. "I'm not kicking the table."

Mary and her sister both glanced around the room, bewildered. A strange rushing, roaring sound swept all around. Not only the table, but also the cupboard, casements, and rafters began to shake. Mary's mother screamed from somewhere outside. In the nick of time, Mary and her sister hid underneath the table as pewter plates rolled like weapons and pottery rained down from the cupboard, dashing to pieces on the floor. In the midst of it all, a gigantic boom split the air like the firing of a cannon. The house creaked and groaned and threatened to collapse around them.

Once everything became still again, Mary and Sarah crept slowly to their feet. Most of their mother's venetian glasses lay in shards upon the floor. Their father's clock had fallen too, but a basket of linen lying below had saved it, along with several of the glasses. Outside, birds filled the sky, yet everything resonated with a strange silence. Circular waves ran through the surface of the water across the river to the Great Island.

Over the next several days, tremors could be felt, swaying trees and anchored ships alike. Settlers throughout Pascataway grew more terrified.

"Britania," Mary's father said to her mother, "something is surely amiss with God's wrath upon us all. Seeing that there's no shortage of the faithless and lawless here in Pascataway, we'll go upriver to worship at the Bristol Meetinghouse this Sabbath, lest we bring further judgment upon us."

The Bristol Meetinghouse was the only church in the region and the parish of the Reverend Burdett, who had come to Strawbery Banke to officiate Nicolas's burial.

"If you think it best, John," her mother replied.

-- 7 --

The Log Meetinghouse

The settlement of Bristol lay seven miles up the Pascataqua River. Pommery Cove, composed of warehouses and fishing flakes, lay near the southern end of its peninsula above which the forested spine of a hill extended northward between the Fore and Back Rivers, extensions of the great Pascataqua confluence and the Great Bay to the west.

"An ideal spot for the Hilton brothers' fishing company that arrived here in 1623," Mary's father said as they drew near. He pointed to another smaller forested hillside across the river in the province of Maine. "And there it is, Britania, girls—our new home, where my plantation will be built. Up there near the narrowest part of the river."

It looked like a nice-enough spot, Mary thought, from a distance. She liked that the river still smelled like the sea this far inland, though the welling and boiling of its tidal current terrified her. She and Sarah had sat crossing their fingers, arms, and legs the entire voyage to protect against an earth tremor taking their craft down in a giant whirlpool. They were greatly relieved when at last her father tied them off at the town dock.

A cart path wound along the Fore River and up into the woods. No one seemed to be around. Even the solitary ship anchored in the cove seemed to be deserted. As they passed by an occasional dwelling, it felt eerie not to see a single soul. The path led away from civilization, deeper into the wilderness. Just when they thought their directions had only led them to a rustic parsonage, a bit farther along the path and over the hump of a mossy ledge, a rather humble meetinghouse appeared, perched in the corner of a meadow. Made of logs, its steeply pitched roof rose to a point above a doorway, through which a congregant or two were still filing.

Once inside, it became evident that Mary's father had not been alone in his thinking, for the hall was full to overflowing. Women and children slid closer together on an already-crowded bench to make room for Mary, her mother, and Sarah. Mary's mother placed Hannah on a blanket at their feet. They had to move over again as Lizzie and Rebekah arrived soon after, having come with Nicolas Shapleigh in another boat. Back in England at St. Peter's, families sat together, but here men and women sat separately. Mary's father, Nicolas, and the male servants sat up front with the other men. In front of them, from among the many rows of coifed heads, Mary recognized Goody Foster and her brood, who had sailed from England with them. Mrs. Foster turned around and waved. It felt good to be greeted by a familiar face.

It was exciting to be at a real church service again, but it didnot take long, pressed in tightly among so many, before Mary's eyes sought the space above. Two open casement windows lit the hall on either side. She could see leaves through the right one and blue sky with puffy white clouds through the left.

The congregation stood up as Reverend Burdett entered and walked the narrow aisle to the pulpit. Mary hoped he was as nice as their beloved priest back in England. But once everyone sat down, the round blue eyes that stared out from under his black cap exuded anything but a warm and friendly manner.

"*When the wicked man turneth away from his wickedness that he hath committed*," the reverend began in a loud ecclesiastical voice, "*and doeth that which is lawful and right, he shall save his soul alive. Because he considereth and turneth away from all his transgressions that he hath committed, he shall surely live, he shall not die.*"

Then he opened up his Bible and cleared his throat slowly and deliberately. "Good people of Pascataway." His voice softened, but his face quickly drained of any imagined pleasantness. "The first Epistle of Saint John, the second chapter, second verse: '*He is the propitiation for our sins, and not ours only, but also for the sins of the whole world . . .*'"

As the reverend's riveting gaze began to burn holes into the souls of those seated before him, Mary found it more comfortable to study the seam of the bodice directly in front of her. It consisted of nice straight stitches over which her eyes ran again and again until the seam itself became painful to look at. She glanced up. The reverend's expression looked incredulous; his voice grew ever more frantic and accusatory.

"Pray tell me, good people, did Christ satisfy the sins of the *devil*? Yet the whole world will believe *themselves included*. And did Christ satisfy for the sins of the whole world in this respect? Art thou a drunkard? Art thou a whoremonger? A swearer? A profaner of the Sabbath? And thinkest *thou* that Christ died for *thee*?"

He paused. A beam of sunlight from a casement lit the glistening spittle at the corner of his mouth. There was nary a sound. Everyone held their breath, shrinking from his omniscient gaze as it roved madly about the room. He began to swing his head slowly side to side, his eyes half closing, his voice deceptively soft again.

"No, no—we must speak of the merits of Christ *limitively*. And that 'the world' in the text prealleged is to be taken restrictively *for the elect only*. And to such sinners, an extension is blasphemous, popish, and ridiculous! Yet such doctrine is enough to draw thousands to eternal perdition," he finished with obvious sarcasm.

A gigantic bee began to buzz up in the rafters. Mary had never seen one so large. She followed it with her eyes as it dipped and hovered.

"Look at the seventeenth, eleventh of John, the ninth verse: '*I pray for them, I pray not for the whole world*.'" The reverend looked up from his open Bible and fixated silently upon his congregation, all sitting perfectly motionless, including the wee ones in the back being held much too tightly by their mothers.

The bee buzzed more loudly, and Mary saw it drop downward, perilously close to the congregation. Mary's mother nudged her with her foot, and Mary quickly averted her gaze back to the reverend.

He continued, "And how did He *die* for the whole world, that professed He would not so much as *pray* for the whole world?" His tone of voice was now smugly self-righteous.

Minutes added into hours, and by noontime the congregation felt holy indeed from three hours of scathing sermon, psalms, and prayers. Mary's family made their way to the door, where the Reverend Burdett stood greeting everyone on their way out.

"Any more *miraculous works*?" he said to her mother, placing his hand on top of Mary's head. His touch gave her chills.

"Nothing of the sort," her mother answered.

Her parents turned to file past, but the reverend seemed reluctant to remove his hand. Mary looked up at him. He was staring down at her, a cold, hard look in his eyes. He let go. Mary hurried after her parents, very afraid.

Once out of the meetinghouse in the brightness of midday, her father set off to Emery's, the local tavern with Nicolas and Tom. Mary followed her mother and Sarah to the crowd of women and children seated on the shady moss-covered ledge. She tried her best to eat a few bites of bread and cheese, but her appetite had vanished.

Mary set off up the lane to see where her father had gone, but she didn't get very far. A group of boys blocked the way with their games. Mary recognized Anthony Nutter, the bully from the ship. He looked bigger and meaner than ever, his red mop unmistakable. She quickly walked back down to the meetinghouse, hoping he hadn't seen her. Sarah had already made friends and was playing Ring o' Roses in the meadow. Mary wanted to be alone.

She walked to the meadow's far end where a spring bubbled up, its water clear and sweet. As she followed its freshet through cattails and reeds down toward the Back River, a small green frog drew her attention. She caught it and it sat on her palm, unwilling to leave, its markings glistening gold in the sunlight. Mary smiled, imagining it sitting on her shoulder for the afternoon service. That would be just what she needed. She set the frog back down in the water, having to nudge it off her palm gently with a finger.

All of the frogs seemed to like her. She dangled a long weed to tease them, and one of them leapt out of the water to snap the end of it in his mouth. He wouldn't let go, so Mary pulled him around through the water until he tired, and another frog snapped up the end of the weed with its mouth. The frogs took turns, vying for the weed. They made her laugh.

When she tired of the game, she continued through a fringe of woods to a narrow inlet of the river where a fishing shallop and several canoes lay drawn up on the bank. Across the water on the opposite shore grew dense, desolate forest. Mary was glad she was near enough to the meetinghouse to see it through the trees, but she really didn't want to go back for the afternoon service. *Perhaps I could feign an illness?*

Low tide had exposed a strip of beach. She picked up a flat stone near the water's edge and let it fly with unpracticed aim. The stone skipped once on the water's surface before dunking out of sight. She picked up another one and swung it more forcefully. It skipped three times. She could do better yet!

Then something hit the water next to where her stone just had. It skipped smartly across the surface many times. She whirled around to see a boy standing up on the bank.

"I didn't know maids could skip stones," he said, sending another one skimming elegantly over the water.

"Well, now you know better," Mary answered, her cheeks growing hot.

The boy stepped down to the beach and began to search for more skipping stones, which he stuffed into a leather pouch at his waist. He looked a few years older than she did. He wore a Monmouth cap, and the tiny brown freckles splattered across his nose lent him a mischievous air.

"Where d'you live?" he asked.

"At the Point across from the Great Isle."

He dropped a stone that wasn't flat enough. "Spruce Creek?"

Mary nodded, watching him wipe the sand off a nice flat one. "But we're moving up here. My father's bought land across the Fore River."

The boy raised his brow. "I live across the Fore River. My name's Francis Small."

Introducing herself, Mary watched Francis skip more stones. He was good at it, she had to admit. One of them skipped twenty-one times. The current of the Back River flowed smooth and perfect. As much as she wanted to, she dared not attempt to throw any more stones in front of him. This annoyed her somewhat.

"Francis, why aren't you gaming with the other boys?"

The stone he threw dunked out of sight after only two skips. "Bumratty! Well, why aren't you with the other maids?" he snapped.

Put off, Mary turned to start up the riverbank. She'd come here to be alone. Francis was just a sneaky show-off, and she'd gladly be rid of him.

Then a question made her stop. She turned around. "How did you sneak up on me like that?"

He grinned at her. "Just like the Indians do."

Now he had her full attention. But Francis wasn't going to part with his secret so easily.

He looked up at some horse tail clouds in the sky. "We're in for some rain. I've an ache in my broken bone." He rubbed his forearm and began to roll up his shirtsleeve inch by inch, examining his arm closely.

Mary gasped. His naked wrist was interlaced with livid red scratches and white scars.

Francis held it out proudly, welcoming her to view it. "Got in a fight with a bear."

Ridiculous, Mary thought. "A bear? I don't believe you."

Francis looked at her through squinted eyes before breaking into an impish grin. "Nah. Actually, 'twas my coon. I raised him from a kit. He likes to play rough, and it worries my madam somethin' awful. Broke my arm when I fell out o' a tree."

"So tell me, how do the Indians walk without making a sound?"

Francis narrowed his eyes again, taking her in as though he were trying to decide if she were worth telling or not. *Exasperating*, she thought, ready to leave.

Then with a toss of his head, he motioned for her to follow him. “It’s easier if you’re barefoot or wearing moccasins,” he told her over his shoulder. “But mostly, you’ve got to roll on the outsides of your feet like a fox does. *Feel* the silence of the ground in your feet and *all over—breathe* it in.”

Feeling silence . . . breathing silence . . . what she did best! Mary couldn’t stop smiling—this was more fun than she’d ever had.

“See the forest across the river?” Francis pointed to the dense forest Mary had noticed earlier. “It’s Pennacook territory. There might be some of ’em watching us now.”

They entered the woods that edged the meadow. Mary walked so silently behind Francis that he turned around a few times to make sure she was still there. She could tell he was impressed. They practiced until the beat of the deacon’s drum put a stop to their game, summoning the congregation back to the meetinghouse.

Bravely, Mary returned. Seated once again on the crowded bench, she felt happy despite the remaining three hours of evensong with the Reverend Burdett. Even when the floor began to shake, the casements rattled, and the whole meetinghouse rode dizzying waves like a ship at sea, she didn’t scream or cower like most everyone else. She was getting used to it all now. With the reverend’s ensuing tirade about their sins and God’s anger, evensong went on much longer than usual. Mary was careful to hide behind the person sitting in front of her.

After the service, her father introduced them to a new acquaintance he had met at Emery’s Tavern during the dinner hour: a man named Edward Small and his family. Mary smiled at Francis, neither of them letting on that they’d already met. The Smalls would be their new neighbors soon enough. Her father had hit it off with Edward Small as Mary had with Francis and the two men planned a trading expedition.

“Anglican minister or not, the service reeks of separatism,” Mary’s father complained to her mother once they were back out on the river, heading home. “In my opinion, this separatist plague is likely the true cause of all this calamity. The timing of this last convulsion certainly points toward this being the case. We shan't be going back."

This relieved Mary considerably, and she tried to put her interaction with the reverend from her mind. But the fact still remained that her family would soon be living just across the river from Bristol, and this worried her.

Back at the Point, Mary practiced her silent walk alone in the woods. She allowed her body to melt into the bracken and evergreen boughs as they slid past her skirt. Walking up the castle rock, her bare feet seemed to sink so deeply into it that she scarcely felt its cool, rough surface. She sat down upon its top. A light breeze ruffled the beech leaves overhead. A peacefulness spread through her body. She sat like this for a while, happy just to be.

A squirrel mouse climbed her skirt to sit upon her bended knee. It looked at her with bright inquisitive eyes in which Mary could almost see her own reflection.

"What do you think?" she asked the sleek timorous creature. "Will I be safe upriver?"

-- 8 --

Trading Expedition

The moon hung low like the eye of a cat, and mist swirled off the water's surface. The canoe moved quickly toward the region known as the Newichawannock to the Abenakis and its Indian village of Quamphegan at the Salmon Falls. Migwah's people. A place Mary's father knew she longed to see.

They had stopped to pick up the Smalls along the way as her father had planned on the Sabbath. She'd overheard Edward grumbling to her father about his bringing her, that she'd hold them up and cause problems. This had hurt her feelings. Francis seemed less friendly as well, as though he agreed with his father. Resting against the pile of trucking cloth, Mary quietly determined to prove them both wrong.

The day grew brighter by the minute and birds began to twitter. At a fork in the river where the Cocheco flowed into the Fore, Mary stared curiously at the remains of a palisade. It was Thomson's trading post, the oldest one in the region, from well before the Hiltons' time. Now it was a rather ramshackle homestead surrounded by hillocks of Indian corn, beans, and squash. Farther upriver, they passed a gundalow harvesting salt hay in a grassy tidal cove as the first rays of sunlight struck the water. Mary's father and Edward exchanged greetings with the men on board, but they didn't stop.

As they rounded the next bend, Mary could see a dwelling ahead in the distance, its upper casements open like dark staring eyes above its palisade. "Newichawannock House," her father told her, "owned by Mason, who called much of the province of Maine his own until he died a few years ago. His employees have taken over everything now." On their right, he pointed out Pipe Stave Landing, the wharf for the upper river.

Passing by Newichawannock House, they entered a stretch of rapids. Mary held the gunnel tightly. "Not bad at all with this flood tide, Mary. You wouldn't like it much in the middle of the ebb," her father said. "Lots of white water." Francis looked back over his shoulder and grinned.

They passed by the mill where their corn was ground, and a fording place of giant stones called Little John's Falls a bit farther on. Then all signs of civilization disappeared. Mary could sense they were close. The river grew narrow, winding through a tunnel of trees. On the right, the forest climbed up a steep hillside.

She glimpsed an Indian wigwam, a rounded structure of tree bark. A dog yipped, and naked children ran down through the trees. Smooth-skinned faces with black eyes stared back at her through the ferns on the riverbank. A midchannel island lay ahead. Indian boys were up in its trees, swinging out on vines, dropping gracefully into the water. Their unabashedness amazed Mary as did their ability to swim like fish. And it wasn't just little boys—she blushed to see the genitals of little girls among them. The day was waxing hot and humid, and the water would feel so good . . .

She remembered being five years old and pulling off her wool stockings while seated on the stone quay of the River Exe. Her skirt gathered in her lap, the water had felt so cool and delightful on her feet. How it sparkled when she kicked, how happy she'd felt. And how terrible it had been when her mother grabbed her, scolding and punishing her about baring her legs in public—"sinful, shameful"—while the boy fishing nearby smirked.

Past the island, the river opened into a large pool of water above which whitewater cascaded over rocky falls where the tide could reach no higher. Here and there, a great salmon leapt, clearing the surface on its way to the spawning grounds upriver. Several older Indian boys stood knee-deep upon the falls, ready with long spears and baskets.

On both sides of the river here, wigwams and cornfields lay scattered. On the right bank, the main part of the village clustered on a long sloping hillside from which water flowed downhill in narrow, convenient rivulets. Outdoor cooking fires burned, and the air smelled of woodsmoke and wildness.

With some of the children still swimming alongside, they landed where the Indian canoes and dugouts lined the shore. An old man approached, and Mary's father and Edward began to converse with him in Abenaki. Mary and Francis soon found themselves surrounded by children and dogs. Mary smiled at the Indian children, and they giggled, reaching out to touch her clothes. The dogs sniffed at her and Francis and were especially interested in Francis's shoes. They pressed their noses to his feet no matter where he moved them, which made the Indian children laugh. "My coon chews on 'em," he said to Mary with a sheepish shrug.

She studied the village. Indian women were hoeing cornfields up on the hillside, some with babes strapped to their backs. Their calf-length deerskins hung loosely, their hair held back with bands. So few men seemed to be about. She would be very disappointed if she didn't get to see Migwah.

Near the edge of the river, a firepit smoldered in front of a low rounded wigwam. Presently, a slow, muffled drumbeat began to sound from within. Alarmed, Mary looked to her father and Edward, but they seemed unconcerned.

"Where are all the sannups?" Francis asked just as the sound of chanting reached their ears.

"Hear 'em?" cried his father. "Inside that giant oven, cooking themselves alive. When they've had enough, they'll be throwing themselves in the river 'til their skins stop steaming."

Mary stared at the wigwam. She wouldn't have believed it if she couldn't hear the chanting. She watched in amazement as dozens of half-naked men poured out the wigwam and into the river, water steaming indeed from their brown skin and shiny black hair.

Migwah emerged from the water to greet them. His eyes brightened when he saw Mary. In Migwah's presence, the Indian children stayed a respectful distance away.

Soon, the men were sitting on rush mats in the shade of some large trees near the landing place. Mary's father and Edward traded iron tools and blankets for the few beaver pelts that could be found for them. Mary and Francis stood off to one side.

"English from Strawbery Banke—Wannerton—come two days past," Migwah explained. This news didn't leave her father or Edward very happy.

The great chieftain Sagamore Rowls joined them, sannups flanking him on either side. Old man that he was, his eyes—gone almost gray in color—seemed to be all-seeing in his wrinkled face. A white deerskin blanket intricately beaded in wampum draped his shoulders, and eagle feathers crowned his white hair still damp from the river.

"Paakuinoogwazian," the chieftain said slowly, nodding to those present.

Migwah commenced with a blessing. He raised his medicine pipe in four directions, fanning sacred tobacco around each person with an eagle's wing. Then he called Mary over and blew a stream of tobacco at her forehead. "Kwassis oligo," he said.

Francis looked envious until Migwah called him over and did the same.

The blessing was an honor Mary would never forget. Others might call them savages, but she knew differently. There was a natural order of relating in the group that seemed so civilized, so wise and considerate, as though the men's hearts and minds were one and the same.

Despite the hospitality of their hosts, the absence of pelts left her father and Edward anxious to move on, and they soon took their leave. Mary crossed her fingers they would find more. She worried Edward would blame her for the lack.

"We can try Basil Parker's," her father said. "He'll know where to find pelt if anyone does."

Edward nodded in agreement, and they returned back downriver. Just past Little John's Falls, they turned the canoe up into the Asbenbedick, a tributary that fanned out into channels. The current moved more slowly here, branching through a lush, overgrown valley where vines festooned the trees and the air smelled like honeysuckle.

Giant ferns and grasses loomed over the narrow waterways, and rustling on the banks betrayed the presence of unseen creatures. A giant snake slithered across the water's surface in front of them and disappeared into the reeds.

"A sacred place to Rowls's village," her father said as they passed under a great white pine felled as a footbridge. It led to a steep rocky hill that rose up out of the heart of the valley. "Not many English dare travel up these waterways, but it'll save us time to do so."

"The place smacks of sorcery. I don't trust it one bit," Edward said.

Mary loved the hallowed mysteriousness the place exuded. They didn't encounter any other human presence, but once she thought she heard a distant melodious laughter, though it could have been a bird.

Up ahead, the current grew stronger, flowing out of a rocky gorge shaded with hemlock. Here, they unloaded and portaged the canoe, the bundles of trucking cloth strapped to the men's backs.

Francis carried the muskets and Mary the basket of food she'd packed. The roar of rushing water dropped away below as they moved precariously up the incline. As the terrain leveled out, the silence of the forest pressed in on them, broken only by the trilling alarm of a squirrel.

The trail soon joined up with a well-used cart path, where her father and Edward rested in the shade and drank from the jugs they carried. The day had become very hot and humid.

Wiping his brow with his handkerchief, her father nodded down the path. "Down that way, Mary, is Pipe Stave Landing, what we passed earlier today. It's a much longer portage from there."

"We'll sup at Spencer's Tavern on the way back, eh?" Edward suggested. He no longer seemed as unfriendly as he had earlier. Mary was beginning to tire of the expedition and wondered how much farther they'd have to go. But to show this would prove Edward right. She would just have to bear it.

A short walk brought them to Basil Parker's, where flies buzzed about the pelts nailed to the side of the house and stretched out on a gibbet in the yard. Mary's father and Edward entered the dwelling, only to reappear a few minutes later with an Indian man of a surprisingly short stature.

Mary started when she saw him. The man's left eyelid was sealed shut, and scar tissue raked down half his face, a livid red.

"This is Piniwas," her father said to them, "our guide."

"Where're we going?" asked Francis.

"Up the Asbenbedick, about a two-hour journey. Mary, Goody Weare said you could stay and help out here."

What might have been appealing to Mary only a short time ago now sounded highly unattractive. She didn't want Edward to believe she'd jinxed them at Quamphegan Village and that they'd only found furs because she'd stayed behind.

"Sir, I'd rather go with you."

A hint of a smile crossed her father's face. "Very well, if that's what you'd prefer. But I don't recommend telling your mother about our extended journey."

The men shouldered the canoe down a sloping bank that met up with the river above the steep rocky gorge. The river's flume, which dropped away out of sight, provided an ever-present thunderous roar while to their right the river serpentined dark and smooth out of the forest.

Piniwas retrieved a canoe he'd hidden in the brush, and Edward rode with him while Francis took over his father's position in the bow of their canoe. As they rounded the first bend, the signs of lumbering diminished. The forest, thick and impenetrable on either side, began to enclose them. The river narrowed enough that Mary could have thrown a stone across.

It felt comforting to have Piniwas as a guide, but even in his world things weren't always safe and predictable, as his scarred face certainly showed. Mary thought of her mother and her sisters for the first time that day. If only they could see her now. The thought made her smile.

It was past noon when they tied the canoes to a partially submerged log to eat their dinner: cold pork, biscuits with butter, fresh garden snap peas, and a little basket of wild strawberries Mary had picked for the trip. As they ate, she tried to get a better look at Piniwas's face, but to her embarrassment, her gaze was met by his one good eye.

He grinned between mouthfuls. "Awasos," he said. "Bear,"

her father translated. "He was attacked by a bear."

The livid red and white claw marks were etched deeply into his flesh. Mary noticed Francis's ears go pink. The real thing was nothing short of horrific.

She graciously offered the last strawberry to Piniwas.

They resumed paddling upstream against the sluggish current, and Mary's father pointed out a small brook flowing into the Asbenbedick. "That's the freshet which flows from the marsh I purchased from Rowls this spring." Marshland meant winter fodder for cattle and horses and was as valuable for a planter as a woodlot. "The marsh lies beside the encampment of my 'Indian captors' this past winter. How different it all is now," he mused.

A short distance upriver, Piniwas directed them over to the bank, where they hid the canoes in the underbrush behind the exposed roots of a windfall. Another brook flowed into the river here, rushing down over roots between the trunks of trees. They set out on foot, following the brook's course before turning off to traverse yet another tributary, which flowed down through rocky woodland.

The terrain grew steeper, and they began to ascend the side of Mt. Agamenticus. Through the trunks of trees, a valley of treetops appeared spread out below. They stopped to rest and admire the view. A hawk sailed smoothly and effortlessly below them. Mary foundit a wonderful, heady feeling being up so high. Her legs felt tired, but she forced herself to keep pace with the men. So far she hadn't given Edward anything to complain about, she hoped.

Finally, they reached a camp high on a rocky ledge. A single bark wigwam with an outdoor firepit and a dog, who greeted them with its curious nose. Off to the side, seated upon some rush mats, two women were scraping pelts. A man looked out of the wigwam.

As Piniwas had promised, there was beaver pelt available, though still not as much as Mary's father and Edward would have liked. The men didn't look happy as they had carried a great deal of heavy trucking cloth along and didn't relish the idea of carrying it all the way back, but they began to barter.

"Swassis . . . Abi spiwi nai," one of the women called to Mary in a soft nasal voice.

Mary walked shyly over to the Indian women. The younger one, her teeth very white and even, smiled and handed Mary a grass bowl holding pieces of a dried pinkish-white substance.

"Mili, mili!" a half-naked Indian boy cried, appearing out of nowhere.

Mary hesitated, but the women both nodded and smiled, bringing their fingers to their mouths. She put a piece to her lips and bit down. It gave under her teeth, its bitter taste immediately recognizable as spruce gum. At first, it was all she could do to keep it in her mouth without making a face. She tried pretending to like it to see if that made a difference.

The boy chewed his with obvious relish. He sat with the dog on a nearby ledge to watch the bartering. Not wanting to appear rude, Mary discreetly dropped her piece in the brush when she thought no one was looking.

As the trade goods moved about in circles, the bolt of bright red cloth caught the attention of the women. Speaking excitedly to each other, the elder of the two stood up and approached the men. The Indian men immediately stopped what they were doing andfocused their attention on her. She spoke to them and returned, looking pleased. It struck Mary to see the stature the woman commanded. She couldn't imagine her mother interrupting one of her father's trades to tell him what she wanted.

Wanting very much to extend her friendship in some visible way, Mary pointed to a pelt and made a scraping motion. The women nodded and handed her a small muskrat pelt along with one of their sharp-edged stones. Mary set to work trying to shave off hardened lumps of fat and gristle. It was much harder than it looked and left her knuckles scraped and bleeding.

By late afternoon, they began the return journey, newly acquired pelts and leftover trucking strapped to the men's backs. The heat of the day had ushered in a dark and threatening sky to the west, and the sound of thunder rumbled in the distance. A cool welcome breeze fluttered the undersides of leaves and billowed Mary's linen skirt. Piniwas guided them back the way they'd come. They hurried downward, hoping to make it to a lower elevation before the storm hit.

Suddenly, Piniwas halted. He gestured for silence, listening intently. Mary listened too. She could hear nothing but the wind in the trees and the rushing of her own pulse. Then ahead of them, from behind the trees, another Indian appeared, breathing heavily as though he had run a great distance. He spoke quickly with their guide, after which he continued on at a run up the mountain.

Something was wrong—that much was clear. Piniwas changed direction and picked up the pace considerably. Mary's father fell back to the rear, his gaze sweeping the woods. Thoughts of a prowling beast filled Mary's head, like the bear that had taken off half of their guide's face. When they reached the edge of a swamp at the base of the mountain, Piniwas spoke to the men in Abenaki, gesturing until they both nodded. Then he turned and vanished.

The storm was growing very dark, and flashes of lightning split the sky.

"What's happened?" Francis asked his father.

"Tarratines," Edward answered.

"A war party," Mary's father explained. "Evidently, they're passing through the area now."

Fear pricked Mary's insides; this was worse than she'd imagined, far worse. The Tarratines were a tribe of Wabanaki from the north who were hostile to their Abenaki neighbors as well as the English. She'd heard talk of them around the hearth late at night when she was supposed to be sleeping. There was no knowing what might happen if they ran into such a party.

"The question is, do we camp here and wait, or do we press on back to our canoe?" Mary's father said.

Before a decision could be made, cracks of lightning split the sky, unleashing a violent deluge. Mosquitoes whining in their ears, they took shelter in a grove of hemlocks as the storm raged about them.

Hungry, tired and uncomfortably wet, Mary wished she'd stayed behind at Basil Parker's. Her father must regret bringing her now, she thought unhappily.

The storm passed to the east, leaving a soggy, much cooler twilight. The men decided to follow the edge of the swamp, searching for the origins of the brook that would lead them directly to their canoe, as Piniwas had said. They would take their chances. There was little talk, everyone listening intently for any unusual sounds.

Swamp water rose up dark and fetid around Mary's ankles. She struggled to pull her feet free of the muck without losing her shoes. Her clothes were wet and heavy, and she had to keep the hem of her skirt lifted to prevent snagging. The going was slow for all of them as the men and Francis carried the heavy trade goods.

They surprised a moose and her calf, who watched them warily over the reeds and bracken. No need to worry, mare moose, Mary thought, glad that the cow and her little one were safe from musket fire for the time being.

Hordes of swamp flies and mosquitoes blackened the air. Francis walked in front of her, his arms swinging like a windmill, swears and oaths spouting just under his breath. His carriage struck Mary as funny, and the quiet laughter that shook her midriff helped her forget her own pain and the blisters that were growing larger with every step.

Francis must have sensed her mirth, for he gave her an annoyed look. The trickles of blood running down his temples from the biting flies reminded Mary of Jesus at his crucifixion. No, not Jesus—one of the thieves. Yet she found it easier to let go of her anger toward him now. And as if he could read her feelings, Francis extended his hand to pull her out of a particularly awful spot.

They had been slogging around the periphery of the swamp for what seemed like an hour when they found themselves at the far southern end of a beaver pond. Knowing the brook they were looking for ran northwest from the swamp, the direction they had come from, the men were dumbfounded.

"We must have walked right past it," Mary's father said.

"Damned beavers have made a mess of everything," Edward agreed.

Daylight was fading fast, but a shaft of light broke through clouds on the horizon, casting an amber glow across the landscape. They backtracked through the trees along the outer fringe of the swamp. Too soon, the shadows deepened all around. The only saving grace was that the swarms of insects began to abate.

Mary could hear the sound of running water—a soft musical gurgling that seemed to be everywhere. Poking about, the men speculated the water ran concealed beneath their feet under the layers of fallen trees, roots, and ferns that must have at one time been held together as a beaver dam. And indeed, much farther out on the periphery, they finally found the brook as the blackness of night closed in. They followed its sound to guide them.

The bone-chilling howl of a wolf rose from behind them in the swamp. Mary pressed in closer to the others, glad for their company. The going was much more difficult in the dark, and she stumbled over the roots and vegetation, her feet and legs numb. Her body felt so tired that her movement began to take on a dreamlike, surreal quality, with branches poking at her eyes and snagging her clothing.

They had been making their way for some time, slowly and apprehensively, hoping they would not be so unlucky as to encounter any of the war party, when the sound of the water once again became confusing. With some splashing and groping, it became apparent that the brook they were following divided itself into two branches.

"I'll wager it's the one to the left. There were two brooks on our way up the mountain," Edward said quietly.

Mary's sleepiness suddenly vanished. She waited for her father to disagree.

"The left seems to be the larger of the two as well," her father reasoned. "Must be. Let's go."

Mary's feet stayed rooted to the spot; she couldn't move. She knew it was the other branch that led back to their canoe, and this brook did not feel good to her at all. For the first time in her life, she saw through her father's infallibility, and this brought to the surface strength she hadn't known she possessed.

She spoke out boldly, as loudly as she dared. "No! That is not the way."

She no longer felt like herself, but a disembodied voice in the dark. The shapeless black silhouettes of her companions froze; she could sense their doubt, the workings of their minds.

Please, please, God, have them believe me. They *had* to—she sensed their very lives depended on it. Someone began to splash along the other branch. Her panic rose. If she had to sit down and fuss like an infant, she would rather do so than go in that direction.

With all the resolution she could muster, Mary repeated herself a second time. She heard them all stop.

The black, shadowy specter nearest her spoke. "Perhaps she's right, Edward." Her father's support gave her hope, yet she could still feel the doubt of the other two hanging in the balance.

"'Tis the right fork that leads to the canoe," she said again with conviction. The fact that they couldn't see her gave her confidence and made her voice all the more powerful.

"Her senses are usually exact," her father explained as tactfully as he could. Mary could hear him step into the right fork. "The water's flowing in the wrong direction. She's right."

Begrudgingly, Edward Small consented.

Thanking God, Mary now found herself in the lead, breaking invisible spiderwebs with her forehead, searching for secure footing, pushing past branches and through thickets. She knew it was even harder for the men and Francis with the loads on their backs. The gurgling of the brook did little to cover the sound of their snapping branches and footfalls.

"Shh . . . nary a sound!" Mary whispered behind her, slowing the pace further, using the silent walk Francis had taught her.

The night felt damp and chill, and the brook seemed to go on forever. Eventually there was another juncture where the brook forked again. This time, Mary led them along the left branch.

"The water's flowing in the right direction," her father said quietly.

Soon the cadence of the brook changed to that of the faster falling water.

"Hark the sound," her father whispered, laying a hand upon her shoulder. All four of them crept along more cautiously now, almost silently, until they could see the light of the rising moon between the trunks of trees, glimmering on the surface of the river below.

A chill swept through Mary's body; for as they watched, dark silhouettes of figures in canoes, one after the other, glided past quickly and silently upriver.

In the shadow of the forest, the four of them did not dare move or hardly even breathe, thankful that the falling water had masked their footfalls. They waited a while before daring to uncover their canoe. Once under way, they kept to the shadow of the shoreline, moving slowly, cautiously.

Though it was great relief to rest her exhausted body, Mary could almost taste danger. Sure enough, they had not been paddling long when a strong sense of foreboding overtook her. "Stop—we must hide at once!"

The men were quick to respond this time. Even in the intensity of the moment, she could feel that Edward and Francis felt differently about her than they had before. In a respectful sort of way, they listened to her now.

They steered the canoe into a bower of overhanging bushes, and waited in silence. Before long, three more Indian canoes passed by. So close were the craft that the natives' war paint was visible in the moonlight, as were the numbers of dark scalps swinging from the shafts of their paddles. Mary could have sworn that one of the sannups looked directly at her as a moonbeam caught the corner of his eye.

The rest of the night was spent tied in that leafy bower, the four of them arriving at Spencer's Tavern near Pipe Stave Landing after sunup. Goody Spencer was very kind and made up beds for them, drying their damp shoes and stockings in the hearth.

"I cannot believe they took you along," she said to Mary, shaking her head. "Heavens, I've seen everything now."

At noon that day, they all sat in the tavern, eating steaming hot pottage. Mary's father and Edward recounted their adventure to a roomful of grave rivermen. Word was the Tarratines had attacked an Indian village farther to the northwest in Pennacook country and had come back downriver yesterday afternoon, skirting Quamphegan Village at the falls.

"Too many gathered at Quamphegan this time o' year for such a small war party," Thomas Spencer said.

Mary's father nodded. "I counted twenty sannups in seven canoes, but some may have passed by before we got to the river. What's your estimate, Edward?"

"Sounds about right. They looked like murderous devils." He shuddered. "I was the worse for having spent the night knee-deep in a cursed swamp with wolves howling 'round. But I'll tell ye, if it weren't for John White's young maid here, we wouldn't be speaking to you now."

With all eyes in the room fixed upon her, Mary wanted to crawl beneath the table. This was certainly unexpected—she'd been so afraid that Edward Small would hold it all against her.

"She has the gift of prophecy, she does," Edward continued. "A good thing indeed you brought her along, John."

Mary's father smiled proudly, and both Edward and Francis looked at her with a newfound respect. She'd indeed proven them wrong. But some in the tavern looked at her much less kindly, and she was grateful when the arrival of a stranger in military dress diverted everyone's attention. At first, Mary thought he'd come because of the Tarratines, but it soon became clear his visit was for quite a different reason. Mason's widow had sent this soldier to take stock of her late husband's property, which was unfortunately most of the land thereabouts.

The men in the tavern grew taciturn. This was the land upon which most of them had homesteaded, building dwellings and planting fields. The newcomer was not at all welcome, and he knew it.

He turned to Francis. "You look strong and capable, lad," he said. "I'm in need of a young man such as yourself."

Francis sat up straighter, obviously delighted to have been paid such a compliment.

Edward Small removed the pipe from his mouth and frowned. "Just what are you proposing, Captain?"

"Can the boy drive cattle?"

"Yes, sir, I drive our cattle from the woods every night," Francis said.

"Ah, then I think you may be just the candidate to help me drive Mrs. Mason's cattle to market in Boston."

Edward Small looked from the captain to his son and back. "That would depend upon the terms of your employ."

The Smalls stayed behind to discuss business, and Mary and her father set off homeward alone, enjoying each other's quiet company until another canoe approached around a bend in the river.

"Crawley," her father scoffed. "Wannerton's knave. I'd bet my horse he's here to see what pelt we've got."

As they drew near, Thomas Crawley shipped his paddle. "Been a murder at the Banke!" he called over. He took a drink from his flask and wiped his mouth with the back of his hand.

"What happened?" Her father's paddle thunked down behind her on the gunnel.

"The widow Gyles been found with 'er neck broke. Strangled."

The news rendered Mary instantly weak and nauseous.

"Do they know who's responsible?" her father asked.

"Nay," Crawley answered. "But 'tis no surprise. The old gammer was a thorn ta many—'tis a wonder she lasted 's long as she did."

-- 9 --

Midsummer

Along the Bristol hilltop, carts lined the high street, and a bearded fiddler enlivened the crowd near Emery's Tavern. Mary hadn't seen so many people gathered together since leaving England. The excitement felt infectious. Most of Pascataway, as well as sailors and even some Indians, milled about.

She and Sarah sat across the lane from the tavern, minding the bags of wool their father and his servant, George, had brought from the new storehouse across the river. One of the bags was open, its creamy curled locks on display in the bright sunshine. Mary reverently picked a dried leaf out of the wool—a small organic token of Devon. There were still so few sheep at Pascataway.

A wave of guilt washed through her. The death of the widow had certainly left her with an intensified sense of fragility. The mortality of creatures, both human and animal, seemed so cruel. She looked at the fenced yard behind them that contained the large livestock. Beyond, a couple of bulls were staked a distance away, snorting and stamping at each other.

The food smells were tantalizing, fresh from hearths and bake ovens. She and her sister shared a pasty their father bought for them before he made his way into Emery's Tavern to conduct business. Mother was off shopping among the other stalls with Hannah.

A sailor with a hornpipe joined the bearded fiddler. They began to play faster and faster. The mood ever merry, a jigging contest began, raising the dust down the lane. Mary's feet tapped faster and faster too. She wished she was allowed to dance.

Francis Small made his way over to them. He squatted down next to her and looked covertly around. "I've got something for you and your sister." He loosened the cuff of his sleeve and extracted several small apples.

"Where'd you get them?" Mary asked.

"Came from Hilton's orchard." Francis pushed an apple into each of their hands.

Instinctively, Mary tucked hers under her apron. "Hide it, Sarah."

Even though Francis had been hired to drive Mrs. Mason's cattle to Boston come fall, Mary sensed he was still like the other boys when it came to pilfering apples.

Sarah hid her apple behind her skirt.

Francis looked put out. "I won 'em fair and square! Hilton's nephew John Roberts had 'em."

Mary wanted to believe him. "Really?"

He nodded. Mary could see as Francis walked away that his sleeves hung heavy with more fruit. She slipped the apple into her pocket. Sarah was already eating hers.

"I'll be back," she said to her sister. "Mother said that Goody Emery is in want of some wool and that we should save her some."

Sarah nodded.

Mary found Goody Emery by a fishmonger's cart. Goody Emery's eyebrows flew upward. "Yes, indeed, child. Must not forget the wool. I'll be over shortly."

Mary was hurrying back to her sister when she caught sight of Francis again. He beckoned frantically to her from behind a haystack near the animal yard, putting his finger to his lips. Seeing that no one was paying any attention, she went over to him.

"What is it?" she asked.

"You're not going to believe it." He danced around in sheer excitement before grabbing her hand and pulling her along behind him. Mary couldn't help but follow. He felt like a brother to her since the trading expedition.

"Where're we going?"

"You'll see . . ."

Well beyond the animal pen, a few drays and carts clustered a distance away from the high street. Francis led her over to them.

"Under here," he said, dropping on all fours and crawling beneath the nearest cart.

"Underneath?"

"Just do it."

Mary crouched onto her hands and knees and followed him. There wasn't much room to maneuver, and she had to bunch her skirt up over her knees to do so. But Francis was ahead of her, so it didn't matter. He came to a halt on his stomach, and she crawled to a rest beside him.

"Look!" he said, pointing. In front of them in the weeds, just beyond the back edge of the cart, a shiny amber pool about the size of Mary's hand glistened.

"What is it?"

"Honey, a whole kilderkin of it. Hungry?" Francis stretched out his arm and scooped up some of the spill with his fingers. "Here, damsels first."

Mary let the honey drizzle off his fingers onto her own. Sarah could take care of Goody Emery. What a discovery Francis had made!

The two made short work of the spill. When it was gone, much to Mary's consternation, Francis slid out from under the cart, crouching low. She wondered if he hadn't caused the spill in the first place.

"Here, Mary, hold out your hand."

"Francis, you shouldn't . . ."

But she couldn't resist the stream that coiled down, so thick and sweet. They ate until the sound of voices approached. Francis barely made it back under the cart before a pair of boots and the hem of a skirt came to a halt directly in front of them.

"Those that fish for a living, being apostolic-like in profession, are surely blessed by God and perhaps hold His favor more often, I say . . ."

The voice of Reverend Burdett. Panic rose in Mary's breast; it became hard to breathe and she didn't dare move. Honey oozed between her fingers, dripping to the ground. What if he were to catch them stealing honey? It would be very bad. She tried pretending she was someplace else.

The reverend's companion giggled. The woman's gray flannel skirt had red-braided trim like one of the fishmonger wives wore. Perhaps the reverend hoped for a good bargain in fish, Mary thought. But what he said next made her hair stand on end.

"And yet there is a great evil in our midst that perhaps only a burning or drowning might cure."

"Oh?" the woman gasped. "Pray tell, that I might keep from harm."

"Unexplainable occurrences which disturb my mind greatly—rogue snowstorms destroying seedlings and the earth quaking for days—likely set off by a dead man coming back to life, of which there were eyewitnesses. A diabolical, insidious parody, methinks, of the ascension."

Mary's mouth went dry—her family had just moved to her father's new plantation right across the river. This was not good, not good at all!

"Oh," the woman gasped.

"Quite evil, yes. And reports of prophecy and other such scandalous happenstance have set me on edge of late. Forgive any impropriety . . ."

Muffled sucking sounds began next, catching Mary completely off guard. Francis's expression withered; he looked like he might be sick. But the reverend's words left Mary still as a block of ice. She stared at the ground, praying they wouldn't be discovered. A spider moved in the weeds beneath her arm. She didn't even flinch. Then she heard Francis give a barely audible groan. Mary looked up to see a thick stream of honey pouring down onto the ground in front of them, the two adults seemingly oblivious. The woman's skirt lifted disgracefully, showing her stockinged calves. Then the bodies in front of them leaned heavily into the cart, and the flow of honey stopped. Mary and Francis exchanged looks of alarm.

"We must make haste to a place more private . . ." the reverend grunted as his companion sighed.

When the way was clear, Mary and Francis made their way out from under the wagon. Mary washed the damning stickiness off her fingers in a horse trough.

Back at the family's stall, Goody Emery had arrived and was examining the wool. Mary tried to act calm as though nothing had happened, though her pulse was still racing.

"Oh, lovely, lovely," Goody Emery remarked, feeling the thickness with her hand, hoisting the bag to feel its weight. "Do you have any black? Oh, there you are, Mary, my dear. Hmmm, you look a bit flummoxed. I'll take the black one and this white for six shillings each."

Oh dear, Mary thought, she'd noticed. Mary shook her head. "Seven shillings, tuppence for each, if you please, madam." She tried not to sound breathless. Her father had said she should accept no less. A good thing she'd made it back in time.

Goody Emery frowned, but other women were now examining the wool on either side of her. "Seven shillings, tuppence it is, then," she said and paid Mary in coin. "I'll be sending my son over for them shortly."

All of the bags of wool sold. Mary's mother soon appeared, her face radiant. "Children, your father has bought me a loom!" She set Hannah down. "An old Danish one, but 'twill work well enough." Her mother had been known in Tiverton for her beautiful weaving, but her loom was one of the things that had not come with them. "Mary," she said, "please use some of Goody Emery's coin to purchase two cones of sugar and a bottle of olive oil. I'm in the mood to celebrate."

Glad to have a chance to think, Mary made her way down the crowded lane. *No one need know what she and Francis had done or witnessed. God help her that the fishmonger's wife wouldn't know whom the reverend was speaking of. It's best to pretend it never happened. Perhaps the reverend would forget as he seemed to have been rather drunken.* This last thought made Mary feel better; and as she passed by the musicians, who were rendering the lilting notes of "Cuckolds All a Row," her feet skipped despite herself.

At first, she didn't pay any attention to the distant shouting that reached her ears. No one else did either, for that matter. Then the shouting became screams and shrieks, and the crowd around her scattered. People crawled up onto stalls, carts, whatever they could find. An enormous sow, the largest Mary had ever seen, came running through the middle of everything, snapping her jaws at anything or anyone in her path.

Mary climbed the nearest tree stump, which unfortunately was not very tall. *Oh no*, she thought. But there was nothing better nearby that wasn't already taken. The animal had to be Mr. Furber's, the one that had tried to bite a little child's arm off a month ago. The child had almost died from fever.

The sow upset a root cart a short distance away from Mary, turnips cascaded between its legs. It chomped at them furiously. Mary saw her chance to escape to something higher; but as soon as she jumped to the ground, the animal gave a snort and headed straight toward her, its mouth gaping open, strings of drool trailing from its jowls.

Time stood still. It seemed like the behemoth froze in full charge. Mary heard the crowd's shrill screams in sporadic spurts, and then the sow was upon her. The beast stopped and calmly began to snuffle her nose at Mary's basket. The crowd, armed with boards and standing on carts all around, began to murmur.

The sow snorted and swung her head away to charge once more in another direction, and people's screams started up again.

Mary ran to the safety of the dooryard fence surrounding Emery's Tavern. Once through the gate, she turned to watch the pandemonium. The sow made short work of gorging herself, upturning stalls and carts. Folk stood by helplessly. A swing of the matriarch's head and she was belly deep in fish, baring her teeth at a fishmonger, making fearsome, ungodly noises. The enraged man was trying to beat her off with a rake, the buttons of his jacket all sprung. His wife came running and to Mary's horror, she saw that the woman's skirt with its red-braided trim was covered with matted leaves and twigs. Reverend

Burdett jogged by too, his suit of clothes covered with the telltale same as though they had both been tarred and feathered.

The whole festival proved mayhem. Emery's Tavern emptied out, men grabbing whatever was handy for weapons. Mary could see her mother and sisters at the top of the dray cart filled with salt hay across the way. They waved at her. At least they were safe. She looked anxiously about for her father. Then the sound of laughter made her look back over her shoulder.

A group of boys stood a short distance behind her in the dooryard, slapping their knees in mirth. In their midst was the dark-haired Roberts boy, half a head taller than the rest. He wore a derisive smirk upon his face. Anthony Nutter stood next to him, doubled over with laughter, his flaming hair a shaggy mop.

Mary knew instantly who was responsible. She turned her head away, but not before John Roberts's eyes had met her own. Mary could feel his stare boring into her back. Aware of Roberts's likely stolen apple pressing against her thigh, she wished it would drop right through the seam of her pocket and roll away.

By the time order was restored—the enormous sow roped and dragged home with the help of a dozen men—the boys had disappeared.

Having overheard the reverend, Mary's fear returned in earnest. In bed at their new home across the river that night, the hanging at Strawbery Banke haunted her dreams. But it was the Reverend Burdett who stood tarred and feathered with leaves in Captain Wannerton's stead, his roving eye searching the crowd as the noose dangled emptily.

Mary deemed it best to keep what had happened to herself. How would she ever explain to her mother what she'd been doing and what the reverend had done and said? It would surely worry her madam into one of her fits or worse.

Accompanying her mother to the Small homestead for a neighborly visit, Mary decided to ask Francis what he remembered the reverend saying. Perhaps she hadn't heard it right. She found Francis in a nearby field, digging out stones. As she walked over to him, a large ball of gray fur made a beeline for her out of nowhere, its black-striped tail held straight out behind. The creature sat up on its hind legs to greet her, waving its paws in the air and making a chortling sound. It had an adorable catlike face with a longer tapered snout and a black mask around its eyes.

"This is your pet coon?"

Francis looked more surprised than she was. "He's not usually this friendly."

The raccoon dropped to the ground and turned on its back, exposing its belly so that Mary could rub it. She laughed. What a delightful animal—its soft leather hands curiously explored her hand. "Such a sweet thing!"

"He usually bites everyone," Francis said. He wiped his brow with his forearm and rested his hands on his wooden shovel, looking at her sidelong. His freckled face and tousled hair normally lent him a friendly and mischievous air, but that was not the case today. He looked afraid. "I don't know, Mary, I don't know . . ."

Mary felt her heart sink. "About what?"

He looked away.

Oh no, Mary thought. She sensed he was questioning how she knew things that other people didn't and why his raccoon liked her so much.

"I saw you bewitch those frogs at the meetinghouse spring the day we met."

"What? Bewitch? They were just friendly—they wanted to play." It didn't feel good, his questioning. Francis was supposed to be her friend.

"Those frogs are impossible to catch. They've never let anyone near 'em." He looked at her suspiciously. "The night we were lost, when my father went to follow the left branch of the brook, remember?"

She nodded—how could she ever forget?

"He went back a few days ago and looked to see where that branch led." A wave of emotion washed across Francis's face. He averted his gaze and took a sharp breath, trying to compose himself before he continued. "It led through a screen of bushes to a straight drop of about forty or fifty feet onto jagged rocks. The brook fans out there so there's little sound. My father said in the dark like that, there was no way he would have escaped with his life."

Mary tried to convince Francis of her innocence and blamelessness, but his father's beliefs seemed to effect Francis strongly. She and her mother left the Smalls a short while later. Her mother seemed angry.

"Mary, follow me." Her mother led her into the woods off the cart path. Deeper they went until she found a clearing in the trees. Here, her mother turned, her expression terrible to behold. "As though the Tarratines weren't bad enough, Goody Small informed me of what occurred at Spencer's Tavern."

Mary looked down.

"Your father made no mention of it to me, of which I'm not surprised. The gift of prophecy—heaven help us now!"

"Madam . . . 'twas only Edward Small who spoke so."

"Only Edward Small," her mother scoffed. "Half of Pascataway must have heard by now. This is a disaster! Your great-grandmother lost her life because of her knowledge of 'unnatural things.'"

What? Mary looked up at her mother. She knew very little about her great-grandmother.

"Your great-grandmother was hanged for witchcraft by Queen Elizabeth's soldiers. My mother—your grandmother—didn't want you to know. She didn't want you to be afraid of your gift. But I think it's high time you knew." A look of fixed determination on her face, she took Mary's hands in her own and pressed them together. "Verily, we're going to do even better. We're going to pray now, child, pray to God to cleanse your soul of prophecy and all other unnatural things."

Her mother pulled her downward. Mary sank to her knees in damp moss, her heart bleeding. As her mother prayed aloud, Mary did what felt best: She silently thanked God for her gift that kept her and others safe and helped to heal the sick. She prayed that God would continue to bless her as her grandmother had taught her. Her sweet, dear grandmother, who'd accepted her for who she was and had always encouraged her. And she prayed for her great-grandmother, who had suffered such a terrible fate. Mary had always hoped that her mother would start to praise and laud her gift; now at last she understood why her mother was so afraid. She prayed for her mother too.

-- 10 --

Come What May

Margaret stood on the storehouse doorstep. "Oh, help me," she sobbed. "Thomas has th' ague, and I fear he'll die—and me with child!"

The dog days of summer were upon them, and many were ill.

Mary felt badly for Margaret—mostly because after the widow Gyles's death, she'd married Thomas Crawley. With her mother away tending to other sick neighbors, Mary packed a basket with the herbs and supplies she would need. Since the trading expedition, nothing seemed beyond her. Off she went to help Margaret, leaving Sarah to mind Hannah and the house.

The Crawley wigwam proved cramped and mean. It smelled of something half-spoilt, and tools lay carelessly about in the wood shavings strewn across its earthen floor. A ship's carpenter by trade, Thomas Crawley built shallops for a living when he wasn't drinking in the taverns.

"He doesn't like it if I move his tools," Margaret apologized. "'Tis only temporary lodgings. He's soon ta build us a house." But at present, the man lay on a bed sack against one wall, fish-belly pale, muttering unintelligibly.

Mary simmered a wort of barks: bayberry, birch, and snakeroot—remedies Migwah had shown her. The Native remedies were much more effective than the traditional English centaury, chamomile, and feverfew. Pascataway augue was bad, and what grew hereabouts naturally made the strongest medicine.

When they propped Thomas up to dose him, a silver half groat slid out from under his shirt. It looked strangely familiar until Mary remembered the one just like it found in the Shapleigh warehouse.

"Does your husband always wear such a necklace?" she asked Margaret quietly.

"He never takes it off. It's his good luck charm. Why d' you ask?"

"I saw one like it once somewhere else."

An hour later, Thomas Crawley was much improved. Margaret had gone out to fetch some fresh water, so Mary decided to say something to him. "Sir, 'tis strange, but the necklace you wear is exactly like one left by thieves in Mr. Shapleigh's warehouse."

At first he hardly registered her words; but then his fingers fumbled clumsily at his chest, and he pushed the half groat back under his shirt. "Couldn't 'ave been mine then, now, could it?"

But Mary did suspect Thomas Crawley, and she could tell he knew it too.

"Nosy little wench needs to mind her own business if she knows what's good for her," he snarled, pulling his blanket over his shoulder and turning away.

How dare this nasty man say such a horrid thing! The ill often said things they didn't mean, she'd heard her mother say many times. Getting a grip on her anger, Mary decided to ignore the discovery. She'd come to help Margaret, not destroy her. She needed to do good works—that was the most important thing. Her patient's ague was getting better. What else could she help him with?

"Does your husband grind his teeth at night?" she asked when Margaret returned with the spring water.

"Oh, somethin' terrible."

"I thought so. I'll leave some black walnut and clove. Simmer him a heaping teaspoon daily in a cup of water for the next fortnight, stop for seven days, and then do it again for ten more." Mary poured a good measure of the dark powder into one of Margaret's bowls with a little smile. "It's vermifuge."

❧

Living just across the river from Bristol was not easy for Mary. She hoped and prayed the Reverend Burdett had forgotten all about "the great evil in their midst." The underlying fear and anxiety around this tortured her daily. She welcomed the deep snow that winter, which kept most along the river housebound, for the greater security it brought. However, this winter was not as comfortable or cozy as their first had been. By mid-January—and Mary's tenth birthday—their dwelling proved almost no better than the camps of those harvesting the king's pines on the log train. Mary's mother threatened to sail back to England rather than suffer through the rest of the season in such a miserable, cold estate. However roomy it was for stockpiling goods, the storehouse was not the best design to weather a New England winter. Its chimney interfaced with an outside wall, heating only part of the large main hall—and not very efficiently at that. The structure had been modeled after their old fishermen neighbors' storehouse dwelling, which Mary's father had thought ideal.

"Britania, Billings and Landers are quite happy with the arrangement," her father argued. "And their goods stay absolutely fresh." They were all huddled around the hearth, trying to keep warm.

"At the expense of frostbite," Mary's mother replied. "John, fishermen are so used to cold, it wouldn't bother them unless their drink froze. And I recall that Billings and Landers kept their drink in the corner of their hearth."

All told, to keep his family in comfort and health, Mary's father pushed to finish a proper dwelling house. It was situated handsomely on top of the nearby hill overlooking the river. A fine clapboard house with diamond-paned windows and a second story overhung in Tudor fashion, with carved wooden finials ornamenting its outside corners. The house proved as remarkably cozy and pleasant as they could want, with an enormous central chimney and walls of draftproof, whitewashed daub.

The move freed up space in the storehouse, which Mary's father aptly used to good advantage. His business had flourished, yet he needed to find another source of supply as Alexander Shapleigh had recently died. He wanted to take Mary with him on a business trip to Boston, to find a new merchant and carry Alexander's death certificate to the clerk of writs to be registered as a token of friendship. He told her mother that Mary's writing skill would come in handy. Mary knew it wasn't really her writing skill that her father hoped to employ. Still, with the trading expedition mishap, Mary's mother staunchly refused, much to Mary's disappointment.

Her father made plans to go alone. But on the morning of his departure that May, Nicolas Shapleigh called him out at the last minute to help translate an Indian deed up at Black Point, a distance east along the seacoast. The trip to Boston would have to wait.

That evening, Mary made her way across the hill in the damp twilight to the chicken coop to shut them in for the night. The hens were unusually flighty, and the rooster began to crow. She looked about uneasily. Was it an animal they were afraid of? Then she saw a blaze of bright yellow flame through the trees below along the river—a shallop with a torch landing at her father's dock. Someone must be hoping to fetch her mother for physick. She would go warn her they were coming.

Chickens in their coop for the night, she started back toward the house. Strange that there were so many voices making their way up the hillside. She stopped to listen. One voice rose above the others—unmistakable, loud, and authoritative.

Mary started to run. She yanked on the latchstring and leaned into the heavy door of the house. It swung inward. She found her mother in the parlour. "Please don't let him take me!" she cried, out of breath.

"What in the heavens?" Her mother stared at her.

"Reverend Burdett is coming with lots of men."

Her mother's demeanor quickly changed. "Run, child, run and hide yourself well!"

Mary flew from the house in a panic, icy claws of fear tearing at her chest.

A dense thorny thicket bordering the woods past the barn felt safe enough. She crawled deep underneath the brambles, which scratched her hands and snagged at her cloak. She curled into a ball, burrowing down into last year's leaves and humus, and pulled her hood down to conceal her cap. Mary's heart pounded so loudly in her chest that she grew afraid the men would hear it. She tried to relax, to slow her breathing.

There were at least five or six of them, from what she could see by the light of their torch in the search that ensued: the reverend, the Bristol constable, and a crew of burly sheriff's men. She was glad George and their new servant Peter were there to protect her mother and sisters. They'd already gone to bed for the night, but they'd certainly be awake now. *Oh, if only Father were home.*

The reverend's men searched everywhere, inside and out, the torch even sweeping slowly along the edges of her hiding place. They were gone a long time before she finally dared to come out, her body numb and cold. The nearly full moon lit the landscape from high above. Staying mostly in the shadows, she crept back to the house.

Inside warming by the kitchen hearth, Mary sat with her mother, who looked weary and traumatized. Her mother wrung her hands, "Let's pray your Father will be home soon."

Peter and George had gone back to bed, as had Mary's sisters. It was late. Very late.

The sound of soft rapping at the door sent Mary skittering behind the woodbox in a second, but the voice she heard at the door was a woman's.

"Mary, you can come out now," her mother said quietly. "It's all right. It's safe."

Standing before her in her mother's kitchen hall was none other than Goody Walford, the herbwoman of Great Island. The one with the witch bottle.

"I tried to warn you, but the reverend got here first," Goody Walford said. "My husband got wind Burdett was commencing a witch hunt. I'm glad to see they've gone off empty-handed." She nodded at Mary. Her eyes narrowed. "They'll be back sooner than later. Likely at daybreak with a hound. I'd recommend making your daughter scarce for the time being. If you'd like, my son Jeremiah and

I can take her down to our place. He's waiting at Cammock's Creek with our canoe. They've got guards on the river by your dock."

Go with Goody Walford? The world had turned on its head.

A short while later, Mary followed Goody Walford out into the night. The woman could walk swiftly despite her gait, Mary learned, as they made their way to the cart path. Mary felt almost invisible, dressed in her good black clothes and her dark wool cloak. Her white cap and collar were safely stowed in her bandbox under one arm, and a basket of food from her mother was on the other.

They walked in silence. A screech owl called in the forest nearby, and peepers sounded from the marsh. The events of the last few hours seemed surreal. It was hard to believe her gravest fear had happened, and she'd escaped.

Then a noise ahead of them in the deep shadow made Goody Walford suck in her breath. A torch blazed suddenly, and a figure stood blocking their path.

"Who d' we 'ave here?" The voice sent Mary's skin crawling. The edge of a sword glistened, and a man stepped forward, pressing its tip to the front of Goody Walford's bodice. "Where d'ye think ye're going?"

Goody Walford stepped back instinctively, shielding Mary, and raised her staff in defense. With a deft backhand, the man sent her staff flying.

"Don't move another muscle, or I'll run ye through." He raised his sword to Goody Walford's throat. *This can't be happening*, Mary thought wildly.

"Shame on you, treating women and children so," gasped Goody Walford. "Where are thy manners? I've never seen the like—"

The tip of the sword began to wave in front of Goody Walford's nose. Then Mary noticed a tall figure appear behind the man. The swordsman sensed it as well, only too late, for there was a dull thunk and he sank to the ground.

"Mind, speak little," Mary's father said, setting down the butt end of his musket. He dragged their unconscious attacker to the side of the lane and tied him securely to a tree with rope the man had on his person. Then he ground out the torch, but not before Mary had found Goody Walford's staff.

Edward Small had tipped her father off when he'd arrived back at the Shapleighs' a short while ago, he told them. Goody Walford filled him in on the rest.

"That settles it. I'm taking Mary to Boston with me. What else can be done with all this madness? Burdett and his demon crew—it's a blessing I missed my passage this morning. You and Mary wait with your son at Cammock's while I pack what we need. I shan't be long."

He returned a short while later with both his musket and his pack. "Strange," he said, "the rogue I tied to the tree seems to have angered a raccoon. The creature's inflicted a few good bites from what I can tell."

With the moon lighting the river, Mary and her father had to lie flat in the Walfords' canoe. Jeremiah, a young man of sixteen, hugged the shoreline, trying to stay in the shadows and as far from other craft as possible.

"We lived on a hill just across the Charles River from Boston a few years back. I loved it there," Goody Walford reminisced. "Only when the place became overrun with Puritans did we leave. May I say, sir, that circumstances sometimes point out clever folk regardless of blame. Once in Boston, it might be best not to come back."

Mary wasn't sure how she felt about this. She wondered if her father would be able to put up with the Puritans. This did not bode well for a move to Boston, if that was what they had to do.

As they drew abreast the town dock at Strawbery Banke, another craft approached them.

"Hark, my mother's ill!" Jeremiah called out. Goody Walford bent forward clutching her midriff and began to moan loudly, interspersed with fits of coughing. It worked brilliantly. They were left alone.

In the small cove on the Great Island, Mary and her father safely disembarked. They rested in the Walfords' kitchen hall. Goodman Walford took the canoe back out to inquire about a passage south. There were only two merchant craft anchored off Strawbery Banke.

As luck would have it, Mary and her father boarded the *Dove* early that next morning before sunrise, Mary's father agreeing to pay the captain in gold coin. It was a small pinnace with a crew of three bound for Marblehead with a cargo of board and locally harvested salt.

"*Salt*?" her father cried, making his way below. Salt was risky cargo as any moisture to reach it was quickly absorbed, rendering the granules heavier and heavier. Salt packets had been known to be driven straight to the bottom of the sea by an errant wave. But there was no better alternative, and her father relented. The sooner they left, the better. " 'Tis in God's hands, and we'll pray for a safe passage."

In the meantime, they made themselves as comfortable as they could upon the firkins and board belowdecks, stowing away their belongings.

The captain stuck his head down the hatchway. "Tide's turning—won't be much longer before we depart."

The sound of oarlocks could be heard outside. "Ho there!" hailed a voice.

The captain disappeared. "Good morrow, mate," they heard him say.

"Ye haven't seen a man with a young maid hereabouts, have ye?" asked the voice from the water.

Mary's father held up a cautionary hand. They sat perfectly still. Mary held her breath. *Oh dear God—we're so close to making an escape!*

"Can't say I have," the captain answered, as stalwart an old salt as the best of them.

The oarlocks resumed and faded into the distance.

Her father grinned.

Mary took a breath.

-- 11 --

Points South

The *Dove* weighed anchor with the turn of the tide and sailed out through the Great Island gut. Once in the open sea, Mary and her father came above deck and made themselves as comfortable as possible against the windward gunnel. Mary hadn't passed this way since their arrival. Back then, Pascataway had seemed so desolate and foreign. Looking back at the Great Island, she marveled at the fact that it now felt like home. Well, it had been her home, she thought sadly. Everything had happened so fast.

Out across the expanse of choppy gray water, whitecaps were forming. On the horizon she could make out the Isles of Shoals to the southeast, smudges of leaden blue. They tacked by Pannaway and the old palisaded stone house, the oldest house at Pascataway, which looked much as she remembered it the day they'd arrived.

The wind picked up, and Mary huddled against her father. She hoped the seas would remain calm. But as the *Dove* plied southward, a swell began to build. Sheaves of salty spray flew across the deck, and waves smacked the bow, jarring the teeth and backbones of those aboard. Mary grew afraid.

"This is why I'm not a sailor," her father said with a grimace.

"Looks like we're in for a bit o' weather!" the captain called apologetically in their direction.

"God protect us with cargo such as this!" Mary's father shouted back, one hand on the little Bible he kept tucked inside his waistcoat.

The weather continued to worsen; Mary began to pray, wedging herself more firmly against her father's side, her feet slipping on the deck slick with seawater. A crew member kindly handed them a grimy oilskin, but the cold spray still stung her cheeks, and the wind whistled through her cap. Her teeth began to chatter. *Please don't let it get any worse.* But the seas continued to mount. Then the skies opened up, and rain poured down; lightning flashed everywhere at once in the gloaming, the sky an eerie purple green.

On the voyage from England, Mary had been able to talk herself out of seasickness, but that wasn't the case now. Nausea overcame her in the ever-building seas, which purging did nothing to ease. To drown no longer felt like such a bad alternative. There was not much the crew could do other than try to keep water from seeping into the hold. The seas being so steep, their best choice was to run with it. A wave crest broke with great force, and Mary felt her entire body lift off the deck, the sea threatening to sweep her away until she felt her father's viselike grip on her arm.

Eventually, the wind eased, and the spray stopped flying. But the seas remained mountainous and rolling. Grateful to be alive, Mary sat wet and shivering. The pinnace was listing heavily to port, and the captain sent his crew below to shift the cargo as best they could.

"Just a mean squall—she's blown over a'ready!" he called out from the steerage.

Mary's father sat stiffly by her side. "I thank our heavenly Father."

The sky was a dramatic mix of stormy white and purple-gray clouds through which apertures of lucid blue-green sky peeked. Against this backdrop, the tall sails of a ship appeared off their stern, making straight for them. As the pinnace rose skyward on the next crest, Mary pointed in alarm. The captain's expression made her blood run cold.

She watched in terrified disbelief as a Dutch privateer overtook them. The ship gained on them rapidly, towering above them, even though they were steering straight toward the treacherous rocky shoreline in an attempt to escape. Shots were fired at them, falling wide with a hiss into the waves. Just when all seemed hopelessly lost, the brig changed its bearing and turned to the eastward, leaving all of them giddy with relief. Any discomfort Mary had felt paled in the light of such emancipation.

"We warn't worth her trouble," the captain said, his face relaxed back to its usual stern countenance. But farther out to sea, the distant sails of another vessel could be seen, the privateer in hot pursuit.

Mary's father wrapped an arm around her and held her close.

The Little Harbor at Marblehead was a welcome sight. Sheltered behind some small islands, a curved sandy beach covered in fish flakes and storehouses greeted them. Along the face of a rocky cliff, small thatched dwellings clustered together, above which a backdrop of dark tangled woods loomed.

Mary stood on the shingle, looking back out to sea. A full moon was rising, large and silvery in the deepening dusk, the sky to the east having cleared. Relief and gratitude to be alive and on solid ground flooded through her.

"We'll certainly thank God tonight in our prayers," her father said.

They were welcomed into the largest house, its diamond-paned windows aglow with candlelight. It was the only inn and ordinary Marblehead had, but a good one. Goody Maverick, with her brood of little daughters, took Mary under their wing. A large iron pot bubbling in the hearth filled the parlour with the delicious smell of fish chowder. Mary's insides felt wretchedly hollow, and she gratefully accepted a bowlful along with a dry smock and warm blanket. Goody Maverick kindly rinsed and hung her wet clothing in the kitchen hearth, pressing Mary's cap and collar. Mary's mother's basket of food had been lost overboard in the squall.

The men in the ordinary took the news of the Dutch privateer with a potent silence.

The innkeeper, Moses Maverick, a friendly man with a commanding presence, was the first to speak.

"Someone needs to alert Salem on the morrow. This is the second report we've had of it in a fortnight."

With the civil war back in England, privateering and piracy up and down the coast was on the rise. It was fast becoming a serious problem and not just one concerning foreign vessels.

But for now, Mary felt safe. Her eyelids grew heavy as warmth and nourishment settled her stomach and limbs. Goody Maverick led her over to a pallet that had been set up for her in one corner. Mary knelt to say her prayers. It felt blissful to relax and pull the soft linsey-woolsey coverlet up to her chin. The voices in the room grew loud and magnified. Falling fast through a weightless nothingness, Mary relaxed more deeply.

"Just further makes the need for a strong defense," Moses Maverick's voice boomed. "We need a fort on the point here between the two harbors. Naugs Head doesn't do us any good."

That was the last thing she heard.

The next day they left Marblehead on foot, Mary's father politely declining a passage by sea. Moses Maverick would accompany them as far as Salem, eager to report the Dutch privateer to the local magistrates. He urged Mary's father to visit his brother Samuel on Noddle's Island near Boston. Evidently, Samuel loved to entertain visitors. Mary's father extended an invitation to the Mavericks to visit Pascataway. Their hosts had been kind and more than generous. Goody Maverick had even packed a new dinner basket for them.

They followed a footpath up the rocky cliff to the top of a hill, where a small meetinghouse sat perched above the harbor. From there, the path sloped down the back side of the hill, past a pond, through the woods, and along the shoreline until they arrived at the Naugs Head ferry.

Just the thought of setting foot in the boat made Mary uneasy, but the short stretch of water before them looked flat and calm. On the opposite side, she could see the village of Salem spread out along the shore.

The ferryman turned out to be several sheets to the wind despite the morning hour, and their course was unsteady, going so far as to spin in a complete circle near the Marblehead shore.

Mary gripped her seat like a limpet. Her father drummed his fingertips on the thwart, his face a storm cloud. They weren't having much luck with boats.

"I surely wouldn't mind having a pull at your oars, mate!" Moses offered cheerfully.

"Nay, Master Maverick, I won't hare of sich a thiingk. Jes res' awhile and let this ol' man doo his dooty!"

Finally arriving at the town dock, they disembarked among the warehouses at the waterfront. Salem was much larger than Marblehead or any of the Pascataway settlements. A small fort protected twin coves of fishing flakes, and the dwellings were spread out a distance from each other, connected by several thoroughfares. In the middle of the village sat a good-sized meetinghouse, a sturdy stock and pillory built next to it.

"Many who arrive here to stay find themselves more comfortable over in our little settlement, rustic as it is," Moses said with a wink.

Walking down Salem's wide main street, Mary was proud of her father's friendly yet refined manner that attracted many a pleasantry from the strangers they passed. Their clothing had dried crisp and clean in Goody Maverick's kitchen hearth, and escorted by Moses Maverick or not, being anonymous was certainly fun. Mr. Maverick soon took his leave, but not before finding them an oxcart heading south on the Bay Road, delivering supplies to the village of Lynn.

The road proved to be nothing more than a cart path that followed an old Indian trail, winding through a hilly, wooded landscape of oak and sumac. Mary was glad they weren't on foot, and they arrived at the village of Lynn in two hours' time. It consisted of a cluster of dwellings, a smallish meetinghouse, and a comfortable-looking ordinary.

"Where the magistrates traveling to the general court often stay," the drover said. "But tha's a better place for ye just a few furlongs down the road. 'Tis where I be going. Ye won't be disappointed."

They rolled on, fording a narrow place in the Saugus River at low tide. On the opposite bank, they passed a row of English-built wigwams about which congregated groups of rather destitute-looking folk. Mary looked away, horrified as an old woman squatted to relieve herself in plain sight. The place reeked of the debauchery and lawlessness that many settlements had at their fringes, populated with those suffering from broken families and other misfortunes. She was glad the cart continued onward.

At a cluster of several well-kept dwellings with lush gardens, the cart did come to a stop. Here a banquet table sat in the shade of an enormous chestnut tree. Mary was amazed to see the trivets of pottage, bowls of stew, roasted fowl, flowery salads, and a suckling pig on a platter in contrast to the poverty they'd just passed. A few people clustered around the feast, shooing away the flies and talking excitedly.

"Welcome!" a stout goodwife cried. "Ye've arrived timely. 'Tis almost noon."

The drover saluted her back.

To their delight, Mary and her father were welcomed to the banquet, eating dinner with the community, rich and poor alike. The wigwams, they learned, were temporary homes for new arrivals who would be striking out on their own in time. A local tannery employed many of these settlers, and it was the tannery's custom to provide a weekly feast for the community so families didn't go completely hungry.

They spent the night nearby, their host a blacksmith and his wife. The smithy spoke enthusiastically of the bog iron found nearby and how the river was an ideal place for an ironworks. He said the governor's son had gone back to London to gather the undertakers and materials necessary to begin an operation. This incited Mary's father's curiosity, and he talked with the man for hours.

Mary was glad she had eaten her fill at dinner that day, for the haslet on which they supped was near rancid. She slept fitfully that night, her stomach unsettled and the bed sack infested with bedbugs. Morning could not come soon enough.

At daybreak, she and her father set off again on foot along a forested road. The sky looked white as goose feathers, the trees partly concealed by a vaporous mist.

"We'll be making Boston yet, my wild rose. We're within half a day's journey," her father said happily.

They walked along in silence. The road proved swampy in areas, and Mary's shoes and skirt hem were soon sullied with mud. She stayed close to her father's side, listening for any strange birdcalls or rustlings in the undergrowth. The natives were known to be less than friendly in these parts south.

By the time the road brought them to the rocky summit of a tall hill, the mist had cleared. They stopped short in amazement. Spread out before them lay a vast sunlit marsh that stretched away to the south and west as far as the eye could see. Below them, a network of tidal estuaries curled toward the sea to the east, and the air smelled strong and salty.

"Rumney Marsh," her father said excitedly. "Look," he pointed to several blueish hills rising above the horizon. One had a wide ridgelike crest. "That must be Trimountain, the isle of Shawmut. Boston lies at its foot, m'dear."

Following the road down into the grassy plain with renewed enthusiasm, they came to the first narrow estuary over which a plank bridge spanned. As Mary's father crossed ahead of her, the weathered boards shook and wobbled from side to side. Mary froze, the movement threatening to jettison her into the water. She could see fish and crabs scuttle quickly away beneath.

"Come, Mary, 'tis stronger than it looks." Her father started back toward her.

"No!" she screamed as his footsteps jostled the bridge even worse than before.

He halted midbridge, and his laugh rang out as she ran lightly across to join him.

The sun shone brightly upon the endless reeds and tall grasses of Rumney Marsh. They walked on again in silence, hearing only the call of waterbirds and the trill of red-winged blackbirds. Indian trails intercepted the road from time to time as worn footpaths, and Mary wondered more than once if the birdcalls were really birds. It felt as though they were walking farther and farther from civilization and she found it rather incongruous, albeit comforting, to come upon an English fence with a gate stretching across the road.

"I thought somebody'd have taken advantage of this ready-made grazing land," her father said, opening the gate so they could pass through and then fastening it shut again behind them. The hollow clunk of a cowbell was another giveaway. Since Rumney Marsh had many small hills and valleys, the plantation, if there was one, stayed hidden from view.

The road to Winnisimmet wound around the sides of several forested hills, a welcome shadiness above the marsh; and in an hour's time, Mary and her father stood on the bank of the Mystic River, gazing across the water at the Trimount several miles distant. Mary's father raised the tattered flag up its pole to summon the ferry. The Charlestown Peninsula where the Walfords had once lived lay perhaps only a mile across the river's mouth, but it took some time before they could see a boat headed their way.

While they waited, Mary brushed the dried mud from her skirt and shoes with the help of a teasel frond and changed into her good band and cap. Her father whistled happily as he cleaned the stubble off his jaw with his straight edge. "Looking like a bearded Puritan is beneath my dignity."

The ferry proved to be a flat-bottomed scow with a lateen sail and sweeping stern oar. It felt good to sit and rest after their long morning walk. The ferryman was a friendly fellow, thankfully sober, asking about Maine and other points north. They crossed the mouth of the Mystic River, between the Charlestown Peninsula to their right, a settlement of marshy hillsides dotted with sheep, and Noddle's Island to their left, where they could see a large plantation.

"That be Samuel Maverick's," the ferryman told her father. "Royalist and Anglican, he is." He paused and then said with a wink, "A veritable thorn in the side of our magistrates. Good man all the same."

"So I hear," her father replied with a smile.

Mary noticed he looked appreciatively upon the Noddle's Island plantation. Goats and cows grazed, and a small pinnace lay at anchor. It looked quite hospitable. Mary wouldn't mind a visit herself, but it was Boston her father had come to see.

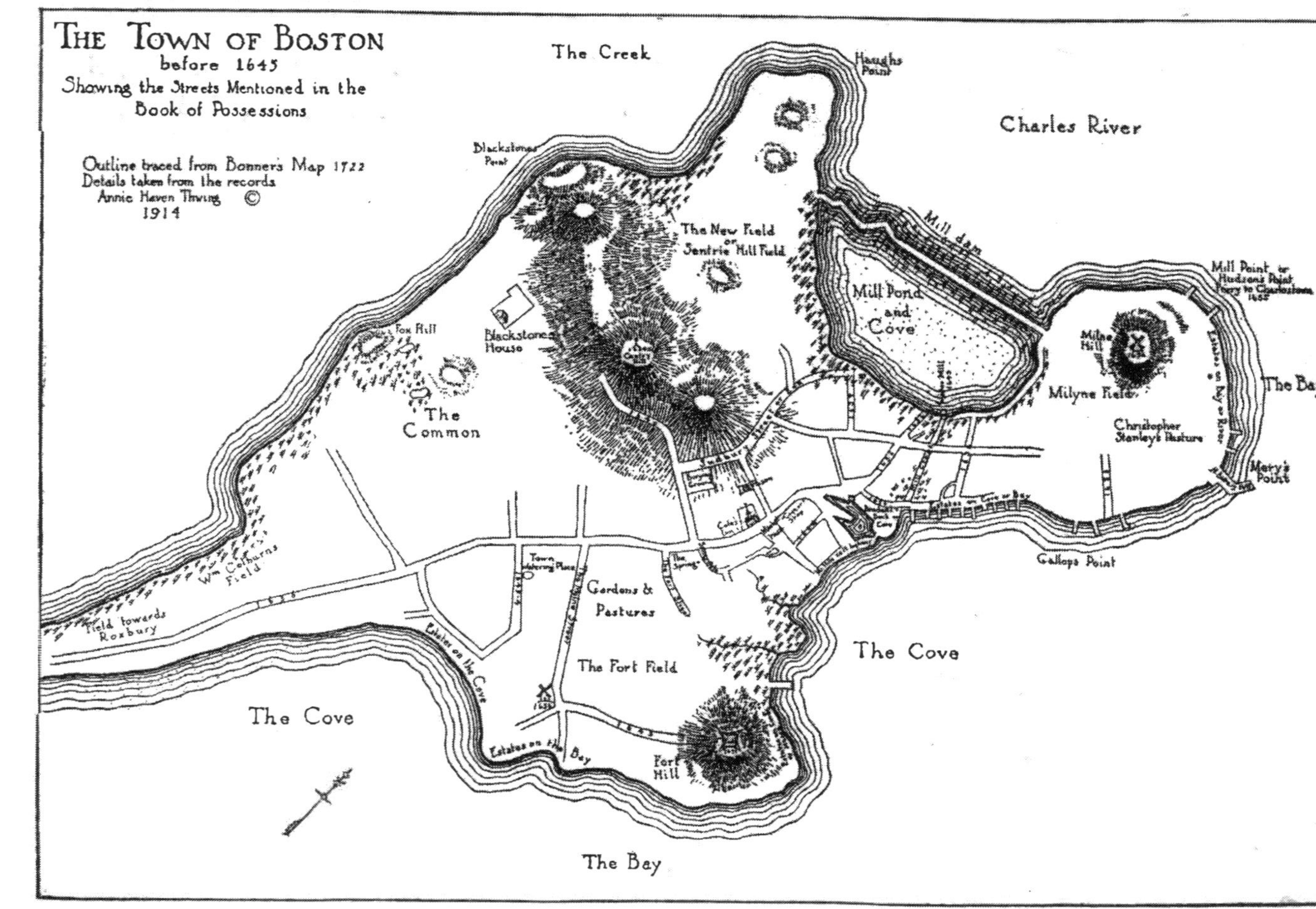
THE TOWN OF BOSTON
before 1645
Showing the Streets Mentioned in the
Book of Possessions
Outline traced from Bonner's Map 1722
Details taken from the records
Annie Haven Thwing ©
1914
The Creek
Haughs Point
Charles River
Blackstones Point
The New Field or Sentrie Hill Field
Mill dam
Mill Pond and Cove
Mill Point or Hudson's Point
Fox Hill
Blackstones House
Milne Hill
Milyne Field
The Bay
The Common
Christopher Stanley's Pasture
Mary's Point
Estates on Cove or Bay
Wm Colburns Field
Town Watering Place
The Spring
Gallops Point
Field towards Roxbury
Gardens & Pastures
Estates on the Cove
The Cove
The Fort Field
The Cove
Estates on the Bay
Fort Hill
The Bay

-- 12 --

Boston

A strong breeze blew across the bay, whipping the water into a fine chop. Cold and wonderful, the breeze smelled sweetly of the sea and wicked the moisture from Mary's clothing. She studied the town of Boston as it grew near, her stomach fluttering with excitement. Many rooftops and a tall steeple clustered beneath the slopes of the Trimount and its summit of three green hills. The island itself looked like a half-submerged great chair with peninsulas stretching out to sea like protective armrests around a cove where ships lay at anchor. Trees were scarce except those she could see in gardens and orchards.

The ferry landed on the nearest peninsula. To Mary's dismay, her father ignored the cheery-looking inn nearby that smelled of fresh baking and made straight for the town that looked yet another mile distant. She forced her tired legs onward. The road took them up a hill with a windmill on top, sails sweeping around in the breeze. Sheep and cattle grazed about a weed-covered common, and Mary could see small thatched houses down along the shoreline. Some looked abandoned, and a fair number were little better than wigwams. They walked along the side of a large tidal pond to a bridge of heavy timbers that spanned the mill creek and an expanse of low swampy ground. The mill caught her father's attention, and to Mary's annoyance he changed course to investigate.

"A fair piece of work," he said, admiring the craftsmanship. "But what will they do with all this swamp hereabouts? Hardly a place to build a town. Would be an immense labor to fill it all in."

Finally, they crossed the creek, and the lane curved toward the town dock. Clouds of gritty dust made Mary cough. The wharves smelled strongly of fish and tar. Sailors and longshoremen were loading and unloading, and lighters were coming and going. Carts, rope, and barrels were everywhere. She trailed behind her father, who skirted the periphery, trying to find a clear path around it all.

Just ahead of them on a large rock sat a party of Indians with painted faces. When she and her father drew abreast, the fiercest-looking one leaned forward without warning, frowned, and pointed a stick at Mary. He was staggeringly tall, even sitting down. Amulets and weapons dangled from his body, and his hair stuck straight up like a hackle on the crown of his head. Those with him grew quiet.

"You eat!" he demanded, holding the stick out so she could take it. Mary froze.

Her father stopped in his tracks. Turning around, he addressed the men in Abenaki. "Gagwi ni?"

The sannups looked surprised, but they obviously understood, for they answered back in their own language.

"Go ahead and try it, Mary," her father said calmly.

She accepted the stick without qualm, well used to sampling the things Migwah handed her. It tasted delicious—a spiced venison jerky. The Indians laughed and slapped their knees, mirthful at their little joke.

Her father tasted some too. Then he bought a bundle, which pleased the natives even more. "A good thing to carry with us." He stuffed the jerky into his pack. "Quite a handy and toothsome travel food." Mary thought so too.

Her encounter with the local Indians leaving her a bit ruffled, Mary walked closer to her father's side up the hill from the wharves to the market square. Ahead, Boston's new meetinghouse steeple graced the crowded marketplace.

"Ah," her father said, "proof that Old England has indeed begun here in the New. Makes Strawbery Banke's new meetinghouse look small and provincial."

The market was a wide dusty square with a thoroughfare on one end, lined with shops of all kinds that led straight down Market Street to a wharf on the waterfront. All sorts of vendors with baskets, barrows, stalls, and animals milled about, hawking their wares.

"Fine writing ink and quills!" a man yelled over the crowd.

"Hot eel pies!" called a woman's voice.

Being midday and near the dinner hour, some official-looking magistrates began to issue forth from the meetinghouse door. The crowd parted for a gray-bearded man in an opulent white ruff who looked especially grim under his tall felt hat. He was flanked by two plumed servants carrying halberds. Another magistrate wearing a crimson doublet and walking with a cane also caught Mary's attention. The man laughed and joked with a bystander in a warm and friendly manner. Mary began to enjoy herself.

"Fair oranges and lemons!" sang out a youthful fruit peddler wearing a wide-brimmed dutch hat. He began to juggle his wares from a small handbarrow, adding more and more pieces of fruit to his airborne circle, which he then caught deftly one at a time. Onlookers gave their hands, and he bowed with a flourish. Then he gave Mary one of his oranges. She curtsied a thank-you, but her father grabbed her shoulders and hastily steered her away. Mary tucked the orange in her pocket. She hadn't had one in such a long time.

A loud shouting made everyone jump. As the crowd jostled and parted, a man puffing from exertion, his sleeves rolled back past the elbows, carted by the largest deer Mary had ever seen—a magnificent creature with reddish-brown fur and an enormous rack of antlers. The deer's tongue lolled out of its mouth, and its large plum eyes were half-open and drying.

"Make way! Make way!" the man cried. Others tailed him excitedly.

"A maccarib," her father said with certainty as those around them began to talk about what it could be. "Very rare about these parts."

Mary had neither seen nor heard of one before. It looked different than a moose. Someone in the crowd caught her attention. She looked back through the sea of strangers—had she just seen a familiar face? Odd. Maybe she'd imagined it, for whoever it was seemed to have disappeared.

It wasn't until the crowd began to thin that Mary noticed the man in the pillory next to the meetinghouse. His head and hands stuck through the holes in the locked boards, to which his ears had been nailed. Blood crusted the sides of his head, and his hair was splattered with tangled offal and other filth. A placard displayed his crime upon the stock post: *Imprudence*. She stared in horror.

"One thing I'm glad Maine does not have," her father said quietly, "though our neighbor Bristol has built one now."

Mary wondered if that was what Reverend Burdett would have done with her. Or the gaol? He'd mentioned a burning or a drowning—both prospects much too frightening to think about. She shuddered. A memory of Tiverton High Street came back to her: that of a man and wife seated side by side, their ankles held in the stocks. Her grandmother had brought the couple food and drink wrapped in a cloth. It hadn't been like this at all.

"Sir, it's terrible what they've done to that poor man," Mary whispered.

"I quite agree."

Once her father finished scrutinizing all the market had to offer, they walked down the street to the sign of the mortar and pestle. Inside the shop, a long counter stretched. Upon its surface sat a brass scale, some knives, and cutting boards. The smell of spices and exotic medicines tantalized. Mary and her father slid in behind others to wait their turn as the apothecary was filled with patrons.

Mary studied the dozens of ceramic pots, vials, and jars upon the shelves of the back wall. There were rows of bottles of varying hues, from clear to yellow to brown, and others of pickled animal parts. One glass canister was coiled with what looked like dried snakes. The largest glass bell jars especially drew her attention. They were filled with different kinds of leeches—some small and black and others large and brown, their wicked toothy mouths suckered onto the sides. She would hate to be the one to have to reach into those jars, though she knew the creatures to be helpful with cleansing the blood and humors.

"May I help you?" a middle-aged woman behind the counter, wearing a pair of pince-nez spectacles, asked her father.

Mary read from the list her mother had dictated: first was *calamine powder*. The clerk scooped the lovely pink calamine from a barrel in the corner into a small cloth bag and weighed it on the brass scale. Next were *chalk* and *Chinese borax* and then *rose water*, which the clerk poured into a small glass bottle from one of the vials, sealing its plug with beeswax. The wild roses weren't aromatic enough at Pascataway for Mary's mother to make her own. Mary's father bought some orange flower water to surprise her mother with. It was delightful to be able to pick and choose from such plenty instead of making do with what the latest ship had brought in. Mary's father also purchased a pound of saltpeter to make gunpowder as an apothecary's quality usually far exceeded the standard.

"Mistress," her father inquired while Mary placed their purchases into Goody Maverick's basket, "would you be so kind to suggest where weary travelers may find suitable hospitality here in Boston?"

"You know the General Court's in session?" she said. "Most places are full—you've picked a hard time for a visit. Try the Anchor across from the town dock. They might have room."

Mary's father thanked her, and they turned to make their way out the door when a tall gentleman entered the shop with a screaming child slung over his shoulder. The child's hands clutched at its ears.

Patrons immediately stepped aside, ushering the man up to the counter, where the shop clerk went right to work grinding with mortar and pestle, her helper reaching for pots in a panic. Mary's father made his way to the door, but Mary stayed rooted to the spot and addressed the gentleman as best she could between his charge's earsplitting screams.

"What he needs, sir, is a few drops of cider vinegar put into each ear. It will stop the suffering at once. It works every time."

The gentleman did not seem to hear her, but the clerk did. "What did you say, child? Cider vinegar?"

"Yes, a few drops mixed with a little warm water."

Perhaps it was the simplicity of the remedy, for the clerk immediately set down her pestle and squeezed a few drops of vinegar water from a cloth into the little one's ears.

The remedy worked magically: the screams subsided to a whimper; and then the exhausted child fell soundly asleep. The entire shop breathed a sigh of relief, and Mary skipped happily out the door after her father.

"Wait a moment, Mary," her father said when she joined him. "Wait right here." He directed her toward the next shop, out of the flow of foot traffic. He did not look happy.

"Sir? What's the matter?"

"That's exactly what I'm going to find out," he said.

Mary watched in disbelief as, with two long strides, her father grabbed the shoulder of a man who had just emerged from the apothecary—the shoulder of someone they knew.

Thomas Crawley tried to bolt, but her father held him fast. "Since when do you make it your business to follow me around Boston, Crawley?" he said angrily.

Mary stared open-mouthed, shocked by her father's behavior. It must have been Crawley she'd seen in the market. Strange that he was here too.

Crawley sputtered, held prisoner by her father's fist hold on his jerkin. His face turned and fixed strangely upon her. *Is he trying to tell me something?* She took a step in his direction, and he began to struggle wildly. *He is afraid of me.* Mary could hear her mother's reprimand for such a careless public display. Thankfully, here in Boston, no one knew who she was. Well, almost no one.

"Wannerton sent you here?" her father said a little less loudly, for the altercation was attracting the attention of those on the street.

"Aye, Wannerton'll make a deal with you for a price," Crawley croaked.

Mary's father relaxed his hold on Crawley's jerkin. "Oh, he will, will he?"

"He'll take care of Burdett ta keep your daughter here from harm."

"Take care of?"

"The cap'n has 'is ways."

Spying on my business affairs is certainly one of them." Her father snorted. If I see you following us again, you'll regret it. Get thee gone!" He let go of the man with a tempered push, sending Crawley backpedaling down the dusty slope of the street.

"I swear there's nothing Wannerton won't do for gold," her father said, picking up his pack and musket. "Unfortunately, I may have no alternative."

Mary wished her father hadn't been so rough with Thomas Crawley. They walked back up through the market and down toward the town dock. She hurried by his side, afraid the Boston constable might approach, but they made it to the ordinary without incident.

The Anchor was as crowded as the market had been. The innkeeper shook his head. "No room here. Ye might try the Red Lion, but you're more'n welcome to share our board."

The savory smell of the cooking got the better of them. They sat down at a long table with a roomful of patrons of all ranks and stations. There were chargers of mutton and beef, bowls of creamed Indian corn, platters of salted cod, and loaves of bread for all to share. The innkeeper poured them a pot of small beer from a pitcher. Sharing a trencher with her father, Mary sat beside him on the bench, the tradition of sitting above or below the salt depending on one's rank ignored; guests sat where there was room, elbow to elbow.

Mary observed two manservants carrying an enormous side of ribs in a roasting pan. She tapped her father's sleeve. "Sir, is that the maccarib?"

Her father raised his eyebrows. "It could be—yes, I believe it must be, or one just like it."

There was little conversation at the table due to the fact that most were strangers to one another. They were a rather mixed bunch: an Indian dressed like an Englishman, a number of longshoremen, a dark-skinned Spanish type, a sailor and his wench, some laborers. Sitting to the other side of her father, however, was a man ofrefined appearance who tipped his hat politely in greeting.

"Pardon me, my goodman," the fellow said. "I believe I happened to observe quite a frightening encounter of yours earlier today—a group of savages making themselves a nuisance to your young maiden at the dock square?"

Mary's father nodded and swallowed his food. "Yes indeed, my goodman. A bit disconcerting perhaps, but they meant no harm."

"You speak their language?"

"Yes . . . well, not exactly. I speak an Abenaki dialect, but we understood each other well enough."

"Quite an advantage," the man mused. He wore a sky-blue satin doublet and a tall felt hat, yet his hair fell to his shoulders, and his jaw was shaven like her father's. He seemed very interested to hear they were from Maine. Upon learning that Mary's father was looking for a merchant connection, he said he could possibly be of some help in that regard.

Mary listened to the conversation as she ate a second helping of Indian corn. To have a full stomach felt wonderful after their morning's journey on foot.

"Are ye rooming here at the Anchor?" the man asked her father.

"No, 'tis evidently full to overflowing. Would you happen to know of another place?"

"As a matter of fact, I do—'tis where I'm lodging. Just straight down the street to the right of the cove. Last house on the corner at Goodman Bendall's." He smiled. "Mind, tell him Henry Powning sent you."

They found Bendall's readily enough, a house on the town cove whose upper story overhung the street below. Edward Bendall was not at home, but a servant fetched his wife, who said there was room available. Standing in the parlour, Mary could hear the voices of children in the kitchen reciting catechism.

Leaving their belongings behind in safekeeping, they followed Goodwife Bendall's directions to the clerk of the writs. "I shan't think you will find him there today," she'd said. "'Tis the week of the General Court."

As Goody Bendall forewarned, the clerk was not to be found at the modest dwelling that fronted Cornhill Street with *Town Clerk* painted on a shingle above the gate.

"Well, at least I now know where to find him," her father said.

Cornhill Street stretched the length of the peninsula; and to the north, behind the thatched houses and gardens that fronted the street, a commons swept down the back side of the island, upon which sheep and cattle were grazing. Mary and her father walked the length of Cornhill all the way to the town gate on the narrow sandy isthmus that connected the island to the mainland and then back again, past the governor's house. The air in town was smoky from the many chimney fires, and the dust that rose in the lane stung Mary's eyes.

"Boston isn't so very far ahead of Pascataway, but it does leave us with a lot to be desired when it comes to goods," her father said.

As they walked back toward the town center, the grassy green summit of the Trimount beckoned. Up past the graveyard, Mary and her father went, excited to see the top of Shawmut's highest point. But as they continued along the path bordering the commons, the sight of a hanging tree with numerous frayed ropes came into view. Mary broke into a cold sweat. She hoped Thomas Crawley would hold his tongue; no one else in Boston knew their business. She and her father hurried past. Still, this worried her as they made their way along the narrow cart path that climbed steeply upward. Until they gained in elevation and Mary spied a lush garden on the hill's southern slope. Its fruit trees were large and in abundant blossom, almost concealing a small private dwelling in their midst. Her eyes grew wide. Something about the place felt magical and eased her fear. That's where I'd like to live, she thought.

Sentry Hill, the tallest of the three summits, rose ninety feet above the sea. The view from its top was spectacular. The wind blew harder here, but the air was clear of the smoke and dust from down below. A beacon marked its highest point: a tall pole upon which an iron pot of tar stood ready to be set alight and raised at the first sign of trouble. A sentry stood watch—or should have been standing watch, for they found him asleep in his tent.

"We'll wake him when we leave," Mary's father said quietly. "With England's civil war, there's little chance of our king sending an army to take back the Massachusetts Bay Charter—what Boston fears most."

Mary walked to the seaward edge of the hill where lovely English grass grew thick underfoot. She scanned the horizon for a fleet of the king's ships or maybe the Dutch privateer, but only a few small sails were to be seen amongst the bay islands. The ferry was making its way to the landing place near the mill pond. Beyond the town cove's flanking peninsulas, six or seven large ships swung at anchor like a flock of wooden waterbirds. Below the hill, the meetinghouse steeple rose skyward, its gilded flag pointing windward. She shuddered to think that one could almost fling themselves on top of its weather vane if it were any closer.

She loved this green high-rising mound of a hill dotted with bright yellow dandelions. She sat down in the grass. Inside her pocket, she found the orange she'd been given earlier that day. She peeled it and began to eat it slowly, savoring its juicy sweetness.

Her father walked over and excitedly pointed out the fort at Castle Island and the village of Cambridge before sitting down beside her. "I've been given the name of a local merchant, a certain Captain Keayne, to solicit in regard to my business. Yet having made the acquaintance of our friend Henry Powning, I am wondering who might make the better prospect."

Mary thought of the soft-spoken man in his sky-blue doublet. "Henry Powning would, Father." She handed him a section of orange.

"Really? Hmm . . . interesting . . ."

They sat peacefully for a minute until an angry shout startled them. "Who goes tha?"

Mary and her father hastened away from the overly fierce sentry who, obviously embarrassed to have been caught napping, told them in no uncertain terms to leave.

At supper that evening, they were pleasantly surprised to be served very tasty maccarib while they learned more about their host. Edward Bendall operated docks, warehouses, and lighters in the harbor. He was currently salvaging cargo from the wreck of the *Mary Rose*, a merchant ship that had gone down the summer before in the deeper water and was obstructing the harbor. His invention of a diving bell made from a great barrel was the ingenious means of salvage: it trapped air beneath the water's surface, allowing the diver to breathe.

Mary's father's new acquaintance, Henry Powning, was there; however Mary was surprised to see the magistrate in crimson velvet whom she'd seen in the market earlier that day. Mr. Richard Saltonstall was his name.

"A marvelous invention, to be sure," Mr. Saltonstall remarked to their host. "Men swimming below as the fish. Amazing, most amazing!"

Mary ate her supper with the men in the parlour, listening to Edward Bendall speak about his salvage process. She found the conversation utterly fascinating. Maybe it wasn't so daunting after all to swim on the water's surface if some were actually swimming under the water with the fish, she mused. She caught a glimpse of the Bendall children peering at her curiously from the kitchen doorway.

Mr. Saltonstall continued on. "With most of the crew on the *Mary Rose* lost, I'd hate to run into their ghosts down there on the bottom—horrors!" He shivered. "But tell me, Edward, what's this I hear about shooting a bar's worth of gold coins out of a cannon? Needless to say, thou hast made dreams come true for some of the rougher sort here in Boston. I hear crowds are still scouring the mudflats at low tide."

Unfortunately for Bendall, a salvaged mass of knotted rope had been found to be a stash of treasure after his gunner fired it for sport from a signal cannon, spraying the Boston waterfront with gold coins.

"One cannot say I'm not a philanthropist, now, can they?" Edward retorted, playing along before furrowing his brow and glowering with mock derision. "God knows I could have used it."

"And the moral of the story," Mr. Saltonstall continued, "all strangely heavy and natty flotsam should be examined thoroughly, whether hidden in petticoat pockets, cannons, or under the deacon's floorboards. Ha ha!" He slapped his knee and stamped his foot, only to grimace a second later. "Agh—my gout!"

"Richard, you're detestably right when it comes to strangely heavy natty flotsam. But as you have graced us with your presence, I'm curious, has talk of the sow at Goody Sherman's left your ears sore?"

Mr. Saltonstall raised a hand in abject protest. "Please, Edward, methinks all of Boston's ears are sore! Aye, and 'tis not over yet by any means—the deputies voted in another hearing. Folk are desperate for Captain Keayne to get his hand slapped." Hearing this about Captain Keayne, Mary was glad her father had met Henry Powning.

Mr. Saltonstall sighed, shifting in his chair. "But to answer your question, *no.* I'm here because of your bounteous board and beer, my friend. To say nothing of our commiserations." He winked, and Mary saw him glance surreptitiously toward her father and Henry Powning, who were engaged in an earnest business discussion at the other end of the table.

When the men were finished eating, a maidservant appeared to clear the table and pass a finger bowl so that all could wash their hands. Mr. Saltonstall spoke to her. "Would you be so kind as to bring me a footstool so that I may elevate my foot?"

The girl replied affirmatively. Hearing this and seated on a footstool herself, Mary brought hers over to Mr. Saltonstall before the servant could oblige.

"Why, thank you, my dear," he replied, smiling at her and hoisting up his fine leather shoe. Mary could see that his ankle looked very swollen.

"Sir?" she asked.

"Yes, my young maiden?"

"You need to take lemons for your gout—lots of them. Take some ground up whole with honey every day. It will help."

"Ho ho ho! A practitioner of physick have we here? Lemons, hmm . . . Did you hear that, maidservant? Does Goodwife Bendall happen to have any lemons in her larder? I shall try your suggestion, little practitioner. No harm in that, eh?"

Mary smiled. She liked Mr. Saltonstall.

He turned to her father. "Our host tells me you and your daughter hail from Pascataway. My dear sister's husband, a certain Captain Cammock, is late of that region, now of Black Point."

"I'm delighted to say I've had the pleasure of his acquaintance." Mary's father tipped his hat.

Goodwife Bendall entered the parlour with her eldest daughter. Where her husband sported longer hair in cavalier fashion, she was his antithesis: plain and somber, reflecting nothing but the highest of Puritan virtues.

"I beg your pardon, Goodman White, but we've lodgings for your daughter with mine own if that pleaseth you?" And without further ado Mary found herself in the company of the Bendall children.

-- 13 --

And So It Is

"Don't mind him," said Freegrace, who seemed so grown-up at fourteen. "He just wants attention."

Her brother, Restore, was seven years old and had recently been "breeched." That is, given his first pair of breeches to wear instead of the customary ruffly gown of early childhood. This rite of passage had modified his behavior most annoyingly, or so his sisters let her know. Restore was moaning and making all sorts of horrid noises as though he were being murdered.

"If thou keebst thad ub, id mighd ribby habben!" Hopefor told him. She and the youngest sister Moremercy had terrible colds, their noses red and runny. Mary wished she had her mother's elderberry syrup to give to them.

"Neber, neber!" Restore teased back pinching his nose, somehow still deemed young enough to sleep in the girls' garret bedchamber. He wore his locks long like his father and strongly resembled his sisters in his nightshirt.

Mary sat in her smock, wrapped with her blanket upon her bed sack. Freegrace sat behind her, brushing Mary's hair so smooth and shiny with boar bristle that it felt silklike to touch.

"I'm going to give you a beautiful hairdo," Freegrace said dreamily. She worked with a quiet, determined concentration in the candlelight. "A lady would wear her hair like this or maybe a duchess."

The girls oohed and aahed. It pleased Mary to have their company, but it bothered her to have her hair brushed out in front of the boy. That didn't seem to bother the Bendall girls in the least, their own curly blonde locks cascading down their backs. Mary tried to pretend indifference, her back to Restore. "Ouch!" she cried when Freegrace grazed her scalp with something sharp.

"Oh! So sorry, Mary."

Mary could feel the warmth of the older girl's breath on the side of her neck, and despite all the fuss and discomfort she was being put through, she liked her. Freegrace had the light hair and gray-blue eyes so common in English girls, but also a peaceful, studied manner about her that was different. She plaited and coiled Mary's hair into two sections, one above each ear. When she had finished, Mary touched them gently with her hands. It felt like she had mushrooms growing out of her head! The Bendall girls seemed to think she looked ravishing.

A small rusted square of looking glass was proffered, and she held it up to her face. The reflection stunned her. She barely recognized the girl staring back. The last time she'd seen herself in a looking glass, she'd been much younger. The reflection in her hand of smooth brow and cheek flashed to a pretty line of nose and lip. Then to a glistening brown eye, translucent and fringed by long dark lashes. The eye stared back in surprise, filling the frame in the glow of the candlelight.

"She loogks lighke a brincess!" little Moremercy cried, only to double over in a fit of sneezes.

"Eeeew!" cried Restore, shielding himself from his sister with his blanket.

"What dost thou think, Mary?" Freegrace asked anxiously. Mary held the looking glass back a distance to see her whole face. Her hair, despite how funny and pulled it felt, did look elegant. She didn't want to stop looking. She began to feel more grown-up and sophisticated. "Methinks I like it." She handed Freegrace back the piece of looking glass lest she appear vain.

Freegrace beamed.

Mary had thought initially she'd take out the hairstyle at night, pretending it was an accident while she slept. Now she was afraid the hairstyle wouldn't stay in. She opened her bandbox to find her nightcap and saw a length of ivory silk ribbon that had the special embroidered white lace pattern unique to her family. On impulse, she handed it to Freegrace. "Here, this is for you."

Freegrace took the ribbon. "Oh!"

"Led us see, led us see!" the younger girls cried. "Ooooh . . ."

"Careful not to sneeze on it," Freegrace instructed sternly, holding it out for her sisters to take a closer look. "Thank you ever so much, Mary!" Her pale face shone radiantly even in the dimness of the garret.

It didn't take long for the Bendall girls to pull out all the swatches of lace, ribbon, and embroidery that they didn't dare stitch to their smocks but stashed away to be coveted in private. Boston was very strict about too much finery unless you were very wealthy. A neighbor would complain to the authorities if ribbons were seen on the laundry line or at the very least think badly of the family. Chaste and pious women dressed plainly.

The sound of a footstep on the stairs below sent them into an instant flurry of hiding everything away.

"Children . . . have you said your prayers?" their mother called up.

"Yes, madam, we're just now," Freegrace answered.

Tying on their nightcaps, the Bendall children scrambled to their knees on the cold, hard floorboards and, placing their hands together, began to recite their prayers. They said a lot more prayers than Mary usually said, and by the time they got to the very last one, Mary was shivering from the damp chill of the evening creeping up from the floor:

I in the burying place may see
Graves shorter there than I,
From death's arrest no age is free
Young children too must die.
My God may such an awful sight,
Awakening be to me!
Oh! That by early grace I might
For death prepared be.

Now I lay me down to take my sleep,
I pray the Lord my soul to keep,

If I should die before I wake,
I pray the Lord my soul to take.
Amen.

As they finished, everyone snuggled under their blankets, and Freegrace blew out the candle.

In the darkness, Mary found the foreign noise from the docks and streets made it hard to sleep. At home, she would be listening to a chorus of spring peepers. The thought subdued her with a stab of homesickness. She would love to show her hair to her sisters. She patted the sides of her nightcap, feeling the firm coils of hair, hoping they would stay neat for the morrow.

Soon, the sound of rhythmic breathing told Mary the others were asleep. Trying to keep her hair intact, yet desperate to get comfortable, she turned onto her side.

Someone's fingers touched her elbow. "Are you awake?" Freegrace's voice whispered.

"Yes."

"That ribbon's so lovely. Did you embroider it?"

"No, my grandmother did. It's my family's pattern."

"It's beautiful, and she's very skilled, your grandmother."

"Thank you. She's good at lacework, but she spends most of her time practicing physick."

"She's an herbwoman?" Mary could hear the interest in Freegrace's voice.

"Yes, she is, a very wise one. She taught me the way of herbs before we left England."

"Oh," Freegrace breathed. "I would like to know more about plants and flowers. I love the commons. I take my sisters and brother whenever my madam allows us. Did your grandmother come with your family?"

"No, she's still in England. I miss her terribly."

The sound of distant laughter and the slamming of a door from the street below filled the ensuing silence.

"Do you believe in magick?" Freegrace continued sleepily.

"You mean natural magick?" Mary whispered back.

"Yes," Freegrace said softly.

Becoming very sleepy herself, Mary wasn't sure how much she should say. "My grandmother taught me it was up to us to unlock God's secrets," she said. She regretted it as soon as she'd said it, but Freegrace showed no signs of fear or judgment.

Have you?" her friend whispered in awe.

No . . . not since England."

Mary heard Freegrace sit up in her bed sack. "Oh, Mary, but you *must*!"

Memories of the alchemical experiments in the garden smokehouse came back to Mary with a pang of intense longing. How she missed her grandmother. Freegrace was right—she must.

The girl leaned in closer. "I'll tell you what I saw in the commons," she whispered ever more quietly. "It was summertime and beginning to grow dark. I was a ways behind my family—I really didn't want to go home as the night was so beautiful and warm." Her voice became barely audible. "I looked up into the trees and saw a circle of light that was just . . . sort of floating. I watched it until it disappeared from sight. What do you think it was?"

"Sometimes I see flashes of light that I think are angels," Mary whispered, much less sleepy. "I used to see fairies when I was little."

"Really? I know whatever I saw was very, very good. It wasn't evil, but my madam wouldn't understand. No one here would understand. I haven't dared tell anyone before. You won't say anything, promise?"

How well Mary understood. "I promise, cross my heart and hope to die. Freegrace, whose house is on the back side of the Trimount, the house hidden away with the beautiful orchard?"

"'Twas the Anglican reverend Richard Blackstone's—Boston's first settler, though he left a long time ago."

"I think you'll find fairies there," Mary said. She yawned. Above the Bendall house, the moon shone high over the Shawmut Peninsula, rendering the town of Boston shades of deep violets, browns, and grays—its surrounding waters black as ink. One by one, as fires burned low, smoke trailed gently from chimneys into the damp salt air. Far out at sea, the Dutch privateer set her course for New Amsterdam, unseen by the sentry on the hill.

The last thing Mary heard before drifting off to sleep was the town crier passing by on the street below, ringing his bell.

"One o'clock, and all is weeell!

❧

The clerk of the writs stared at them grimly over a pair of spectacles that magnified his eyes. His snow-white beard spread like a napkin down his front, falling beneath the table, while his beaver felt hat rose to an impossibly high point. Mary's father doffed his hat, and Mary curtsied uncomfortably.

"And how may I be of service to you?" the man queried, his voice tight and civil.

"I've come to register the death of Mr. Alexander Shapleigh, late of Kittery, in the province of Maine," her father answered.

"Maine . . . Mr. Alexander Shapleigh . . . Shapleigh . . ." The clerk ruminated. Unfolding the parchment, he peered through his spectacles at the death certificate Mary's father had brought with them. Then he came stiffly to his feet and lifted a great leather-bound ledger off the tall cabinet of drawers, the only other piece of furniture in the room other than his table, chair, and several wooden benches.

"Please have a seat," he said in a milder tone.

Mary's father pulled up a bench to the clerk's table. Mary sat on a bench back against the wall. She smoothed the sides of her cap with her hands, feeling elegant and fashionable. Just knowing her hairdo was there gave her tremendous pleasure.

The room had one small window casement, but even with the door wide open to the sunny side yard, the clerk was having trouble seeing. Eventually he found what he was looking for. "Alexander Shapleigh, merchant, Kingswear, Devon," he read from his register. "Yes, I believe Boston is much obliged to him for sending goods, and reasonably too, some half score years ago, if my memory doesn't fail me. God rest his soul. We must stand on ceremony here." The clerk picked up a little bell that sat on the tabletop and gave it a brisk ring. In a moment, a servant appeared. "Joanna, procure us drink. We've official business," he said.

While her father and the clerk of the writs conducted their official business, Mary visited the garden behind the house. Purple lilacs were blooming. Burying her face in one of the blossoms, she breathed in its essence. Her whispered conversation with Freegrace from the night before came to mind. She thought of her grandmother's crucible turning its flesh-melting smoky white, the smell of its acrid scorch, and the excitement of never knowing where the end result might lead. The purification of one substance into another, hoping for that magical elixir that would heal the sick. She would start with some of the flaky translucent mineral embedded in the rocks and barter with Migwah for a stone pot. Nama would be proud.

Mary skipped back up to the house. Peering in at the door and finding her father and the clerk still at their business, she stepped out through the front gate onto Cornhill Street. A horse cart rattled by, but a rain shower overnight had quelled the dust. On the opposite side of the street, another lilac bush hung over a dooryard fence. Crossing over, she breathed deeply of one of its blossoms too and sat on a stone horse mount to watch the everyday world of Boston go by. She recognized the boy with the fruit cart coming down the street. He stopped short when he saw her, his entire face lighting up.

"Good morning, fair maiden." He doffed his dutch hat and bowed low with a flourish. Mary smiled and stood to curtsy back. He was older than she was, a slender youth dressed in worn breeches and a threadbare blue coat. She liked his smile.

He proceeded to juggle his oranges and lemons in a mummer's dance, much more intricately than at the market, thoroughly showing off. The fruit flew under his arms and between his legs and high in the air. He made her laugh. Then he used his hat to catch each piece neatly one after another.

"Here, would you like to try?" He reached into his hat and handed her an orange and two lemons.

He stood close by her side and instructed her to toss one into the air and quickly pass another over to take its place. It was harder than it looked, and Mary kept dropping the third fruit to the ground.

"I'm sorry," she apologized. "Maybe I shouldn't try any more. I'm afraid you won't have any left to sell."

"No, no. You'll get it. It just takes a bit o' practice, really."

She tried again until a flying lemon narrowly missed a passerby, who glared at them disapprovingly.

"Apologies, madam!" the boy called after the woman.

His name was Daniel. His mother had died on the voyage to Boston, and he lived with his father and brother. Mary could tell that he liked her; a boy had never acted so nice to her before. He turned to the lilac bush and picked her a hasty nosegay.

Then he hovered close, a prospect that both terrified and excited her. Was he going to try to kiss her? She wasn't sure how she felt about that. A strange tension filled her breast.

But the lad never had a chance. Her father crossed the street in three long strides, grabbed Mary's arm, and pulled her away with him down the street. Mortified, she had just enough time to toss the orange she was holding back to Daniel. He caught the orange, a forlorn look clouding his face.

Walking back down Cornhill Street, Mary began to feel tired of Boston with all its busyness, smoke, and noise. The novelty was wearing off, and the realization that she may not be able to go home was sinking in. She missed her mother and sisters, and Inky her cat. She missed George and Peter, even the cow and the chickens.

Back at the Bendalls' for the dinner hour, they were served a delicious cod stew.

"John," their host Richard said over his trencher, "there's news from Pascataway just arrived this past hour to the town dock."

"Good news, I trust?"

"I'm afraid not—it's not the best sort of news at all. It concerns a reverend by the name of Burdett who's also the governor of Bristol."

Mary's father sat bolt upright in his chair. No! Mary thought. *Where can I hide? The Blackstone house—they wouldn't look for me there, would they?* She gulped a mouthful of ale to wash a sharp piece of bread crust down her throat and began to choke.

"Rather lewd, I'm afraid," Bendall continued. "Disgraceful . . ."

"Reverend Burdett?" her father exclaimed.

"Yes," their host replied. "Word is he's fled Bristol for parts north—Georgeanna, they say. It's quite the scandal."

"Fled?" Mary's father repeated.

Mary stopped choking.

"Run out of town by his own parishioners for indecency and fornication with his two maidservants, among others."

That evening, the mood was merry in the Bendalls' parlour. "My dear, you've cured my gout!" Mr. Saltonstall raved. The swelling in his foot and ankle had noticeably disappeared. He reached into his breeches pocket and pulled forth a round bronze object. "Please accept this as a token of my gratitude. I've been mulling over perpetual calendars of late. A hobby of mine."

He handed the object to her. Its heavy weight surprised her. On its upper face lay a relief of concentric rings with elaborately cast figures, designs, and roman numerals—a coded calendar of sorts. It was very beautiful and old. No one had ever given her such a special gift.

"Thank you, sir," she gasped.

"I'll bet you can figure it out." He winked.

They left Boston the next day, homebound. Mary's father was anxious to depart before the Sabbath, loath to set foot in the Puritan meetinghouse. After bidding their farewells to the Bendalls and Sir Saltonstall, they bought a few more supplies and walked down Market Street to the wharf. Mary's father was in high spirits, for Henry Powning had agreed to a visit to Pascataway. Henry was looking for just the right place to open up shop and had a merchant connection already in place. Her father hoped Henry would see the potential of his location.

Waiting on the wharf to be rowed out to their ship, Mary studied the top weight Sir Saltonstall had given her. It conjured up images of the wise philosophers of ancient Greece and Rome of whom she'd read in the rectory's library back in Tiverton. Such ancient glory lost to the mists of time always struck her heart with longing. Was it really just a calendar, or did it hold other secrets? She turned it around, trying to decipher its face.

Her father's eyes twinkled. "Here's something I picked out for you, my wild rose." He pulled a little green velvet bag out of his waistcoat and handed it to Mary. She loosened its silken drawstring, and into her hand tumbled a silver comb.

"Oh, sir, it's lovely—thank you so much!" She'd never before been given such lovely gifts.

Her father looked pleased. "I wanted to get you something to remember our trip by."

He had indeed, the only problem being that she didn't want to touch her hair until she'd shown her elegant hairdo to her sisters. Freegrace had fixed it up for her again that morning. She solved the matter by sliding the comb right up behind one of the buns on the side of her head underneath her cap.

Casting off from the wharf, the tender rowed them out toward a sloop bound for Pascataway, carrying rope and other marine supplies. The fear was gone; the tide had turned, and Mary could feel it. A fair wind would sail them home. As the stretch of water widenedbehind them, Sentry Hill receded slowly into the distance. The meetinghouse spire and town—with its narrow lanes, blooming gardens, and characteristic lay of the land, as well as all of its inhabitants—would eventually be lost to time and history itself. No differently than ancient Greece or Rome.

❧

Back home in Pascataway, the good citizens of Bristol, incensed past the eyeballs by the whole Reverend Burdett affair and anything the man had espoused, conveniently forgot—and quickly at that. Goody Walford said that luck was on Mary's side now.

Mary's father began preparations for Henry Powning's visit. Mary helped him by writing lists of all the inventory in his storehouse. Inside the hall of what had once been her family's dwelling, hardware lay upon shelves of wooden board or stacked up neatly against the walls. Mary also began a list of the inventory her father needed to send back to London with his merchant.

She unrolled a piece of parchment, weighted its corners with beach stones on her father's desk, and readied her quill and ink. Her father's first customers of the day had just left when another one appeared at the door.

"Morning," Thomas Crawley said, stepping over the threshold and tipping his hat in greeting. He seemed surprised to see Mary there and looked away from her nervously. Mary winced to think about how rough her father had been with him in Boston.

"Good morning, Thomas. Anything I can help you find?" her father asked.

"A chisel if you've got'n. Have ye heard the news?"

Mary's father stopped to stare at Crawley. "News?"

"Aye. News that may please ye to know."

"Indeed? And what might that be?"

"Wannerton's been shot dead."

"What? Are you telling me the truth?" Mary's father looked dubious.

"Aye, shot dead playing games with the French military rivals La Tour and d'Aulnay up in Penobscot. A trade deal gone wrong. His greed got the better of 'im in the end. Not that Wannerton didn't deserve it."

"Still, a shock to hear . . . tragic." Her father shook his head. "Well, he certainly made good use of Alexander Shapleigh while he could. This means you won't be shadowing me anymore, right?" he joked.

Many folk blamed Crawley for performing Wannerton's dirty work. That must have been so in some cases, but Mary knew her father believed Crawley to be a coward at heart and highly unlikely to murder anyone. A sneaky, tractable sort who drowned both his sorrows and loathing in drink.

"Ahhh . . . you're in luck." Mary's father picked up a chisel from among his assortment of tools. "It'll set you back all of two shillings."

Crawley weighed the chisel in his hands. Satisfied, he began to grope in his coin purse.

"I'm curious, Thomas, did Wannerton have a hand in the widow Gyles's murder?"

Crawley's nose jerked up, and his mouth spread in a sort of grimace. "Don't know for sure but could ha' done. I'll tell ye that the widow Gyles's 'usband didn't drown fishin'."

A wave of nausea sifted through Mary's stomach. Crawley paid her father the coins.

"You're busy with carpentry work?" her father said, changing the subject.

"Building a shallop for Mr. Waldron." Mr. Waldron was an up-and-coming magistrate across the river in Bristol, invested in the Indian trade, as Wannerton had been.

"Better for him than Wannerton, I'd say."

Crawley snorted. "Can't say there's much difference 'tween the two."

PART II

PASCATAWAY, 1646

-- 14 --

Cupid's Arrow

A light breeze fluttered the leaves of the forest. The heat and humidity so insufferable in weeks past had finally let up, and the air felt pleasantly warm and dry. Mary sat back on her heels, breathing in the fragrant smell of the pine needles cushioning the ground beneath her.

This was her secret place—a small hidden clearing by the river with a moss-covered stump for a seat. Holding a bouquet of Indian paintbrush blooms, she let them drop one at a time into a bowl filled with spring water on the ground in front of her. *Love . . . happiness . . . joy . . . and magick.* She held a piece of clear quartz in her hands and, asking God's blessing, added it too. She loved making these simple elixirs. After a few hours in the sunlight, she would pour the liquid into a glass bottle, preserve it with some brandy, and seal it with a wooden stopper and beeswax.

Though petite in stature, she'd grown into a striking young woman of sixteen. Her smooth brow was tinged with warmth from the sun and her hair fastened back at the nape of her neck beneath her cap. She'd worked in the hearth all that morning, and the sleeves of her smock were rolled carelessly past her wrists. Her legs were bare, her feet tied loosely in open-sided latchet shoes as comfortable as the old black-felted bodice and blue linen skirt she wore. She'd been tempted to leave the house barefoot before reminding herself of the sharp sticks and pinesap that stuck to her feet.

Mary stretched her arms overhead luxuriously, allowing a breathy sigh to escape her lips—it felt so good to be alive! Every so often, her life felt completely different from what it just had, and how she thought or looked at things changed too. Only in the moment when she first noticed the change would she reflect on it until another such similar shift happened. Now was one of those moments, and she looked about, feeling the newness of everything.

Above the brush lining the riverbank, the top of a haystack floated by on a gundalow. Beyond, on the opposite bank, rose a sloping hillside of fenced fields, houses, and outbuildings belonging to what had been the village of Bristol, then changed to Northam, and now was called Dover. The Maine side of the river hadn't changed so much, yet the rest of the world certainly had: The king was a prisoner in his own country, and the Reformed Church had taken control of England, banning the Anglican Book of Common Prayer. Foreign ships cruised off the coast thicker than ever, their spyglasses set on the timber and furs of New England. Without the Massachusetts Bay Colony and its outlying coalition, the small settlements in the province of Maine had little support or defense. Yet they clung tenaciously to their independence and prayer books, content in their proximity to their much more powerful neighbors to the south. That much had stayed the same.

Mary was carrying her bowl to a patch of sunlight when a creeping awareness on the back of her neck told her she was not alone. Not again, she thought with irritation. Some of the neighboring boys seemed to have made a game of it of late. She knelt to set the bowl down and, turning by degrees, looked about discreetly: there was no one to be seen.

She was about to dismiss it as her imagination when a twig snapped. The clearing was surrounded by a tangle of brushy woods. Was it an animal? A catamount had killed a neighbor's goat only a week ago . . .

She stood up, her pulse racing. It was a distance back up the hill to the safety of the house, but whatever was here had cut her off. Turning in the opposite direction, Mary walked with measured steps toward the river. She would throw herself into the water if she had to—it was fairly shallow here.

Another noise came from behind, and Mary bolted. A glance over her shoulder confirmed something moving in the brake, and she tore blindly ahead in a panic. Pushing through the brush, she almost fell into the river, catching herself with a scream. Seeing that some people out on the water had heard her and their attention was fixed upon her, she ran farther along the top of the steep bank and hid behind a leafy hazelnut, too afraid to feel self-conscious. There were unmistakable sounds of something following her.

In less than a minute, two boys, Warwick Heard and Charles Frost, pushed their way out onto the bank with smirks on their faces. Gone were the pain-inflicting slingshots of their childhood, replaced by muskets carried over their shoulders. First sheer relief, then anger flooded through Mary as she watched from her hiding place.

Noticing they had an audience, the boys ignored the onlookers and began to follow the bank in her direction, whistling, feigning innocence. Mary remained hidden until she could have touched them before bursting out at them with a hair-raising scream.

Their eyes widened, and their mouths gaped open. Warwick jumped backward so that he lost his hat and had to cling to roots to keep from slipping into the river. The hoots and laughter from a nearby fishing shallop had the boys instantly crimson past their ears.

"Shame on you, spying on me like that!" Her hands on her hips, Mary tried to sound angry. She really wanted to laugh.

"Spying on you?" Charles spluttered, looking as incredulous as he could muster.

"Oh, don't tell me—you mistook me for a rabbit?"

Warwick grappled with his musket and pulled himself up, his shoes and stockings soiled with rank greenish muck. "We're after pheasant!" He snatched up his hat up before Charles could step on it.

Mary folded her arms across her chest. "Oh, so I look like a pheasant?"

The crew in the fishing shallop nearby were still laughing and joking, and an older man's voice called out, "She got yar tails, boys! Hee-haw!" He slapped his thigh with a resounding smack that carried across the water.

Charles and Warwick wasted no time disappearing back into the woods.

A canoe paddled over near to where Mary stood. "Are you in need of some assistance, fair maiden?" A young man grinned up at her. His teeth flashed white against his skin, bronzed from the sun. The two other fellows in the canoe ribbed each other.

Mary felt her cheeks grow hot. She hadn't intended to attract attention unless she really was in danger. The stranger removed his hat with a sweep of his arm, his brown locks falling to his shoulders. He was strikingly handsome.

"No, thank you. I can manage," she replied shyly. Giving a quick curtsy, she turned and disappeared herself.

Making her way up the stump-covered hillside toward home, she laughed to remember the looks on the boys' faces as she'd jumped out at them and laughed again to think of their retreat. Yet it was the handsome stranger and his smile that she couldn't stop thinking about.

Back at her father's house, a surprise awaited her in the kitchen hall. A large man with a mop of sandy-colored hair, whom her mother, looking flushed and happy, was feeding and fussing over. A linen dinner napkin was draped over his shoulder.

"Mary, do you remember your uncle Samuel? He's just arrived from England."

Her uncle sat filling her father's great chair. His jowls looked in need of a good shave, and the sleeves of his doublet, originally of a fine gold satin, had been rendered water stained and greasy.

"*Little* Mary? This surely can't be you?" his voice boomed. "Why, you're almost grown!" He looked from her to her sisters and back. "Britania, all your little maids have fairly blossomed in this new land."

Sarah and Hannah stood leaning shyly against the woodbox and smiling politely. Both were smaller versions of their mother with their fair hair and green-gold eyes. Mary looked like her father, or so everyone said. She did not smile.

Uncle Samuel was the son of her grandmother's second husband, the draper. He looked different from what she remembered as well:

his face had grown in size, as had his paunch. He dug hungrily into the generous piece of venison pasty her mother set in front of him.

"Delicious, Brit. I see you haven't lost your knack with victuals."

Her mother looked pleased. "Our venison here is much tastier than that back home."

Uncle Samuel ate everything Mary's mother set in front of him: bread, cheese, eggs, salad, apricot tarts—the filling of which Mary had made that day—as well as a joint of cold mutton, all the while complaining about the scanty spoiled fare he'd suffered shipboard.

"Only water to drink—putrid, slimy stuff . . ."

"Brother, you must replenish your strength as you'll certainly need it here." Her mother poured him another pot of small beer and set down a wooden charger with the half-carved duck they'd eaten at noon. Despite all he'd just swallowed, Samuel set to work on it greedily, pulling off the meat with his fingers and cracking the bones to suck out the marrow. When he finally finished, he settled back in the chair like an overstuffed pillow, wiped his hands, filled his pipe, and began to smoke.

Her mother took his napkin. "Until you find a place of your own, you're welcome to stay with us—that is, if John has no objections."

"Thank you, sister, most kind, most kind." Her uncle sighed with satisfaction, smoke trailing from his nostrils.

A softer look passed over Mary's mother's face. "So tell me more about how my madam is faring?"

"Right busy for an old woman—physick, midwifery, making herself useful. She sent along a box for you and your girls. It's in my chest."

Mary, her mother, and sisters opened the box together. Neatly folded on the top were four beautiful lawn collars and matching caps, embroidered in the family's cut lace pattern.

"Bless your grandmother! I'm amazed her sight's still sharp enough to do this." Her mother held the collars up one at a time so they could all admire the intricate needlework.

Mary quietly drank in her grandmother's essence, which radiated out of the box and streamed off the linens. Love sewn in with every stitch. She wondered what her dear Nama was doing that very moment back in England, wishing it had been her to arrive and not their uncle.

The rest of the box was filled with herbal concoctions, ointments, and remedies; however in the very center underneath it all, pinned to something wrapped in cloth, was a small piece of paper with the name *Mary* quilled upon it. As her mother lifted the heavy object out and set it on the table, Mary knew instinctively what it was.

With her mother, sisters, and uncle looking on, Mary unwound the cloth slowly, resenting the fact they were all watching and fearful of how she would explain. As she pulled away the last layer, exposing the old Hessian-made ceramic pot, her sisters and uncle immediately lost interest. But her mother stared at it quizzically. It was her grandmother's crucible of special slow-fired porcelain that could withstand great heat, melting mineral and metal alike.

Mary's mother picked it up and turned it over, revealing its scorched bottom. "An odd thing to send all this way. Strange old bird, your grandmother." Raising a critical brow, she set the pot down and turned her attention back to the box to examine its remaining contents.

Mary picked up the crucible, scarcely believing she was holding it again. Her throat constricting, she wrapped the pot up in the cloth and climbed the stair to the chamber she shared with her sisters. She placed the crucible carefully on the bottom of her box, next to her bronze calendar, wiping the wetness from her cheeks. She would examine it later in private, but her grandmother giving her the crucible could only mean one thing—and that made her very sad.

Saturday being market day across the river in Dover, Mary and Sarah set off with the extra garden produce, their mother keeping Hannah home to help with the baking. Carrying baskets, the girls made their way down the hillside path to their father's storehouse. Henry Powning's Trading Post next door was already open for the day, and they waved at him. Henry had a wife and two little children now. Mary's father liked to say that bringing him to Kittery was one of the best things he'd ever done. Between the two stores most goods were covered, and business was brisk.

At the ferry, the girls found seating along the sides of the flat-bottomed craft with other market-bound folk, the livestock on board tied front and center. Mary relaxed with her basket on her lap, her straw hat dangling down her back. She gazed out across the water, watching the mist on the river's surface swirl upward in the sun's early rays, content in her dreaminess. The ferryman swept them quickly around and across with his large stern oar, the passage taking only a few minutes.

On the Dover side, as everyone stood jostling to retrieve their goods, someone on the landing dock gave Sarah a hand up. Then they gave Mary a hand up too. With sun spots in her eyes, it wasn't until she stood on the dock that she realized whom the hand belonged to. It was *him*, the young man with dark hair from the canoe. He smiled down at her, his brown eyes lively, his face smooth-shaven. He bent forward and brushed her hand with his lips. She tried to pull away, but he wouldn't let go.

Her sister stared with eyes like goose eggs.

"So we meet again," he said softly, so only she could hear.

A shiver of excitement ran through her body.

"Get movin', you two!" a man barked, trying to push past them with a cart.

Reluctantly, the young man let go of her hand. Cheekbones searing, Mary walked with Sarah and the rest of the market crowd up the hillside lane. She turned back to look at him; she couldn't help but do so. Her feet no longer touched the ground, and a blissful sensation that felt almost painful filled her breast. He stood staring after her with his face aglow. Her heart smoldered.

Sarah began to giggle.

"Hmmph! What makes you think I'm even interested?"

Sarah giggled all the harder until Mary had no choice but to giggle herself. Their laughter incited a dirty look from a goodwife hoeing in her garden nearby.

Mary floated up the rest of the steep lane to the high street at the crest of the hill. They continued down the length of the peninsula toward Pommery Cove. Sarah was talking, but Mary wasn't listening.

The market at Pommery Cove lay behind the shoreline docks and warehouses. Merchant ships now regularly brought in goods from England, Spain, Virginia, and the Caribbean, which, along with the local produce, made the market a festive and stimulating place—especially if sailors were in port with a hornpipe or fiddle.

In joyous spirits, Mary set her basket of vegetables down next to the other women selling their goods, and she and her sister spread out a blanket to sit upon. In the harbor, the *Charles* of Dartmouth lay at anchor, a brig of four hundred tons, dwarfing all the others. It had come in by way of Barbados.

Goody Emery greeted them, proffering a stoneware jug. "Here, dearies, lend me your fingers. You must taste some o' this wondrous concoction!"

Mary caught a dribble of the black conserve.

"Ye favor it? 'Tis called molasses. Came in on the *Charles*. Made from cane sugar down in the Caribe Islands."

"Delicious." Mary noticed Goody Emery's shrewd eye linger on her momentarily.

She smiled; it was hard to stop smiling. The sun began to beat down, and she pulled on her straw hat. The day was beautiful, and to everyone's pleasure, the resonant notes of a bagpipe began to reverberate from the harbor's edge. Some of Sagamore Rowls's sannups encircled the player, utterly fascinated, until one of the Indians prodded the instrument with a stick. This miffed the player considerably, and he stopped playing. It made Mary and others laugh to see the fellow looking so nervous, knowing the sannups to be friendly and meaning no harm.

A pair of breeches stopped in front of Mary's basket. She looked up to see the Roberts boy. He had grown so tall and large. He squatted down on his haunches and removed his hat, staring at her intently.

Mary looked down into her basket, allowing her hat brim to shield her face from sight. *What was happening today?*

Roberts's calloused fingers stroked the clean white skin of a parsnip in front of her. "These must be sweet indeed if you grew them with your own hands."

"Yes, very sweet—grown at the hands of my madam."

His fingers hesitated. "Yet you helped her grow them, did you not?"

"God helped her grow them, not I."

John Roberts lifted the brim of her hat with his forefinger and peered impudently underneath. Mary slapped at his hand, and he let go.

She could feel the attention their interaction was drawing from those nearby. Young men did not usually shop for garden produce. The gossips were salivating.

"*Mary White*," he said, standing up, "what's the price for a dozen of your *sweet* parsnips?"

"One penny, *John Roberts*."

He stood silently. She glanced up to see him looking directly at her. He laughed to have caught her eye. Mary tried not to laugh back, but the whole thing was so hilarious that she couldn't help it.

"Ah, so now you please me," he said.

She stifled the urge to throw the parsnips at him.

Goodwives were sidling in like peabirds, trying to get an earful. Mary lifted the bunch of parsnips and held them out to him. Roberts took them, looking amused. He tucked them under his arm and reached into the coin purse at his belt. He held out a silver penny.

Mary let him drop it into her hand. "We thank you." Coin was hard to come by, especially for dooryard vegetables. Women mostly bartered.

"I thank *you*, Mary." But he wasn't finished. He squatted back down and, grabbing Mary's wrist, pushed something into her hand. Then he stood up and, with a spring in his step, strutted away, whistling while swinging the parsnips like a cony by the ears.

Mary looked down into her palm to see a shiny silver shilling. She closed her fingers over it as one of the gossips bent to look.

"He has a fancy for thee, maid," Goodwife Emery chortled, winking.

-- 15 --

Abel and Cain

At noontime that day, the White household sat down to dinner. It was a pleasant meal, with a late summer breeze airing the hall, the casements flung wide and pies cooling on the sills. All seemed well with the world, and Mary felt very happy.

"How was the market today, girls?" her mother asked, passing a bowl of salad.

"Somebody gave Mary a present," Sarah blurted before Mary could answer.

As all eyes turned upon her, Mary kicked at Sarah under the table. It would have been spot-on if Uncle Samuel's knee hadn't been in the way.

"Aaagh!" he yelled, his mouth full of food.

Her father ignored the outburst and looked at Mary sternly. "Well?"

Mary lowered her spoon. She had no idea what her father would think or do about it, and the thought scared her. "A shilling," she answered as casually as she could as though it were no reason to be excited or make a fuss.

Uncle Samuel stopped chewing, "Oh my!" He leaned forward on the table, a piece of food clinging to the corner of his mouth. "John, your maids are like flowers to the bees!"

Mary wished she'd kicked a lot harder.

Her father pretended not to hear him. "A shilling? Who gave you this?"

"John Roberts, sir."

"John Roberts," he repeated. Peter, her father's servant who was just a few years older than Mary, shifted uncomfortably.

Hannah piped up from Mary's side. "It's because he likes her, Father. Lots of boys like Mary."

"Yes, Hannah, I suppose they do," he replied, forgiving the transgression of his youngest. "It looks like I'll be keeping my musket fair and handy."

"Oh fie!" Mary's mother cried, swatting her husband playfully with a dish towel as she rose from the table to fetch the stewpot. She ladled another serving onto Uncle Samuel's trencher.

Uncle Samuel sighed contentedly, patting his stomach, "'Tis a fortunate man, Brother White, who has such attractive daughters. Think of all the dowry ye'll save!" He clicked his tongue before resuming his repast.

Over the next few days, Mary kept a lookout on the river, hoping to see the young man who'd kissed her hand at the ferry; but she saw no sign of him. When her mother sent her across to Dover to help Goody Emery at the tavern, the Emerys' African maidservant being away visiting family, Mary was delighted. She'd been waiting for an excuse to take the ferry again, but to her disappointment, she saw no sign of him there either. She arrived at the tavern somewhat melancholy.

This did not go unnoticed by Goody Emery, who never missed anything, even in the dire heat of her bake oven. "Things with your beau can't already have gone sour?" she prodded. Goody E, as she was affectionately called by many, was one of Dover's most prolific gossips.

Bristling on the inside, Mary shook her head. "John Roberts is *not* my beau, madam."

"Oh?" Goody E's forehead wrinkled. "There's many a maid who'd be glad to court *him*, deary. Speaking of courtin', banns have been posted on the meetinghouse door today, and there's speculation the fellow still has a wife in England." She bent to pick up a couple split logs to feed the oven. "Ow!" she moaned, clutching the small of her back. "It's fetching all th' water. I tell ye, I do miss Molly. But she went to nurse an ailing relation, you know." Goody E's painful back worried Mary. It needed some sort of realignment, not an herbal remedy.

To a running commentary of local hearsay, Mary helped Goody E and her daughter Becky bake and brew up a storm. She liked to cook at the tavern as they always let her create dishes as the whim took her. The Barbados molasses proved a tasty addition in the pumpkin pies, to which Mary also added cinnamon, ginger, and nutmeg—a combination she liked to use that always brought compliments. The afternoon flew by, and the tavern began to fill with patrons.

"Mary dear, would you carry a stewpot out just this once?" asked Goody E. "I know your mother would be none too pleased, but she wouldn't have to know, would she?"

Mary's mother had made it clear that Mary was not to have anything to do with the tavern, but Mary could scarcely say no with Goody E in such pain.

She skirted the wainscoting, following Becky, slipping by the men crowding the tavern after a hard day's work. She set the trivet pot inside the hearth and turned to leave but found her way blocked. Mary looked up—it was *him.*

"Good evening, Mary White," he said, smiling. "John Woodman at your service."

His shining brown eyes held hers—a luminous translucence of the greater fire and spirit her soul craved. He reached for her hand, and this time, Mary let him take it. His touch melted her insides, and she forgot all about the tavern until Goody E's shrill screech split the air, and the proprietress all but dropped a stack of trenchers. Goody E pulled Mary back to the kitchen hall by her elbow, the crowd parting like the Red Sea for Moses and the tavern resounding with laughter.

Mary didn't care. *John Woodman—so that was his name!*

Back in the kitchen hall, she floated in absolute reverie, her cheeks flushed and eyes sparkling.

"Oh my, deary, you've got it bad," Goody E fussed and fumed. "And that fellow is such a handsome devil. Oh dear, *oh dear*. Don't let your mother know—she'd surely have my hide, she would. *James*!"

she hollered. "Escort Mary White down to the ferry and see she gets on safely." James was Goody E's son about Mary's age.

As Goody's strong arms pushed her out through the entryway, Mary's gaze again sought John Woodman's through the tavern door. He was staring back at her, smiling. Mary sighed and felt herself lifting farther off the ground.

Darkness had fallen, and despite the coolness of the evening, crickets serenaded from the sides of the lane. Mary lifted her face to the heavens alight with countless stars winking and blinking magically. They seemed to match how expansive she felt: more brilliant and happier than ever before. James Emery carried a lantern, and they walked along in silence past fields and dooryards.

When they turned downhill toward the river, James cleared his throat and spoke. "If I were you, I'd stay on John Roberts's good side."

"That's up to my father," she said, annoyed that James would both broach the subject and distract her from her reverie. James worked as a servant for Richard Waldron, who was now a leading magistrate of Dover. James knew much about the people and the town—perhaps a little too much.

They stood on the dock, waiting for the ferry. The lantern's dim yellow light encircled their feet, full of the looping, darting shadows of moths.

"Tell me, James, where is John Woodman from?"

He answered slowly, almost unwillingly. "From Newburytown, I think, or Oyster River. I've heard both." Oyster River was a settlement off the Great Bay, not too far from Dover.

"Is he a planter?"

"A trader."

The ferry drew near; its creaking oarlock grew louder, its lantern brighter.

"John Roberts's father was the most liked governor Dover's ever had," James continued. "They're relations with the Hiltons and have connections with those who matter most. Lots o' maids favor John Roberts." He sounded so much like his mother.

"You say John Roberts is one you'd not want to displease. Does that include displeasing yourself to do so?" she asked, her annoyance sharpening her tongue.

James was silent.

The ferry drew up to the dock, and Mary bid James Emery thank-you and good night. Across the river, she could see a light shining from her father's storehouse—her father was waiting for her. She would walk the rest of the way home safe in his company.

As the ferry drifted away from the dock, its long oar sweeping the bow around, James Emery called after her: "Nary forget what I've said!"

❧

That Monday afternoon, while Mary and her sisters scutched flax in the barn, their mother appeared with Mary's most elegant bodice and petticoat draped over one arm and a clean folded smock in her other.

"What good progress," she said, eyeing the growing pile of long clean fibers. Her voice sounded suspiciously cheery. "Come Mary, you must change into this. I'm sorry I don't have time to press the ruffles. Thomas Roberts and his son have come to call. They've brought your father along with them from his store."

Mary wiped her hands on her apron. "Why have they come?"

"'Tis nothing terrible." Her mother smiled. "Only to get permission for Roberts's son to visit with you from time to time. 'Tis only a formality."

Only a formality. What if I feel ill? The look on her face must have spoken volumes.

"Behave yourself now," her mother warned. "Let's show your best manners."

Mary unlaced her bodice with trembling fingers. She hadn't expected this so soon. *Perhaps Father would refuse?*

Her mother handed her a towel and helped her change. "I remember when I was a maid and your father asked to court me," she said.

I do feel ill, Mary thought, pressing her hands to her stomach. She followed her mother over the threshold and into the house.

Their guests sat in the parlour around the little Turkish rug covered table, upon which Mary's father had poured canary sack into stemware. As they entered the room, John Roberts and his father both rose, removed their hats, and bowed politely. Mary and her mother curtsied back.

Mary had always liked Thomas Roberts. She remembered as a little girl how he had once patted the top of her head affectionately while speaking to her parents. Thomas's touch had conveyed the warmth of a beloved uncle or grandfather, and she knew him to be a kindly man. But it was different with his son, and this troubled Mary.

During the visit, Mary hardly said a word. Neither did John Roberts, though his glances toward her were happy and possessive as though he were being given a new suit of clothes or a good milk cow. He did look nice in his fancy new doublet and breeches, Mary had to admit. Perhaps she'd feel differently if someone else had not already caught her heart. Her father and Thomas Roberts obviously enjoyed each other's company as well as the sack, and soon it was settled: John Roberts could visit weekly, though never unchaperoned.

Mary didn't dare tell her parents about John Woodman. But as it turned out, she didn't have to worry about this for long. The very next day, while she and her sisters combed the flax in the warm sunshine, a happy whistling tune reached their ears.

"Oh, Mary, it's *him*!" Sarah squealed and clapped her hands to her mouth.

To Mary's complete surprise, John Woodman appeared, walking up the hillside path from the dock.

"Good morning!" he called with a wave of his arm and a friendly smile.

Heart fluttering, Mary tucked her hair back under her cap and walked forward to greet him, her sisters silent behind her.

He doffed his hat and bowed, as handsome as ever, and presented her with a beautiful nosegay of meadow flowers.

Mary thanked him with a curtsy. She introduced her sisters, who stood by awkwardly, forgetting about the work they were doing.

"Mary, I'd like to speak to your father," John said.

"My father's not here, but he will be soon."

They sat down on a log some distance from her sisters, careful not to sit too close to one another. There were so many questions Mary wanted to ask, but at that moment she couldn't think of one.

"Did those lads leave you alone the other day by the river?" he asked.

"Yes, thanks to all of you. I didn't know what was stalking me until I saw them on the riverbank."

"You gave us all a good scare," he said with a grin.

"I suppose I did." Mary smiled back. She stood up, feeling more comfortable. "Come, I want to show you something." She led him over to the nearby orchard, where a round woven basket hung from the branch of a pear tree. She lifted its lid carefully, peering inside first before she let John take a look. Nestled inside on a bed of dried grasses, the squirrel mouse looked up at them, its black eyes shining inquisitively, stripes running down the length of its soft, sleek body.

"My cat was ready to eat him," she explained. "But I couldn't bear it—such a young thing. Look, he doesn't even bite." She stroked the chipmunk gently with her finger.

"You have a kind heart, Mary." He attempted to give the creature a pat with one of his fingers, and it jumped to the other side of the basket. "Most women I know are terrified of mice or anything that resembles them."

"You impress me, John. Most men I know would rather shoot a squirrel mouse than pet one." It was true; she wouldn't dare show Warwick or Charles or any other boy she knew, except for maybe Francis.

"I think he's mended well enough now." She set the basket on the ground, and the chipmunk leapt out and was gone. Mary looked up at John Woodman standing by her side. How sweet the world felt—colors seemed brighter and the breeze fresher. The orchard boughs laden with ripened fruit shone golden in the sun.

"I have something for you, Mary." His voice resonated softly on her heart. "I hope you'll like it." He untied a small deerskin pouch from his waist and handed it to her.

Mary loosened its rawhide tie and drew out a delicate necklace of blue and white shell beads: wampum—Indian currency. The largest bead was carved in the shape of a white dove. "Oh," she breathed, "it's beautiful!"

"Here, let's put it on you."

"And who have we here?" Her father's voice made them start.

John doffed his hat respectfully. "John Woodman, sir, at your service."

Mary's father advanced, mowing scythe over one shoulder,until he and John stood face-to-face. "I've seen you on the river, lad. Where're you from?"

"Newburyport, sir."

It horrified Mary to see her father assuming such a bullying carriage. John, however, stood up to it well.

"So, Woodman from Newburyport, my daughter has work to attend to. And so must a young man like yourself, I would assume?" His tone was cool.

John Woodman appeared not so easily discouraged. He stood near her father's height, yet with a solid breadth of shoulder, a beautiful specimen of a man. He looked her father in the eye in a friendly manner, holding his hat in his hands.

"If you please, sir, I beg your forgiveness for any impropriety. My sincerest apologies. I've come to ask permission to court your daughter Mary."

The world slowed and ground to a stop.

Mary's father stepped away to lean his scythe up against a tree before turning back to face him. "Woodman, I am a devout Anglican and a very particular man, especially when it comes to my daughters, as I'm sure you can understand."

"I do indeed, sir."

"The answer is no." Her father gestured John Woodman back in the direction of his canoe with an air of finality.

No! Mary screamed inwardly. *There must be some misunderstanding!*

She stood atop the hillside where she could see John Woodman depart. Out on the river, he saw her and slowly raised his paddle in a salute. Mary waved back, holding his bouquet of flowers. When he was no longer in sight, she brought the necklace he had given her briefly to her lips: a talisman of love. Why, she wondered, had her father refused John Woodman—and so rudely? A black caterpillar had invaded the cornfields that July, leaving ears full of missing kernels. With harvest nigh upon them, did this have her father out of sorts?

Her father was washing his face at the well when Mary approached him.

"Sir? John Woodman is so very nice and kind . . ." She faltered at the look on her father's face.

"That may be so, Mary." He picked up his scythe. "But I know his father." He strode toward the barn.

Her father's bent continued at dinner that noon. "For the love of God, Britania," he said heatedly while Uncle Samuel was out in the privy, "everyone in the plantations has to pull their own weight. Your brother best either get off his lazy duff and learn to wield an axe or catch the next merchant back to England. I refuse to continue to host such a vain and gluttonous fop."

Her father's voice was known to carry, and dinner proved a tense affair; no one in the household looked happy except for Hannah, immune in her bubble of childhood joy. Mary focused her attention on her youngest sister just to get through dinner.

It was no surprise when, soon after this, Uncle Samuel bought a house and land down in the Baylands, opposite the entrance to the Great Bay along the Long Reach of the river. He continued to stop in to visit however, if Mary's father was not at home, especially around mealtimes.

Mary took to shelling and drying harvest edibles on the hilltop overlooking the river, hoping to see John Woodman. In this, she was not disappointed: John would raise his paddle in passing, and if it was safe to do so, Mary would wave and run to meet him. Her hidden clearing down by Daniel's Creek became their meeting place. Their first rendezvous had sustained her with sighs and blushes over the following day when her father had been home, and she hadn't been able to meet him. But he'd left her a token of his love on the mossy tussock of a stump: a fair heart-shaped stone of amethyst.

Meeting again, John brought her a bouquet of wild grapes. They sat together on the mossy tussock. Mary had never felt happier.

"Aye, Mary . . . I knew it would be this way with us. I knew as soon as I saw you on the riverbank." He reached for her hand.

She let him take it, luxuriating in the warmth of his touch. "How did you know?"

"I don't know how . . . I just felt it."

His answer filled her with delight.

He examined what had been a deep cut in the finger of his other hand. "Mary, you have some wondrous skill. 'Twas purple two days ago, and now 'tis an almost completely healed light pink." He held it out to her.

She looked at his wound, happy to see how much better his finger looked. "'Tis good—plantain poultices are powerful."

In the clearing, they told each other their life stories. John Woodman listened attentively, and Mary told him about her experiments to discover new medicines to help the sick, her grandmother, and about the hidden knowledge all around them in the natural world. It surprised her how easy it was for her to tell him these things.

"The natural world teaches us to sink our roots down deep and to stretch with our hands for the stars! When I'm sad, the trees comfort me. They meet me softly with love—I feel it pressing around my heart." She blushed, never having admitted as much to anyone.

"Mary, 'tis beautiful what you say. I think you're right that the trees and plants are more alive than we think, but I've never thought of how much more. The Indian sorcerers seem able to call on all sorts of things from nature."

"I'm not a sorceress, rather a student of *natural magick*—God's magick."

"Yet thou has rendered me a tenderhearted, starry-eyed wretch—my friends say *bewitched*," he laughed.

Mary smiled—he was teasing her.

She'd never known anyone other than her grandmother who could listen to her without being afraid. "You're much more aware of the natural world's magick than most."

John Woodman blew out his breath. "My father may be considered wicked by some. He's not an overly religious type by any means, refusing to go to meetings. But he has a great respect for nature that has rubbed off on me."

"Oh dear . . . I think I understand. My father said he knew your father. My father's very religious, I'm afraid. But you're closer to my own heart and spirit than any pious youth I know!"

"Mary, we'll find a way. For now, I'm glad we have this place. Your alchemy sounds fascinating. You have such marvelous interests—I'd love to help you if I could."

"Really, you would?"

"Yes, I would."

Mary was so happy she wept.

Meanwhile Roberts came a-courting. Arrogant and proud, the broad-shouldered youth sat with her in the parlour while her mother served them fancy tidbits and sweet Madeira wine. Mary found his visits exceedingly boring as he usually went on at great length about himself and not much else, until one particular visit when he asked a question she found highly disturbing.

"Mary . . . the trader John Woodman—do you ever see him?"

Her pulse quickened. Of course Roberts wouldn't know her father hadn't given permission, but her mother could most likely hear much of their conversation.

"I see him on the river from time to time, but does he visit like you do? No, he does not," she answered, the palms of her hands gone moist.

Roberts's dark gaze, just like the one she remembered from the day the hogs were set loose long ago, stared back at her.

The weather waxed strangely warm for the season. Henry Powning's two infant children came down with a bad case of quinsy. His wife and children split their time between Boston and Pascataway but had left Boston for the summer to escape an outbreak of smallpox raging down there. Mary thought of her Boston friends, especially Freegrace. She hoped they'd all be spared.

The Powning twins lay tangled together, their small faces pale and insipid. As soon as Mary saw them she knew it was more than just quinsy.

"Their tonsils do have spots," Goody Powning said, looking exhausted and scared.

Maryused a tincture of the marsh rosemary Migwah had shown her. It worked much better than mullein and vinegar. As the day wore on, word came back from across the river that many more were sick. Meanwhile, the Powning children, their cheeks now flushed with the scarlet fever rash, seemed to be stable. Mary kept them well covered, knowing a good purging sweat would heal the raising. An Indian oven bath would be the perfect remedy, she mused. The Powning children were soon recovering; but the slow, steady beat of Dover's meetinghouse drum was heard frequently across the water, tolling for the dead.

The harvest continued in earnest; neighbors helped neighbors, working doggedly from sunrise to sunset until the strange warmth of the season came to an abrupt halt with a violent storm the Spanish called a *hurricano*. Water surged and flooded, trees were uprooted in the great winds, and houses were left battered and full of gaping holes. Ships had been cast ashore, having snapped their anchor lines. In the storm's aftermath, the air became cool and fresh as it usually did at harvest time.

In the narrow mossy depth of a well, a crimson maple leaf floated on the water's surface in the shadow of Mary's silhouette. Miniature in size, it came up in her bucket of water. She picked it out, admiring its perfection. The cooler weather would bring welcome relief from all the sickness, but there was something about bringing up this blood-colored leaf that left her uneasy: it was one of *those* feelings again, the kind she knew from experience to dread, and it did not go away.

-- 16 --

A Tragic Circumstance

Lantern in hand, Mary could scarcely see two steps in front of her, the fog being so thick. She was used to milking the cow in the predawn darkness; but this gray world, so enveloping, was eerie. To draw lungsful of air felt labored and painful as though she were breathing underwater. She made her way to the barn, finding her way with her feet. It felt as if she'd not yet completely woken. Her sleep had been restless, full of apprehensive and disturbing dreams.

Inside the barn, she could breathe better. The animals were restless too. The cow almost kicked over the bucket while Mary milked her. Fog seeped in through the cracks, ghostlike beyond the lantern light.

Back in the hall, cheese and bread were on the table for breakfast, and the savory smell of pottage bubbling in the hearth promised a satisfying meal. The cream from the milk would be churned into butter for their dinner. Mary skimmed it into the little churn and closed the lid—churning was Hannah's job. Peter was just finishing topping off the woodbox when her father and George came in, and they all sat down to breakfast after a short blessing. The blanket of fog outside began to disperse as the day grew brighter, but Mary's apprehension did not.

Midmeal a knock was heard upon the door, and Henry Beck the ferryman entered.

"Sorry to interrupt your victuals—there's been terrible hap'nings." He was breathing hard as though he had run up the hill from the landing.

Her father wiped his mouth with his napkin. "What is it, Henry?"

"Some English have murdered an Indian wench, and Hopehood and his sannups are up in arms, calling for blood. Dover's got those who done it in the gaol. Someone saw them burying the body yesterday up past the frigate on the Cochcco."

Mary's father pulled his napkin off his shoulder and stood to follow Henry out. "I'll be back," he said. "George and Peter, harness up the oxen and head out to Hereges Marsh woodlot." His voice sounded grim; anything that would strain the relations between the English and the natives was of great concern.

Mary's mother stood up too. "Goodman Beck"—her voice tremulous and thin—"pray, who is responsible for such a heinous thing?"

"Some traders: Richard Pratt, John Woodman, and a lad named William Biddle is what they're saying. Anthony Nutter saw them burying the body."

Mary rose to her feet, a buzzing in her ears. The room grew black, shrinking down to a pinpoint of light in the center of her vision, and she felt her knees give out beneath her.

❧

The next thing Mary knew, she was lying on a pallet next to the hearth, weak and shivering. Something was terribly wrong, but she couldn't remember what. She drifted in and out of sleep, unable to discern what was real as figures came and went from her side.

She dreamt of brown-winged locusts emerging from the ground to eat the leaves on all the trees. Then they began to eat the hem and folds of her skirt until a great flood tide sucked them out to sea. Mary saw people drowning and ships being broken apart on rocks and a woman being hanged on the Boston Common. She saw an Indian sachem pouring lengths of blue and white wampum into the arms of a military commander and the colors of the French king flying. The Indians were burning houses, only the tall stone chimneys left behind in the smoldering ruins, and Indians taking the scalp locks of the dying. Mary saw things she didn't understand: Pommery Cove had become a flat, smooth surface like a ribbon of rock, over which shiny objects sped so quickly that it made her dizzy, and a giant chimney nearby belched smoke high into the sky.

She saw what she believed to be God: an old man with a long white beard filling the sky, a beatific expression on His face and His arms opened wide. He dissolved into light, merging into the treetops, the fields and mountains, rivers and lakes, into her and all other beings.

Once, she opened her eyes. She saw her grandmother sitting by her side, stroking her forehead. As Mary's fever passed, the realization that her grandmother likely walked the earth no more was painful. Months would pass before her family would get the news.

Sarah told her John Woodman and his friends were still in gaol, awaiting court in Boston. Dover had refused to hand him and his comrades over to Hopehood, who had a violent reputation. Mary quaked just to think about it.

She was sure John Woodman wouldn't murder anyone—it was all a terrible mistake. Yet she knew something had happened. Thinking back to the last time she'd seen him, John had seemed tense and preoccupied. He hadn't stayed long.

When Mary recovered enough to be on her feet again, Migwah and two sannups stopped by the house on their way to trade at her father's store. Only she and Hannah were home. A chill wind almost wrested the door out of Mary's hands as she held it open for their visitors. Migwah looked quite dignified dressed in an English greatcoat.

Mary served them all stew from the pot in the hearth. While the men ate, she spoke to Migwah about John Woodman and his friends: her belief of their innocence and her fears of what Hopehood might do. The medicine man's response surprised her very much.

"Hopehood leave, no?" Migwah said.

"Yes, he's waiting for the trial."

"No." Migwah shook his head. "Pennacooks know who kill woman and will make pay."

An icy tingle raised the hair on Mary's scalp. She swallowed.

Migwah's black eyes held hers. "English in gaol not interest Pennacooks." His sannups finished their meal. He stood up to go.

"The Pennacooks know that John and his friends did not murder the woman?" Mary exchanged a look with Hannah, who'd watched quietly in the corner as Mary fed their guests.

Migwah stopped in the entryway. "White sachem want Indian to forget, punish others for Indian. Indian never forget." He stepped out over the threshold, the wind blowing his long silver hair fiercely about him. He turned back to Mary. "Indian will make right."

Then he was gone.

When Mary felt certain enough time had elapsed for Migwah and his sannups to have passed down the hillside, she and Hannah tied on their cloaks and ventured outside. Hope filled Mary's breast, boosting her spirits. The surrounding maples were splashed with color, and the brisk air took her breath away after having been inside for so long, but her new skirt and waistcoat of an elegant golden-brown serge kept her nicely warm.

A cairn lay alongside an old Indian trail that led from the back side of their hill down to the cart path. The cairn was a pile of stones made by the natives long before the English came. Mary's father said it was used to communicate and that they should never touch it lest they change the meaning. The cairn also lent them a degree of protection, as the local Abenakis liked him.

Standing in front of it, Mary and Hannah eagerly searched for any recent additions. Some of the dyed bones and odd trinkets had been there for quite a while, but today two fresh turkey feathers crowned the top. It was always fun to see what appeared and to guess at its meaning. But to have heard Migwah say the Indians *knew* John and his friends were innocent—that was almost the best news she could hope for.

As soon as Mary could, she visited the Dover gaol. The roughly built structure had a small barred casement at one end through which she hoped to see John Woodman.

"You have no business here, filly. Off with ye!" the gaoler growled as she approached the opening. He sat smoking on a form outside his dwelling, which comprised the other end of the gaol. One hand held his jaw. He was obviously suffering from a toothache and in no mood to be persuaded otherwise.

Mary refused to leave. She stood a distance away until she remembered her shilling. Then she approached again boldly. The gaoler glowered to see her coming back and pulled the pipe from his mouth.

"What now?" he barked.

"There's a coin I'd willingly part with—if I could but have a word with my beau."

"Beau?" He snorted, squinting at her perversely.

Mary steeled herself and lifted her chin.

"Let's see the coin," the gaoler said, his tone changing. Hepried himself off the bench, his hand moving from his jaw to the small of his back, and he walked stiffly toward her.

She pulled the silver shilling from her pocket.

"A shilling, is it?" His eyes gleamed. "A'right then, the coin for a *peep* in the window."

But Mary shook her head. "No, *inside* the gaol."

The old man glanced uneasily toward the cooper's shop down the lane and at the surrounding fields before making a grab for the coin.

Mary drew her hand away. "After!"

"A'righty, but I'll inspect your basket first," the gaoler said, showing his long yellow teeth. He helped himself to one of the pasties before untying a key ring from his waist and unlocking the iron-studded door. "Be quick about it wench," he said, pushing the door shut behind her except for a small crack and standing directly outside.

Inside, the dirt floor was covered with musty old rushes, and the place smelled strongly of squalor. A pile of straw angled upward to the back wall, from which posts sprouted heavy iron chains that fastened to the leg-irons of each prisoner. It took a few seconds for Mary's eyes to adjust to the dimness. She didn't recognize John Woodman until he sat up. His jaw was covered with the beginnings of a beard, his face thinner and pale. It had only been two weeks since she'd seen him, but it felt like an eternity.

"*Mary*? Is that you?"

"Yes, John, 'tis I!"

He took hold of her arms, his grip pleading. "Mary, you *must* believe me—we're innocent!" There was desperation in his face. Even in the gloom, she could see it. It smote her heart to see him in such a state.

"I *know* you are, John."

"This is Roberts's doing," he said through clenched teeth. "I'll *swear* to it! Anthony Nutter's his best friend."

To hear this sickened Mary, and it must have shown on her face.

"Mary, 'tis *not* your fault. Please don't ever think you're to blame."

"John, the Indians know you're innocent too."

This seemed to be the first good news all of them had heard. The other two sat up out of the straw, and Mary relayed what Migwah had told her, which heartened them all considerably.

"The Indian woman's dead body snagged on our fishing net. The best thing we could ha' done was bury her," Richard explained.

"Here, I brought you something to eat." She handed out meat pasties and cheese. John's companions began to eat ravenously. "Please eat, John. Oh, you need a drink?" She looked about to find the water bucket bone-dry.

John stared at her, a smile curling the edges of his lips.

"Your time is up. Now out with you!" spat the gaoler through the crack in the door.

Ignoring his demand, Mary called back over her shoulder, "They've no water! I see you've neglected your duties."

"Out, wench, *now*!" the gaoler hissed angrily. "Or I'll lock thee in too!"

"John, I will get you all out of here, I promise," she whispered, picking up the empty water bucket.

As the gaoler flung the door wide, Mary parted hands with her love reluctantly, the gloom swallowing him as she stepped out into the light of day.

The old man slammed and locked the door, his face a blotchy purple. "The coin, and be off with you!" He held out his hand.

But Mary stood her ground with the water bucket, facing off to the gaoler's indignant glare. "First, they need drink—at the very least some water."

"Bring drink to me, wench, and I'll see they get it!" he snarled.

"I'll fetch them water right now."

"Nay, thou will get thee gone!" He waved her away, but Mary went right to the well the gaol shared with the cooper and carried back a bucketful of water, demanding the gaoler deliver it before she would give him the coin.

The prisoners fed and watered, her mind continued to whirl as she walked away up the lane. She would get them out—she had to. By the time she reached the high street at the top of the hill, a plan had already come to her.

❧

The night was dark. Down Nutter's Lane on the back side of Dover peninsula, Francis Small strode by Mary's side beneath a faint glimmer of starlight, a heavy sack slung over his shoulder. Mary stood back in the shadows while he knocked softly on the gaoler's door. She could hear the gaoler's voice mumble from within.

"A delivery of drink for the prisoners," Francis said.

Chair legs scraped the floor, and a crack of dim orange shone behind the doorframe. "From whom?" the gaoler demanded.

"A young maiden who told me you were expecting it."

There was a pause.

"Right. Well, bring it in then," the gaoler said. He opened the door so Francis could enter. Mary could see him squinting at Francis's whiskery face, trying to place him.

Once back outside, Francis sat with Mary up the hillside from the gaol, under a pine tree as they bided their time. Mary was glad she'd worn her black woolen cloak as it was cold. Francis said he hardly felt the cold nowadays, used as he was to so much time outdoors up-country. His employ driving Mason's cattle to Boston year's back had led him into the life of both a trader and guide.

"It shouldn't take very long," Mary said.

Francis grinned. "Audacious of you, Mary. I know of no other maid who'd attempt such a thing."

"I only pray my sisters don't discover the pillow beneath my quilt isn't me."

The night grew still and silent.

When they deemed enough time had passed, the two approached the gaol house. Pressing their ears to the door, they could hear the sound of muffled snoring. Francis pried the latchstring out using a nail he'd brought but found the door bolted securely on the inside.

They walked around to the side of the dwelling. Above them, next to the chimney, they made out the shape of a small shuttered casement. Francis reached up to pry at it with his fingers. To their relief, it gave inward; and in less than a minute, Francis had pulled his body up and in.

Mary waited, crossing her fingers that Francis would find the ring of keys. It took longer than she'd expected before she heard the door open quietly and the clink of keys in Francis's hand.

"Had to cut the ties off his breeches," he whispered.

They had the gaol door open in no time. It took a bit of fumbling to open the leg-irons of each prisoner in the dark, but Francis had it done soon enough. Though the three men were weak in body, their gratitude of sudden freedom knew no bounds. John Woodman held Mary close as they made their way down to the Back River, not knowing when they would see each other again. An Indian canoe awaited there, Migwah and his sannups as escort.

In the adjacent room the gaoler slept on, thanks to the soporific effects of wood betony and lemon balm, oblivious to the fact that his kidneys had been given just the right dilating purge to pass the stones that so wracked him. He would also wake to find his toothache quite cured. Other things wouldn't be so right for him, but Mary felt it a fair-enough exchange, all things considered.

The news of the prisoners' disappearance spread the next day. Gossip was that Hopehood had taken his revenge after all. The gaoler blamed it on the Indians. Mary was glad she knew differently.

However, until John Woodman and his friends' names were cleared, they could not return.

Along the Pascataqua, flaming color dressed the forest, sweeping back to the distant violet-blue mountains. Mountains in the up-country where Mary knew John and his companions would take refuge. For this, she was grateful.

Mary stared at the cairn from under the hood of her cloak. A cold drizzly rain was falling, the path beneath her feet lined with a wet carpet of bright yellow leaves. She'd heard nothing from John in the week after his escape. In the absence of news, she'd imagined the Indian cairn to be a place where such information could easily be overlooked. It would be safer for him to communicate Indian-style. She stared at the pile of stones, matted leaves, faded bones, and broken seashells. Nothing looked newly placed, but she stared at it all the same, willing something to appear.

"Halloo, Mary!"

She started and turned to see a man coming along the cart path on horseback, visible through the half-bare trees. He reined his horse to a stop. It was Francis, looking every inch a trader with his unshaven chin, deerskin leggings, and bedraggled gray coat.

"I have news!" he called.

Her heart beat faster. She ran down the rest of the trail to the cart path. "From John Woodman?"

"Nay." Francis shook his head.

Mary's heart fell. Some sort of sign—anything that would let her know her beau was well and sound—was all she wanted.

Francis looked at her gravely. "Roberts is bragging about how he and Nutter convinced the constable that John and his friends committed the murder. Those two know your friends are innocent—they set them up. Roberts is screaming glad to have Woodman out of the way, and you'd best be careful."

❧

Dover's Michaelmas festival was in full swing, the musicians playing and the crowd in high spirits. But Mary did not feel much like being there. John Roberts was looking everywhere for her while she avoided him like the plague. Seeing Roberts in the distance, she hid behind the corner of Emery's Tavern.

"Mary, my sweets! How fare thee?" said Uncle Samuel's booming voice. She jumped. Uncle Samuel stood behind her, swaying on his feet, returning from the middens out back. "Why's such a comely maid as yourself all by her lonesome?" he slurred.

"Oh, Saaamuuuuel!" cried a woman flouncing out the tavern door. The burn mark on her jaw looked much less livid dusted with flour. Rebekah stopped abruptly to see her. No longer so bone thin and pinched looking, the old Shapleigh servant had rouged her cheeks and lips with crushed mulberries like a harlot.

"Darling, this is Mary White, my niece." Mary

curtsied politely. "Good day, Rebekah."

Rebekah drew herself up and returned the greeting without looking Mary in the eye.

"So ye are acquainted then? Come in and join us, Mary. We'll have a drink—aghhh!" he yelled. Rebekah must have goosed him.

In the flirtatious chaos that ensued, Mary made her escape. Her uncle and Rebekah—she never would've guessed. Now if she could just avoid John Roberts . . .

Before she could take a step, he was upon her.

"There you are, Mary. I would think you're trying to hide from me," John Roberts said in an accusing tone, his jaw jutting out sullenly.

-- 17 --

Wolf in the Fold

On All Hallows' Eve, groups of young men roamed the fields and woods in hopes of catching a glimpse of a wandering spirit. They carried makeshift turnip lanterns to light their way, carved with ghostly faces and casting creepy shadows. In every hearth, a fire blazed. Apples and nuts were washed down with strong brew while tales of spirits and strange happenings left small children wide-eyed and afraid to go to bed. All traditions of Old England not so easily abandoned, even by the Puritan towns.

Inside the Whites' dwelling, Mary's mother sewed by firelight while her father smoked in his great chair, conjuring up another story. George had fallen asleep sometime during the last tale, his head leaning back against the wall. Peter sipped his ale slowly. He was the younger of her father's two servants and would have rather been out and about with the other lads.

Mary sat at the table, writing in her journal by candlelight, pausing to watch her sisters push chestnuts back into the coals at the edge of the fire—a game all English maidens knew well. Would their future husbands be faithful? Her sisters perched on their stools with apprehension until Sarah's popped with a loud snap. Laughter and the sweet smell of roast chestnut filled the hall.

"Mary, will you play crack nut?" Sarah asked, anxious for another go.

Mary shook her head, no. Her initial elation at John Woodman's escape was now tempered by the realization that she would not be seeing him for some time. She sighed, her gaze settling on the bronze top in front of her with its perpetual calendar, which she used to weight paper. *Will it give me the date of my beloved's return if I sleep with it under my pillow? I will try it and see.* She pulled out the sketch she had drawn of his likeness, shielding the drawing with another piece of paper to hide it from prying eyes. It captured enough of him to please her. She gazed at it longingly before hiding it away again inside her leather binder.

Excusing herself, Mary stepped outside into the deepening twilight. The moon was rising behind the pines to the east, its yellow face large and luminescent. The crisp air smelled of autumn and woodsmoke. Somewhere in the distant mountains to the north, John was breathing it too. The thought gave her comfort.

She looked up to see an evening star shining brightly. Sometimes stars sparked within her an indescribable glimpse of something so magical and elusive that it was hard to comprehend. Perhaps a tiny glimpse of heaven . . . But tonight, trying to open to such a feeling only made her heart ache more.

Mary walked over to the well. Folklore said maidens were supposed to see their future husband's face in a well at midnight on All Hallows' Eve. It wasn't even close to midnight, but she thought she'd try anyway.

She peered down into the blackness. As her eyes adjusted, she could make out a circle of brighter blue down below, the reflection of the deepening sky, and the dark shadow of her head's silhouette. She waited, hoping to see John Woodman's face staring back at her, but nothing happened. It really must have to be midnight, she thought, disappointed.

Mary looked down again, this time imagining his face, until a sound from behind her caught her attention. She straightened. A hand clasped over her mouth, and she was pulled close to a body smelling of drink and tobacco.

"Mary," a voice hissed in her ear, "'tis me, John Roberts."

Her heart pounding, she relaxed a little, letting her breath escape. His hand let go of her mouth. She tried to step away, but he wouldn't let her.

"What's wrong?" he said glibly. Mary did not trust the tone of his voice at all. "You're safe now that Woodman's received his just revenge." It was too dark to see Roberts's face, but he laughed under his breath. "Pennacooks tortured him and his friends. He won't be bothering you any longer."

Hearing this, Mary could only think of how much she hated Roberts until it occurred to her that it could've just happened. *No, it has to be a lie. I know better!*

Then to her horror, Roberts fastened his lips over her mouth. He pulled her so tightly against him that she couldn't breathe. He tasted of spirits and sweet corn, and the pinch of his teeth against her lips was painful as though he were trying to devour her alive.

Mary pushed hard at his chest. He relaxed his hold. She stepped backward, but he pressed forward.

"Oh, Mary," he said softly.

Again, she stepped backward, only to be blocked by the well. He pressed her body against the hard stone. Once more, he tried to fasten his lips on her mouth.

"No!" Mary thrust the heels of her hands against his chest as hard as she could.

He stopped. "What's wrong?"

"Don't!"

"Why not?" His tone sounded resentful and angry.

"John Woodman and his friends are *innocent*!" she choked out. "*You* set them up."

John Roberts stepped back. A sense of fear crept over Mary. She could feel him measuring her words. When he spoke again, his voice was different.

"A lot to say for a wench who brews strange potions down by the river."

Mary swallowed. *So he knew.*

The sound of the door latch clicked up at the house. Roberts left her then, taking off into the woods seconds before a welcome glow of lantern light revealed the dooryard.

Mary walked toward her father, trying to look as though nothing out of the ordinary had happened. She felt violated and unclean, terrified of what her father would think of her if he found out what had just happened.

"There you are. You've been gone awhile." His voice sounded relieved, yet he looked at her shrewdly.

"Yes, sir. I needed some air."

Behind her on the threshold, her father raised the lantern, searching the shadows of the dooryard before following her in and bolting the door securely for the night.

Bluish hickory smoke hung low along the riverbank while kitchen gardens withered and cornfields lay fallow. November was slaughtering time, when planters killed the livestock they would be unable to feed over the winter and preserved the meat by salting and smoking.

The cold gray weather did not help Mary's spirits. She spent her days inside, weaving household items on the loom, finding solace in the imaginings of her mind.

Shoes arrived for Mary and her sisters from England. This helped to cheer her somewhat. Hers were a lovely pair of green silk with gracefully arched heels to be worn on Sundays or special occasions. The outlines of their feet had been charcoaled the year before and the imprints sent back to a cordwainer. Her new shoes reminded Mary of the lovely green taffeta skirt she wore as a child. The skirt had been handed down to Sarah and then Hannah. Mary was now using diamond-shaped bits and pieces of its undamaged fabric to quilt into a counterpane for her marriage bed. The fabric reminded her of Tiverton, her grandmother, and the magic of what had been much of her early childhood. Mary's father alsopresented her with a dowry chest, handsomely carved with her initials. Into this she packed her household linens as they grew, neatly pressed and folded.

Then a letter arrived from England, confirming what Mary already suspected: her grandmother had died. "Peacefully, in her sleep," the letter said. Hundreds from the village and surrounding countryside had attended her funeral at St. Peter's in Tiverton.

With her grandmother's death confirmed, everything seemed more meaningless and hollow than ever, and it only grew worse.

One dreary day, upon returning home from helping a sick neighbor, Mary heard company in the parlour. An odd time for a visit, she thought, being not even midmorning. Hearing Uncle Samuel's laugh, she supposed he knew her father was not at home and had decided to take advantage of it.

A shock awaited her that in retrospect she should have seen coming: seated next to her uncle, all cozied on the settle, was none other than Rebekah. The maidservant's dark locks coiled out from under her cap in the flirtatious manner of a strumpet, and the burn mark on her jaw was again dusted over with flour. At least she hadn't gone overboard with the crushed mulberries. Rebekah affected well a meek and girlish show, wearing her Sunday best and drinking from one of Mary's mother's green Venetian glasses—very different from the sullen, calculating girl Mary knew.

In the kitchen hall, fetching another platter of edibles with Sarah, Mary seesawed her shoulders in mockery. She and Sarah could hardly contain their laughter.

"Perhaps they're quite fit for each other," Mary whispered, batting her eyelashes.

"*Stop*!" Sarah hissed.

"Nieces, come join us in a toast to my bride-to-be!" Uncle Samuel cried, his glass held high as they returned with a laden platter.

Rebekah marrying into their family left Mary more than a little worried.

"Your uncle seems very happy, and that's all that really matters," her mother said once their guests had departed. "Rebekah is sure to be better behaved as part of our family."

Mary hoped her mother was right.

John Roberts still came courting. The fact that Mary now loathed him seemed to make him all the more attracted to her. She made it a point to explain to him that she often prepared herbal remedies out of doors as her mother needed their hearth for cooking. She wasn't sure he believed her. When the snow lay deep and men began their winter logging, Mary relished the peace, for his visits became fewer for the season.

January marked Mary's seventeenth birthday. As she was born under the sign of Aquarius, her grandmother had always said Mary was a visionary, ahead of her time and a force to be reckoned with. Her grandmother had meant it as a good thing, but Mary felt who she was to be more a curse than a blessing—and lately not so very much a force at all.

As winter drew to a close, snowmelt filled the streams, and the sunny thawing days seemed balmy. On one such day, the earth breathing forth its sweet breath, Mary passed along the steep clay riverbank with her basket where she'd so satisfactorily turned the tables on Charles Frost and Warwick Heard the summer before. Usually, she thought about her first encounter with John Woodman here, of how he'd smiled at her and what they had said. But today she thought about the two boys. She smiled at the memory of their fright, but tears filled her eyes. Charles had shot and killed Warwick the week before, mistaking him for a goose picking herself in the Great Marsh at the head of Sturgeon Creek. Warwick's coattails had blown up in the breeze as he was readying to shoot. The sun had set, and neither had known the other was there. Mary was not really that surprised but grieved nonetheless.

On the end of a rocky spit where a colony of mussels clung to the base of a boulder, she let her tears fall into the briny shallows. *A river of tears*. The thought soothed her. The river shared her sadness now too.

With her basket of mussels, Mary made her way back toward shore. The tide had turned, and its waters flooding over the spit forced her to use the larger rocks as stepping stones. She looked down into the clear water growing deeper by the second, the stones beneath the surface a jumble of beautiful colors. Something unusual caught her eye; she pulled up her sleeve and fished it out.

It looked just like a sawed segment of femur bone, possibly human, soft and creamy white, grooved along the sides, though it was solid where the marrow would be. Mary dried it off on her apron. Perhaps it was so old it had turned to rock like seashells seemed to do. There were other similar pieces scattered about. There wasn't much time to spare as a widening gap of water had already formed between the last stepping stone and the shore. She retrieved what she could and leapt none too soon. Within seconds, the spit disappeared completely beneath the surface.

That night, hearing her sisters' footsteps mount the staircase below, Mary placed the femur-like stone under her pillow, hoping to learn something about it from her dreams. Sarah and Hannah readied their sleeping sacks, neatly laying out their skirts and doublets for the morrow; then they all knelt to say their prayers. When they were finished, Mary blew out the taper that lit the space with its tiny flame. A light gust of wind brought a shower pattering softly on the steeply pitched roof. Mary lay still, listening. The stone, based on the doctrine of signatures, would certainly heal or strengthen the bones of the body; she thought of her crucible with growing excitement.

As her sisters' breathing took on a deeper, more rhythmic pattern, she retrieved the stone and held it gently between her palms, feeling its essence and its silky talc-like feel. "Bones of our great Earth Mother," she could hear Migwah say.

❧

It was in the merry month of May, when the fruit trees were in blossom, that news, the first of its kind in New England, reached Kittery. A woman in Windsor, Connecticut had been hanged for witchcraft. Mary's mother took it as a bad omen.

Indeed, the summer heralded a strange pestilence that infected all the land, English and Indian alike. Those afflicted grew weak and listless, the illness dragging on for weeks. Corn ripened on the stalk unharvested, and marsh grass grew long. Mary and her mother were kept busy while Sarah and Hannah tended to the animals, gardens, and the keeping of the house.

"Dr. Fernald says those he bleeds or feeds cooling drinks seem to die," Mary's mother told Bertha Frost, handing her a cup of steeped yarrow. "Heat is best to break a fever."

Bertha's husband was the latest casualty. Mary had come with her mother to help and to visit with Anna and her sister Catherine whom Mary had helped birth years ago. The Frosts' new homestead lay a distance from the river, situated upon a hillside at the head of Sturgeon Creek, overlooking the Great Marsh below.

"I trust your judgment implicitly, Britania," said Goody Frost, who was with child again, holding the medicine to her ailing husband's lips.

Mary found it shocking to see the intimidating man lying so weak and infirm. She helped her mother apply a mustard plaster to his chest and pile on enough coverlets and rugs to keep out the chill of the coldest winter's night, though it was a hot and humid day in July.

"Mother says I may be able to apprentice next summer," Anna told Mary with excitement. She was now eleven years old, and she watched carefully all that Mary and her mother did. "Should we feed my father warming foods too?" she asked.

"Actually, no," Mary replied. "He has an excess of yellow bile—too much fire, hot and dry, and the plaster we've administered is hot in the fourth degree. So when it comes to food, we want to balance it with a little cool and damp, but only the first degree—no more than that. Salad and fish or pears and plums are good, but he probably won't have much appetite."

Mary's mother nodded approvingly.

Nicolas Frost's face grew very red, and beads of sweat laced his temples—exactly what Mary and her mother wanted to see. It was always a good feeling when one's patient responded how they were supposed to.

Charles Frost stepped in at the threshold and walked over to where his mother sat. He'd fetched Mary and her mother by cart that morning. He looked as grim and closed as he had been for months despite the fact that the day before he'd been acquitted by the court in the shooting death of his best friend, Warwick.

"Your father is perspiring now. 'Tis a very good sign," Mary's mother explained to him.

Bertha glanced up at her eldest, showing no sign of sadness for what had lately befallen him. "What have you a mind to do?" she asked.

I'll be mowing the lower field if you need me," he replied. Then with a polite nod to Mary and her mother, he left.

Turning back to Mary's mother, Goody Frost sighed. "So how hath ye been keeping, Britania?"

"Well enough, Bertha, with all this fearsome pestilence. I'm glad to hear of Charles's acquittal. 'Tis such a sad business. You must be relieved the trial is over."

"Methinks 'tis why my husband has come down ill," Goody Frost answered.

The Frosts had certainly been through a time of it, though not nearly as bad as the Heards, with the loss of their son.

The sound of an approaching horse in the yard caught everyone's attention, but it soon faded again into the distance. Charles stuck his head back inside the doorway.

"We've had a visitor?" his mother asked.

"Treworgy returning from the court. Kittery's been granted a township."

That afternoon, Mary returned home alone. Nicolas Frost's fever had cooled, but her mother would stay on to make sure there was no relapse. Mary sat behind Charles on Bertha's pillion, the heels of her lovely green shoes hooked on the slipper stirrup. Charles urged the mare into a trot, and down the long sloping hill toward Sturgeon Creek they went, the Great Marsh stretching ahead. A view which must pain Charles terribly, she thought. Gone was his exuberant boyish manner. Mary couldn't help but feel the pall that surrounded him.

They passed by the Heard plantation for the second time that day. There was no sign of anyone other than a slow trail of smoke drifting up from the chimney. Charles urged the mare into a canter, and they quickly left it behind. Mary clung tenaciously to the little wooden rail behind her cushioned seat.

As soon as they were hidden by the trees again, Charles slowed the mare to a walk, his shoulders visibly relaxing. He looked back at her. "How are you faring there, Mary?"

"Oh, managing well enough. 'Tis good to have the horse walk for a change."

She thought she saw Charles smile as he turned his head away. She felt a mild vexation. He wasn't the one perched sideways on a pillion!

Twisted ancient cedars ran along the edge of the marsh through which Sturgeon Creek meandered. Migwah called them "the tree of life."

"Charles, would you mind if I cut some cedar boughs?"

In answer, he steered the mare over to one of the trees. Pulling out his hunting knife, he cut Mary an armful. Thanking him, she rolled them in her apron, hoping the fragrance would help lift his spirits. Charles urged the mare on at a walk, the smell of fresh cedar potent in the heat.

The horse carried them up from the intervale and into woods of large stately elm and beech. The green shade of the leaves felt cool and lovely.

"So tell me," Charles asked, "have you received any word from your friend John Woodman?"

He looked back over his shoulder again and cocked an eyebrow at her, some of his old flair sparking in his steady gray eye.

"It's been some time," Mary replied.

"No worries, Mary. I mean no harm. I suppose I feel reckless enough to tell you I know of his innocence." He reined in the mare to a very slow walk, reaching down for the saddlebag.

"You do?" Mary tried to keep her voice casual.

Charles pulled the stopper from his flask. "Drink?"

"No, thank you. How do you know he's innocent?"

Charles took a long swallow. When he answered her, it was through gritted teeth, his tone tight and angry. "Let me say it's just a good guess."

Mary stared at the back of his waistcoat, not knowing whether to believe him or not. "Is that all it is, Charles . . . a guess?"

❧

News of Ferdinando Gorges's death soon reached the province. With both Gorges and Mason—the original patentees—now dead, Maine was more vulnerable than ever to being swallowed up by Massachusetts Bay, whose Puritan church had banned the Anglican Book of Common Prayer. Massachusetts had also banned many of England's age-old customs and feasts, including the celebration of Christmas. The future of the province looked rather tenuous and bleak to its inhabitants.

But to Mary and her mother, the ship that brought the news of Gorges carried news far more grave: Cromwell's men had begun to kill "witches"—namely, women of herbs and physick, whose healing knowledge stemmed from ancient Celtic lore. A massive hunt was under way in Old England, and hundreds had already been put to death.

"I'm so thankful that Grandmother did not live to suffer Great-Grandmother's fate," Mary said.

"We must thank God in our prayers," her mother answered, "and pray for us here in New England as well."

-- 18 --

Apprentice

Five rows tabby and five rows twill make a lovely design in red and yellow, Mary thought happily, working on the loom in the parlour. She'd become mildly proficient at weaving, and her feet knew the patterns without having to think. She pushed the shuttle through the warp, rhythmically pressing the foot pedals and snugging up the linen thread with the beater, admiring the neat, tight rows until she heard a noise. Mary looked over to see her mother doubled over her spinning wheel, arms holding her abdomen.

"Madam!" she cried, extracting herself from the loom.

Her mother labored longer than usual this time, unable to speak. "'Tis a female problem," her mother always said. "Naught much to be done for such as it."

Her madam's many sleepless nights had taken their toll of late, midwifing eleven births in a span of months. One of the births had been Rebekah's firstborn, a son named Elias, afterRebekah's father; and another had been Bertha Frost's new son, Nicolas Jr.

Mary held her mother's shoulders and rubbed her back, giving what comfort she could until the worst was over. In the kitchen hall, she poured her mother's medicine into a cup. Black cohosh root, a remedy Migwah had shown her that helped more than any of the English herbs, but it had not healed her mother's condition. She thought of the bone-like stones that lay upstairs in the bottom of her chest—perhaps they would. She would love nothing better than to use her grandmother's crucible to effect a remedy, but it would have to be done in secret, if at all.

Back in the parlour, she handed her mother the cup.

"Thank you, Mary. I'm doing better. Why don't you join your sisters at Rebekah's?"

“But, madam, you’ve had one of your fits.”

“Nonsense, I’m well enough now. Go and enjoy yourself.”

Reluctantly, Mary donned her cloak and muff and picked up her sewing basket with its sections of her beautiful quilt. Her mother wanted some time alone—that much was clear.

In the bitter cold, she followed the icy track along the river past the Small’s old plantation. Francis’s parents had moved out to the Isles of Shoals, selling their plantation to Antipas Maverick, a younger brother of Moses Maverick of Marblehead. He had taken up her father’s invitation a year or so back and fallen in love with Kittery. Mary crossed the slippery fording place at Cammock’s Creek, choosing her footing carefully. Rebekah had continued to invite friends to gather at her house to sew and gossip after the birth of her son and her lying-in. It had become a sort of fashion with the younger set, especially with Mary’s sister, Sarah—a fact Mary found disconcerting since her own relationship with Rebekah had shown little sign of improvement. She was not very keen to join the gathering.

Well, she thought, she would likely see Lucy and Abigail Treworgy, nieces of Nicolas Shapleigh who had recently arrived to live at their uncle’s house. They were close to Mary and Sarah in age and had brought with them fancy new-styled clothes and news of Old England embroiled in civil war.

Mary pulled the latchstring on Rebekah’s door. Sounds of excited laughter could be heard from within. “Who’s there?” Rebekah called.

Mary stepped into the warm kitchen hall where a group of young women sat around a center table that filled most of the room.

“Good afternoon,” she answered cheerfully, happy to be out of the cold. She ignored the hardening of Rebekah’s expression.

“Come, Mary, look at what Lucy’s brought,” said her sister Hannah.

A length of deep crimson velvet fabric lay draped across the table. It called out to be touched, the luxurious richness of its varying tones mesmerizing. Few wore such fabric hereabouts, at least in public. The Puritan church certainly shunned such fabric.

"Our aunt Alice gave it to us. She used an ell of it to make our uncle a new waistcoat," Lucy explained.

Mary ran her hand across its plush surface, admiring its thickness. Men could get away much more easily with wearing such luxury. It certainly wasn't above Nicolas Shapleigh's status. "Are you going to make something from it, Lucy?"

"Mother says I can make a bodice to be worn at home," Lucy said proudly.

"Oh, how I wish," sighed Mary Small, Francis Small's sister, with dreamy longing in her voice. She was the next oldest to Rebekah and had stayed behind at her father's old plantation to work for the Mavericks.

Mary draped her cloak over the back of the settle with the others. Anna Frost made room for her on the bench. "I'm glad you came, Mary," she whispered, her eyes sparkling.

Mary smiled back, giving Anna's hand a friendly squeeze in return. Anna would start her apprenticeship with Mary and her mother that spring. Goody Frost said her daughter had been talking about nothing but.

"If there are any bits and pieces left over that you could spare, I'd like to trim my nightdress, pray?" Sarah's voice piped up.

"Oh, me too!" Hannah cried.

"Yes, to be sure, I'll save them for you," Lucy told them generously while others in the room looked a little envious, wishing they'd thought to ask.

Mary's sisters beamed. The cloth was the most beautiful thing most of those present had seen in a long time.

"Imagine," Mary said, "courting your beau in such a gown."

The room filled with girlish tittering.

She saw herself in a fashionable gown with a low-cut bodice and flowing skirt. How beautiful she would look, and how it would delight John Woodman . . .

"Speaking of beaus, have you seen John Roberts lately?" Rebekah's blue eyes covertly mocked. She sat sewing and rocking little Elias's hearthside cradle with her foot. The tittering grew louder. Rebekah's mouth twisted into a little smile.

Mary felt sure Rebekah knew her true feelings. Sarah must have given her all the details. Refusing to give Rebekah the satisfaction of getting to her, Mary thought of her beloved again; then with a dreamy secretive smile upon her own lips, she shrugged nonchalantly and pulled her sewing from her basket. The tittering grew louder still.

"Oh, look at Mary's beautiful quilt piece!" Anna said.

"Thank you, Anna."

"Lovely . . ." others echoed and complimented.

Rebekah sniffed. "My husband spends as much time as he can with me and Elias."

"You are so lucky, Rebekah. My beau is off fishing at the shoals." Mary Small sighed.

"Lucy, what about Humphrey Chadbourne?" Abigail teased with a giggle, looking sideways at her sister, whose face immediately began to color. "I think Humphrey fancies her," Abigail told the gathering.

Everyone looked at Lucy, who quickly changed the subject. "Mary, we left our madam with such an awful headache. What should she take for it?"

Reminded of her own mother's recent fit, Mary let her sewing drop to her lap. "Has your madam had such before?"

"Yes, and her usual rose water and vinegar hasn't worked at all."

"She thinks she might need to be bled," added Abigail.

Mary frowned. "Does she feel cold, or does she complain of feeling hot?"

"She complains about the cold and stiffness in her limbs," Lucy said.

"What about biliousness?"

"I think only her head grieves her."

"Well," Mary mused out loud as Anna Frost listened attentively, "I'd say she needs a remedy hot in the first degree and only slightly drying. Your madam should use feverfew syrup taken with warm water. If you don't have any, we have a goodly supply."

A log shifted in the hearth and startled baby Elias, who began to cry. Rebekah picked him up to breastfeed. Fussing, he pulled away.

"Sarah," she snapped, "tell your mother that I need more of *her* medicine for Elias's colic." Cradling her crying babe in one arm, Rebekah stood and reached for a basket that hung on a rafter above.

The movement roused a clandestine creature hidden among the hanging foodstuffs. A dark flutter of leather dropped downward, and a bat hovered over the red velvet cloth. Shrieks and bench-upsetting scrambles set the creature into a panic. Gnashing its teeth and squeaking audibly, it began to dive about the room, narrowly avoiding the human occupants.

"Out, out! Let us out!" screamed the Treworgy sisters, who were first through the door, the others on their heels.

Mary could hear them all outside in the snow. At least Elias had stopped his fussing.

"Oh, if only Samuel were home," lamented Rebekah.

"We c-could all go d-down to Everett's T-Tavern?" Mary Small suggested, her teeth chattering.

"It's too far without our cloaks," lamented Abigail. "And I'm already f-freezing!"

"Where's Mary?" Anna asked.

There was a brief silence.

"She must still be inside . . ." Hannah's voice sounded husky.

With the fear and chaos gone, the bat came to rest on top of the settle. Mary gently placed a blanket over it, scooping it up. She stepped out over the threshold with the blanket in her arms. It was funny to see the others all clustered together, looking terrified.

She smiled at them. "You can come back inside now."

"Not if there's a bat in there," screeched Rebekah.

"Mary, how could you scare us like that?" her sister Sarah cried.

"Scare you? I was taking care of the problem." The group recoiled instinctively as the blanket Mary held began to move. She opened the blanket gently, and the bat's dark form fluttered up and sped away.

The girls' faces gaped with astonishment, all except for Rebekah's, whose pursed lips and narrowed eyes belied a different sentiment.

Mary and her sisters made their way home together later that afternoon as twilight deepened the icy track along the river to blue. "Mary, you shouldn't do such awful things," Sarah said once Mary Small had left them at the Mavericks'. "Methinks Lucy and Abigail are afraid of you now."

"Oh, and Rebekah will prate that the bat is my familiar?" Mary scoffed. "Methinks Lucy and Abigail were grateful not to suffer frostbite."

"It could have attacked you," Sarah said stubbornly. "We were all so scared—it had such horrible teeth!"

"Methinks 'twas a brave thing that Mary did," Hannah defended.

But Sarah ignored her. "Mary, why can't you be like everyone else for once?"

"You mean stand there helpless and cowering in the freezing cold?"

This angered Sarah. "Everyone thinks you're strange, and I'm so tired of making up excuses. You know, Mary, Rebekah is not such a bad person."

Mary could hardly believe her ears. "Fiddlesticks! Don't you see the looks she gives me? Rebekah knows how I feel about John Roberts, thanks to you! You heard her—'my beau'! She ignores me and my physick. She's mean, spiteful, and nasty. And she tries to act as though she knows what's best about everything!"

"And I think she *does* know best about many things," Sarah retorted, pulling away and walking quickly on up ahead by herself.

The year of 1648 started out much more hopeful for Mary, as Anna Frost began her apprenticeship, staying at the White plantation four days each week. Another pair of hands was very welcome, and Anna's friendship a comfort, for as Mary had feared, Sarah had become fast friends with Rebekah.

The news reached Kittery that a woman in Connecticut had actually confessed to witchcraft. Troubling, yes, but Connecticut was a long distance away. Then in midsummer, when the fields and forests were at their peak, news arrived that hit much closer to home.

Mary poured an electuary mixture of honey, vinegar, and powdered dandelion root into a glass bottle on the long trestle table in the kitchen.

"It looks delicious," Anna said.

"'Tis. Taste the spoon if you'd like. It makes a powerful vitality syrup once it's left in the sunlight for a few days."

"I don't understand why some folk are so suspicious of plants and medicines that God made to be so good for us," Anna said.

"It doesn't stand to reason, does it? You've seen yourself how those who don't use our physick fare poorly compared to those who do."

Mary's mother entered the kitchen hall. She set her medicine basket down and collapsed into the great chair. Her complexion looked peaked.

"Madam, are you ill?" Mary and Anna both stopped what they were doing.

"Oh . . . 'tis terrible, shocking news." She held a hand to her heart. "They hanged a midwife and practitioner of physick on the Boston Common a few days ago."

"A *midwife*? But why?" Mary wished Anna did not haveto hear.

For using medicines to cure the sick," her mother said sadly. "I was afraid of this. If Cromwell's witch hunts themselves have not crossed the sea, the sentiment certainly has." She leaned forward on the table, holding her head in her hands.

"But, madam, that's not a reason to hang someone. Surely, there must've been another?" Mary could see the confusion on Anna's face.

"Oh, hearsay is she made her neighbors sick as well as their cattle, and those who refused her physick became worse—worse beyond anything natural."

Mary cringed.

"And," her mother continued, "they say that the same day and hour of her hanging, there was a very great tempest in Connecticut that blew down a great many trees and other things."

"But, madam," Mary pointed out, "there wasn't a tempest of any sort here in Kittery."

After this, Anna did not come for a week. Mary sensed the hanging must have been the one she'd seen in her feverish dreams, but she had little patience for the happenings in Boston or the Connecticut towns. They were not Kittery. She knew the local families she treated adored her. She had only ever helped them—and greatly so.

Goody Frost knew this too, and soon, Anna returned.

That summer, Mary began to wonder if she would ever see John Woodman again. She'd received his messages from time to time through Migwah or Francis. Little did she know that his return would come soon—very soon. Yet at an unimaginable cost.

The sun had barely risen over the tops of the trees when Mary and Anna set out to wildcraft in early summer, dew sparkling on all the grasses and leaves. The cairn caught Mary's eye as they ran down the path on the back side of the hill. She stopped abruptly in front of it. A few brightly colored bones had been added to the chest-high pile of stones, giving it a festive look.

"What is it?" Anna spoke in a hushed voice, coming to a halt by her side.

Mary was proud of the cairn. "Our hill used to be an Indian gathering place, and this marker is one of the ways they leave messages for each other."

Anna's eyes grew wide. She looked afraid. "Do they pass by here often?"

"Yes, they do." Anna looked very uncomfortable with Mary's answer. "Well, not that often. Mostly when they come to trade with my father. You really must meet my Indian friend, Migwah. He's a medicine man, a *medeoulin*, and has taught me a lot about the plants here." Meeting Migwah would certainly help Anna be more at ease, she thought. "Haste, before the dew dries," Mary cried and dashed away again in the lead.

The mood once again merry, the two girls ran on until they reached a meadow just off the cart path. Mary navigated her way through a patch of thorny raspberry bushes to a fiery orange cluster of flowers. She broke off a small sprig, handing it to Anna.

"Pleurisy root. It looks like milkweed, but its stems are hairy, and there's no milk sap. It's for chest congestion and coughs. You can see by its signature—like air sacs of the lights, yes?"

Anna nodded, fascinated.

We harvest its roots in the fall when they are the most potent and the plant has dropped its seeds. Only the dried root should be used—the fresh is much too strong otherwise."

A small animal peered at them from over a fallen tree, then darted noisily into the bracken. Mary went over to where it had been. "Sometimes the animals show us too."

Anna followed her apprehensively.

Sure enough, on the other side of the fallen tree, a fuzzy green stalk with hooded purple-blue flowers was growing. "Skullcap! How perfect—my mother will be pleased. We have little left."

Mary picked one of the small flowers from its stalk and held it out to Anna. "I want to show you something, but it's to be kept a secret between you and me only—yes?"

Anna nodded.

"Touch your lips and the tip of your tongue to it and breathe in its essence."

Anna did as she was instructed. Mary had familiarized her with the stock of herbs and medicines they kept and how they prepared their tinctures, infusions, decoctions, salves, ointments, and distillates; but she had saved the best for last. This remedy made her mother nervous because it was such invisible magic, but Mary found it most helpful for changing a patient's mood and mind-set.

"What do you feel?"

"I feel . . . more relaxed?"

Mary smiled. "Skullcap *is* a relaxant, a tonic for the nerves. I will show you how to make a special elixir from its blossoms—what I like to use along with the preparations. It's one of my secrets."

Anna's face shone with excitement.

At the far end of the meadow ran the upper reaches of Daniel's Creek. When the girls had collected what they needed, they stopped to rest upon the thick pine needles between the gnarly roots of its bank. This was another one of Mary's favorite spots, where she and her mother and sisters went to bathe privately in the heat of the summer. The creek broadened out into a slight cove, shallow and nonthreatening. The girls waded, holding their skirts up above the surface, minnows nibbling at their ankles, the water so cool and inviting. Shiny mica pieces on the sandy bottom winked and glinted in the patches of sunlight that managed to penetrate the forest canopy. It was a peaceful place whose silence was only broached by the ethereal tinkling notes of a hermit thrush.

They rested on the bank afterward. Mary's gaze alighted on a trillium growing an arm's reach away. Its three characteristic petals were white, its center purplish.

"Ah, trillium root stops bleeding in childbed and is what my madam uses most now. Here"—she plucked a leaf and bruised it with her fingers—"give me your hand." She applied the bruised leaf to a bramble scratch on the back of Anna's hand, a raised, puffy welt. "The leaves are also good for treating bugbites, and the Indians eat them boiled as food."

Anna watched in amazement as her scratch began to flatten and become less red.

"Here, why don't you breathe in the essence of this one? You don't need to pick it."

Anna touched the center of the flower with her tongue.

"What do you feel now?"

"I feel—it's funny." Anna sat up and looked around. "I feel like I am sitting with you here now. Not that I didn't know I was before . . . It's just I'm more aware of it somehow?"

Mary's eyes lit up. "Yes! It draws the soul back down into the body and helps us become more present. I'll show you how to make the special flower elixirs next time you come."

❧

Bang! Bang! Bang! The sound of pounding barely registered to Mary's consciousness and became a part of her dream until she awoke sleepily. The night was terribly hot and humid. Waking in a sweat, she threw her sheet off to cool down.

"Constable White," she heard a voice from outside the house say, "I'm here to fetch you—be quick if you would."

Mary awoke further. She could hear her mother trying to rouse her father down below. Her father had been voted constable for Kittery and was very unhappy about it. Nicolas Frost had been the constable but, being elected a townsman, had abandoned his post.

"John, wake up. You're being called for."

She heard her father cross the parlour down below, making his way unsteadily in the dark to the door.

"You're needed for an arrest down at Everett's. There's been a fight. A fellow's hurt bad. Dr. Fernald's been sent for."

Hot summer nights could certainly bring out the worst in people.

"John, please be careful," her mother pleaded.

Mary prayed he'd be all right. Constables frequently had a rough time of it and were occasionally beaten up themselves.

But nothing could prepare the Whites or anyone else for what came late the next afternoon. The sound of musket fire echoed against the Dover hillside from the mouth of Sturgeon Creek and did not stop. Most people took to their houses, too afraid to go out. Mary, her mother and sisters stayed together in the kitchen hall as her father had instructed while he gathered up a few brave souls from the neighborhood to investigate. The men were assembled in front of the house when Warwick Heard's father arrived.

"White! Thank heavens!" John Heard called as he reined his horse. "It's Frost's wife and daughter—kidnapped by Indians. Frost and his sons are on their flank but are well outnumbered."

"God help us! What tribe?" her father asked.

"Pennacooks, methinks, painted black and yellow."

An arrow of fear struck Mary's heart; they knew no Pennacooks. Bertha and one of her daughters. *Not Anna—please not Anna!* The like had never been known to happen in Kittery before. If a crime could be blamed on an Indian, it was considered beneath the law, unpunishable, and kept out of court. The English often used the excuse to get away with crimes up to and including murder. But the Indians truly had, for the most part, left the region's English alone. Just as they had with John Woodman and his friends.

It wasn't until the next morning that her father returned home. He collapsed in his great chair, having been awake all night. They were all too afraid to ask, but Mary's father told them what had happened. Slowly, painfully, and reluctantly.

"We advanced as it grew dark but couldn't get close without coming under a barrage of bullets. The Indians had a great fire burning across the Sturgeon Creek mouth. 'Twas sunrise when we managed to make it to the camp. The red men must've slipped away just before dawn. Nicolas Frost and his son Charles beat us to it. We found Charles sobbing and retching in the bushes—can't blame him. 'Twas a horrible sight by the smoldering bonfire, the remains of Frost's wife and his daughter Anna. I'm so sorry—I'm so very sorry."

❧

"Mary!" John Woodman stood in the dooryard, his face weather-beaten and ruddy, grinning his handsome grin. It took Mary a moment to recognize him—she could hardly believe her eyes.

"*John*?" She ran to him. His arms enfolded her in a warm embrace, which her mother and sisters, who followed on her heels, did nothing to stop. On the contrary, they looked happy too.

"'Tis a good thing my father isn't home," Mary said, laughing through her tears.

John Woodman laughed himself and hugged her tighter. "Perhaps now your father will change his mind."

What a great comfort John's presence was to Mary in light of the recent happenings, but in his embrace, her face suddenly clouded with pain.

John held her at arm's length. "What's the matter?"

"John, I may have you back, but my dear friend Anna is dead. I have such remorse . . ."

"Mary, listen to me. What happened was a tragic shame, but nothing to do with either one of us." He brushed her tears gently away with his thumbs.

She knew in her heart that he was right. But to think about her friend was too much for her to bear. The look in Anna's eyes as they had stood at the cairn that day haunted her. Somehow her friend had known she had reason to be afraid. Why couldn't Anna have been at their house that day instead? *Why* had the Indians killed her and her mother instead of her father?

"A terrible, ghastly shame," Mary's father said later. "But 'tis the Indians' usual way to seek revenge. They bide their time, and then an eye for an eye, a tooth for a tooth—a dead man cannot suffer, can he?"

The Indians who committed the crime were indeed Pennacooks from the up-country, according to Sagamore Rowls. Migwah had told Mary no less. Rowls also cleared John Woodman and his friends publicly of any wrongdoing. Their residency with the natives had suited them well; for they brought back enormous piles of furs, had learned the language and deepened their trading connections, proving that those who had been all too happy to eliminate the competition had been sorely thwarted. And in John Woodman's case, in another way as well.

But the murder of Bertha and Anna had ripples that grew.

Mary found it disturbing to witness Charles Frost hardening from all the anger and hatred he carried. Charles began to channel his energies into becoming a good soldier, his loathing toward all Indians worn on his sleeve. Mary also felt for the rest of the Frost children, especially baby Nicolas, who was not yet one year old and had been on his mother's milk. Not surprisingly, the kidnapping and murder were ignored by the English authorities, though the occurrence did not sit well with the community. Fear settled on both sides of the river. Such things had happened before down in Massachusetts Bay, but not in Pascataway, not in recent memory.

Perhaps to ease Mary's grief or to keep a closer eye on her, Mary's father finally granted John Woodman permission to court her. To have her beloved as a guest in her father's house made Mary happier than anything ever had, and her mother was exceptionally kind and gracious, serving the best of everything. John Roberts still came courting despite Woodman's return. Mary felt Roberts's continued attention was more about competition than anything else. She certainly was not very friendly with him, but that didn't seem to matter.

That summer was a time of many endings and new beginnings. Tragically, Goody Emery's back had given out whilst leaning over a laundry tub, leaving her with burns so severe from both the scald and the lye that she died within the day. Anthony Emery sold his Dover tavern, unable to bear being there without his wife.

Mary's father found that as constable, he couldn't run both his store and his plantation to his satisfaction. He built a smaller storehouse on his plantation and sold his large storehouse and outbuildings, along with an adjacent field and marsh, to Anthony Emery. Anthony also bought the ferry from old man Beck and transformed John White's old storehouse into an ordinary aptly named Cold Harbor, in keeping with the English tradition of unheated sleeping quarters. Much to Mary's father's chagrin, he was kept busier than ever as constable with yet another Kittery tavern.

News soon reached Pascataway that the king of England was imprisoned by Sir Oliver Cromwell's Parliament. It was an outrageous scandal—not that it changed much of anything in New England: he was still king, whether he sat in a prison or not. But when the news came that the king had been beheaded, the inhabitants of Kittery were shaken indeed.

The townspeople soon realized that it would be better to join the much more powerful Confederation with Massachusetts and her allies by choice, and have it on their own terms, than endure what looked like an inevitable takeover. Many new families of wealthy, influential Puritans were moving to the region from the south and had been for some time. Still, there were many old Anglican planters attending Kittery's town meeting who stubbornly disagreed, Mary's father among them.

-- 19 --

Pascataway's New Arrivals

Mary began to sew, weave, and collect her dowry in earnest after John Woodman's return, wanting to have everything ready ahead of time. She was still deemed young to marry. Too many younger wives died in childbed.

Preparing for marriage and housekeeping was not an easy endeavor for most in colonial New England. Women were on average twenty-four years old and men twenty-eight before they had accumulated the resources to do so. Women were still scarcer than men, and men often had to return to Old England to bring back a bride. The lack of women was made worse by the English civil war and Cromwell's deportation of prisoners to the colonies.

In the winter of 1650, a local man named Richard Leader handpicked several dozen Scottish prisoners off a ship in Boston Harbor. Leader had recently settled in Pascataway, finding its resources splendid for his business ventures and life on the fringes of Puritan control easier. He put his new Scottish indentured servants to work felling trees and building a mill, sending them up and down the river delivering board, fetching supplies, and hiring them out to those in need. Leader had been granted the rights to the falls at the Asbenbedick River and its surrounding forests by the town of Kittery and had a plan of building a great works of a dozen saws.

Mary's first glimpse of his Scots was out on the river. Big, sturdy, intimidating fellows, whose laughter and strange Gaelic tongue reached far across the water as they floated mast pines downstream in the ice floes. Women peeped out their shutters. Men took notice too, for servants like these were exactly what every planter needed: soldiers captured at the Battle of Dunbar by Cromwell's forces. Hardy survivors, by the look of them, many standing near six feet tall.

Mary's father took ready advantage of Leader's Scots and had soon settled on his favorite, returning home one dinner hour with the fellow. One of the youngest, not more than eighteen years of age, youthful in build and well above average in height. A nice looking, quiet lad, with bluish-green eyes and thick golden hair. William Thomson was his name. At the dinner table he only spoke when spoken to, in an accent unmistakably Scotch.

"William, please let me serve you another helping of meat, and do help yourself to more bread." Mary's mother fussed, filling his trencher with seconds and thirds. Word had gotten out as to how the Scots had suffered at the hands of Cromwell's army.

"Feed him well, my dear. The lad works as hard as any I've ever seen," her father chuckled. Within the week, her father had bought William Thomson's indenture off Mr. Leader. George's indenture had expired, and her father needed another servant to work alongside Peter.

William proved strong as an ox. He and Peter soon had the upper hillside cleared of trees all the way down to the king's pines at Daniel's Creek, William felling three for every one of Peter's. The Scot would often pause in his labors to help Mary and her sisters with their chores as well. He helped them gather beechnuts, climbing to the highest boughs, and would carry the water bucket to the house for them if he was nearby. William was eager to please and seemed to take pride in taking on extra chores and responsibilities for everyone.

"That Will, he's one good worker" or "William's more responsible than my own son would be," her father repeated often.

Sometimes upon hearing her father praise the Scot, Mary would feel a pang of sadness that her father had never had a son, and she was glad he had William. Then there were times when she felt the opposite too.

On a midsummer evening, the woods along the river lit golden with the last of the setting sun, Mary walked back up the hill toward home. She felt happy, her face still flushed from John Woodman's parting kiss, when William appeared ahead on the path.

"There you are, Mahry—just making sure tha you're safe." He looked at her shyly, quickly glancing away from her gaze.

She could tell her eyes spooked him. "Truly I'm safe, William. I'm safer with John Woodman than I am with anybody!"

William blushed. He usually stayed off at a respectable distance when either of her suitors would visit, pretending to mind his own business. In truth, he was keeping a careful eye on her for her father. This irked her, especially tonight. Mary marched past him disdainfully, blowing off steam.

It's not William's fault. I shouldn't take it out on him. Mary stopped and waited for him to catch up. They walked the path side by side. She knew very little about him outside of the fact that he'd been captured by Cromwell's forces.

"William, what part of Scotland are you from?"

His eyebrows raised. "Highlands—me family are McTavish. Not so many of us left naow."

"I'm sorry. The battle must have been horrible. Do any of your relations know you're here?"

William shook his head. "I think na."

Up on the hillside, he helped her get the chickens into the henhouse for the night. The light was fading fast.

"William," she said as the rooster followed the last of the hens, "would you like me to write your family a letter so they know you're alive and well?"

"Aye, I suppose I would—if you knew Gaelic, Mahry."

"Surely, someone could translate the English?"

William didn't answer.

She bolted the coop for the night. When she turned around, it was with shock that she realized William was crying. "Oh, I'm sorry . . . I didn't mean—"

Shaking his head, he sniffled, wiping away his tears with his hand. "Me uncle died on the end of a pike thrust by a guardsman. Cromwell's cavalry attacked us just before dawn, after a night spent oot in the rain and having naught for warning. Fighting on foot, me brother and I held out until . . ." He paused to steady his voice. "Until he went down protecting our ensign. Ayh sat by me brother and held him 'til he died . . . his life's blood bubbling from his mouth. Ayh could nah leave him—could nah flee with the others. When the sun burned off the mist, the waters of the burn were runn'ng raed, and the Scots army was nah more." He hung his head, ashamed. "Better for them that's left not to knaow. I want to forget . . . Ayh'm sorry, Mahry."

"Nay, Will, please don't apologize," Mary said softly, the intensity of his description having taken her breath away. "'Tis good to talk it out, as terrible as it was."

He told her then of what followed: of his capture and brutal one-hundred-mile journey on foot, with most of his clothes stripped away and the only food raw cabbages, roots and all, grabbed from roadside fields. Housed in the cathedral at Durham with six hundred other Scottish prisoners, he and the others were forced to burn pews to keep warm as the season grew colder. Guards stole their food rations, and many prisoners died of dysentery as there was no clean water to drink. After a month in the cathedral, Will was among those taken down to London. Here, they were kept in chains on board a ship called the *Unity* and ill-used by the crew while waiting to set sail to New England.

The winter passage had been rough and cold, and they were made to work with poor food and little clothing. Many died at sea. In Boston Harbor, when Richard Leader came to his rescue and that of sixteen other Scots, giving them warm clothes to wear and good food to eat, William and his Scottish brethren were grateful indeed.

Hearing the outpouring of grief on William's part and the horrors of what he suffered roused a great sympathy in Mary. She resolved to treat him more kindly from then on.

In November of 1652, the town of Kittery officially submitted to the governance of Massachusetts Bay. Heads of households were summoned to Everett's Tavern at nine o'clock in the morning to sign the petition. Many were quite unhappy with the turn of events, but the transition was made easier by the fact that Kittery would be able to retain its religious freedom even though its governing magistrates would answer to Massachusetts Bay—a privilege other towns to the south had not been so lucky to keep.

Kittery residents had to admit it was a comfort to be officially within the protection of their larger neighbor to the south. Trade and shipping continued to flourish and expand, New England sending out its own ships to trade with the Dutch and Spanish even as English ships were forbidden to do so by Cromwell. Faster than ever, many new faces and families settled the region. More skilled craftsmen arrived, and settlers became less dependent on imports. Strawbery Banke, now a flourishing seaside town, changed its name to Portsmouth; and the face of Pascataway changed for good.

❧

January 16, 1652, marked Mary's twenty-third birthday. She was certainly of age. Lately, there was desperation in John Woodman's face. Both he and John Roberts had asked for her hand, only to be turned away. Mary's father said neither yea nor nay, but told them that when he decided his daughter was ready, he would consider their plea. If a young man was ardent enough, he could wait.

It had begun to feel absurd to her, as though her father would rather she stay a maid for the rest of her life. She made sure her father knew whom she wanted for a husband. John Woodman even had his own house at Oyster River, off the Great Bay to the west of Dover. Mary had all her household linens ready, neatly folded in her dowry chest along with pots, dishes, and other chattels that had been set aside for her housekeeping. She had learned all the cooking, sewing, and weaving skills that she needed to be a good wife.

The evening of her birthday, Mary's mother came to her rescue as the family sat eating supper by candlelight, the deep snows of winter outside.

"Sir? I have my dowry set and ready," Mary said, not knowing how else to broach the subject.

Her father said nothing.

A sigh escaped her mother. "Methinks, John, that our eldest is quite ready for housekeeping."

Mary's father did not answer her mother either but continued to eat as though he had not heard either of them.

"Oh fie!" said her mother, setting the wooden top back on the pot in the hearth embers. Straightening, she walked over to the table center where Mary's father was seated and began to knead his back and shoulders with seldom-demonstrated affection. "Oh, John . . . 'tis time. Mary is more than ready."

Much to Mary's surprise, her father's body visibly relaxed under her mother's hands. He set his spoon down upon his trencher, and Mary could see that his eyes looked watery. Both Peter and William looked down at the table. Mary's sisters looked as surprised as she was.

The next day, after the dinner hour, all others were excused from the kitchen hall except for Mary. She waited on the edge of her seat, opposite her parents at the table, her hands fidgeting nervously in her lap.

"Mary," her father began, "your mother and I have decided that you are ready for marriage."

Her heart leapt to hear those words. *Oh! If they only knew how my heart aches for John Woodman. It has grown almost unbearable.*

"William Thompson will be your future husband," her father said. He pronounced 'Thomson' the English way as he had never done before.

Mary sat motionless, her eyes fixed upon the table salt. She felt dizzy. *It can't be real. It must be some cruel joke.*

"I know that Will is not the one you hoped for," he continued. "But your mother and I agree that he is strong, capable, and responsible. He would make an ideal husband, of which we have proof enough."

Mary found herself floating upward, spinning, separate from the weight of her body. Her father was still talking, but she barely heard him with his first words still ringing in her ears—words that took a good while to fully sink in.

❧

In the dying light of the embers, Mary tied on her shoes and stepped into her wool petticoat and doublet. On such a cold winter's night, the entire household slept in the parlour, and the floor was strewn with sleeping bodies about her parents' corner bedstead. William lay farthest from the hearth, snoring lightly. She felt so heartsick and betrayed. William would understand why she'd left; he knew where her heart lay. Mary hoped her parents would be able to forgive her. All she had to do was push the canoe across the ice until it found an open channel, then navigate around Hilton's Point and over to Oyster River. She could do it. She'd go to John Woodman tonight and demand he carry her off! He had even suggested it himself not too long ago.

With a sorrowful glance about the room, she slid stealthily past the wool curtains in the doorways to the hall, where she filled a foot warmer with embers from the hearth. She would need some warmth out there. The night was bitterly cold. At least there was a good moon to see by. Mary pulled on her wool cloak and grabbed a pair of thick leather gloves that lay drying on the woodbox—William's gloves. Her father would find him another pair. All wrapped up, she lifted the foot warmer by its chain. She turned to go and jumped with fright.

Her father stood in the kitchen doorway, pinning the wool curtain to its side. "Where do you think you're going?" His sleepy eyes burned holes through her. He took hold of her arm and sat her down roughly in a chair. "I should whip you soundly!"

Mary's mother came into the hall, her sleepy face disbelieving.

"How in God's name dare you oppose me?" Her father trembled with rage.

"Mary, how?" gasped her mother, placing a calming hand upon her father's arm.

Mary could hear her sisters crying in the next room.

No one slept much the rest of the night. Mary curled herself tightly into a ball under her covers, wishing she were dead.

The next day, the banns of Mary and William's intent to marry was nailed to the Kittery chapel door, and the aching sadness closed in miserably upon her.

❧

A weak winter sun had forced its way through the clouds earlier in the day, but now the sky looked gray and lowering, smelling like snow. A match to Mary's mood. She stood down by the river, gazing past the jagged shelves of greenish ice that angled upward like teeth toward the open channel. Mary didn't mind that her toes were aching cold. It felt good somehow.

The chickens flocked about her, hungry for the ground samp she carried. They'd followed her all the way down the frozen hillside.

Maybe John wouldn't show up today. It terrified her that he might.

When John Woodman's distant shout from the river did hail her, it filled her with sorrow instead of its usual joy. She watched him pick his way through the ice floes, dread flitting about inside her stomach.

She'd tried to close him out of her mind, to barricade her heart. But the sight of him made her pulse quicken and a warmth sear through her cold breast like a knife. She watched him despairingly, her feelings unraveling. *Does John even know Father has promised me to William? Maybe he doesn't . . .*

He stopped out of breath, a few feet from her, the chickens scattering. His handsome face looked tormented, his jaw muscles working. His eyes searched hers. "Mary, is it true?"

She looked down, a wave of humiliating sorrow and confusion washing through her—if only this was some monstrous dream that she could pinch herself awake from this instant!

But it wasn't.

She nodded, terrified to look him in the eye.

John turned his head away toward the river, swallowing visibly, bitterly. His Adam's apple quivered with outrage and grief. Mary felt it all.

"No, he's making a mistake!" He stared at her disbelievingly, then took another step toward her, removing his hat, holding it to his breast. Snow began to fall around them. "Talk to him, Mary," he pleaded. "You mean more to me than anything . . ." He looked at her beseechingly and knelt down on one knee in the snow.

"I have, John. I've tried. He won't hear me. You know how he is." She shuddered, averting her gaze. Tears spilled from her eyes and bounced off the rooster's plumage. "I tried to leave—to come to you the night before last."

"But how?" He glanced from her to the river and back, horrified realization dawning that the attempt could have taken her life. "Mary, come with me now," he said in earnest.

She shook her head. She felt so twisted and shattered inside; a sort of numbness was beginning to set in. A resignation to the whole situation. "You talk to my father," she answered. "I cannot dishonor his wishes."

"Mary . . ." John said softly, rising to his feet. With his finger, he lifted her chin so he could see her face.

Seeing the love, hurt, and pain in his eyes was too much for Mary to bear. She pulled away and turned her back to him, throwing handfuls of chicken feed angrily into the snow. Her feet felt unpleasantly frozen and wet; she had stayed out much too long.

"Mary! You have more say in this than I have. Go to your father and tell him how you feel!"

She shook her head sadly. "I cannot change my father's mind. Please . . . just leave me alone with the chickens." She didn't know what else to say. She began to walk away from him.

"I won't accept this!" he yelled.

Frightened, Mary began to walk faster. "Talk to my father!" she called back over her shoulder, hoping to appease him somewhat. *This is much too hard for me. I should not have come here today.*

John came after her and grabbed her shoulders. A tussle ensued between them. Mary's cap pulled loose, and her silver comb fell into the snow, her hair tumbling down over her shoulders.

John stood still, holding her in an embrace, enraptured. For a brief aching moment they came together face-to-face, before Mary struggled out of his grasp, reaching for her cap.

Exposed and humiliated, a rage began to build inside of her.

John stepped backward awkwardly, picking up her comb. "I'm sorry. I didn't mean t—"

"Go away!" she screamed, snatching her comb from his hand. "Leave me be, you . . . you . . ." Tears of hurt and anger streamed afresh from her eyes. Tears that in reality had very little to do with him.

He backed away slowly, bewildered, his expression remorseful.

Mary picked up the samp basket that had scattered its contents all over the snow, to the chickens' delight. Pulling on her hood, she ran back up the snowy hillside trail toward home without looking back.

Left alone with the chickens, John Woodman punched the air with his fists. He threw his hat down and stamped upon it violently.

Then he sank to his knees in the snow, his face in his hands.

-- 20- -

Wedding

The last patches of snow were melting from the dun-colored hillside overlooking the river. Mary sat alone on a log next to the henhouse, half concealed by the wild bower of leafless coppice that cascaded over its roof, her body bent and wracked with sobs. Thinking about John Woodman was more sadness than she could bear, but she couldn't seem to help it.

She would marry William Thomson soon—*Scottish* William Thomson, her father's servant. Sure, there was a certain something between them—mostly on William's part—but nothing close to what she felt for John Woodman. Still, this something had not been missed by her father. He knew William adored her, his master's daughter. She frowned. Her father had married his master's daughter too. Grief coursed through her yet again before she surrendered, exhausted.

Having cried her heart out, she sat still awhile, feeling a calm emptiness.

The landscape lay before her, as still and placid as she, its colors and forms amazingly vivid and clear. Behind the fringe of budding trees, the river ran a silver gray below, and the air smelt sweet of damp earth and brine. A chorus of peepers sounded from the surrounding marshes. Usually, she loved this time of year, watching the greening of the meadows and woods.

Wiping her tears with a damp handkerchief, she looked to her left where the hillside sloped away down to the grove of king's pines on the banks of Daniel's Creek. Peter and William had felled the forest right up to them on a straight line, exposing broken needle-less branches. Their boughs at the top, however, were still a beautiful deep green. It soothed Mary to look at the pines, to feel their towering presence. At her feet, the chickens clucked and crooned, cocking her a sympathetic eye as they scratched for bugs in the undergrowth. She blew a tiny spider off her sleeve, watching it sail away on its silken thread.

The sound of someone coming up the path from the river below reached her ears. She sat frozen, not having the wherewithal to hide herself better, hoping whomever it was wouldn't notice her.

It was William, and he saw her right away.

"Mary," he said, striding over.

She dabbed at her eyes again. He was supposed to have gone with her father. Well, he knew how she felt—there was no need to pretend otherwise, was there?

His boots stopped in front of her for a moment before he sat his strong, muscled body down beside her on the log, uninvited. "I ken ye are not happy," he said with quiet resolve. "Ye would ha' chosen another."

Mary struggled to hold back a fresh welling of tears.

"I want ye to knaow I will make ye a gewd and gentle husband."

Finding her composure, she stared at her fingers interwoven tightly in her lap. Of course he would. He had always treated her with respect and kindness . . . almost a kind of reverence.

"That," William continued, "I can promise ye."

Mary looked up at him, daring to meet his fair bluish-green eyes before looking away. To see her like this must be hard, she thought. She began to feel badly. William had been through so much. She should not be so unkind; this, after all, was not his fault.

She drew a deep breath, and something within her let go. William looked so earnest and vulnerable; his cheeks flushed with humility.

"Aye, Will, I know you will."

❧

Spring training day on the Dover sheep pasture was a particularly grueling one. In an absolute downpour, William and his fellow Scots had been put through unceasing drills to show the Dover militia what they were made of, and it only rained harder and more furiously as the day progressed. Afterward, the Scots gathered in a local tavern for a pot of brew, the place packed full of wet and hungry militia. Perhaps not the best place for William to have gone.

Three of his friends—Alexander Maxwell, James Barry, and Niven Agnew—had brought him home. They were brave souls who'd been his fellow Covenanters, fighting for religion, crown, and king in what had once looked to be certain victory. The horrors they'd suffered would certainly bond them for life.

His comrades holding him up on all sides, William gimped into the kitchen hall, wracked in spasms of gut-wrenching laughter, his lip split wide open and bleeding down his chin.

"He's gone mad!" Maxwell exclaimed.

Hearing this made William howl all the louder. "If this is wha' mad is, Ayh'll take it any day."

Mary couldn't believe her eyes. "Who are you, and what have you done with William?"

"Ayh feel good, Mahry . . . Ayh can't remember *ever* having felt this good," William crooned.

She applied boiled comfrey root and gave him some rockrose elixir to drink. She hoped he'd heal quickly—their wedding was not much more than a week away.

"Whatever happened?" she asked the other Scots.

"The other fellow got it worse," Niven Agnew began.

"Oh, much, much worse," James Barry confirmed. "You should ha' seen him strugglin' like a beetle, arms and legs kickin' as Willy dragged him to the door." All of them laughed. "One swing of his arms sent Roberts rollin' like a log 'cross the muddy dooryard 'til the ash barrel stopped him cold, the back of his doublet rent right down the middle."

"Roberts? Just who was this other fellow?"

"Your favorite disgruntled suitor," William laughed.

"John Roberts? Oh dear!"

"Trust me, Mahry, he deserved it, calling you a witch. Don't worry, there's not much of his arrogant nose left to get out o' joint."

"How did this happen?"

"Ayh think the old Scotch ballad of Lochnagar was somehow to blame," Alexander Maxwell said thoughtfully. He held his chin, screwed his mouth to the side, and nodded in an impish manner.

"Or Maxwell himself," said James Barry.

"Nah, truth is Roberts is just a poor loser," said Niven Agnew.

"With a nose where his ear was," agreed William.

❧

Mary looked up at William, standing by her side. He looked handsome in his new suit of clothes and polished boots. He still had a thin faded crescent underneath his eye, but it would have looked a lot worse without her comfrey.

He was now her husband. They stood in the yard at Kittery House chapel, where the Anglican reverend Thomas Millet had just officiated. The sun shone brightly for the first time in almost a fortnight.

"Any more rain, and I'd be building an ark!" her father had joked that morning in a surprisingly good mood.

Between the different friends and family members congratulating them, Mary's eyes sought the river. *Maybe John Woodman is there, watching from a distance . . .*

But she was now another man's wife.

Her father had forbidden William to consummate their marriage until he deemed the match sound. This was just fine with her. What would have been a natural expression of passion for a certain other person was now a prospect somewhat frightening that she dared not dwell upon.

A sun-warmed breeze brought the smell of blossoms from the orchard. Bees were humming, birds nesting, and the woods and fields were lush and green—things that normally made her giddy with delight. She thought of the garden table back at her father's house, laden with the small green melons grown early under earthen pans. Of the music to come—four musicians: a fiddle, two fifes, and a drum her father had hired—and the dancing. She had the reception to look forward to.

Mary curtsied elegantly in return to Uncle Samuel and Rebekah. Their son, Elias, now four years old, clung behind Rebekah's skirts.

Mary smiled. "Elias?"

He peered around at her shyly.

Mary felt beautiful with her tresses elegantly coiled upon her head and crowned with a wreath of blue iris, white lilac and lily of the valley flowers. A violet-blue silk ribbon wound around the wreath, its ends danglingbehind her slender neck. She'd chosen the flowers not only for their scent and beauty, but also for the vitality, peace, and joy they offered. The fabric for her wedding dress had been ordered several years before. Its bodice and sleeves were a cream sarcenet décolleté, as was the fashion, embroidered with small textured flowers and curling vines in a range of violet blues and greens—her mother's skilled handiwork. Her fine holland chemise was just visible at the edge of the décolleté and fell elegantly from her sleeves to her wrists in the family's cut lace pattern. The bodice fastened down her back with several dozen pearly-glass buttons. Mary's father, particularly fond of nice clothing himself, hadn't spared any detail in his eldest daughter's raiment. Mary's petticoat was a lovely matching violet-blue satin, her slippers a cream rosette sarcenet with gracefully arched heels, and her stockings were of the finest French silk.

She hoped John Woodman would catch a glimpse of her. She'd crafted her wedding attire to please him, after all. Her eyes moved to the river again until she noticed that William had followed her gaze. She lifted her nosegay to her face, breathing deeply of the lilac and lily of the valley that matched her headpiece. She shouldn't think of *him*—at least not today.

Arriving home from the chapel by horse cart, Mary's father handed her a small package. It was wrapped in white-embossed paper and tied with the same violet-blue silk ribbon she wore in her hair. She unwrapped it with trembling hands, uncovering a leather-bound book with a gilt title: *The Book of Secrets of Albertus Magnus: Of the Virtues of Herbs, Stones, and Certain Beasts.* Teary-eyed and choking back a lump of emotion, she thanked her father, amazed that such a book even existed.

But there was something else everyone was excited about. Her father ushered her into the parlour, where something quite large lay covered with a sheet.

"Go ahead and uncover it, my wild rose," he said. Her family stood by smiling, along with some close friends and neighbors who were helping with the food.

Mary looked around at William, her parents, and all the happy faces. She never wanted to forget this moment. Sunshine poured in the open casement lighting the room brilliantly, and birds were singing in the bush nearby. Her father's clock ticked from the wall next to the door, and the celebration outside was ready and waiting.

She pulled off the sheet.

Underneath sat a chest of drawers. Her eyes grew wide, for upon its surface were painted flowers and vines in bright colors. Mary had never seen a chest so beautiful.

"Go ahead, open a drawer," her father prompted.

She pulled one open to find the inside sectioned off into twelve smaller compartments to hold different herbs and medicines. "Oh!" she gasped, tears of joy filling her eyes. She could not imagine a better gift. She hugged her father, then her mother. Her parents looked choked up and teary-eyed themselves.

William, of course, was not forgotten. Her parents' gift to him was a house and land lying just north along the river, past Cold Harbor Ferry and Henry Powning's trading post, where the cart path curved to follow the shoreline of Sturgeon Creek. A fair house of four chambers and attached barn, built with an allotment of board that had been her father's payment from the town for his service as constable.

Soon the high, clear notes of the musicians' pipes, the resonance of the fiddle, and the soft rhythm of the drum filled the grassy dooryard, and the guests began to arrive. All was so beautiful and the mood so festive that Mary could not help but enjoy herself. She danced light on her feet, the music stirring her soul, the thought of her medicine chest and book making her truly happy.

Food was served on outdoor tables, and neighbors arrived laden with dishes. The little melons were exquisitely sweet and refreshing, cut in half and eaten with spoons. Their green flesh looked tempting and jewel-like, set on a raised platter surrounded by bright red strawberries, flowers, and leaves.

The longest table, consisting of linen-draped plank boards, stretched out in front of the front of the dwelling. On the left center was the bride's cake, covered with sugared spring flowers and flavored with rose water. On the right center sat the groom's cake, dark and fruity, flavored with rum. The rest of the table was covered with all manner of dishes—platters of meats, breads, salads, and puddings—and in the very center, a punch bowl of traditional wedding mead.

Relatives, guests, and their servants all helped out, replacing dishes as soon as they were eaten with those that lined the kitchen hall table, windowsills, and hearth, awaiting their turn.

Nicolas Shapleigh and his wife, Alice, arrived to cheers as they drew up in their horse cart laden with two kegs, a large one of ale and a smaller one of fine canary sack. The first thing Nicolas did was raise a toast in the bride's honor.

"To the virtuous bride! Long may she live and heal our sick!" Everyone cheered and gave their hands.

Mary's heart felt gratitude.

Almost two hundred guests—which swelled to many more by evening's end—ate, drank, and danced in traditional English fashion. Some Mary hadn't seen in a very long time. Lizzie, the Shapleighs' old housekeeper, was now Goody Trickey, living across the river at Bloody Point, married to a shipwright.

"Congratulations, Mary! I wish ye happiness and many, many children, m' dear!" Lizzie was still as large and capable as always. She had her whole brood with her. The older ones were running about, grabbing pasties off the tables, while the younger ones clung to her skirts and breast, fussing and drooling.

Mary smiled graciously and thanked her, thinking happily of the meadowsweet root that she had already begun to take to stop her fertility. She would have children when she herself was ready, God willing.

And there was yet another reminder: Lucy Treworgy, now Goody Chadbourne, far along in her first pregnancy, was there with her husband, Humphrey.

"I hope you and your mother stay sound and able. I should be in childbed soon," Lucy said nervously. Humphrey put his arm around his wife's shoulders. He had built a fair house at Sturgeon Creek on land he had bought from Lucy's uncle.

"As soon as we get the word, we'll come swiftly," Mary reassured her.

Nearby, Charles Frost stood talking with James Emery. Charles was in training to be a military officer, a position he took very seriously. His tall frame and stern carriage contrasted with his father's, who laughed and joked with his new wife, Joan, and other guests by the ale keg.

A crowd of young people were gathered in the orchard, Mary's sisters among them. She could see little Nicolas Frost Jr. and his sisters, Catherine and Elizabeth. Mary felt such pity for little Nicolas to have lost his mother at such a young age. But when she realized Nicolas was trying to skewer frogs with a stick at their little spring-fed pond, she flew over to put a stop to it. His sisters apologized and promised to keep an eye on him.

When the guests had eaten their fill, the musicians picked up the tempo with a hornpipe, and Mary found herself lifted into the air by William through the dancing crowd. Then the groomsmen, six of William's Scottish friends, grabbed her from him and ran around with her on their shoulders, keeping her from William in jest, pretending to make off with her, which made everyone laugh. Then they lifted William too.

For he's a jolly gewd fellow,
for he's a jolly gewd fellow,

for he's a jolly gewd fellow,
and so ye say of thee.
And so ye say of thee,
and so ye say of thee.
For he's a jolly gewd fellow,
for he's a jolly gewd fellow,
for he's a jolly gewd fellooow!
And so ye say of thee!

As twilight fell, the festivities and merrymaking continued, with people coming and going. Fireflies set the woods and hillside twinkling like the stars above, and a bonfire was lit.

Around the fire, a strange, wicked-looking woman began to dance, whom Mary soon recognized to be none other than her friend Francis. His outrageous antics—preening, flirting, and the lifting of "her" skirts—created uproarious laughter.

The festivities went on long into the night and were still going strong as Mary took her leave. She gave William a parting kiss.

To the great disappointment of the groomsmen, there was to be no bridal bed, the custom of the attendants helping undress and "tuck" in the bride and groom. They begged and cajoled Mary into at least throwing her bride garters. To appease them, she did.

James Warren caught the garters with a triumphant yell. He and the other Scots, having drunk their fill, were singing Gaelic tunes of a rather suspicious nature, teetering on the verge of being asked to leave, of which they were long past caring.

By the time Mary lay down to sleep in the upstairs chamber of her father's house, it was well past midnight. She relaxed, listening to the merry voices and songs of those revelers still around the fire. Her sisters lay on either side of her, happy and exhausted. In a week or so, when her father deemed they should, she and William would go to housekeeping to start a life of their own. She held her sisters' hands, feeling nostalgic, not wanting to think about what was coming to an end.

Together, they drifted off to sleep.

As the cock crowed the next morning, Mary awoke. She moved to the gable window to survey the scene below and saw her husband leaving what remained of the bonfire, stumbling blindly for his bed sack in the parlour. His three remaining groomsmen—Niven Agnew, James Barry, and Alexander Maxwell—were rolling themselves like logs down the steep hillside path to the dock, howling like coots and bandits.

"Who needjs laigs? Nah Ayh!" Niven shouted, his mood ever merry.

"Las dawg thair mans th' oars!" cried Alexander, freeing himself from bushes halfway down the hillside, only to throw himself into another rolling pin–style spin and gain the lead.

"Lil hair o' th' dawg, methinks!" James hollered.

Luckily, none of them stood a chance of revival once they'd come to a stop in the dew-wet grass at the river's edge. Sweet English clover, planted so thick and comfortable, the air so pleasantly warm . . .

Fortunate indeed, for they might have all drowned otherwise.

-- 21 --

Greylock and William

Mary and William's new house near the mouth of Sturgeon Creek had diamond-paned casements, a high-pitched roof, and a front door that sat just back from the lane connecting it with all the other homesteads along the Kittery side of the river. Mary's quilt graced their bedstead in the corner of the cheery whitewashed parlour: a work of art with much of her past sewn into it as fabrics. Mary was especially proud of her kitchen hall with its enormous hearth and her beautiful herb chest in the far corner, above which were built rows of shelves. Next to her herb chest, a second door on the left side of the house opened out directly into the kitchen garden. Mary had asked for the door as the house was being built. When this door and the window casements lay open, the southern light and sweet air of the midsummer mornings permeated the room pleasantly. Bunches of drying herbs hung from the rafters, and a set of new cast-iron pots graced the hearth. Family and friends had been paying their customary housewarming visits, complimenting her new abode.

This particular morning, Rebekah and Elias had come to call. "I see you've made yourself quite at home." Rebekah eyed the shelves, which already boasted pots of ointments and bottles of elixirs, electuaries and tinctures. "Doesn't it frighten you to hear of Goody Knapp being hanged?"

Mary looked at her relation whose blue eyes held narya mote of real friendliness. Goody Knapp was the latest in the line of women from Connecticut accused of witchcraft.

"Practitioners of physick and witches are two completely different things," she calmly replied. "Why would news of Goody Knapp's misfortune frighten me?"

"Hmm . . ." Rebekah lifted her brow mockingly.

Elias sat between them at the end of the table, eating cake with a focused intent.

"Elias has a good appetite today," Mary remarked as the boy finished his last bite.

"Wouldst you like another piece, sweetheart?"

"Yes'm," he answered, with a furtive glance at his mother.

Elias always seemed to be ailing with one thing or another. Mary knew that her own mother had been concerned for some time, being the one Rebekah always consulted for physick.

"Be careful, Elias. You know how ill you felt after Goody Thompson's wedding." Rebekah brushed her son's curls back offhis forehead in a mollycoddling manner. She'd been picking at her own serving of cake, cake that other visitors had complimented up and down. Rebekah turned back to Mary. "I heard talk your father was putting on airs by serving dainty melons and such."

"Oh? I'm sure everyone enjoyed them. I thought they were delicious."

Rebekah appeared not to hear her, taking a sip of the fine canary sack Mary had placed before her as though it were vinegar. When her relation's thin, angular frame finally disappeared through the gate pulling Elias behind her, Mary shut the front door and drew in the latchstring with a sigh of relief. Some peace and quiet would do her good. Smoothing her skirt, she tied on her work apron.

Walking back through the kitchen and out the side door, she noted with satisfaction that all was in order inside and out. A bushy close had been left between the garden and the lane and offered a lovely privacy barrier. The day was gloriously sunny, the beehive humming with activity, and the garden she'd planted earlier that spring was flourishing. As she wound up a bucket of water from the well, her gaze swept over the young orchard William had planted between the house and the river. She imagined the boughs heavy with ripened fruit and her rosy-cheeked children who'd laugh and play beneath. *When she was ready, of course.*

'Twas not as bad as she had feared, her first night with William. Yes, it was painful, and she'd bled as she'd been warned about.

But she enjoyed the feeling of his hands so intimate with her body, stroking its smoothness and cupping the roundness of her breast, his lips exploring her as if she were a piece of succulent fruit. His lust and desire for her was intense and overwhelming—just to think on it built a pleasant tension within her. Such intimacies created a connection and appreciation of her husband that had been missing. But sometimes she couldn't help but think of John Woodman. *What would such intimacies have been like with him?*

Today William was off working for her father, as he did many days. If he wasn't building, repairing, or farming, he was loading and unloading lighters or making deliveries. He'd be exhausted when he came home in the evening, and it concerned Mary because there was so much here at his own homestead that needed tending. But being left alone during the day was perfectly fine with her.

The Pownings and the Emerys were their closest neighbors, the trading post and ordinary lying just downriver across a little inlet. However Goody Powning and the children still spent most of their time in Boston; and Becky Emery, Goody E's daughter, and her ever-trusted maidservant, Molly, were kept very busy with the tavern.

Mary weeded and watered for a while, thinking of all the things she needed to do. There was only one thing that felt inspiring and exciting—something that she'd wanted to do for the longest time.

She hurried back into the house. This newfound freedom to act on her own desires made her giddy, even ecstatic. From her medicine chest she selected one of the bone-like stones that left such a silky softness on her fingers. She tried to crush it with her mortar and pestle, but she found the material surprisingly harder than it looked. Fetching Will's hammer from the barn, she cracked the stone into pieces on the hearth, hammering it down into a fine silky powder. I don't need the crucible at all for this, she realized. Amazed at the simplicity, she added the powder directly into a pot ofboiling water.

Mary had wasted no time in reading her wedding present about Albertus Magnus's secrets. In the writings of the fourteenth-century monk, she found a correlation between the herbs he mentioned and her own experience of their subtle yet potent effect. Yes, celandine cleared communication, and yarrow made her feel protected and less vulnerable. Albertus knew everything had a voice—not necessarily one he could hear with his ears, but one that he could feel nevertheless.

The brew turned to a bubbling milky mystery, and Mary's excitement began to build. *What will this long-awaited creation bring?* When the contents had cooled sufficiently, she drank a little. It was innocuous enough, she decided. Not much of a taste at all—only perhaps a bit gritty when stirred—but its effects were most interesting. She felt a calming and strengthening, and it seemed to sharpen her mind almost right away. She funneled her creation into the glass bottles she had on hand, added a bit of brandy, and sealed them with beeswax. Then she proudly lined them up across the top of her medicine chest.

Flinging the garden door wide again to the light of day, she admired her work. It turned crystal clear as the residual sediment settled—a perfect alchemy. The corner of her eye caught the scattering of the little wrens and flycatchers from the dooryard before the sunlit doorframe was blocked by the figure of a man.

"Kuai." He nodded. It was Migwah. She'd not seen him in months.

"Kuai," she answered, hoping he hadn't seen her start. Migwah's hair was now a snowy goose-feather white, and he was wearing his Native skins.

He held some roots out to her. "For *behanem* sick with child," he said.

Mary blushed and welcomed him in, thanking him for the roots. Of course she would never tell him about the meadowsweet root. Her mother had brought the seeds with them from England.

Migwah was alone; it was unusual to see him unaccompanied.

"But where are your sannups?" she asked.

"Trading post." He gestured in the direction of Henry Powning's.

Mary fed him the pottage left from breakfast and a salad of newly sprouted greens, herbs, and flowers from her garden. Migwah watched her silently as she prepared it, sitting in William's chair. "No husband here watch over you?"

"No, William's working on the river."

"Not good leave young *behanem* alone," the *medoolin* said, shaking his head.

"I like being alone." Mary set his meal before him. "Besides, I have my family down the lane, and there are neighbors nearby."

"Indian wife choose if keep husband or no."

"Indian wives can choose to keep their husbands?" Mary was surprised.

"Unh-honh—if husband no good, they make leave."

"How do they do that?"

"Leave husband's moccasins outside wigwam."

Mary laughed, wondering if he was teasing her. "Truly?"

But Migwah looked serious. The thought of a husband finding his boots on the doorstep and having no choice but to leave seemed absurd, but the more she thought about it, the more she liked the idea. Indian women certainly were better off in some essential ways.

She saw him looking at the new bottles lined up on top of her herb chest. "Ah, you must try my tonic." She poured him a cup from what was left in the pot.

He tasted it carefully before asking what it was. Mary handed him a piece of the stone. He turned it over in his palm, admiring its texture. "Sacred stone, bones of the mother," he said and swallowed the rest of the cup. "Good medicine."

A few days later, Mary was in her kitchen garden harvesting snap peas, when she looked up to see Migwah once again. He stood a short distance off where a moment before he hadn't been.

"Oh, kuai!" she called.

Migwah nodded in greeting and began to make an odd clicking noise with his tongue. Out from behind him, a fuzzy gray puppy came running. It ran over to Mary, and she knelt to rub the little dog's soft ears and snout. It melted under her touch, licking her hands, panting with excitement. "What a sweet creature!" she cried, smiling.

Migwah grinned, his black eyes sparkling. "Yo, gagwi ki-oh' nah."

"For me?" she cried with delight. "Oh, thank you, Migwah! Oolioonі!"

This time, when she offered Migwah a meal, he declined. Instead, he spoke to her in Abenaki that she did not completely understand, his lined face betraying a glimpse of what looked like sadness. "Oodoza, Jon Whytt, kinikinik volcanda kottliwi kwahliwi tapsiwi. Adio, ooli nanawalmezi."

Then with a nod of his head, he departed. She watched him go, his gait ever graceful for his age. A troubling sadness stirred within her until the puppy jumped against her skirt for attention.

She named the dog Greylock. He soon proved to be a wonderful companion, warning her when anyone or anything approached with his growls and body language, as Indian dogs didn't bark. He followed her everywhere she would let him.

"Ayh wouldna ha' guessed our firstborn ta look so like a dog," William teased.

One of the first things William had done after they went to housekeeping was to trade four acres of marsh for a mare he named Ginger, who was his pride and joy. Ginger's halter hung on the wall inside the house when it easily could have hung in the stable.

"I'm just relieved our bed isn't big enough for a horse!" Mary teased back.

Privately, she wondered if William himself would grow to be the size of one: his wedding clothes were already looking small. True to his word, though his size grew ever more fearsome, William was kind and gentle with her. She found herself happy enough married to him.

Just once she went back to the little clearing by the river. Her feet led her there—she couldn't help it. Had John Woodman been back since, she wondered? What if she were to find him there? The thought made her heart race. But the clearing was closed in by bushes thicker than ever, and the mossy tussock looked as if it had never been sat upon. It made her feel sad.

With Greylock as her constant companion, Mary spent hours of the day gathering plants in the surrounding meadows and woods. Collection basket over her shoulder, she watched the dog's lithe young form trot ahead of her, alert and sniffing the air, dashing off for brief excursions into the undergrowth. Her pharmacopeia grew, and she began to enjoy her life more than she ever had.

Mary went to Daniel's Creek almost daily in the heat of the summer. Its cool, clear waters still fanned out shallowly in the hidden cove, the bank as blanketed with pine needles as ever.

Only a few sunbeams reached the water this time of year, and the air was lovely and cool in the shade. She waded into the sandy shallows, the pull of the current and the nibble of minnows a delight against her legs. She watched Greylock frolic and swim into the deeper water, where the current moved faster. He was such a good swimmer that she didn't have to worry.

She practiced her feeling sense and found that much like breathing into the earth through her feet as Francis had once shown her, connecting with the earth deepened her awareness and offered a protection that was beyond explanation. Once, two wolves had appeared on the opposite bank, Greylock's hackles growing high. The wolves ignored them and moved away as soon as Mary grounded herself. Other times, she knew as soon as Greylock did, that they should turn around in their travels and not go any farther.

That summer, those to whom she gave her tonic flourished, healing quickly, sometimes miraculously. The sicker someone happened to be, the more powerfully it worked, bringing back many from the very brink. Mary found that her flower elixirs worked nicely with the tonic, bettering her patients' mind-set and emotions. It was easy for her to feel which remedy someone needed. She would pick the blooms fresh with morning dew and let them float in a bowl of spring water in her kitchen garden, the light and warmth of the sun transfusing their essence. Mary began to make reserves of these elixirs, preserving them in brandy.

The first very sick patient she used her tonic with was Richard Leader, the man who had come to the rescue of William in Boston Harbor, bringing him to Pascataway. Fetched by a servant to Leader's house at Strawbery Banke, Mary admired the multitude of hollyhocks that graced its garden gate. The Banke itself, now known as Portsmouth, looked much more like an English village than the rough settlement it had been years before.

Shown into a chamber behind the parlour, she found her charge delirious. "Ahhh . . . the great work," he said as she entered. "You must expect it exceeding black into the glass over fire . . ."

Leader's wife stood by his bedstead. "Please forgive his transgressions . . . The fever has disturbed him. His passion is alchemy, you see," she said almost as an apology. "I sent for you as some womenfolk here say you're quite clever."

"That's very kind of them," Mary said trying to conceal her excitement. *Alchemy—a kindred spirit. How wonderful!*

Her patient began to rant, his voice rising and falling in dramatic oration. "If it be not black, proceed no further, for it is unrecoverable: it must be as black as the raven's head."

Mary gave him a dose of her tonic laced with heal-all flower that she sensed he needed. Funny how her own alchemical panacea would be first used on a man yearning to discover alchemical secrets—God's natural magick. She wondered if he'd discovered anything special himself.

Mr. Leader quieted down for a minute before blurting, "Matter and composition doth begin to purge!"

Mary decided that, raving or not, she liked the man. Perhaps he would tout her remedy. Perhaps with such an interest, he would help her open the eyes of others to the healing powers of alchemy. She felt terribly excited.

"A stink like unto graves newly opened," came his voice, deadly serious. Then with a sighing finish of "That sign of perfect whiteness . . ." he drifted off to a steady slumber. Mary didn't even need the bayberry bark that she often used in a case like this.

It didn't take long for his feverish fit to pass, for the perfect whiteness of healing to take the place of the foul, black humors of his illness. To Mary's disappointment, Richard Leader did not recognize her healing work for the alchemy that it was. Still, Mary delighted that her tonic had proven itself an effective remedy, especially against fever and delirium. Young and childless, she was henceforth kept busier than ever by the womenfolk, many choosing her services over those of Dr. Fernald, the only schooled doctor of the region.

Sadly, Migwah's visit to her house that June was the last time Mary ever saw her mentor and friend. At the turn of the season, her father brought news of his passing. Greylock placed his head on Mary's lap and looked up at her, his eyes compassionate and forlorn.

Mary felt very alone.

As the fall turned to winter that year, William, such the slender youth at his arrival, continued to fill out until his muscular chest rivaled the size of a kilderkin. Few would be foolish enough to pick a fight with him now.

"What in heaven's name are you feeding him?" Mary's mother fussed. William had outgrown the set of clothes he had been married in and was now outgrowing another larger set besides.

"I wonder if we shall have to consult a sailmaker for his next shirt," Mary mused.

Her mother gave her a steely eye, not finding the joke so funny.

However light Mary made of William's growing size, there was something about him that did trouble her. She sensed a certain dissatisfaction in him, one that perhaps had been there all along—a particular look, an unseeing stare told her his heart was restless. He had really just been a boy at his arrival and had appreciated being taken care of by her parents more than anything. But now he began to look to other things, she sensed, dreams of his own making. It was only natural at Pascataway, seeing that those who went adventuring inland to trade with the Indians amassed fortunes. William had always done what was expected of him and more, and she knew he always tried hard to please her father. But what did he want for himself? She couldn't blame him. If she were a man, she would have gone off adventuring long ago, like Francis or John Woodman.

William arrived home one evening in March with a nasty head cold and a bad temper to boot. He'd worked on the river all day in the rain and sleet, floating the thawing mast pines to the dock in Portsmouth. Dangerous backbreaking work.

Mary had just set a strong spiced posset before him when Greylock looked up from his spot by the hearth and gave a whine and thump of his tail. That usually meant one of her family was near. Sure enough, a minute later the sharp rap of her father's walking stick sounded upon the front door.

Oh, please don't be coming for William—not on a night like this! She had a sinking feeling that was exactly what her father had in mind.

Her father entered, his usual energetic self, hat and cloak dripping wet from the weather and walking staff in hand.

"Please, Father, have a seat," she pressed. "I shall fix you a nice hot posset. The weather's not fit to be out in!"

He stood in the entryway and abruptly held up his hand. "No, my dear, no time for such. There's business to attend to." He looked to William, who sat staring fixedly over his mug into the firelight, hat off and wet hair sticking up wildly in all directions. "Will, I need you to go at once to Pommery Cove to fetch goods that arrived this afternoon on the *Eagle*. I'm afraid they might not last the night otherwise."

"Father," Mary pleaded, "Will's got a terrible cold. He's not fit to go."

"Nonsense! A man like him can hold his own. Come, William, let's suit up and be gone. Those casks are better locked in my storehouse sooner than later."

Mary watched helplessly as William rose slowly to his feet and gave his nose one good blow with his handkerchief. Without looking at either her or her father, William tied on his cloak and grabbed his hat, both of which were dripping wet, and followed her father out into the night.

Mary spent the evening awaiting his return. When three hours went by and there was no sign of him, she began to grow very anxious. *I really should have protested further against his going out. Father can be so hard and unreasonable when he has his mind set on something.*

She set down her sewing, and Greylock sat up with a whine. "Come Greylock, let's go to my parents' and see what could be keeping him."

She and Greylock made their way down the cart path in the dark. Sleet stung Mary's face, and the lantern flame danced and sputtered as the wind gusted violently. Tree branches lay across the cart path everywhere. It was indeed a wretched night to be out.

Her mother opened the door. "Mary, you shouldn't have come out in this!"

"Where's William? He's been gone for hours!" Mary stepped into the familiar warmth of her mother's kitchen.

"Your father has gone to look for him. He never should have called William out on a night like this, but you know how he gets. There's little one can do to change his mind. Your husband's as strong as two men put together."

Her mother fixed her a hot drink of mint and hyssop, and they sat waiting by the fire, the rest of the household asleep. The wind gusted forcefully, rattling the casements.

"A nor'easter for sure, tsk tsk," her mother assessed, shaking her head.

It must have been near midnight when they heard what sounded like a sea shanty above the wind. Greylock began to wag his tail. Mary stood. *That's William's voice, thank God!*

In he came, eyes half-closed, as wet as a drowned rat and hardly able to stand on his feet. Stumbling, he would have landed on his face if the great chair hadn't caught him. Her father followed him in, his mouth a grim set line.

The three of them barely managed to get William into the chair, where he sat smiling broadly and reeking of brandy before collapsing onto the table and passing out cold.

"What in the light of God is this?" Mary's mother gasped as William drooled like a baby on the table rug.

Mary had never seen her father so angry—well, maybe once. He paced the hall, pulling off his wet garb, shaking with rage. "I should call the constable!" He stormed. "My ungrateful son-in-law has defied my orders, squandered my goods, and is now so overtaken in drink he would drown himself in his cup!"

"John, calm thyself, dear," Mary's mother said, pulling up the other chair for him. "A cup of mint and hyssop will do you good."

"No, something stronger. *No*, not brandy—certainly not brandy!" he bellowed as Mary's mother made haste to pour his request.

William began to snore, oblivious. Her father's new servant, Thomas, appeared, groggy with sleep.

"Harness up the gelding, boy, and cart this oaf home," Mary's father commanded him. "I'll not have such debauchery under my roof!"

Needless to say, William was on his best behavior in the following weeks. And then when all had seemingly been forgotten, her father caught William gaming with friends at a tavern when he should have been returning from a delivery.

Mary could only stand quietly, cringing inside, as her father vented. William's actions were shameful and embarrassing, yet the control her father had over her husband was becoming ridiculous. William needed to be a man in his own right and not her father's errand boy.

In all fairness, there were others besides William who begrudged her father—some for the price they paid him for much-needed goods and others for the fact that he and his family always got first pick and never had to wait in line. And then there were those still seething from his year as constable as, true to her father's nature, he'd been most thorough. Grudges aside, her father's outspoken Anglican Royalist allegiance rubbed many across the river the wrong way. But her father was not alone when it came to this. Other old Anglican planters of the region also felt the effects of being steadily outnumbered by Puritans settling the area.

Through all of this, there were those who sympathized with and supported William. Lieutenant Raynes of the Kittery militia was one. He had high hopes for William's military career. All the Scots excelled here, and in recognition of their abilities, the town of Dover in 1656 granted those who had been freed from indenture parcels of land. William's grant lay across the river past the Cocheco Log Swamp and ran all the way back across the peninsula to the Back River. About the same time, Mary's father, not to be outdone, had the house and land he'd given William at his wedding formalized with a deed at a Kittery town meeting.

As time went by, the discord between Mary's husband and her father began to settle on its own. Partly because Mary's father now spoke to her and not to William when he disapproved of anything. A change that Mary did not particularly like, but one in which she could help keep the peace.

In April of 1656, the evil long feared by Mary's mother crept perniciously into the region. It slithered from tongue to tongue, bedding down with slugs and toads, until it had reached every doorstep in Pascataway and Goody Walford found herself accused of witchcraft. This was not the first time their friend had suffered such an accusation. The first time, only one person had accused her, and the court had fined them for slander. This time, seven people testified against her.

Seated at Mary's table, her mother looked pale and distraught as she was wont in such circumstances. "In light of what is happening in Portsmouth, we must be especially wary of what we say to the ill and their families."

"Of course, madam." Mary sliced the last of the soft overwintered beets from her root cellar. "What has Goody Walford been accused of this time?"

It's perfectly dreadful. Goody Trimmings is saying she heard a rustling one night, and Goody Walford stepped from the woods, dressed in a red waistcoat and petticoat, an old green apron, and a black hat. She says Goody Walford asked her for a pound of cotton. When Goody Trimmings refused, Goody Walford told her something terrible would happen because of it. Then Goody Trimmings says she felt a bolt of fire hit her back, and Goody Walford turned into a cat and vanished. This happened a fortnight ago, and Goody Trimmings is still having numbness in her legs.

Mary felt a chill run up her spine. The image of Goody Walford holding a witch bottle skyward that morning many years ago flashed before her eyes. Their friend was certainly very clever, but blameless, as they all were. "What can we do to help her?"

"Well, I'm afraid there's more terrible news that concerns all of us."

Mary stared at her mother. "What is it, madam?"

"Someone deposed to the court that Goody Walford belongs to a coven of witches who practice diabolical deeds up and down the river."

Mary set down her knife. "Certainly, that doesn't include us—unless healing the sick is considered diabolical?"

Her mother shook her head. "Mary, heed that we are both suspect. We must not assume people consider us blameless. Don't forgethow 'twas when we arrived. We must be extraordinarily careful."

"Mother, those we have healed and keep in good health would not wish us harm."

"My dear daughter, one would hope . . . People can be so quick to condemn, as well we know. I think witch bottles are in order."

This coming from her mother!

To protect themselves, Mary and her mother got to work, each making their own. Goody Walford must certainly have prepared one herself. Sharp, rusty pins and nails went into the bottles first to deflect negativity and ill fortune. Hair and nail clippings were added and brimstone for strength against the darkness. Then cloth hearts pierced with brass pins and sea salt for purification. A length of red ribbon for protection, as well as wine and urine. Finally, spit for consecration, and they sealed the stoppers with white wax.

At sunrise the next morning, they buried them on the southern hillside past Mary's father's orchard, facing Portsmouth. Any negativity directed toward Mary and her mother would be drawn to the witch bottles instead and thwarted.

That summer, Mary heard that John Woodman of Oyster River had married an Irish girl whose father had been the first settler to climb the Great Carbuncle, what the fishermen called the peak of shining white seen rising far inland from out at sea on a clear day. In the early years, the Carbuncle was rumored to have been made of diamonds and silver and was instrumental in attracting adventurers to the region.

Mary was happy for John, despite her own sadness and regret. She privately hoped that the fact that his wife's name was also Mary was not pure coincidence.

Much to Mary and her mother's profound relief, the witch bottles seemed to hold their own and nothing of consequence stemmed from the local witchcraft trial. Perhaps it was the fact that so many were accused or because the accused knew how to use witch bottles. Whatever the reason, Mary and her mother were grateful indeed.

Wary of slugs and toads, Mary resumed her focus on her physick and midwifery with more discretion until the day Greylock began to sniff at her peculiarly. Only when she found herself on her hands and knees, vomiting for no good reason, did she understand. Either the meadowsweet had failed her, or she'd been careless with the witch hazel. Whichever it was, it really didn't matter now. She was with child. Perhaps it was time anyway—she was not so young anymore. Mary eased her morning sickness with the black haw root Migwah had shown her before his death. She'd been treating other women with it ever since with good results.

William of course, was very happy with the news of her pregnancy, as was the rest of her family. But now that she was expecting, her father began to demand William's help more frequently again, taking him to task; and things grew tense between the two men once more.

In all of this, Mary decided it would be better to have her husband at home and not at her father's beck and call. Maybe, she thought, a little covert intervention on her part would help the situation. Her flower elixirs could work wonders.

She picked the blossoms early one morning. Buttercup for William's sense of self-worth and esteem, fairy lantern to ease his mind. What else could she find? The remedy called for something stronger. William needed a bit of gall, something that would fortify his resistance more substantially. She wandered about until she spied some pink yarrow growing at her feet in a rocky fissure—the perfect addition to balance William's sensitivity, strengthen his sense of self, and protect his heart.

That night, she readied his field jug for the morrow.

At seven o'clock in the morning, Mary made her way to her father's field, where William had been laboring since sunrise, raking the drying meadow hay into stooks.

William smiled to see her. She set his field jug in the shade and hung his breakfast basket from the branch of a tree. He wiped his brow and removed his sweat-soaked shirt, spreading it to dry in the sun. Then he walked uphill to meet her at the meadow's edge, slaking his thirst with a good swallow from the jug.

"How fare thee, my love?" he crooned, giving Mary and her midriff an affectionate glance.

"We are well. Please be careful in this heat."

"Must get this done, or we'll have your father to reckon with."

Mary had just disappeared back into the forest, headed for home, when she heard the familiar creak of her father's hay wain. Her father always seemed to know exactly when to arrive, for the stooks were now ready to be forked into the wain and carted away. Mary frowned. William hadn't yet had more than a bite to eat.

"Ho there, William!" she heard her father call. "No time for slacking when a man's got a baby on the way."

Mary stopped and returned to the forest's edge to watch, careful not to be seen.

William said nothing. Drinking from his jug, he walked back down into the field, set it down, and grabbed the pitchfork he'd left stuck in the ground. Still naked from the waist up, he began to fork the nearest stook into the wain. A weaker man might have reacted in anger a long time before with the way Mary's father treated him.

Her father stepped down to the ground. "You've an indecent amount of flesh showing, William." He looked away, surveying the field.

William normally would have made haste to put his shirt back on, but he did no such thing. He continued forking large heaps of hay into the wain. Mary could see the indiscretion did not gounnoticed. Meanwhile, William worked like a behemoth, his torso glistening with sweat.

Glaring at his son-in-law, Mary's father picked up the field jug William had left in the stubbled grass nearby. Taking a drink, he smacked his lips.

Oh dear, Mary thought.

"I said, William—if thou hast ears—get thy shirt back on, man!"

The back of William's neck grew dark red, but he continued tossing up pitchforks of hay, ignoring her father. Mary sensed William's Scottish heritage was being blamed for his behavior.

Glowering, Mary's father took yet another swallow from William's jug.

"Well, thou hast finally proved thyself capable when it comes to my daughter's happiness. Are thou taking care of all that needs to, boy? Can thou husband like a man?"

Her father's words brought Mary's hand to her heart.

William worked faster. Mary could plainly see he was trying to ignore her father's demeaning words and patronizing insult in using the familiar pronoun. This was a disaster. Mary could almost hear William's mind talking back, telling her father exactly what he thought of him. Then suddenly, still breathing hard, her husband stood still while her father continued to berate him.

"Thou should be thanking me I gave you Mary," her father ranted before he realized that barrel-chested William, whose arms andlegs were strong as tree trunks, stood glowering before him, holding the pitchfork by its shaft with its three prongs pointing directly at him.

Her father's mouth opened and shut noiselessly. He stepped backward.

"Hold thy tongue, manny!" William spoke in a slow, steady cadence through his clenched teeth. "I am neither thy servant nor thy son and perhaps more man than ye will e'er be!"

Mary was horrified. She watched the blood drain from her father's face. "How dare you speak to me in such a manner!" he sputtered, aghast, completely taken aback. "After all your dear mother and I have done for you, treating you like our own son!" His eyes were on the pitchfork William held.

"Done for me? Ye have kept me at thy beck and call as a servant. How can I possibly husband my own?" William snorted.

"*Ingratitude*! Oh, how it would crush your mother, and she so weak in body . . ."

Mary felt a pang of guilt to hear this. William ignored it, pressing his point.

"You have other servants and now Sarah's betrothed, Adrian. Why am I the one to always do thy bidding?"

"Nonsense. I use them as well as thee."

"Like hell thou do!" William stuck the pitchfork forcefully into the ground. Snatching up his shirt, he marched away, leaving his father-in-law with a meadowful of stooks to be loaded and carted to the barn.

Mary fled down the path toward home, hoping to get there first.

A fierce shame descended upon William. He, of course, was the one who would pay. He had been weak; he had lost control. It was inexcusable behavior. Mary took full blame for it herself, though she dared not tell William what part she had played.

John White's feathers were not easily smoothed, as incensed as he was. He took William to court for rebellion against him and Britania, that it might teach him a lesson through the sting of his pocket as well. William hadn't a chance; it was the old and established against the young and penniless. A bond of twenty pounds was taken out against his future good behavior, and he was fined thirty shillings plus the cost of the court, another five shillings.

The sum of money was a hard hit, but William's wealthy militia officer came to his rescue. Being on the younger side himself, he paid the thirty-five-shilling fine, much to William's surprise and gratitude.

"Only too glad to do it," Lieutenant Raynes explained later. "Don't like to see the deck stacked so unfairly, my goodman."

The silver lining in the whole affair was that Mary's father finally began to back off and respect William's boundaries. It was long overdue, and Mary and William both enjoyed the newfound peace.

"Welcome, Jane, and thank you for coming the distance," Mary's mother said to a visitor at her door one afternoon, a visitor Mary and her mother had been expecting.

A much older-looking Goody Walford than Mary remembered entered her mother's kitchen hall. Wearing a black hat and green waistcoat and petticoat, Goody Walford cut a dignified appearance despite the fact that her lean had worsened over the years.

"'Tis a pleasure, Britania. Thank you for inviting me. 'Tis God's will for certain," she said, nodding in reply to Mary's curtsy. "I see you are with child," she said.

Mary smoothed the visible bump in the front of her skirt with her hands. "Yes," she answered, smiling.

"And about time it is too," her mother said happily.

The women commenced their visit over peach pie and fresh-pressed perry.

"A blessing a neighbor was with me at home that fateful evening," Goody Walford told them. "The court dismissed the charges, but all those who accused me have not changed their minds. Many folk are still fearful—as is their wont to be, as ye well know. I'm glad Thomas is a selectman. Times have changed. There are those who would be more than happy to see us all hang. Delicious pie, Britania."

"Thank you, Jane. How well we know indeed," Mary's mother said. "I believe hearing of so many hangings of witches in years past has affected people's minds. They question whether our plantations are really immune."

"Our witch bottles are certainly working well," Mary said cheerfully, cutting into her pie with her spoon. "Perhaps some have come to their senses."

"Don't count on that, m' dear. Folks are fickle and not to be trusted," said Goody Walford. She took a sip of perry. "Matter of fact, years ago at Strawbery Banke, my daughter saw one from your own party pulling down the fence that housed those sheep."

"What?" Mary and her mother cried in unison.

"Yes, indeed. We didn't tell you as we thought it best to keep what we'd seen as recompense." She cocked an accusing eyebrow in Mary's direction. "In case a sneaky little maid were to wag her tongue about what she'd seen."

Mary blushed. Goody Walford *had* recognized her those many years ago! How embarrassing.

"For heaven's sake, Jane, *who* would have pulled down that fence?" Mary's mother said in disbelief.

"Was one o' the maidservants—the tetchy one with the sour face and dark hair," Goody Walford said with a nod.

-- 22 --

The Quaker Women

On a cold, frosty evening in early January 1659, Mary's first child, John Thompson, was born. Mary thought he looked just like William, his big blue eyes following her around. She was pregnant soon again, and William II followed—cherubic, his head soft with blond peach fuzz. The great magick and mystery of how a woman could lie with a man and create such perfect little human beings? Birth was a sacred, divine miracle. It disturbed her beyond measure to think that some were so frightened by it that they thought it evil; a husband killing his wife and newborn child in a fit of terror after witnessing the birth was not unknown. One more reason midwifery was so important.

Mary no longer bothered with the meadowsweet root. Being a mother was the pinnacle and greatest blessing of every woman's life, and in this, she was no exception. It meant less time for gathering herbs and healing neighbors and more time spent washing, feeding, and taking care of her own; but the rewards of motherhood outweighed it all. William took great pride. He worked harder, taking on extra jobs on the river to cover the added expenses of food and clothing.

During these years, great change was afoot in Old England. Oliver Cromwell's Commonwealth had come to an end with his death, and the Crown had been restored. Repercussions swept through the colonies, the Royalists as delighted as the Puritans were unhappy. But Puritan and Royalist alike grumbled when New England merchants suddenly found themselves subject to taxes and restrictions once again under the authority of the new king, Charles II.

Those in New England who challenged the power structure of the Puritan church and the Massachusetts Bay government were seen as increasingly more threatening. The Quaker, Mary Dyer, fighting to repeal "the wicked law of religious intolerance" with her martyrdom, was hanged on Boston Common—a warning to others who followed the Quaker path and its "blasphemous negating of authority." And as though for good measure, three more witches were tried and hanged in Hartford, Connecticut.

William and Mary, like the rest of Mary's family, attended the Shapleighs' Kittery House chapel every Sabbath. The Shapleighs boarded the reverend and his family, to whom the Kittery Anglican community paid a tithe. Uncle Samuel and Rebekah were the only family not in attendance as they had joined the new Congregational, or Puritan, meetinghouse across the river.

On a Sabbath in early December 1663, when Mary's boys were very small, two Quaker women visited the Kittery chapel: Mary Tompkins, a tall kind-faced woman, and Alice Ambrose, who, though being little and crooked, was bright and sunny with what she professed to be the Spirit of the Lord.

Mary was intrigued, and she was in good company; there was gossip all over Kittery as to what had occurred when the two Quaker women had visited Dover. Word was the doctrine the women preached had left Dover's Reverend Reyner speechless and fretting without proper refutation. This didn't trouble the Kittery Anglican community in the least. After all, they already knew the Puritan doctrine to be flawed.

Mary found the Quaker women's manner kind and gentle. However, they did not remove their hats in greeting to anyone. The fact that this caused offense to many in the congregation became apparent soon enough.

"Master Millet, I wonder if you'd be so kind as to discourse with our guests? I'm quite curious to hear what they have to say," Nicolas Shapleigh requested enthusiastically after the service. Nicolas was always ready to give anyone their fair shake.

A hush descended upon the fifty-odd parishioners crowded into the small second-floor chapel.

"Goodman Millet," Mary Tompkins addressed the reverend straightaway before he could respond, "thou art a minister of Christ?"

"But of course I am a minister of Christ," he answered.

"If so, thou wouldst not own such a title," Mary Tompkins replied, shaking her head with great seriousness.

Reverend Millet's expression clouded. "I have heard that ye deny magistrates and ministers and the churches of Christ."

"Thou sayest so," Mary Tompkins replied calmly.

"And ye deny the three persons in the Trinity," Millet continued.

To which Mary Tompkins, in answer, spoke to the congregation, who sat listening in rapt silence. "Take notice, people, that this man falsely accuseth us. For godly magistrates and ministers we own, and the churches of Christ we own, and that there are three that bear the record in heaven—which three are the Father, Word, and Spirit—that we own." She turned back to Millet. "But for three *persons* in the Trinity, that is for thee to prove."

"I will prove three persons in the Trinity," the Reverend Millet said hotly.

"Thou sayest so," said Alice Ambrose sunnily, "but prove it by the scriptures."

"Yes," he replied. "By this, I will prove it: where it is said, '*And he is the express image of his Father's person.*'"

"But," Alice said, "that is falsely translated."

"Yes, that's true," Nicolas Shapleigh interjected. "In Greek, it is not *person*, but *substance*."

"But," said Millet, "it is *person*, and so there is *one* person!" The reverend was looking pretty flustered now. Mary felt sorry for him.

"Thou sayest so," said Alice, "but prove the other two if thou canst."

"There are three *somethings*," Millet blurted, whereupon he threw up his hands and stomped out of the room. "These women are wolves. I won't put up with it!"

"Come back! Do not leave thy people amongst them thou call *wolves*!" Mary Tompkins called after him. The reverend kept going, the sound of his footfalls stamping down the stairs. She turned and addressed the room. "Is this not the hireling that fleeth and leaveth his flock?"

The congregation burst into argument amongst themselves until three burly men scooped up Mary Tompkins, and making towards the door, threw her down the stairs headfirst.

"Stop it at once!" Nicolas Shapleigh cried, but too late.

Hearing a dreadful thump and bump, Mary hurried over to the doorway, peering past the men, not knowing what she'd find. To her amazement, the tall Quaker woman was standing on her feet at the bottom, brushing herself off and seemingly unhurt.

"God protects His children!" Mary Tompkins cried, her voice clear and triumphant as she climbed back up the narrow staircase.

"'Twould have broken her neck if she wasn't a witch," one of the men said to the other two.

As Mary Tompkins reached the top of the stairway, the three men caught hold of her again and cast her down the stairs a second time. This time, she did not get up.

"I'm outraged!" Nicolas Shapleigh cried, pushing through the congregation to the top of the stairs. "Manhandling God's servant in the Lord's chapel—I'm *sorely affronted*!"

Mary squeezed past the knot of confused men and flew down the stairs to where Mary Tompkins was seated at the bottom. One of her arms seemed to be injured, but there was a smile upon her face. "Aye, the Spirit has kept me from grievous harm yet again."

But Mary was not so certain. She helped Mary Tompkins to her feet as the parishioners filed out. She noticed many cast the woman a sympathetic eye, though some glared angrily, including her own father. A few even scowled at her too.

"If it please you, Goody Tompkins and Goody Ambrose, I would be delighted to receive you as our guests so that I might make amends for such uncouth and ungodly behavior," Nicolas Shapleigh said, beside himself with embarrassment.

Mary stayed behind at Kittery House while William took their boys back home. She made a poultice for Mary Tompkin's bruised and swollen elbow with what comfrey and calendula Goody Shapleigh had on hand, adding some fresh bugleweed she found growing outside the chapel door. She soon saw that Nicolas and Alice Shapleigh were as interested as she was in what the women had to say. The Spirit that flowered in these women was unmatched by any they had ever seen.

The very next Saturday afternoon, Mary's father paced the length of her kitchen hall, his staff in hand. As it was baking day, the table was covered with cooling pies and loaves of bread. Mary held her youngest little Will, while her eldest John stood by her skirt behind the table, out of his grandfather's way.

"*How dare he*!" her father stormed, but Mary didn't mind. For once her father was not disparaging her husband, and she found it a relief despite his agitation.

"Alexander would roll over in his grave!" he ranted. "His son, *a Quaker*! Reverend Millet let go—our chapel gone to Sodom! What's an Anglican to do? And we thought the Puritans were a problem! Huh . . . they're no match for these women!"

Mary's boys watched their grandfather pace, his staff thumping hard against the wood floor with every other step.

"Surely, Reverend Millet will agree to preach in one of our homes?" Mary suggested, trying to calm him down.

"Agree? The man's pride is scathed. He and his family left Kittery two days ago. The reverend vowed to return to England rather than suffer any more ridicule. I can't blame him."

"I'm sorry to hear that, sir."

Greylock's behavior and the click of the door latch told her William had arrived home. But if William was surprised to see her father, he didn't show it. He hung his musket and Ginger's bridle upon the wall. "Good afternoon, John. You look fit to club a man o'er t' head w' that stick o' yourn," he joked.

This only served to send Mary's father into another five-minute tirade.

William did his best to placate. Mary could tell he too was delighted not to be the subject of his father-in-law's wrath. "I give you my word, John, we've no intention of becoming Quakers."

Excitement flopped like a dying fish in Mary's breast. On the contrary, she was quite interested and had been meaning to talk with

William about it. *Oh, why did he have to say such a thing?* Little Will struggled to get down. She let him go. Her father had stopped his pacing and thumping.

Mary's brother-in-law, Adrian Frye, had no such qualms. Mary was glad she hadn't been with her father when he found out Adrian and Sarah had decided to give the Quaker faith a try.

The authorities across the river in Dover reacted the worst to the Quakers. Called back out to Kittery House on a cold and snowy December day, Mary found Mary Tompkins, Alice Ambrose, and a third woman, Ann Coleman, in a terrible state. The deputy of Dover, Captain Richard Waldron, had ordered them stripped naked from the waist upward, tied to the back of a cart, and cruelly whipped in the freezing cold and snow. Their nemesis the Reverend Reyner, and others stood by, laughing vengefully. But that was only the beginning. They were to be taken through a total of eleven towns, whipped in a similar fashion in each until they had left the Massachusetts Bay jurisdiction. Fortunately, at the third town, Captain Walter Barefoot who accompanied them, managed to become the constable's deputy. Receiving the warrant, he set them at their liberty and brought them back up to Major Shapleigh's. Captain Barefoot and Nicolas Shapleigh were friends.

Mary found the Quaker women singing happily together as they sat wrapped under blankets at the hearth.

"Here she is, Mary Thompson, the one to patch our wounds."

"Nice to meet you, Mary. I've heard many wonderful things about you," said Ann Coleman, a very attractive younger woman.

The three were so cheerful that Mary was completely unprepared for what she found beneath the blankets. Their flesh had been brutalized with a corded whip that cut through the skin, in some places right to the bone. She tenderly washed their wounds with yarrow and comfrey and loosely bandaged them with clean cloth that Alice Shapleigh provided. Mary had known men with less than half so many stripes to cry out, but not these women. They sang and laughed, oblivious to the pain. Nonetheless, she gave each of them a cup of nettle mixed with her tonic and laced with pain-relieving impatiens elixir.

"I wouldn't let Captain Barefoot touch us after receiving such wonderful care for my elbow, sister." Mary Tompkins smiled.

No wonder Captain Barefoot had been less than friendly as she arrived. He'd ridden off in a huff. It would embarrass him terribly to have his services refused in front of the Shapleighs, especially as he'd been the one to free the women from their sufferings. He was a surgeon—handy for amputation or the pulling of teeth or even the cutting of hair, but not for physick. Captain Barefoot liked to think otherwise since Dr. Fernald had died and old Dr. Reynolds had sailed back to England, leaving Pascataway without a physician.

Mary was proud of the fact that more families across the river in Dover had started to call on her. There were at least a dozen herbwomen at Pascataway now, including her mother. Her practice was still growing because her patients got better. If they had a will to live, she could save them, and saving them was what made her feel better than anything else.

Mary's Quaker friends were hardly on the mend when the wife of Richard Waldron, the Dover deputy responsible for the women's gross abuse, called for Mary to treat an ill servant. Mary went for the servant's sake.

"He's not used to such climate," another household servant told her, escorting her into a back extension off the kitchen. "He's come from the West Indies. Salomon is his name."

The man lay shivering under a thin blanket near the hearth, his coal-black face slick with sweat. Wiry gray hair curled at his temples, though his body looked as fit and strong as someone much younger. His fever was building, and Mary could tell he was freezing cold.

She turned to the maidservant. "Please bring a sheet and more blankets. He needs to stay as warm as possible until his fever breaks."

Mary wrung out a clean cloth in a basin of hot water and gently wiped his face. He looked up at her, barely able to crack open his bloodshot eyes. "I will have you well soon, Salomon." She smiled and patted his arm. She diluted syrups ofburdock, bayberry, and yarrow in a cup of warm water and added a good dose of her tonic and self-heal. Salomon was shivering so violently that his teeth clacked audibly on the rim of the cup, but he drank her medicine down. Mary had no sooner dosed him and covered him warmly than the master of the house arrived with Captain Barefoot.

"He's the best one I've got, and I'd loathe to lose him. Spare nothing 'til he's sound," boomed Richard Waldron.

"I'll see to it immediately," Captain Barefoot assured him.

If Captain Barefoot was surprised to see Mary, he didn't show it. She was certainly surprised to see him. *Surely, Richard Waldron is aware that Walter Barefoot violated his warrant with the Quaker women?* Strange how Walter seemed to keep in good graces with both Nicolas Shapleigh and Richard Waldron when those two men were at such odds with each other.

"Ah! Here's my patient," Captain Barefoot said. "Not looking so cleverly, is he?" Ignoring Mary, he pushed her herb basket to the back side of the table and set his surgeon's case down in its place. Captain Waldron stood watching near the door, an intimidating presence if ever there was one.

Mary noted Salomon's shivering was already subsiding. She went about her business, determined to stay, regardless. She refreshed the cloth on her patient's forehead, wondering what sort of miscommunication had led to both her and Walter being summoned.

"Surgeon Barefoot has arrived. Ye clear out so he might treat his patient!" Waldron commanded.

The servant girl backed away, her eyes on the floor. As she slipped out through the door, Goody Waldron brushed past her and into the room.

"Husband, I've brought in Mary Thompson, the renowned herbwoman from Kittery."

Captain Waldron's brow raised slightly, and he cast an appraising eye in Mary's direction. Behind his cold expression, she sensed a powerful shrewdness as well as something dark and disturbing. She curtsied politely, lowering her eyelids.

"Humph . . . very well. As long as she does not impede Captain Barefoot." He turned on his heel and exited the room as though his mind were already on matters of greater import.

Goody Waldron walked over to her sick manservant. She seemed a kind woman, opposite in many ways to her husband. She looked down at Salomon with a pitying face, her arms folded beneath her shawl. "'Tis a shame he doesn't speak English."

Meanwhile, Walter Barefoot went to work. He opened the lid to his surgeon's chest, revealing a lineup of knives, calipers, saws, and gouges terrible to behold. "Oh yes, my *lovelies* . . ." he crooned. "Won't be needing all of you here, but one never knows!" He ran a forefinger over their shafts before stopping on a sharp knifelike lancet. He pulled it from its fastening, and held it up, admiring it.

Salomon's eyes opened wide, and he began to shake violently again, much to Mary's chagrin. Walter Barefoot tapped the blade with his finger. Then setting the lancet down upon the table, he turned to his patient, assessing him from afar in an inscrutable manner.

"Looks like a little bleeding would indeed be most benefic," he discerned.

"Oh dear," Goody Waldron said nervously, looking from Mary to the surgeon and back.

How predictable, Mary thought angrily. "Captain Barefoot, he's already been remedied. A good rest is what he needs most."

"I have to agree with Goody Thompson," Goody Waldron nodded. "Captain Barefoot, why don't you come to the parlour for a little refreshment?"

Walter Barefoot ignored the invitation. He pulled on his collar and cleared his throat. "I've been hired to do as I see fit, mistress. Now if you will kindly fetch me a bowl, I will purge his blood." He picked up the lancet with an ominous frown and advanced.

Mary started to rise to her feet, but Salomon reached out, which must have been difficult in his condition. He gripped her arm. "Nooooaa!" he protested.

"Now, now, thy master knows what's best for thee." Walter Barefoot began prodding with a finger for a good vein on the man's foot.

Salomon disagreed. Weak with fever or not, one well-placed kick with his muscular legs sent Walter Barefoot flying straight backward into a cupboard with such force that a heavy brass mortar fell from an upper shelf right upon the crown of the surgeon's head. He slumped to the floor as though all the life had gone out of him.

"Oh, Lord have mercy!" cried Goody Waldron, dropping the bowl she had chosen, which smashed to pieces at her feet.

She and Mary dashed over to where the very still Walter Barefoot lay, his stubborn, authoritative personality reduced to a quiet nothingness. Mary loosened his collar, feeling for his pulse. "He's fine—just struck into a stupor."

Goody Waldron drew a breath of relief.

"I see I've got two patients now," Mary said with a little smile.

Over the next several days, Mary nursed Salomon back to health. She liked him; he had a singular depth about him that resonated with her. Then she learned from a household servant that Salomon was not indentured as the rest of them were. He was a slave.

It was common practice to sell one's self into indenture for survival's sake, but to have one's freedom permanently taken against one's will? On whose authority? God would not condone such behavior. It made no sense to her no matter how she looked at it, and the more she thought about it, the more incensed she became. It was a violation of the most outrageous sort. An evil, contrived act of dominance that only served the slave owner in becoming richer and lazier.

As Salomon learned to speak English, Mary learned that he came from a long line of African witch doctors. His tribe had been conquered by a neighboring tribe when he was a boy. Sold to Dutch traders, he'd been brought to a sugarcane plantation in the West Indies.

Despite some outspoken criticism, Mary learned that other wealthy merchants of the area had begun to quietly collect human possessions—Africans who had been conquered and enslaved by their fellow countrymen and then sold to white traders. But in Africa, no one was expected to be a slave for life.

Mary was called out in the wee hours to treat the Quaker women yet again before their wounds had even healed. How much longer could they take such abuse and come away with their lives? In the Shapleigh kitchen hall next to a blazing hearth, she cleaned and anointed the cuts and bruises on Alice's face, abdomen, and arms.

"Two burly brothers, the constables, each held one of my arms and dragged me facedown through the snow over tree stumps and bushes for over a mile," Alice told her. "Their elderly father followed behind them, crying and lamenting that he was the father of such wicked children."

Mary listened with a clenched jaw. Alice looked as if she'd been beaten with a stick! The Dover constables were John Roberts and his brother. Their behavior didn't surprise Mary at all.

"Their poor father is a kind and just man," Mary Tompkins added. "But they ignored him shamelessly and fetched us all one at a time to Thomas Canney's house—oh, another wicked one—where we were denied food and treated ill. Then yesterday morning, they dragged us down the steepest part of the hill, through the deep snow to the river—me on my back over stumps."

Mary peered down the back of Mary Tompkin's smock to see extensive purplish-black and green, and her healing stripes reopened. The woman continued, "They said, 'They would now do such with us that we would trouble them no more.' And when Alice refused to get into the canoe, they threw her into the water!"

"Thank the grace of God that I can swim," Alice added with good humor.

It amazed Mary to see that these women really were unfazed by their sufferings. That the light of the Spirit so filled them that they actually thrived on such martyrdom. No one could force them to think or be to his satisfaction. What joy and freedom were theirs! God did not judge them but danced among them, supported them, loved them—the enlightenment of which was profoundly dizzying. An intense desire to join them flooded Mary's being.

"Well, 'tis miracle enough the cold water didn't kill you alone," Ann Coleman cried. "They meant to take us down to the river mouth and cast us out to sea. But they didn't get far, for a tempest suddenly arose, and they were forced to turn back with us, keeping us prisoners at Thomas Canney's again in a cold chamber. Alice's clothes froze like boards!"

"Yet the Lord protected us so we were not killed," Mary Tompkins finished. "For they turned us out into the bitter cold and snow at midnight, thinking to have dispatched us by such wickedness. The hand of the Lord who keeps those who wait upon Him has preserved and upheld us, and we find ourselves again well provided for at Kittery House."

It was the last time Mary would ever see these three brave women who all but burst at the seams with verve and Spirit, though tales of their exploits reached her ears from time to time: trials in the stocks at Hampton, mishaps at Newbury, and surviving Boston surely by divine intervention before heading south for New Amsterdam and Virginia.

Mary might have joined them were it not for her children. She made her way home later that morning along the cart path. Fresh snow had fallen overnight, deep enough to have protected her Quaker friends from the stumps had it fallen the day before.

Ann, Mary, and Alice's Spirit left Mary uplifted and resolute, full of passion and energy. The women spoke their truth so fearlessly. Oh, how good that would be, she thought. It occurred to her that she *could* speak her truth. She didn't have to run off with the Quakers. She already had the respect and admiration of so many. *If they can do it, so can I!* Resolution burned through her—she too would speak her truth. She'd always known all things were equal in God's eyes.

Ahead of her along the cart path came two horse and riders. Side by side, they each followed the broken snow made by the runners of a sleigh. Mary recognized the bay mares instantly and sensed the arrogant pride and self-righteousness that projected from the cloaked riders like the advance of an army. It was Captain Richard Waldron and Reverend Reyner, the sight of whom usually struck fear into the hearts of Kittery inhabitants.

They must be on their way to Kittery House, Mary thought. She wished she could warn Nicolas, but he could hold his own. After all, his sister had married into Dover's founding patriarchy. Family ties interwove both sides of the river.

It was customary for a woman who was not of noble birth to give way to a man on the road no matter how low his status. To step aside so that he might pass, averting her eyes for modesty's sake, was something that was taken for granted by even the very least of men.

Loath to be swallowed by a snowfall deeper than her waist, Mary kept right on walking into the path of the oncoming horse and rider, which happened to be the reverend. She greeted the men as they grew close, looking straight into their faces with a peaceful conviction.

"Good morrow, gentlemen. The snow is beautiful in the trees, is it not?"

With a very unecclesiastical curse, Reverend Reyner reined his horse up onto its haunches to fall back behind Captain Waldron's. Mary continued up the snowy lane, hidden behind her long hooded cloak. She could feel the men's bewilderment and anger, but something had changed: she no longer cared.

Two days later, Mary was returning home early in the morning from a sick call. In hindsight, she should've turned back to her neighbor's house when she saw the set of fresh cat tracks crossing the path a quarter mile back. It was too late now. She could sense its raw wildness before she even knew it was near.

She stopped, every nerve in her body on alert. A movement of snow up in the woods to her right caught her eye. Then she saw it, motionless on the rise above her. Enormous and tawny, its eyes golden, white muzzle and tufts at the ears. *Oh, why did I leave Greylock at home?*

It came toward her, its movement liquid, its gigantic paws weaving an undulating line. She'd never come face-to-face with such a large unpredictable predator. It stopped about ten feet from her and began to walk an arc around her.

Intuitively, Mary knew her fear could only hurt her. She relaxed and connected her heart with the earth through her feet. There was nothing else she could do. The catamount stopped then and stared back at her. *It* certainly wasn't afraid.

They stared at each other for a short while. Then the big cat gave its chest a quick lick and, with a whirring noise, leapt off into the woods across the trail. Mary stood still for another minute to be sure the cat had truly moved on before she continued on her way.

The animal had been there to tell her something, that she was sure of.

She would need to be fearless.

-- 23 --

Portent of Disaster

The gathering of women, seated on forms and chairs, filled Mary's kitchen hall. They looked up expectantly at Mary as she stood in front of them, curious as to why she'd called them all together.

"Dear friends," she began, "I will start by saying that my heart has called me to reach out to all of you. Truth be told, and strange as it may sound, we've been taught to repress our inherent wisdom." The familiar faces of her neighbors stared back blankly, confused or downright uncomfortable—her words were almost unthinkable to those primarily concerned with survival and the daily duties of feeding and clothing their families. Still, she pressed on.

"We have turned away from our natural connection to all that is: the earth, the animals, even from each other. 'Tis what Christ meant when He said we must be as little children—to come from our hearts with love and grace, not with fear and judgment—to access the kingdom of heaven."

The fire crackled and popped loudly on the cob irons.

"Does not God's wrath hold any fear for you?" a neighbor questioned, Mary's discourse ringing of blasphemy to many of those present.

"God is not to be feared, nor is He wrathful but is an intensely loving real presence inside of us all and everything that exists, whether acknowledged or not."

"I agree with Mary," said Sarah, the only family member present. "Just look at the Quakers—they understand this. They don't need a priest to connect to God or tout a covenant of works for our salvation. 'Tis through divine grace we aspire to the Kingdom of Heaven."

All knew what suffering the Quakers endured, how the laws of the land proclaimed against them. Yet how they rose above this time and time again defied explanation.

Mary nodded, smiling at her sister. *It is wonderful that Sarah understands.*

"Us women are taught to be afraid," she continued, "and forced to abide by the laws of our society without question. Why, even Native women have more say than we English! All an Indian woman has to do to end her marriage is leave her husband's moccasins outside the wigwam."

The women tittered to hear this.

"And such a loving, grace-filled God would never desire His beloved children to enslave one another." Mary could sense her last words angered some. No matter, she thought. Infused with direction and purpose, her stature would surely support her until enough had opened their eyes. Spirit was on her side.

Indeed, Mary might have found herself in entirely different circumstances if her knack for healing hadn't garnered her neighbors' appreciation and loyalty. They readily put up with her idiosyncrasies in exchange for her physick. Only from Mary's own relations—namely, Rebekah—did she ever have any sort of trouble, and mostly of the slanderous kind. Darts still flew covertly from Rebekah's prating lips to those who would listen, or so others told her. Mary was glad Sarah had come to her senses and long since quit the friendship.

A handful of the women present understood what Mary was saying. It was a quiet awakening of sorts, involving only a few households on both sides of the river. The women talked amongst themselves, most too afraid to instill any real change at all, but talk they did. However, Goody Pinkham of Dover became quite passionate about it all—not only leaving her husband but also walking out of the Dover meetinghouse in a huff during Reverend Reyner's sermon. As a result, she was sentenced to sit in the town stocks. Mary and the other goodwives sat with her to ease her pain, to which the Dover constable wisely turned a blind eye.

"Mistress Mah-re!" a voice called. Mary looked up from gathering pickleweed on the riverbank to see a boat gliding toward her.

It was Salomon grinning over his shoulder, trailing a fishing line behind the boat. The African looked happy, his grizzled locks worn up under a Monmouth cap. Mary adored him. In Salomon she'd found not only a kindred spirit, but also a man who respected her as an equal, as Migwah had done.

"Salomon," she greeted. "You're fishing?" She hadn't seen him out in a boat before.

"Oh yes, Ayh've got to catch m'self supper."

"Richard Waldron doesn't feed you?"

"No more he does."

"What?"

Salomon laughed, showing his fine white teeth. "Ayh'm a freeman now."

"You are?"

"Mister Waldron's heart seized up, so Ayh simply boiled him some willow bark. Now would ye look at me—a freeman with a piece o' land down by the river—a wigwam, a garden, and this here ole fishin' boat."

"Oh! Salomon, your news has made my day. I'm so happy for you!" Perhaps Mr. Waldron was coming to his senses after all.

"But, Mah-re, Ayh'm concerned 'bout you." Salomon's smile faded. "You got the menfolk over on mah side o' the river stirred up, an' Ayh don't like the looks of it."

"I know, Salomon." She sighed. "You're a freeman now, but I'm not a freewoman, am I?"

Mary's beliefs were no great surprise to those who knew her. Passing goodwives squawked indignantly to see Mary's children hanging out of trees or spending hours of the day building miniature villages of sticks and stones in the dooryard. Such idleness was deemed sinful to those used to seeing small children drop spinning wool for hours on end or shelling peas until their fingers bled. And then there were the animals: all manner of furry or reptilian creatures injured by plow or scythe, nests brought down by felling trees, a young thing left orphaned by a planter's dog. Despite the raised brows, Mary took care of them all, allowing them to mend before releasing them back to the wild.

Motherhood was as unsuccessful in keeping Mary housebound as marriage had been, even after her third child Robert was born. She would take her three little boys with her while wildcrafting in the woods and meadows. She loved to play "Babes in the Woods" with them, the popular English ballad of two little children lost in the woods who die of cold and hunger. Mary delighted in watching her "fair innocents" totter along behind her, struggling through the vines and brambles. It made the heart-wrenching story more real to her and gave her the emotional satisfaction of changing the ending.

John who knew the game well by now, proudly pushed through the bushes behind her, being tall enough to see his way, while Willy valiantly made his way along behind John as best he could. Little Robert struggled to keep up with Willy, then lost sight of his brother and began to wail, his gown all caught up in a brier. Lost until Mary's arms swooped down to the rescue, kissing his berry-stained face.

The creek was one of her boys' favorite places to go. On the path winding through the meadow, they would first gorge themselves on blackberries, Greylock scouting ahead, rousting out critters. Then in the shade of the great old white pines that grew along the creek's bank, they would remove their shoes and stockings and wade into the cool water, splashing and trying to catch minnows. It was shallow enough in the little cove for all to enjoy it safely. They were forbidden to go near the creek's middle, where it became deeper and the current was strongest. Greylock was the only member of their party who knew how to swim, and swim the beloved dog did, shaking the water out of his coat to the screams and laughter of the boys.

One August day, Mary and her boys spent an afternoon at her parent's home. Mary helped her mother put up preserves from the orchard while the boys had a marvelous time picking fruit, playing, and exploring. Upon leaving of course, they had to inspect the Indian cairn, another favorite thing to do.

"Ooh, look at that scary bone! Is it a person's?" her son John asked.

"Willy, remember not to touch. No, John, they're all animal bones. Remember, boys, you're *never* to touch anything here. The Indians have placed everything just so, and it might give a very wrong message if it's disturbed."

"Mother, John found a special rock today," Willy said.

"He did?"

"Yes, Mother, look!" John said proudly. He held up a beautiful piece of heart-shaped amethyst with clear purple crystals. The rock looked startlingly familiar.

"That's lovely, John. Wherever did you find it?"

"We found a secret place," Willy chimed in.

"You did? Where?"

"Mother, it's our *secret* place," John explained.

"Yes, our *secret* place down by the river," Willy added enthusiastically.

"I see. Can I see the rock again, my darling?"

Mary took it in her hands. It had been years since she'd held it. She knew exactly where the boys had found it and where their secret place was. "It's a special rock, indeed," she said, handing it back to her eldest, looking away to conceal her emotion. She wondered how life was treating John Woodman. She had heard he'd had children too.

The following summer, a boy of twelve, a neighbor's child, sat in Mary's kitchen hall. He had a fishhook sunk through his thumb and was trembling from fright.

"This'll teach ye to be so clumsy, Reform!" his mother barked. "I figure ye can do something, Goody Thompson?"

"I will certainly try," Mary said.

"Better than fetching the surgeon Barefoot," the woman said to her son with an ominous laugh. Then she turned to Mary. "Reform's scared to death of 'im! Your time is coming nigh, I see."

Mary smoothed her round tummy. "A few more months, God willing. Now, Reform"—she placed a soothing hand on the boy's shoulder—"calm thyself, dear. Let me take a look, just a look. I'm not going to touch it just yet."

She gently examined his thumb: the flesh was red and swollen, and the sharp iron hook had gone clean through next to the bone. The barb would definitely need to be removed to extract the hook without grievous damage.

Mixing a dose of chamomile with a large dollop of honey, Mary added her heal-all elixir to clear the boy's shock. Reform drank it down without complaint, and when he'd calmed significantly, she took up the shears William used for trimming his homemade iron nails. Reform looked away, biting his lip.

John, Willy, and Robert were crowding around in innocent fascination. "Shoo, outside please," she ordered.

Holding the shaft of the hook as steady as she could, Mary pressed the shears firmly together. To her surprise, the barb snipped right off, ringing against a crock and falling to the floor. Greylock rose to his feet and stuck his nose at it with a wag of his tail.

John, who'd not gone far, picked it up and handed it to Reform. "Here's the tip if you want to save it."

"And here's . . . the rest of it." Mary pulled the hook out before Reform even knew it. Smiling, she set it down on the table in front of him. Then she gently cleansed the wound with her comfrey tincture before applying a thick layer of her plantain salve and tying it up with a strip of clean cloth. Reform looked much relieved.

The sound of a cantering horse on the road reached their ears. No one paid much attention to it until it stopped in front of the gate. A brisk knock sounded upon the door. "I've come to fetch you, Mary," the rider said. "Reverend Reyner of Dover has taken ill. He's asked for you to come."

Mary found the reverend low indeed. His wife, who was kneeling at his bedside, stood to greet Mary as she entered the room. Mary could tell by Goody Reyner's expression that she expected the worst. Her husband lay so still and pale as though death had already claimed him.

"Dr. Barefoot has been here and done what he could," she said, her eyes unfocused and distant. She clutched an embossed Bible to her breast. "My husband asked for you." The woman knelt back down near the foot of the bedstead, praying silently.

An illness involving the kidneys. One, Mary gathered, the reverend had suffered for some time. The servant who fetched her had told her the dose of calomel, which usually brought him around, had failed to do so. He had been bled, purged, and bled again, all the while growing weaker.

Mary brewed up a strong infusion of couch grass, bearberry, parsley, and horsetail along with her tonic and elixirs. As the evening progressed, she was pleased to see her medicine begin to put some semblance of life back into the reverend's complexion.

As the light of dawn filtered into the room, with her patient still alive and sleeping peacefully, Mary allowed herself to doze off on the chair that had been provided for her. It was terribly hard not to lie down and sleep this far along in her pregnancy. It felt like she had just closed her eyes when she was roused by the sound of the reverend struggling to get up. She supported his elbow, helping to steady him as he rose in his nightshirt to make use of the chamber pot. Miraculously, there was no longer any blood in his urine. He would make it, at least this time.

"Reverend Reyner, I'm glad to see you're getting better," she told him. "You must rest now and continue my medicine."

He lay back down on his bolster with a groan.

As Mary busied herself in the hearth, building up the fire and reheating his medicine, she could feel the reverend's eyes upon her. "Thank you for coming, especially in your condition," he said. His voice sounded weak and unexpectedly mild.

Mary smoothed her burgeoning midriff with some embarrassment, but she could see that he sincerely meant what he'd said. "You're welcome."

The reverend's eyes, lit brightly by the fire, were red rimmed and watery beneath his hoary brow. He looked a far cry from the proud and arrogant man she saw in public, one of the most influential citizens of Dover. Possibilities ran through her mind. If she spoke to him of God's magick and the divine consciousness in all things, would he spurn her now, when her use of it had just saved his life? It was not her usual practice to take advantage of a patient's ear. Still, he'd asked for her physick—on some level, he must have had faith in it. Perhaps she should just leave it at that for now.

Mary ladled a fresh dose of medicine into the reverend's cup. He drank it propped up against his pile of feather bolsters. The sound of a rooster crowing told her the sun's rays were peeking over the horizon. She would not need to stay much longer as others could care for him now.

"I know you have reason to have chosen not to come," he began in the quiet egoless voice of a man who had just come face-to-face with death.

Many people considered him responsible for the harsh treatment of the Quaker women, the women who had embarrassed him publicly and caused many to doubt him and leave his congregation. It was well-known that he commonly referred to their light as a "stinking vapor from hell.'"

"Truth is, I'm not proud of all that has come about, but I do my best as God's servant and ward of this parish. I follow the law and take my responsibility seriously."

"I too do my best, Reverend. That's why I'm here, regardless," Mary answered.

His eyes moved from her face, off into the ether in front of him. He spoke slowly as if he were only musing out loud to himself. "Some covet knowledge such as yours, and others fear it. A woman having such renown to keep death at bay, a woman who has been filling the heads of others with ideas that are . . . shall we say, unusual?" He met her gaze sharply as he finished.

The memory flashed before her of that day when she'd greeted him as an equal in the snow.

"All the same," he said, "I will put in a good word for thee . . ." The reverend's eyes glittered darkly for a moment.

With whom did he mean? God? Or would he tell his friends how her physick had saved him? Before Mary could ask, Goody Reyner rushed in to her husband's bedside, and their private conversation came to an end.

❧

A lit taper in one hand and the hem of her skirt in the other, Mary mounted the narrow stair that led to the upper story. At the top, a dark blue velvet curtain separated the sleeping chamber from household storage. Her children were fast asleep, but Mary enjoyed watching them slumber, the angelic sweetness of their faces and soft breath.

John was growing up so fast. He'd soon be given his first breeches. Muttering unintelligibly, he turned his face away from the light of her taper.

Little Willy and Robert looked like peaceful cherubs; their soft round cheeks and the curve of their lips warmed her heart. She stared at them lovingly, and a longing welled up for her infant daughter. As that all-too-fresh pain wracked her heart yet again, she sat on the floor and wept silently. Her boys had been so excited to have a baby sister. It had been the hardest thing she'd ever had to do—to lay her three-day-old daughter in that small pine box, wrapped in a veil-like shroud.

Stifling a sob, Mary made her way quietly back down the stairs. They were low on small beer; she would brew a batch overnight. She stepped outside into the October twilight with the empty water bucket in hand and Greylock at her heels.

The last of the setting sun cast a ruddy light on the bare tree branches. A wind scattered the leaves that crunched underfoot and whirled about her. Mary pulled her shawl closer. There would be a hard frost tonight, she thought, glad she'd harvested the rest of her gillyflowers.

At the well, she paused to look warily about before lowering the water bucket. For some reason, she felt afraid. She filled the bucket and had wound it halfway up when dread seized the pit of her stomach. Mary ran toward the kitchen door of her house, the bucket falling back down into the well with a great splash.

"Greylock!"

But he was right with her. His hair bristled down the entire ridge of his spine, and his upper lip curled back from his teeth. He came inside with her, and she pulled in the latchstring and barred both the doors. She stood in the middle of the room, trembling and breathless. *What was it?* Greylock paced to and fro, growling, more upset than she was.

Mary built up the hearth fire. The flames grew brighter, lighting the hall. Brewing would have to wait until morning—or at least until William came home. Did she dare tell him? She'd felt unexplainably anxious for a while, and William had been rather grumpy of late. He would likely blame it on the loss of their daughter. And Greylock? He'd say it was the scent of an animal.

But there was something she hadn't told him. She'd happened upon Thomas Crawley locked in Kittery's newly built stocks. He was the first to use them. Margaret frequented Mary's gatherings and had the full supportive sympathy of the other women.

"Goody Thompson!" Crawley had called to her. "I have news that will serve ye to hear."

Mary had stopped in her tracks and looked sidelong at him. This was certainly unusual—the man had been afraid of her for years.

"Come closer," he said. "I daren't speak so loudly. Oh, for a drink of water!"

Mary took a few steps in his direction, not sure whether to t
him seriously or not, drunk as he often was. A water bucke
dipper sat nearby, and she filled the dipper with water. "Wha
Goodman Crawley?"

"There are those who wish you harm."

"*Who* wishes me harm?"

"Those who don't like anything that questions their

"How do you know this?"

"Drink!" he gasped. She brought the dipper to h
drank. "Pah!" he spat. "Awful stuff, water is." Tv

further in the stock, he focused a squinty eye upon her. "Crawley always knows things others wouldn't want him to," he chuckled. Then more seriously, he added, "I would take heed if I were you."

"Why are you telling me this?"

"Don't I owe you a favor, Goody Thompson? It's them other fellows who've got ta worry now," he laughed in an odd relieved sort of way.

Yes, she could have turned Crawley in as the owner of that necklace years ago if that was what he was referring to. Crawley refused to name names, and Mary would have liked nothing better than to have forgotten all about it, but she was not so sure that there wasn't some truth to his words. After all, Salomon had mentioned the same.

Seated on her settle by the hearth, Mary knew William would scoff at anything that came from Thomas Crawley's mouth. He'd tell her she was the fool for having listened, and William thought her friend Salomon just short of mad.

She called to Greylock, who was still pacing. He came to her with a whine, placed his head on her lap, and looked up at her lovingly. She stroked his mottled head and thick ruff, so grateful to have him. Noché, the progeny of her cat Inky, sat crouched in the warmth of the hearth, his eyes open wide to something only he could see beyond the walls of the house. Just down the lane by Sturgeon Creek lay the new house of Sarah and Adrian. But tonight, even that comfort paled against the unease that Mary felt.

If only William were home. He spent most evenings over at Emery's Cold Harbor ordinary by the ferry landing. Funny to think the property had originally been her father's.

Later that night, she heard William at the door, Greylock wagging his tail as he always did. She jumped up to slide the bolt and lift the latch.

William removed his cloak and sat in his chair, stretching out his ng booted legs toward the hearth. He hadn't shaved for several ys. That and his sheer size made him look rough and intimidating, ugh Mary knew better.

"Have you had your supper?" she asked quietly, folding his cloak over the back of the settle.

She'd saved some stew for him in the trivet pot. William usually ate his supper at the ordinary but often ate again when home.

He grunted affirmatively, his eyes resting unfocused on the flames inside the hearth. "Constable was back at Emery's tonight, after Thomas Crawley with a warrant for slandering our justice of the peace, Mr. Rishworth."

"Methinks Thomas Crawley asks for trouble just frequenting Emery's," Mary said. James Emery, who had inherited his father's business, was known for his sharp morale.

"Rishworth manages to stay in the good graces of whomever is in power. Crawley called him a 'lying, flaccid-bellied, pandering eel.' Can't say tha Ayh don't agree." Just last month, the king's commission had taken over the government of Maine en force, officially ending the governance of Massachusetts. All those in power had the carpet pulled out from under them—all except Rishworth, who continued on as justice of the peace, ever deciding Thomas Crawley's fate.

Hmmm . . . maybe I should tell him what Crawley said?

William sat up straighter, drawing in his long legs thick as tree trunks. "Think Ayh will ha' a spot to eat, Mary."

Mary ladled some stew into a bowl and placed it on the table next to him. She sat back down on the settle with her sewing, waiting for William to have a full belly before she told him what had happened that evening.

He grumbled as he ate. "Power-hungry magistrates. By God's blood, I wish the rogues would suck each other dry!" Mary was used to his oaths in private commentary. These were indeed turbulent times as power changed hands. Strange things had been happening up and down the river, things disappearing and people acting oddly.

"William?" she asked when he'd finished his meal. She folded her hands in her lap and looked intently at him. The last time something similar had happened, he'd put her off as though she were being womanishly fearful.

He blinked a few times before his eyes could focus in his drink-induced haze. "Aye, Mary, ye be the witch of Fife, I ken." Even after ten years of marriage, her eyes could still spook him. He turned his face away and shook his head of hair like a dog to get his bearings.

"*William*," she said again, leaning forward in earnest, ignoring his comment. "*It* happened again. *Someone* or *something* was nearby while I was at the well. I was *not* safe! Greylock was terribly upset." As though he understood her, Greylock, lying at her feet, gave a short whine which finished in a growl.

William looked at her. For a fleeting moment she thought she saw concern cross his face. He shifted in his chair. "Oh, Mary . . . nightwalkers, Peeping Toms—probably just some lads. 'Tis All Hallows' soon."

"But, William, there's more. Thomas Crawley told me there are those who wish me harm and that I must beware." Mary cringed to admit this. *How can I get William to believe me?*

"Crawley? Don't tell me ye listened to that besotten excuse for a man. Don't let him succeed in making you a fearful ninny. 'Beware,'" he scoffed. "The man's a liar, Mary, plain and simple."

William grew silent again. He stared into the fire, all trace of concern vanished. The logs shifted and embers fell apart, scattering like deep red rubies.

Mary fought to hold back her misgivings. Maybe Crawley *was* lying, and she *was* imagining things, she told herself, taking what solace she could from the idea that William might be right.

Still, a deeper part of her knew differently.

Greylock opened one of his yellow eyes to stare at her.

Not long afterward, a great and dreadful comet appeared in the southeast sky, a blazing ball of light with a long tail streaming behind it. Seen as an ominous predictor of some calamity, it terrified people everywhere. Reformist ministers claimed it was because New England had fallen away from its divine mission and back into the king's hands.

As fall gave way to winter, Mary watched the comet night after night until it waxed large and brilliant near the end of December. She did not share the blind fear of the comet that many did. Yet standing in the cold and gazing at the frosty night sky, she felt something wasn't right. But what it could be, she was at a loss to name. In January, the comet disappeared as suddenly as it had come.

With the new year at the end of March, little John began his schooling across the river in Dover. Wearing new navy-blue breeches, her eldest acted so grown-up that Mary couldn't help but smile. She went to school with him on his first day, remembering her first day a lifetime ago back in England: her grandmother walking her down the hill to the rectory past Chilcot's school, the boys' recitation carrying from the open casements. She was so proud that John was going to school and would learn to read and write as she had.

The Dover schoolmaster began by having each from the first year write out letters on their slates. John would do well, she knew. She had already taught him his alphabet and then some. He sat proudly on the front bench amongst his peers. Mary sat in the back of the classroom, dressed in her best clothes and her grandmother's exquisite cutwork lace collar and cap. She would stay for just a little while that morning, as new parents could.

The noise of sawing and hammering reached the school. No one minded because it meant a church bell would soon be ringing from the top of the new Dover meetinghouse, the deacon at long last retiring his drum. *Oh, for the sound of a church bell resonating throughout the town and across the river.* Mary's visit to Boston as a girl was the last time that she'd heard one. Before that, it had been in England.

She could not have possibly imagined, sitting there as happy as she'd ever been, with the world perfectly ordered about her, that the Mary who would hear the first peals of that church bell in a few weeks' time would be an entirely different person.

-- 24 --

Servants of the Devil

John, William Jr., and little Robert Thompson said their prayers, kneeling on the edge of their bed sacks in their nightgowns. The upstairs chamber was damp and chill, and Mary tucked them all snugly under layers of rugs and coverlets.

"Good night, my sweetie pies. Sleep tight," she called softly, making her way back to the stair with the candle.

"Don't let the bedbugs bite," John piped up, sending his little brothers into fits of giggles.

"Shhh . . . go to sleep," Mary whispered. Bedbugs were no laughing matter; but the fragrant mint, lavender, and wood betony she mixed into their straw ticking made the bloodsucking insects scarce to none.

Back downstairs, she busied herself wiping out supper trenchers and scouring the bean pot with sand as the fire grew brighter in the fading light. Where was William? He had said he'd be home early this evening. She placed the leftover fried herring in the dutch oven to keep it warm, feeling oddly anxious.

"Here, Greylock, my love." She set down a portion of ripened venison for him, a meal that he usually gobbled straight up. But tonight he sat stock-still in the middle of the room, his ears alert and his hackle bristling up and down his spine. Mary stared at him, her own hair prickling on her scalp. Her almost-forgotten fear from last year rose up anew.

Greylock began to growl, his lip curling back from his teeth. She held her breath, listening intently. *William will be coming home any minute now, won't he?*

A sudden urgent knock at the front door made her jump. Greylock growled even more menacingly, keeping her from the door with his body.

"Who's there?" she called out warily, glad she had pulled in the latchstring.

A man's voice that she did not recognize answered her. "Widow Batchelder's ill with fever, looks to be on her deathbed."

"Mary Batchelder?"

"Yes . . . wants you to come right away."

Something about the news struck her as odd. Or was it the tone of the man's voice? Mary Batchelder was very active in her group of women. If her friend was ill, Mary would go immediately. Sarah could keep an eye on her children.

Before she could ask further, the click of the latch at the garden door caught her attention. She flew toward the door, Greylock ahead of her, but it was too late.

In came two men with kerchiefs tied over their faces. Greylock leapt right into them, latching his jaws onto the forearm of one. The man swore, trying to pry him off with his other hand. Meanwhile, the other intruder came straight at Mary.

She picked up a stool, holding it up as a shield. "Who are you? What do you want? Get out of my house this instant!"

The man started to laugh. Every hair on Mary's scalp stood up.

"Mother?" cried John's little voice from upstairs.

"*Stay upstairs! Don't come down!*" Mary yelled, her heart pounding wildly in her chest.

"Drop the chair, wench, and I won't have to make thee."

She felt nauseous.

"Get the damned cur off me!" screamed the man Greylock had by the arm. The dog's snarls were bloodcurdling. Two more men entered from the back door and began to beat at Greylock with their hands and feet.

Mary had no time to think, for the man who had cornered her grabbed at the stool. She swung its legs into his chest with a thud. He grunted and cursed. Another man grabbed her arms and, with a violent jerk, held them up behind her back. She lashed out with her feet, striking him in the shin. The next thing she knew, she was thrown hard to the floor, and rope was being wound around her wrists so tightly that it cut into her skin.

She filled her lungs to scream, but a cloth was stuffed roughly into her mouth and a gag tied around her face. She thrashed, chin to chest, unable to breathe, until someone pulled it away from her nose. Then her legs and feet were tied together, and she was lifted, a sack of some sort pulled over her body.

From the chamber above, she heard John's worried voice call again, "Mother?"

Please, God, don't let them touch my sons!

It sounded like Greylock was tearing the men to shreds until Mary heard a loud crack and a doglike whimper, followed by a thud. Then silence. *Greylock? Greylock!* she screamed into the gag. *What have they done to my dog?*

"Let's get out of here," someone said.

Her captors lifted her and carried her out into the chill, damp night. Claustrophobia set in as Mary struggled to find air to breathe—any air at all. Struggling only made it worse. She lay limp, dizzy and disoriented, her pulse a militia marching in her head. Such a coarse-woven sack was not airtight, but this one certainly felt like it.

What are they going to do with me? This must be what I've been warned about. But why? What have I ever done? Where is William? Maybe a neighbor will see us and put a stop to it all! Her mind racing, she struggled again with all her strength.

A fierce blow to the small of her back put a stop to it. Searing pain and flashing lights danced hideously in her head. The creak of an oar and the hollow thump of a boat brought her back to her senses. She felt herself set roughly down into its bottom, a rib from its thwarts sticking painfully into hers.

One of the men said something she couldn't hear clearly, and they all laughed.

Mary lay helplessly, listening. There were four of them—four, at least, whom she'd seen. *Did any of them stay behind to harm my children?* That and the thought that they were going to drop her over the side to drown froze her heart. The uncertainty was absolute torture. She began to plead with God for her life and those of her children's. She prayed John would know to run to his aunt Sarah's down the lane. *What if the men have already done something to William? And Greylock, what did they do to Greylock?*

The feel of the boat's keel running aground and lodging fast was a relief, but it only brought up a new set of fears. Mary felt stiff and cold, and sounds echoed eerily. Rough hands lifted her again, carrying her up what felt like an incline. She heard raucous laughter in the distance that grew louder and nearer as they climbed. Soon, there were voices all around.

The next thing she knew, she was tossed like a bag of samp onto a pile of straw, and the sack was pulled off her. Mary sucked in lungsful of air through strands of her hair, her cap pushed back off her head, its strings choking her.

She was inside a barn. A solitary lantern hung from a post, lighting the place dimly. Tongues of fog curled in from the shadows. At least a dozen men surrounded her, and the smell of liquor was strong. Her limbs were cut free, but she barely had a chance to rub them before she was seized by her arms and dragged onto her back, her wrists tied to something above her head.

The men were laughing and jeering at her. She recognized most of them—the shock of which made her blood run cold: magistrates, elders, and selectmen from across the river. Dover's elite. They were also making nasty remarks about her father and William.

"Not so cocksure of yourself now, are 'ee, wench? This is what happens to those who need to be put in their place," one of them slurred. Mocking laughter ensued.

"Remove her gag. Let's see what the whore has to say!"

Someone stepped forward and pulled it off.

"What have I done to harm you or anyone?" Mary gasped, her tongue parched and fuzzy. "I have helped to birth your babes, nurse your sick wives and children . . ."

Some of the men quieted down.

"With the devil's potions thou has, witch!" Richard Waldron spat. He leered over her, pointing a shaking forefinger inches from her face. "Own that thou are the devil's consort—*own it*!" he screamed in a frenzy. The group of men began to mutter darkly.

"No, I will not own what I am not! As God is my savior, how dare you speak thus?"

Waldron's answer was to strike her hard in the face. "Lies!" he roared. "Lies and impudence, whore! We'll show thee what thou are!"

Mary's face felt numb, and warm blood trickled from her mouth. The force of the blow had turned her head to the side, and behind those standing to her right, she saw someone walk into the barn. Sudden hope flooded through her. *He will help me . . . Reverend Reyner will stop this insanity! Certainly these men will stop their drunken evil immediately and shamefully in the presence of God's advocate that I saved from death's very door?* She called out to him; but he looked away, ignoring her, and began to talk to the man next to him.

The whole world felt turned upside down. Nothing made sense. These men were pillars of the community who were supposed to govern and protect.

Her skirt was pulled up and thrown over her face, exposing her to them. She wanted to die, to disappear. She held her legs together, twisting and kicking with both feet. Her screams sounded like they were coming from a long way away. Rough hands held her legs fast, pulling them apart.

Someone lay on top of her, crushing her, lifting her petticoat off her face to grasp at her breast. He rent her bodice and pulled down her smock. His smell was repulsive. She could feel his lips and tongue seek out her nipple as though to eat her alive, and his teeth bit into her flesh.

"Leave some for us!" others cried.

When the rogue had his fill of her breasts, she felt him penetrate her with a violent push, and his body become rigid. Someone pulled him off, a warm wetness seeping out of her.

She ceased to struggle, floating somewhere above, no longer present while others made use of her body, destroying her life and dignity in their perverse hate and drunkenness. “Don’t tell my husband!” her voice screamed over and over again from what sounded like a great distance away.

The voices around her were slurring heavily now. Someone dangled a rope in her face, a noose. “Breathe a word of this, and we’ll be coming back for thee—*with this*!”

❧

Mary dragged her skirt through the shallows, too numb to feel anything. Her first impulse had been to run, but as the sound of the oarlocks faded in the distance, she fell upon the exposed mudflat, too weak to get up. She lay with her cheek and hair pressed into the muck: salty, acrid, primordial slime—utterly nasty, yet a solid and grounding lifeline as she trembled and shook, her breath a rapid staccato.

Slowly, awareness began to creep back into her body. The sky was graying, and all around her resounded still and silent. How unfathomably filthy and unclean she felt.

Mary struggled stiffly to her feet, swaying back out toward the deeper water, allowing its icy pressure and pulling current to flush the muck and filth from her body. She stood up to her chest in water that could never wash away the worst of it. It crossed her mind to sink herself down . . . to breathe deep of the cold, dark brine . . . to let the current sweep her away . . .

The horror of leaving her children motherless sent her back to the bank. She steeled herself. *If I can survive what has been done to me, I can withstand anything.*

Shivering uncontrollably, she pushed through the thorny undergrowth. The shallop had disposed of her on a deserted stretch of shore. She felt afraid to go home. *What will I find? My children, my poor dear children? At all costs, William must not find out. How will I hide my shame?*

She found the garden door unlocked. The latch lifted with its usual quiet click. Nothing looked out of place. Someone had banked the fire. There was no sign of Greylock. Miraculously, her boys were all seemingly unharmed, asleep upstairs. Mary hurried back down to the parlour, where she and William slept: the bed was empty.

She changed clothes as quickly as she could, her fingers stiff and hard to control. Somehow she managed to pull on a clean smock and crawl between the linen sheets of the feather bed. Even in the warmth of the bed, she continued to shiver. It was impossible to sleep. Her body felt so sore, achy, and swollen.

William came home soon enough. She heard his boots cross the floor to their bedstead.

"Mary, where ha' you been? The boys said some men came for you that Greylock didn't like, but they didn't know who or where you were going. Was someone ill?"

"Yes . . . I was called out," she lied, her back to him, trying to make her voice sound as normal as possible.

"You left no word!"

Mary turned over to face him, the bedclothes covering her mouth. "I'm sorry, Will. I left very quickly." Her voice was muffled. "I don't feel well myself."

William stared at her. Reaching down, he pulled the bedclothes away from her face, his eyes widening as he saw her lip and all the swelling. He took a step backward, away from her.

"Where's Greylock?" he asked at length, his voice rough and thick.

"I don't know," Mary answered miserably.

❧

Fearing for her life, and those of her husband and children, Mary didn't breathe a word of what had happened. Such matters were not discussed as it was. Still, she could tell that William knew or strongly suspected. He began staying up late, disappearing in the wee hours of the morn, returning at daybreak.

Mary had her own suspicions, especially when word got around that some rogue was knocking holes in boats, pulling down fences, and setting fire to warehouses across the river.

Being left alone at night was horrible. If the men came back for her and her children, who would stop them? They wrote the laws, ran the church, controlled the whole society! They were some of the wealthiest and most powerful men in Pascataway. In her world, there was no such thing as sanity or safety anymore.

Mary's fear and shame kept her close to home. Sick calls went unanswered. Her boys watched her, troubled. For Mary, they were the only good left in her life. Until one evening.

It was late and Mary sat by the hearth alone. Unable to relax, her eyes wide with terror, she listened. The chorus of peepers in the nearby marsh had suddenly gone silent—something had disturbed them.

She waited with bated breath until she heard a noise at the kitchen door. Instantly, every hair rose on her head, and her heart began to pound.

It's them. God help me, I'm sure of it! They've come back for me. She rose to her feet, trembling, not knowing what to do.

Then a second sound arose: a scratching, and with it a familiar, yelping whine.

In disbelief, Mary approached the door. *It couldn't be.*

"Greylock?"

Another whine and the sound of paws stretching up onto the door. In a daze of emotion, Mary opened the door to be greeted by a mass of matted gray fur that was barely recognizable. A much, much thinner Greylock, stinking like swamp and caked in mud, hadcome home—he too had survived! He leapt upon her, his soft pink tongue lapping at the tears on her face.

The joy was mutual; the watchfulness his ears and nose brought, invaluable; his companionship—bliss.

Mary did her best to keep the daily routine for her sons as normal as possible, thanking God she still had her life and now Greylock, her beloved protector. But unresolved questions festered within. *Am*

I evil? Have I strayed from what is righteous? Stars in the evening sky no longer glistened back at her the same way when she looked at them. *Am I to be spurned by the gates of heaven?* The world had lost its luster. Common belief espoused that God punished those who sinned, and part of her had begun to believe those men.

She spent hours on her knees praying and threw herself harder than ever into her housework, trying to keep her mind off everything. Then to make matters unfathomably worse, she discovered she was with child.

People still came wanting remedies, begging for help with the ill. Mary refused them, invariably retreating to the parlour to cry tears of despair, afraid that her family's lives hung in the balance. Then she noticed brown spots on the undersides of her wrists. She stared at the spots in disbelief, the horror of what she knew them to be too much to comprehend.

It had crossed her mind during the attack. The last one to rape her was not yet eighteen years old but had the reputation of hanging about the wharves with those of ill repute. Bad blood . . . syphilis. Never had she thought it would ever happen to her.

Treating herself as best she could with sarsaparilla and other remedies, Mary told William she had pregnancy complications and could not share his bed. Until her symptoms were gone, she knew it would not be safe for him.

Daughters of several neighbors had often come before to help keep house when Mary needed them. Now one of them came daily.

The change in her did not go unnoticed by her family. Mary blamed her pregnancy, but her mother suggested perhaps a doctor should be sent for, one well versed in not only the humors but also the new medicines. One trained at Oxford or Cambridge.

As luck would have it, Mary's father discovered a doctor already at hand on board a ship at anchor in Portsmouth. A certain Dr. Rhoades, on his way to Boston, having left London because of the great plague raging there. Dr. Rhoades agreed to see Mary.

The doctor looked into her eyes and mouth with a special glass and asked her a few supercilious questions. She refused to disclose her illness to him. The outward signs of her infection had by then disappeared, and she knew there was not much hope for a cure.

Dr. Rhoades tried bleeding her with horseleeches and feeding her crab eyes and castoreum, diagnosing her with a severe case of melancholia. In the end, he prescribed calomel and laudanum. But as she was nearing childbed, it was best to wait with the calomel until after she delivered. After Dr. Rhoades left her house, Mary placed both his remedies high on her shelf, where she wouldn't have to look at them.

The doctor stayed on at her parents' home and periodically stopped in to check on her. Mary's mother's illness was worse than ever, though her mother would not admit it to anyone. All the same, Mary sent her son John often with bottles of her tonic for his grandmother.

As Mary's pregnancy progressed, she began to sense an ill wind blowing. It wasn't long before she noticed neighbors strangely distancing themselves from her.

Her sister Sarah stopped over one day, visibly upset. "Mary, you were so right about Rebekah—she's a horrid gossip who speaks badly about others and spreads malicious lies!"

"I won't disagree with you, Sarah. But whatever has Rebekah done to make you so angry?"

Sarah glanced through the kitchen hall door, where Mary's boys could be seen playing in the dooryard. She stepped closer to Mary and lowered her voice. "Its what she's saying about you. She's spreading lies that the babe you're carrying is an Indian's."

Mary felt her stomach clench and her head grow dizzy. She held on to the back of William's great chair to stabilize herself.

"Oh Mary, I hated to tell you. I'm so sorry. I know you haven't been well."

"Why would Rebekah say such a thing?" Mary's voice sounded flat to her own ears. She knew why Rebekah would. Mary's attackers, upon learning of her pregnancy, would spread such a lie themselves to save their own skins.

"She says she's only repeating what she's heard, but I don't believe her. I told her I won't tolerate such shameful, lying slander and that I no longer wish to have anything to do with her."

The speculation worried Mary greatly. Were those who had brutalized her afraid the child would look like one of them? Could her babe be a mixture of all the men's seed? She prayed the rumors would not make their way to William's ears.

Though no longer so prone to late-night absences, William was nonetheless seldom home, busy improving his land grant across the river by the Cocheco Log Swamp. Things remained strained between the two of them.

In childbed late that fall, the labor was the hardest and longest Mary had ever had. Her mother, having stopped her own practice of physick, ailing as she was, acted as midwife, the public speculation surrounding the birth bringing out her maternal protectiveness.

Early morning on the third day, baby James was finally born. Small and weak, this newborn son did not look like Mary's others had, with their pates of blond peach fuzz. He had a full head of dark hair, a fact that frightened her until her mother assured her that James looked just like Mary had as an infant.

Many neighbors came in to see baby James that morning. Word was soon out that he looked as English and fair-skinned as any, but William took one look at his dark-haired son and recoiled.

Late in the afternoon the following day, as Mary lay resting with her newborn at her side, a knock came at the door. She'd dozed off, but somehow that knock wakened her fully. Sarah was with her and answered the door. The sound of voices reached her ears, though Mary could not hear what was being said.

"Sarah, who is it?" she called. Baby James awoke and began to cry. Mary held him to her breast.

Sarah returned a minute later, her face white as her smock. Mary grew alarmed as Sarah was with child herself.

"Sister, you're unwell?"

Sarah shook her head no, in answer and handed Mary a neatly folded parchment with shaking hands.

Willy and Robert came into the room. "What is it, Mother?"

"I bid ye leave as your mother needs her rest," Sarah said faintly, ushering the boys to the door.

The letter was a warrant from the regional court held that very day up in Saco. Mary read it over and over again, trying to comprehend the words that repelled her mind like water on oilskin:

> *Wee present Mary Whitte of Kittery, the daughter of John Whitte, for haveing of a bastard. The court orders Mary Whitte for her offense to have 10 Stripes given her at the post on the 3rd Twesday next May Insewing, being at the court in York.*
> *-Henery Jocelyn} Justice of the Peace*
> *-Robert Jordan} Justice of the Peace*

Was her infant son a bastard? She did not rightly know. Wondering who had presented her and upon what evidence the court had ordered her punishment, Mary crumpled the warrant and cast it to the floor. She slid back down under the bedclothes and curled around baby James. She could hear Sarah crying.

Sometime later, as she drifted back from a tortured sleep, the sound of voices from the hall reached her ears. One was her father's, and the other sounded like Nicolas Shapleigh's.

"I'm afraid Humphrey Chadbourne was not there to put in a fair word, and Jordan was standing in for Jocelyn. 'Tis a shame. The grand jury went on the word of two of their members—and a presentment at that."

"Unjust, lying slander!" her father raged. "Mary has been ailing, and now she's weak in childbed. Ten stripes, I don't care when, would be the end of her!"

"I can do away with the whipping post, John, if not the other. I will speak with Robert Jordan. She won't serve that punishment—I'll make sure of it. You have my word."

There was a pause.

"Well, I'd be grateful for that, Nicolas. Mary will be greatly indebted, that's for certain."

Her father paused again before continuing. His voice rose. "Then to rub salt in the wound, they come after Dr. Rhoades on the grounds that he has been living 'suspiciously' at my abode while he tends to Britania with his physick. Their court order will be the death of my wife!"

"You know, John, you must be wary. The warrant states 'John White's *daughter*,' not 'William Thompson's *wife*.' This is, for whatever reason, also aimed at you."

"For what, upholding God's law? For staying clear of their underhanded dealings?" Her father's voice rose indignantly.

"Yes, I'm afraid, to name a few."

Mary could tell her father was biting his tongue. He was still beside himself that Nicolas Shapleigh had left the Anglican church. Her father had seemingly disowned Adrian and Sarah for converting to Quakerism and, in private, bitterly blamed Shapleigh for misleading half of Kittery.

"Mr. Shapleigh, I'm sorry to inconvenience you with my daughter's affairs." Her father's voice rang with sharp finality.

But Nicolas ignored the tone. "John, your daughter has long since earned it, my goodman. She's healed my family and servants of all manner of sickness and distempers. She's been a great blessing to us all."

But her father was not to be placated. After Nicolas Shapleigh took his leave, he stomped into the parlour, snatched *The Virtues of Herbs, Stones, and Certain Beasts* off the table next to Mary's bed, and threw it into the fire.

All that was left now was the charred spine of the book's binding.

After James's birth, the visits paid by those seeking her help began to dwindle. "Sorry, she won't see anyone right now," her sons told those who still came to the door. There were other herbwomen along the river. "Goody Walford in Portsmouth might be willing to help."

Then her son John came home from school one day, a pained and unhappy expression on his face.

"How was school?" Mary asked.

"Fine, Mother," he mumbled, shrugging. He left his slate and primer near the door and tried to slip back outside.

"John, pray tell, what's the matter?"

"Nothing, Mother."

But Mary could see something was very much the matter. At first, he wouldn't tell her anything, but she kept after him until he finally told her.

"Boys at my school are saying wicked things about you. Why? Why are they saying such bad things?"

"Don't believe all that you hear, John," Mary told him, her voice steady but her heart rent through the middle. To be judged by children, especially her own, was the hardest. She was a marked woman now: shunned, despised, and discarded. It was a long, hard fall from the pedestal where she'd once stood, and she was seemingly powerless to change it. Despair pressed in upon her; and beneath it all was the deep, unfathomable terror of her entire life disintegrating.

That evening she unstoppered the bottle of laudanum Dr. Rhoades had left. It did help, blissfully so, for the week or two that it lasted.

Meanwhile, baby James in his weak condition needed all that she could do for him. In his innocent love, she found both the comfort and defiance to keep her back from the chasm of depression that otherwise would have swallowed her whole. James was her companion in disgrace. Determined not to lose him, she kept him close, swaddled and tied to her breast in a sling. William and her son John ignored the newborn's presence, pretending he didn't exist.

❧

Midwinter that year, on a long, dark night, a servant of Mary's father's came to fetch her. Mary's mother was not in a good way. The snow lay deep underfoot, but Mary didn't feel the cold. She held baby James close beneath her cloak.

Mary found her father and his household sitting vigil in the kitchen hall. In the parlour hearth, a fire had been built up. Mary's mother lay in bed, propped up on bolsters in the far corner of the room.

Sarah and Hannah, both seated near the bedstead, looked so sorrowful.

"Madam, 'tis me, Mary."

Her mother's eyelids fluttered. She smiled faintly, reaching out to hold Mary's hand.

"I shall prepare your medicine," Mary said and made to pull away. Her mother, though her grip proved weak, did not let go.

"I've had the medicine," she said. "Mary dear, there's naught else to be done."

Mary studied her mother in the candlelight. She'd grown gaunt over the last several months, fairly wasting away, a husk of her former self—something Mary had not been willing to admit or even allow herself to fully notice.

"What about the tonic—have you been drinking my tonic?"

"Aye, Mary, and I'm thankful. It's surely kept my body and soul together these past few years." Her mother's grip lessened, but Mary held hers firmer; she was not ready to lose her mother. "Thy gifts have helped so many, child . . . Please forgive me . . . I've held you back," her mother whispered.

"But you haven't, really," Mary said softly. Her vision blurred with tears.

"Life's far too precious and short to worry about what ill might happen." Her mother's breath came shallowly, and a spasm clutched her frail physique.

Mary held her mother's shoulder. *Why, oh why is this happening now? I've been through so much. I'm not sure I can bear anything else!*

"You must promise me now to do," her mother gasped, "as surely God in the heavens made ye to do. Now please send your father in." Such bittersweet words.

As the next day dawned, William and Adrian dug their mother-in-law's grave in the least frozen soil they could find, next to the southern foundation of the hilltop house.

Sitting with her sisters beside their mother's body in the parlour, Mary regretted that she had not done more to help when her mother needed her the most. She felt a terrible guilt that because of her, Dr. Rhoades had been chased away—a guilt complicated and made no better at learning that Dr. Rhoades hadn't let their mother drink Mary's tonic during his residence.

The afternoon after their mother was buried, Hannah paid a visit to the Thompson house.

"Father has not moved far from his great chair in the parlour today. Louise is watching over him, making a fuss," Hannah told Mary. Louise was the wife of their father's overseer.

Hannah had not taken a suitor, though she was more than of age, preferring to live as a maid in their father's house. Mary knew Hannah had been a great comfort to their mother. She and Hannah recounted memories with tears and laughter, feeling once again a bit of the closeness they had shared growing up.

"Mary," Hannah said softly, after a reflective silence, "what happened? You *must* tell me what happened." Beseechingly, she stared at Mary.

Mary felt her heart skip a beat. Their mother had asked her the same thing before James's birth; all she had done was cry, refusing to subject her dear, sweet mother to such wicked shamefulness.

"No, Hannah, I cannot. I cannot do much of anything now."

"Why can't you?" Hannah prodded.

"Because they will murder me . . . and William . . . and our children."

Hannah gasped, her eyes so like their mother's. "Who would do such a thing?"

Hearing the voices of her younger children resounding from their game in the parlour, Mary leaned forward. "Hannah, if they knew I told thee, they would come after you too! There's naught to stop them."

Hannah stared back at her, a look of staunch resolution forming on her face. She rose from her seat and knelt on the floor in front of Mary, grasping Mary's arms with her hands. "Mary, I swear to you, I will not so much as breathe a word to anyone," she whispered.

Mary ached to voice her pain and suffering to a sympathetic listener. But would anyone believe her? No one had seen her kidnapping. Not a day went by that she did not condemn and berate herself for what had happened.

"All right," she said finally, "I will tell you. Please don't give me cause to regret this."

"You have my word," Hannah breathed solemnly.

And so Mary told her. Not in detail, by any means, but she told Hannah enough that she would understand. Before Mary had even finished the tale, Hannah was weeping.

-- 25 --

Aftermath

The Dog Star rose in the east at dawn, and the day waxed seasonably still and sultry. In the treetop canopy, the sound of heat bugs reverberated, mocking the feverish buzzing inside Mary's head.

She sat on the trunk of a felled tree in the shade, holding a limp and feverish baby James on her lap. Not that the shade did much good; there wasn't a breath of air to be had anywhere. James felt more like a rag doll than a seven-month-old baby. Mary picked up the tin cup by her side and poured a small amount of her tonic into his mouth. If she could only get him to swallow some, but the liquid just dribbled back out again.

His body felt sticky and heavy, his usual sweet smell tinged with vomit. A wave of revulsion swept through her. She felt miserable herself, her head as heavy as a rock. It hurt to think.

James's tiny body began to shake and convulse.

"Please, God, don't let him die!" Mary pleaded aloud, terrified.

He lay limp again, limper than before. She held her breath, her head swimming—was he still breathing, or was she only imagining the tiny tickle of air she felt? Then she thought the unthinkable: could it be his soul leaving?

"God, please, no!" she begged in agony.

She cradled James to her chest in excruciating despair, praying and pleading. It was more than she could bear. *Not another one . . . he can't die! I will keep him going with my will, with my mind—nothing else is real.*

She pressed him to her heart. "Please don't go! Please don't die!"

Her face contorted, and her body gripped so that her cries barely issued forth until through the blur of her tears, she realized that she and James were not alone. Two boys carrying fishing poles and naked from the waist up stood nearby in the trees, staring at her. She could feel their judgment in that innocent, yet fascinated way of children who have been told that something is bad or evil and they should stay away. One of the boys she recognized as Reform.

Mary turned her head away. *Why now, of all times, are they here?* New tears of self-pity and shame unleashed, cool in the heat, wetting James's thin cotton gown—James, who seemed too much like an empty shell, a poppet, his small body pressed to her own. She lowered him to her lap and cupped his little face with her hands.

To her amazement, he drew a sudden shuddering breath—*he was with her yet!*

Now if the boys would just go away . . . She glanced up to see that they had gone. For a fleeting moment, she felt envious of them. *How good it would feel to be a half-naked boy, your only concern whether you caught a fish or not for supper.*

Never in her life had she felt so despicable, so judged and full of hopelessness as she did in that moment. Rage flared up within her.

"God help me, that is *not* my truth. I will *not* take it on. I'm *not* an evil person!" she cried out bitterly.

But James had gone still again.

Mary held up the hell of her agony to the divine; there was nothing else she could do. *If God has created all things, then God can experience my feelings too.* She poured her feelings forth intensely. *If He will take my babe, He will feel it too!* "God as my witness . . ."

Something seemed to fall away from her then, to dissolve. Amazed, Mary pulled up more feeling, only to feel it vanish as well. Where there had been so much pain a moment before was now a calm nothingness. Of its own accord, a spark of pleasure burst forth inside her heart.

James moved in her arms and made a louder whimpering noise. She wiped her face in disbelief with the back of her hand. Baby James was staring up at her with concern as though he had completely forgotten his illness.

His fever had broken.

Mary began to resume her physick. Slowly and quietly, yet resume she did. In this she discovered a peculiar thing: the more she forgave and stopped judging herself, the less scorn and judgment she felt from others. She still carried some fear of retribution, but in her heart of hearts, she sensed that those who had sinned against her would be happier to have their families tended to than not. But there were consequences Mary did not see coming.

On a morning the following spring, it was breakfast as usual at the Thompson house. William had taken Ginger's bridle down from the wall and ridden off early. John, Willy, and Robert were eating fried eggs, garden greens, and toasted bread with butter. Mary was packing the older two their dinner basket for school.

"Mother, James isn't wearing his shoes," Robert cried, his mouth full of toast.

"Mind your manners, Robert. James, why aren't your shoes on? The floor is awfully cold."

"He's got something wrong with his foot!" exclaimed Willy, leaning around the end of the table to get a better look.

Little James tottered oddly into the hearth corner and sat down upon his little stool. *How strange*, Mary thought. She lifted the ruffle of his gown and picked up his left foot, but James promptly pulled it away from her. She picked him up and sat on the settle with him in her lap. His foot felt stiff, and his ankle joint was oddly thickened. There was no sign of a bite or infection. Mary stroked his small icy-cold foot, trying to rub some life into it.

When her older boys left for school, she filled the large barrel tub with heated water. James splashed and played to his heart's content, soaking in her tonic, comfrey root, and flower elixirs. Then she tried a clay and plantain poultice, determined to draw out the poison, whatever it was. Heat seemed to help somewhat, but it did little to bring the flexibility back into his foot. Perhaps daily poultices were in order.

Worried, she sent for Salomon. If anyone could help, he could. She'd seen him cure a man's goiter with boiled goat hair and clay. But

Salomon's cheerful demeanor faded as he looked at James's ankle. "Thars not much that Ayh cahn do, Mah-re," he said, shaking his head.

In a matter of weeks, the tragic fact that James was growing lame had sunk in. Life was hard enough with two good feet. How would her son be able to keep himself, much less a wife and family?

But Mary was persistent. The word *silver* kept coming to her. She made an elixir with a silver shilling. It did nothing. She tried heating it in her grandmother's crucible. Again, nothing. Then she mixed a dozen of her strongest herbs together in water with some of her tonic, elixirs, and a silver shilling—a veritable witch's brew. She gave James a little of this to drink and soaked his foot in the remainder. It helped dramatically. His foot grew no worse, and the swelling and pain diminished. She began to keep a supply of this special brew on hand to help him. Silver shillings were often used to keep a bucket of cow's milk from spoiling. Silver obviously had some powerful alchemical qualities. Perhaps James would heal even more over time. A makeshift piece of leather tied around his foot became his shoe.

William offered no support, then again, Mary did not expect him to. But James was bright and full of love, and it was this that finally won his father's heart. This and the fact that William could now plainly see that James was his son.

Her eldest John still ignored his youngest brother. He, more than his other brothers, could remember his mother being looked up to and respected by all. How their games and stories had been fun and lighthearted. How happy they'd all been.

How it had all been before.

One Sabbath, Mary's father invited the family back to his house on the hill for dinner. He had an important announcement to make. Sarah, Adrian, and their infant daughter, Eleanor were also invited. Mary was hopeful: *Perhaps Grandfather White was softening in his old age?*

Hannah had been happy to keep house for their father since their mother's death, along with the help of the farm servants. She had overseen the dinner preparation. It felt good to share a family meal again at the old house. Mary's mother not being there made it quite sad as well. Still, the old kitchen hall was pleasant and cheerful, reminiscent of happier days, with its window casements opened wide.

"Sir, you keep us on the edge of our seats as to your special announcement," Adrian commented cheerily, taking a bite of roast duck. Both he and William had bets on Mary's father relinquishing more of his land. All eyes were on the old patriarch, anxious to hear. Whatever it is, Mary thought, he is terribly excited. Even her boys were quiet, standing at their places. She shifted James on her lap.

Her father smiled secretively, looking about at them all. His hair had long since turned to grayish white, yet he retained a certain youthful regality and a tall straight spine.

"Yes, do tell us, Father," Hannah begged.

"I need a wife," he told them.

Everyone stopped breathing.

"I've sent to England for a bride."

Mary's heart drained of its blood; had she really just heard her father say those words?

Adrian began to choke, and Sarah thumped him on the back until he recovered himself. An uncomfortable silence followed, the shock of his announcement palpable. *How could he?* It was obvious by the looks on Mary's sisters' faces that they felt the same way. Little James began to cry as he tended to do when she was upset.

"Our congratulations, sir," William and Adrian echoed each other.

It was many weeks away, the arrival of John White's new bride-to-be; however even with time to digest the news, nothing prepared Mary and her sisters for the young girl stepping off the boat. She could almost have been Mary's daughter. Lucie was her name, flaxen-haired and very fetching. Mary's father married her the same day she arrived, having posted the banns well in advance.

If Mary's shame and reputation had not completely cut her off from her father, Lucie made sure that she did. John White had always helped his daughters with all manner of sundry things. They had never wanted for anything. This changed as Mary's father indulged his new wife instead. The fancy cloth and ribbons stopped coming, as did the spices, wines, and dried fruits that she and her sisters had grown accustomed to.

Mary grieved privately, feeling disowned and abandoned to see her father put his heart and mind so completely into a new life and relationship. He built a dwelling house for Lucie on his land down near the Point on Crooked Lane, where his first planting field had been. Lucie ruled the roost and wanted to be as far as possible from her new husband's family. But what surprised Mary most of all—astounded her, actually—was her father attending Kittery's Puritan meetinghouse at the Point, as it was Lucie's preference.

William was not unaffected by this turn of events and became more dissatisfied with his life than ever. Mary grew worried; it had never been as bad as this. Lately, the sun was well up over the horizon by the time he rolled out of bed. Now that her father was no longer breathing down William's neck or watching from afar, it seemed that William didn't care much about anything. His days were increasingly spent in idleness, and Sabbath services were missed. Neighbors presented his absences and other misdemeanors to the county court.

The last time she had dosed William with her flower elixirs, the results had been disastrous, but things were bad enough that she decided to try again. This time, it seemed like there was only more to gain, so she began to pour elm blossom into his daily cider to help ease his despair. It worked wonderfully—almost too well.

Mary soon found herself pregnant again; it had been three years since James was born. She prayed in earnest for another daughter, one to whom she could pass on her knowledge and who would eventually help with the keeping of the house. Neighbors' daughter's still weren't as readily available as they once had been.

❧

"Yes, by God's blood, I will swear and bid ye take notice—and I will swear again, goddamn prating filth!" William had bellowed, barely restraining himself from throttling his old nemesis John Roberts at the spring training day in Dover. Niven Agnew taking the liberty of a tight hold on the tail of William's jacket had certainly helped.

Unfortunately for William, his language was reported to the authorities. With so many witnesses in the Dover regiment, he was fined twenty shillings, or ten lashes upon his bare skin. He paid the twenty shillings.

Mary began to lace William's drink with snapdragon to soften his words. But if it was not one thing, it was another, and she had to figure out what he needed on a daily basis until she gave birth to another son.

"His name will be Alexander, after my dead brother," William announced.

Mary had named James herself, hoping to please both her father and husband, when William had wanted nothing to do with the child. James was named after King James I of England, the one who had revised the Anglican Bible and whose mother had been a Scot.

With Alexander's birth, William recovered enough spirit to get back to work. Unfortunately, this did not last. His mood once again became increasingly surly and his temper short. Those concerned for Mary and the children's welfare, making the mistake of stopping in for a visit while William was home, often paid the price with his threats and verbal abuse. William's fines began to add up. Perhaps a mislabeled remedy of Mary's was to blame, but somehow William ended up with debilitating flux for an entire week. Well, she thought, it would certainly help his biliousness—a good purge never hurt anyone. In the darker moments of their marriage, she had once, maybe twice, thought about doing a good bit more.

At the fall court of 1671, not having the thirty shillings to pay his fines, William chose the punishment of twelve stripes given to him at the post.

Mary cleaned out the bloody, coagulated cuts that crisscrossed his broad, muscled back. None had reached bone, but they had bitten deep. All their boys had left the room except for James.

"Aiy-ya! Don't torture me, wench!" William growled, his forearms braced upon the table.

"Sir, can I get you your pipe and tobacco?" James's sweet little face shone full of compassion, wanting desperately to help in some way.

"*Aaahhg*!" William cried through clenched teeth. "What's tha', James? No tobacco, son. But I'll certainly take a bullet from me musket belt!"

"Honestly, William," Mary snapped, "the man who made *nary* a sound whipped at the post, *tortured* by yarrow and comfrey? Hush now and hold still."

Her heart smote as she watched James, now six years old and wearing breeches, hobble awkwardly across the floor as he went to fetch the bullet. His left leg was slightly shorter than his right, and his ankle could not flex much at all, but his remedy had surely kept other potential defects at bay. And for this, Mary was grateful.

Mary shook her head. "All this suffering instead of paying the thirty shillings. I don't know, William . . ."

"I'd hardly call this suffering!" William scoffed, argumentative as usual. "'Tis nothing to wha' I went through 'tween Dunbar and the bloody cathedral, na to mention coming here."

True, Mary thought. It amazed her William and his friends had survived the ordeal at all. *What was it with men, whimpering like children as their wounds are patched, yet ready to tear each other to bits on a moment's notice?*

James returned with the bullet. "Here, sir." He handed it to his father.

"Thank you, James." William took the bullet and bit down on it comically, screwing his face into such outrageous expressions of pain that Mary and James began to laugh. She loved it when William was in good spirits.

She finished anointing the last stripe. "There, my sensitive fellow, your torture is over."

"Ahhh!" William breathed like a dragon.

"For the time being," she corrected.

Their son John walked into the kitchen hall. At twelve years old, his light hair had darkened, and it now made a striking contrast with his light skin and clear blue eyes.

Mary looked him over proudly as he sat on the opposite side of the table from his father. "I've split the kitchen wood, sir," he said. "Could I take the canoe over to the frigate launch?"

"You ha' cut the wood, but wha' about sanding out those hogsheads?"

The excitement on John's young face clouded. The launch of a newly built ship only happened a few times a year and was always a cause for festivity.

"Get those hogsheads scoured clean, and you can go."

"Yes, sir, thank you," John answered, obviously relieved that he could go once his chores were finished.

"Sir, I'll scrub the hogsheads for John if he wants to go now," James volunteered.

"No, James, I want John to do it," William said firmly.

James always went about his chores—chopping and bringing in firewood, emptying chamber pots, herding the cows back to the barn—without complaint. Mary never asked him to bring in water, thinking it too heavy on his leg, but he did it anyway. He often took on his brothers' chores as well, especially John's. Much how his father used to be himself, Mary thought with a sigh.

John stood up and left the room without any acknowledgment of James's offer, much less a glance his way.

Mary could feel James's hurt. She had always believed that John would outgrow the anger he seemed to carry toward his lame brother, but lately, she had begun to wonder.

❧

Migwah may have died long ago, but the younger sannups who used to accompany him had not forgotten Mary's kindnesses. She still found herself hostess to traveling parties of Indians from time to time. A fact that made her neighbors nervous and all the more suspicious and Rebekah's gossipy friends wink at one another. The Native visits always helped Mary feel better. They did not consider her a marked woman. William complained about the expense of feeding so many "heathen" mouths on the occasion that he heard about it through the boys or neighbors. He was never home when they came.

Little James would help his mother serve the Native men, their belts and bands bristling with weapons and the trussed remains of animals, great and small. He passed out trenchers and spoons, poured well water into cups, and hobbled about as best he could. After their guests had taken their leave, he always asked to hear stories about Migwah, the medicine man who'd given them Greylock.

Greylock, grown milder in his old age, warned of approaching Indians in a singular way: he would rise to his feet and walk over to her, all the while looking at the door in an expectant manner, his tail wagging slowly. Since Mary's attack and his subsequent disappearance, he growled wickedly at Englishmen outside of the family who approached Mary's door. The exception was Uncle Samuel. Greylock seemed to have it out for him and would leave him no peace, chasing him and his horse down the lane every time, snarling viciously. Uncle Samuel only passed by on the road now at a gallop, his coattails flying.

Mary had not felt truly well since Alexander's birth. Her bones and joints felt achy, her neck was stiff, and sometimes a sharp pain knifed its way into the base of her skull. Delusions and dizzy spells became frequent and intense. Sometimes she garnered things were happening differently inside her head as she would awaken to find herself somewhere with no idea how or why she'd gotten there. Even her family began to stare at her strangely. She tried to make excuses for herself so as not to worry them, but it certainly complicated things. Her herbs, tonic, and elixirs that worked so well for most maladies had not assuaged this one. She began to drink James's special silver solution daily. It seemed to help more than anything else. With some relief, Mary threw herself into her daily work with redoubled effort.

Her fear of her attackers' return had abated over time. Many of those responsible had moved on. Some were dead. Times had changed. Life in New England was full of trial and strife, and most English memories were blessedly short.

And as though the dog sensed there would be no return for him to protect against, Mary's beloved Greylock finally gave up his ghost—peacefully in his sleep.

Despite her illness, Mary found herself pregnant again. To her absolute joy, she gave birth to a healthy baby girl. Mary named her Judith as that had been her grandmother's Christian name. She had great hopes for her daughter. Yet the abyss soon gaped even wider between Mary and the rest of the world. Little Judith was only six months old when Mary realized its severity.

In the middle of July 1674, on a sweltering hot day, Mary accompanied nine-year-old James and almost five-year-old Alexander to the creek to cool off. She carried baby Judith against her chest in a basket, a pail of soiled breech clouts hanging from her arm. The day had been a peaceful one. Mary thought with pleasure of her son John busy clearing a new field with his father. Her sons William and Robert had both been apprenticed out and happily so—William to a blacksmith named Richard Otis at Cocheco and Robert to the Dover recorder, a man of letters and law. Robert seemed to have an aptitude for letters, much as she herself had.

At the stream, Mary set Judith down in her basket on the pine-needled bank. While the boys splashed about happily, she began to scrub the clouts in the running water, vaguely aware of a funny resonance buzzing in her ears along with her usual headache. Then a sort of floaty numbness overtook her senses, or was it the hem of her smock weighted by the water that made it hard to move?

Her dog shook himself off next to her. "Stop it, Greylock."

Things seemed dreamlike. Her eyes watched tiny gnats fly madly about in the beams of sunlight above the water; time suspended.

Where is Greylock? Wasn't he just here next to me? Then the sound of her boys' shouts and horseplay suddenly made her very nervous.

"James! Alex! Don't go 'round the bend! Stay where I can see you!"

"Mother, the whole stream is shallow!" they called back from out of sight. Shallow or not, she liked to keep an eye on them.

Her nervousness dispersed as quickly as it had come. She finished washing out her little one's clouts, leaving the pail on the bank.

The water was so cool and lovely, and she sat on the shallow bottom to bathe herself in her smock. She lathered a little of the soft gray soap, splashing water up onto her ribs and under her arms. If neighbors were to see her do this, they would think her mad indeed—but it felt so good. The current welled against the small of her back, and the sandy bottom sparkled. Minnows almost transparent, like the water itself, darted about or hung suspended in the current, barely moving their fins and mouths. She looked up again, and her eye caught sight of the swaddling pail. How lucky she was to have a daughter.

But somebody else was sitting on the bank. *Could it be?* Mary blinked. Anna Frost sat, just as she had many years ago in this very spot. Anna smiled and pointed to the pail.

The thought struck Mary's heart cold. In a panic, she scanned the stream with its swirls and eddies. Holding the hem of her smock, she splashed past her boys. They stopped their game to stare at her.

"Where's your sister?" Mary screamed in terror. The buzzing in her head was loud, so loud she could barely stand it. *Was Judith swept down toward the river? Was she drowned? How could I ever have taken my eyes off her?*

Her sons stood thigh deep in the water, just watching.

"Help!" she screamed at them hysterically. "Find your sister!"

Why are they just standing there?

"Mother," James said calmly, "Judith is on the bank, where you left her."

Mary shook her head, holding it in her hands. Sure enough, she could see Judith sleeping soundly up on the bank where she'd left her, plain as day.

What sort of devilish illusions have overtaken me? There is no sign of Anna Frost, and did I really see Greylock?

Back at home later that afternoon, Mary pulled a stool over to her herb shelves. James's silver solution just didn't seem strong enough lately. Stretching up onto the tips of her toes, her hand grasped a bottle thick with dust. Once down, she wiped it off on her apron, uncorked it, and took a mouthful. It tasted awful, metallic and chalky. The calomel Dr. Rhoades had left her long ago. She hoped it would help.

❧

It was late in the afternoon when Mary's son John paddled her across the river to Dover's Saturday market at Pommery Cove. While he waited in the canoe, Mary looked at the different fabrics the stores had on hand. She preferred to come late in the day after the crowds had gone home. After purchasing a good broadcloth to make little Judith a proper winter cloak, she tucked it into her basket and exited the shop into the alleyway. Sunlight lit the dusty lane in front of the buildings; but the alleyway, which opened to the cove, was cool and shaded.

"Mary," said a familiar voice.

She looked over and drew in her breath. John Woodman stood not five feet from her. It had been years since she had seen him—and then only at a distance. An intense spark of love shot out of her heart. She took a step backward.

The corners of John Woodman's eyes began to crinkle, and flashing his old grin, he took a step toward her. He looked much the same. It felt so odd: it was as though nothing had really changed, that they had just seen each other the week before.

He reached out and took her hand. He brought it to his lips, the old sparkle in his eyes.

His touch did what it had always done: melted her insides. Mary thought he looked more handsome than ever in his captain's military jacket, his dark hair swept back, dignified and graying at the temples.

She stood suspended; the well of her feelings rising through layers of joy, grief, and regret—oh, how she had missed him all these years!

John clasped her hand between his own. "Thy beauty has grown ever sweeter, my friend," he said. "I can't help but think on what I've missed," he added quietly, looking into her eyes.

"I'm the one who has missed, John," Mary whispered, her eyes filling with tears. "I'm the worse for it."

John's face clouded, but only momentarily. He held her hand in earnest. "My heart has always been with thee, though thou didst break it."

"Please forgive me, John."

"Father, I've found two ells that are perfect," a girl cried, dashing into the alleyway. A lively, pretty thing, she stopped short to see Mary, her mouth a perfect circle of surprise.

John let go of Mary's hand. "My daughter, Sarah," he introduced. "Sarah, this is my dear friend Goody Thompson."

The girl curtsied politely. She had her father's eyes.

John Woodman and his family still lived at Oyster River, where he had recently built a garrison. It saddened Mary to reflect on what might have been, though it was a great comfort to know that he still loved her. *Despite all the years, despite everything, he loves me! Oh, if only I knew then what I know now.*

When they at last said their goodbyes, Mary made her way to where her son John waited in the family canoe. He had seen the encounter from the dock. "Who were those people, madam?"

"An old friend of mine and his daughter. John Woodman of Oyster River. A very dear old friend."

-- 26 --

Unsettling News

Following the hanging of three Wampanoag Indians in Massachusetts that June, the Indians had first attacked one English town for revenge and then subsequently destroyed another. The colonists to the south were now at war with the Wampanoag Indians. King Philip's War, they called it. The conflict weighed heavily on the minds of most in New England. The Wampanoag had become so dependent on English goods that they'd been forced into trading their land to survive. Land that had sustained their ancestors for time out of mind was disappearing rapidly.

Even though relations with the local Indians along the Pascataqua had heretofore been mostly peaceful, palisaded garrisons began to be built in each settlement as a precaution, and the militias held training days every fortnight.

Always a friend to the English, Sagamore Rowls of Newichawannock had died. His son, Blind Will, succeeded him. Before his death, Rowls had called the local English authorities to a council, demanding that the town of Kittery reserve several hundred acres for his people as the land of their birthright had been taken from them.

Sadly, the town of Kittery refused.

❧

"Mary, it's me, Francis Small," pleaded a voice from the other side of the door.

It was late, and Mary was home alone as usual, James and Alexander asleep upstairs. It had not been easy to open the door at night since Greylock had died.

"Francis Small, who?" she asked.

"For God's sake, Mary! It's me, your old friend. May I come in?"

The memory of the Francis Small she once knew flashed before her eyes. Mary unbolted the door, but not without trepidation.

The man who stepped over the threshold was not the Francis of her memory, but one whose face was weathered and lined. He removed his hat and bowed politely, grinning his old grin minus a few of his teeth, his forehead a shiny dome in the firelight. "I was passing through on my way to Portsmouth and decided to visit the old neighborhood," he said.

Yet after Mary had served him a mug of cider and they had spoken for a while, he admitted to more. "I've just come from Emery's, where I'm staying the night. I regret to tell you that William is quite taken in drink. James put him to bed in the back room to keep him out o' trouble. He's passed out cold now." Francis looked at her intently, his expression concerned in the light of the candle that burned between them. "James Emery gave me quite an earful. Is it as bad as he says it is?"

Mary looked down at her hands folded on the tabletop, though her mind hardly registered them. How was she to answer that question? "You mean William's drinking?"

"That and everything else."

This was the Francis she remembered. Mary sighed. No one else had ever asked before, not even Hannah. He was studying her in the candlelight. She knew she looked worn, her girlish beauty long since faded. "Aye, Francis, maybe worse," she said. "I've had a time of it, as surely you can tell."

He did not blink. "Are you in want for anything?"

She shook her head, embarrassed. "We have enough, thank you."

Now that her father's second wife had died in childbed, he had begun to help Mary and her sisters again. Mary felt sorry for the death of Lucie and her newborn and sad for her father, of course, but she could not deny her relief that things were back to normal again. Lucie had pushed all of them away, and Mary still felt angry about that. Perhaps she and her baby would not have died if Mary had midwifed.

Francis looked about the darkened kitchen hall, his gaze lingering on Mary's herb chest and the shelves above it. Shelves that were not as well stocked as they used to be.

She rose to tend the fire, glad for her father's latest gift: fresh cinnamon, ginger, and nutmeg from the Caribbean. It was nice to have those seasonings back in her pots. She was a good cook. William had never once in all the years complained about his meals.

"Mmm," Francis remarked. "What's that I smell—some sort of succotash?"

"Why, yes. Wouldst thou like a bite?"

Francis certainly wouldst.

Mary laughed and gathered the bed of embers into a nice little cooking pile, enough to heat the remains of supper. William certainly wouldn't be wanting any, at least not tonight. She set the trivet pot over the embers and gave the pot a good stir.

Over his trencher of stew and cold johnnycake, Francis filled her in on the particulars of his life as well as some rather worrisome occurrences that had taken place.

"Mary, what concerns me most is a prophecy that Sagamore Rowls held in high regard," he told her. "So high a regard that his son Blind Will has recently joined our militia. A prophecy that a great war would soon take place between the English and the Indian. One that would at first go in the Indians' favor but would eventually bring about their demise. King Philip's War," he said gravely, "has all the earmarks to be that war."

"To make matters worse, a few days ago, three English sailors drowned Sagamore Squando's newborn son just north of here during a drunken argument over whether Indian newborns could swim or not. They overturned his mother's canoe with their poles in the Saco River, and the babe sank to the bottom, strapped to his board."

Mary clutched her breast with her hands. "They just left the poor child?"

"His mother fished him out, but the babe died soon after in the Indian camp."

"Oh, how tragic! I'm embarrassed to be English!" she cried.

"Now Squando has sworn himself our eternal enemy. Sakokis, the babe's mother, called upon a medeoulin for justice. He called up the Indian devil, and the river's been cursed: *as long as the English live near the river, three of their number will drown each year.*"

A sense of foreboding began to creep in from the edges of Mary's awareness, a foreboding that had been growing for some time. One she had tried to ignore. The local Abenaki Indians were still friendly enough—at least they had been the week before.

"Mark my words, Mary," Francis said grimly, "the Indians are angry here in our province too. There's more to come. We English have gained so much at their expense."

Francis soon took his leave, but the gravity of his warning hung as palpably in the air as the residual smoke from his pipe, blue and suspended below the ceiling.

Mary shuddered. How well she remembered the look of those northern warriors in the moonlight years ago. Greylock would surely come in handy now, she thought.

Feeling one of her spells coming on, she held her temples and willed herself back from the brink. Baby Judith began to cry in her cradle. Mary breastfed her daughter, listening with renewed wariness to the sounds of the summer night—chirping insects, hooting owls, the buzz of mosquitoes at the sash—alert for any sound out of the ordinary. The natives could emulate birdcalls so well that they were almost impossible to differentiate.

The next day, Mary made it a point to check the Indian cairn. The path was overgrown, hardly used since her father had married Lucie.

The cairn was still intact, but only a few old bones and rakish feathers stuck out from between the stones. This was not a good sign. Mary picked up a clamshell lying on the ground and set it back on the pile. Then thinking better of it, she put it back on the ground exactly where it had been. She resolved to check the cairn daily.

She had begun to walk back up the lane toward Sturgeon Creek when the sound of a cantering horse coming up behind her slowed to a trot.

Her skin prickled.

"Mary Thompson?" The voice immediately distressed her. The town constable reined in his horse, whose legs waltzed impatiently sideways.

Mary studied the man's stirrup strap.

"I have here a warrant for William's appearance at the next county court. Pray see to it that he's timely," the man said, handing her an all-too-familiar sealed parchment.

When the constable had cantered away around the curve up past their house, Mary unfolded the warrant. "*For breach of Sabbath and other sundry offenses*," it read. *Not again.* She sighed. William seemed to receive a summons every court session.

On a bright morning early that September, Charles Frost stood in Mary's kitchen doorway. Now a militia captain, he cut an intimidating figure in his blue military jacket with its polished brass buttons and shiny sword hilt. Lately, he had taken to visiting Mary at home, concerned for her and the children's well-being. William, of course, did not like Frost "meddling in his affairs" and had threatened him on more than one occasion. This did not deter the captain, who continued to stop by when he knew William was not at home.

Frost's visits made Mary nervous, being more than aware of the true purpose behind them. She hadn't had an Indian visitor in weeks, but what would happen if they chose to visit while Charles was there? The prospect terrified her.

"Be sure that William pays tithe at Michaelmas, Goody Thompson," Charles said. "Forgive me for saying so, but I suspect your husband purposely won't pay if he hears it from me or the constable."

"I will do what I can, Captain Frost," Mary answered, trying her best to look relaxed when she was anything but, flushed in the heat of the bake oven. *Oh, how she wished Charles would just go away!*

"Don't let me keep you from your labors," he added as if seeing for the first time what she was about.

Mary shoveled out the spent ash and charred wood with the peel while repositioning fresh hot, glowing coals. She'd spent hours that morning preparing the weekly bread and pies, which now covered the tabletop, awaiting the oven.

"I hear you were out late by yourself last night on the road to Berwick," Charles continued. Mary hadn't offered him a seat or any hospitality whatsoever, but he showed no intention of leaving. "A risky endeavor with the Indians riled up. You should never be out alone."

"Sometimes it just can't be helped, Captain Frost. There was no one at the Grant household well enough to see me home, and my own family needed me."

Mary carefully slid the pies one at a time into the center of the oven and placed the loaves of bread in last. The walk home last night had frightened her, but it was not the Indians or the beasts she feared. Mary often hid alongside the path to let other English pass her by, unaware of her presence.

She sealed off the oven with its tin-lined wooden cover and turned the hourglass over. Charles continued to stand in the doorway. She dusted off her hands. "Can I offer you a seat and a drink?"

"No, thank you." Then in an offhand manner that Mary knew was anything but, he asked the question he had come to ask. King Philip's War had everyone on alert—Francis had been quite prophetic. "Any Indians come by here lately to trade with your father?"

"Yes. Friendly Indians my father knows well." Mary hated to tell him even this much.

She still felt anguished about the deaths of Charles's mother and sister when in his presence. Mary could hardly blame him for his feelings, but it was senseless to hold all Indians accountable.

Charles's face hardened at her answer. He stared at the kitchen windows. "I see you have Indian shutters now—William's doing?"

"My father had them joined for us," she admitted.

"Ah! So your father does have concerns?"

Charles enlivened at the news, or perhaps she just imagined it. She wasn't comfortable telling him that the Indians who traded with her father had also warned her themselves. They'd sat at her board and been fed a meal. "They warned my father about parties of Wabanaki from the north," Mary replied cautiously.

The truth was the Indians didn't hold all English in the same light. Indians had a soft spot for Quakers, who treated them as equals, and for those who had always been kind, hospitable, and traded fairly. The natives had uncannily long memories, forgetting neither a kindness nor a slight.

"I would say no party of Indians is to be trusted," Captain Frost said stonily. "Goodman Wakefield thought he was safe. His house in Falmouth was found yesterday in a smoldering ruin, and inside were the remains of him and his family—seven of them. Don't fret. I will spare you the details."

Yes, Mary thought. Falmouth was to the north.

Little Judith tottered into the room from the parlour, holding her corn husk poppet. Seeing Captain Frost, she hid shyly behind Mary's skirts.

"The two young Wakefield maidens were carried away," Frost added. "For the love of God and your family, Goody Thompson, take precaution!"

As soon as he had gone, Mary sat down in the nearest chair. The green and friendly world framed by the garden door seemed suddenly incongruent. Judith, sensing her mother's angst, played quietly at her feet.

As much as Mary tried to think differently, as much as she hoped it would all settle down, something told her that what she dreaded had indeed begun.

Not long after, Mogg Heigon, a towering sachem known for wearing a gaudy red-tassled blanket and beaten copper necklace, besieged the Phillips garrison in Biddeford just to the north. And before the week was out, the violence had spread closer to home.

On September 24, Indians attacked the Tozier garrison up above Quamphegan Village on the Salmon Falls. The Kittery militia was rounded up as the bell pealed nonstop from the Dover meetinghouse across the river.

Most of the neighboring womenfolk took refuge at Major Shapleigh's, but Mary's father thought it best that his family spend the day with him at his house on the hill. Mary, her sisters, and the children watched the militia march up the lane—men and boys, friends and neighbors, William and Adrian among them, as well as Mary's son John who was only sixteen.

That afternoon dragged on much too quietly. It was the longest afternoon of Mary's life. She found herself unable to do anything except sew. Keeping her hands busy helped.

"No news is good news," her father said.

As darkness fell, the men returned. Thankfully, William and her son were among them.

Mary dressed the wounds of an eighteen-year-old maidservant, a survivor of the Tozier garrison who'd been carted back. "All us neighbors were at the Toziers'," the girl recounted, her eyes glazed from pain and fever. "Fifteen of us, I think, mostly children."

Mary winced at the lump the size of a fist underneath her patient's blood-matted hair, over which the scalp had split in a jagged grin. She gently flushed the wound with a yarrow wash. She'd never seen a living person with such head trauma. "What happened then?"

"I just happened to look outside and saw Indians all done up in war paint bearing down upon us. I screamed to warn the others and barred the door. Everyone ran out the back door to the Plaisted garrison. But 'twas too late for me to leave and follow, so I just held the door 'til the Indians cut it to pieces and brained me with a tomahawk."

"You were very brave. Luckily, they used the blunt side of a tomahawk," Mary assessed. "'Tis a miracle you've survived."

"I came to while they were looting the house and ran to the Plaisteds' myself. There were little children who couldn't run . . ." The girl let out a sob. "Two tiny maids. They killed the youngest an' took the other with them."

"Nothing to be done by the time we got thar," William explained to Mary later that evening. "Tozier's in Biddeford with Captain Wincoll and Blind Will to fight Mogg Heigon. 'Twas Hopehood and

Andrew of Saco who attacked his garrison, an' there's no sign of 'em now."

John sat scowling in the corner, oddly silent, his musket propped between his legs.

"How was it for you, John?" Mary asked.

"Militia's a bunch of cowards, madam."

"Oh, I think not, John." Mary looked at her husband and then back to her son. John's scowl deepened into a scornful disgust beyond what she'd ever seen on his youthful face.

"They climbed up the hill, looked around, and that was it!" he scoffed.

William rolled his eyes. "The savages don't need more of a reason to rile up further than they ha' done already." He turned to Mary. "Word is Hopehood's after Thomas Toogood, bent on avenging his family's death. Went to the only house tha' was full o' people to look for him, is my guess."

Mary wondered if she'd heard right. "Thomas Toogood killed Hopehood's family?"

Toogood was not one she would think capable of such a deed, being a small, slightly built man, always complaining about one thing or another. While she'd assisted his wife in childbed, he had thoroughly vexed her with his ways.

"Oh, it's been a running joke for a year or more in the taverns that Toogood is the 'best Indian fighter' in the province," William informed her. "He traded Hopehood a blanket that once covered a relative of his who died of the pox. Hopehood's entire family and half his village then died of the pox. Toogood would have gotten away with it too if he hadn't boasted and bragged 'til Hopehood got wind of it."

Nobody in Kittery slept much that night. The following day, the same marauding Indians returned and burned Captain Wincoll's house and barn up near the falls.

William and John sat in Mary's kitchen hall with Adrian Frye. Their muskets were cleaned, and the harvest was the last thing on their minds. "Truthfully, I'd like nothing better than to hand over

Thomas Toogood and be done with it!" Adrian quipped, peace-loving Quaker that he was.

"Not a bad idea," William agreed. "But then, ye might have to throw in Captain Wincoll and some others to boot. Ayh'm just glad Ayh don't ha' a bone to pick with the savages."

But William changed his tune pretty quickly when he got the news that they'd killed his old friend James Barry. A party of Indians had attacked the Newichawannock wood train on its way to the mill. Three of the nine men working were killed, one of them his Scottish comrade. The two others were the old Shapleigh servants, Eddy Walker and Samuel Biddle. All left behind families.

More news came in the following day. Kittery's Lieutenant Plaisted and twenty armed men had gone out to retrieve the bodies with a cart. As they were loading them, a group of Anasagunticooks leaped up from behind a stone wall and fired a volley. Lieutenant Plaisted and one of his sons were killed outright, and another of his sons was mortally wounded.

The death toll on the English side soon reached sixty men, women, and children in the province. Sadly, Mary watched the once-good feeling that had existed between the Pascataway English and the natives disintegrate into hatred and fear.

-- 27 --

Winter Sunset

December arrived, and with it the Indian attacks came to an abrupt end. The snow lay deep and even deeper up in the backcountry. A bad flu or measles epidemic had hit the Native warriors hard, and they'd begun to feel that the English were just plain bad luck.

This was the topic of discussion around the Thompson dinner table when the immediate family gathered at William and Mary's on Christmas Eve, Grandfather White promising to be on his best behavior toward his kin of Quaker leanings. The hearth blazed with a giant Yule log to help push back the vestiges of fear and anxiety that had plagued them for months.

"The Indians are short on corn." Mary's father spooned himself a large serving of hominy pudding, breaking its surface ofbeautifully patterned dried fruit without the least show of regret.

"Serves them right," Adrian snorted. "Now only the French would be kind enough to give them a handout. A long walk for dinner, if you ask me."

Everyone sat around a table piled high with all the makings of a Christmas feast: platters of roasted meats, roots, and squashes; a wheel of cheese that had been carefully stored away for the occasion; nutmeats; loaves of freshly baked bread; and pies, both sweet and savory—all washed down with a strong cup of spiced wassail.

"Until they buck up again in the spring and we canna get our corn planted," William said.

"We're safe enough for the most part," Mary's father assured. "They still know who their friends are."

"They consider us Quakers their brothers," Adrian agreed. Mary noticed her father give his son-in-law an acerbic eye, which Adrian deliberately ignored.

After the children had eaten their fill, they fled to the parlour to play games before a crackling fire of their own. Mary watched them contentedly from the pine-festooned doorway. Sarah's daughters, Eleanor and little Sarah, were playing nicely with her Judith. Eleanor was weaving an intricate cat's cradle to entice the little ones. James and Alexander were busy at marbles with Sarah's son, William. Her Willy and Robert were engaged in a game of nine-men's morris, one of their favorites. They had both thrived in their apprenticeships.

James looked up at her and smiled. Mary smiled back. Such a handsome young fellow James was, but then, all her children were comely. She and William had done well together that way. Her eldest sat at the hall table with the adults, old enough now to prefer their company. His laughter rose behind her, merrily echoed by others around the table. Glad as she was to hear John's laugh, Mary noticed that the sound of it brought to little James's face a look of longing. It smote her heart that John had never shown James the acceptance and approval James so desperately needed from his older brother. Mary supposed that deep down, John still blamed James for all the shame and torment he'd suffered, for how different everything had become. As for that, John was still angry with her too. He was not always as respectful as he should be, she thought sadly.

The start of a headache began to creep into the base of her skull. *No, please . . . not now.* Christmas carols were starting up around the table.

"I'm feeling sleepy from all the food and need to take a nap, if you don't mind," Mary told Hannah and hastened from the room. She hated to miss all the joyful Christmas spirit. Yet lately, when the spells came on, she had trouble thinking and speaking. She would lose vision out of the sides of her eyes and see devilish dancing lights. Her main concern was to conceal how bad she was from her family.

Even with both hearths lit below, it was cold upstairs. Pulling blankets around her wan frame, Mary shivered violently until an unfamiliar blackness exploded in her brain, and she lost track of everything.

As January began, Mary was not herself at all. She kept inside by the hearth if she could help it, staring off into space for long periods of time. All of her joints were stiff and painful and it sometimes felt hard to move, much less walk. She hadn't the energy to keep her supply of tonic up or even to brew herself any medicine. All the energy she could muster went to taking care of her children and cooking meals.

James, Alexander, and one-year-old Judith were her constant companions. James proved a great help with little Judith, carrying her around on his hip as best he could with his lame foot. He'd never been to school, but Mary had taught him to read and write herself. William said that Alexander didn't need to go to school either, that James could teach him well enough.

Sometimes Mary would awaken from a trance to find herself in strange circumstance. The pot in her hearth full of stones pulled from the riverbank and her hands scratched and bleeding, or her apron covered in wood ash and no memory of why. These times, she would notice James and Alexander watching her with fear marring their young faces.

Toward the end of January, shortly after Mary's forty-fourth birthday during a spell of deep and cracking cold, a sledge driver passing to Berwick stopped and pounded on the Thompson door. Rebekah's son was ill. Rebekah needed help.

"Elias must be seriously ill," Mary told the boys. Rebekah had never called on her before.

William and John were off cutting king's pines, and Willy and Robert were back with their masters across the river. The younger boys would be fine left at home. Only little Judith needed a caretaker despite how good James was with her.

Mary donned her wool cloak and wrapped a scarf around her face. She felt weak herself, and her head ached, but Elias was Rebekah's only child—how could she not go? She bundled little Judith in a blanket and carried her over to her aunt Sarah's not far down the lane. She kissed her daughter's soft rounded cheeks, all rosy from the cold.

"Mama, mama, mama," Judith chanted.

Sarah looked at her aghast from the doorway, an icy wind blasting them on the threshold. "To Rebekah's on such a day?"

Mary handed her Judith and left before her sister could protest further.

Back at home, Mary reached for the last bottle of her tonic. She dusted it off and placed it in her medicine basket with its assortment of herbs. Entrusting James to keep an eye on his younger brother, she set out on foot along the lane, her hands gathered in a wool muff for warmth.

The surface of the snow was a hard, frozen crust and made for slow progress and treacherous footing. Numbness began to creep into her toes but she pushed herself onward. At Cammock's Creek she crossed the fording place by the mill, its giant wheel frozen solid, and called in at Kittery House to warm herself. She found Alice Shapleigh and her servants spinning wool at the hearth.

"Oh! Mary Thompson, what brings you out in such weather?" Alice gasped, welcoming her.

"'Tis Rebekah's son. I fear he's very ill."

"Oh dear. There's an awful distemper this season. We heard this morning that some have died across the river." Alice Shapleigh shook her head. "What troubled times we live in."

Mary gratefully accepted a hot elderberry and rosehip tisane sweetened with honey. As soon as she had warmed enough, she wrapped herself back up. Alice was one of the few who never treated her any differently in public than she did in private.

"Please give my regards to Nicolas," Mary thanked her hostess.

"Yes, dear, I will. 'Tis folly the menfolk are out cutting mast pines. Brrrr!"

From Kittery House, the journey to Rebekah's was another mile distant, up on a hillside above the river, not far from the old Frost homestead in the Baylands. Just when Mary felt like she couldn't survive the cold a minute longer, she made it to Rebekah's door.

Rebekah looked haggard. "You came," she whispered, her eyes glistening.

Elias had been ill for days and did not appear to have much time left. Now a fully grown young man, he looked a lot like his mother. Mary knelt beside him. "You should have fetched me sooner," she rebuked gently.

"Yes . . . I know . . ." Rebekah began to weep.

"I will do what I can. First, help me get some tonic into him."

The two women, weak in body as they both were, managed to prop Elias upright. He choked and spluttered but the tonic went in and stayed down, as did the strong infusion of goldenseal, yarrow, and wood betony Mary gave him. "He will need to drink a cup every two hours," she instructed.

Rebekah nodded, her gaze fixed on her son, her manner softened in the face of losing her only child. It was the worst thing a mother could experience, and Mary would not wish it on anyone. In light of Rebekah's change in attitude, Mary thought this would be a good a time to ask something she'd never understood.

"Tell me, Rebekah," she said, "what has given you cause to treat me as your enemy as long as we have known each other?"

Rebekah glanced up and then away. "I know I have not always been so . . . *kind*," she said slowly.

"*Kind?*" Mary replied.

Rebekah silently studied part of the counterpane that covered Elias. When she spoke again, her voice was low and thick. "My father hardly cared that I existed. He used to beat my madam cruelly," she said. "One day, he came after me and my sister . . ." She shuddered, her fingertips finding their way to the faded burn that still scarred her jaw.

Mary listened, feeling her own anger dissolve as she absorbed Rebekah's words.

"Your father adored you." Rebekah looked straight at Mary, intense pain and longing in her eyes. "You had what I wanted more than anything else in the world." She swallowed. "What I never could have . . ." Her face contracted, and she turned away.

With this understanding, the tensions Mary felt evaporated into a lingering compassionate sadness. The wind whistled without, shaking the timbers of the house.

"Aye, Rebekah," she answered. "I may have had the love of my father, but certainly not my freedom or self-respect. I sacrificed my beloved for my father's love. Aye, I sacrificed my life for it. I didn't know any better at the time."

They sat in silence for a while.

Then Mary drew a glass vial of flower elixir from her basket and handed it to Rebekah. "This too will help Elias. Just a few drops on his temples and under his tongue should do it. You need some as well."

Rebekah nodded, her expression reflecting the vestiges of hope and good feeling that Mary knew to be crucial.

Mary stayed the rest of the afternoon until she saw signs of Elias's improvement. Then leaving Rebekah supplied with plenty of medicine, she packed her basket and tied on her cloak. "Can I fetch you in water or wood before I go?"

"No, thank you, Mary. I can get it myself. You've done enough already."

Words like these from Rebekah!

Wrapped in her cloak and woolen muff, Mary stepped back out into the cold, warmed by the strange new peace that flowed between them.

"Wait, Mary," Rebekah said. "Before you go . . . there's something else I need to tell you."

The way home felt less difficult. The wind had tapered off and night was coming on. Orange streaks of setting sun tinged the surface of the violet snow and frozen river, making it easier to navigate around the deep holes where one might, through haste or carelessness, break a leg.

Elias had a fighting chance, and to have come to such a new understanding with Rebekah was astounding. But it was the last thing Rebekah had told her that had the blood racing through Mary's veins.

It could prove her innocence and clear the stigma from William and the children! Her whole body shook from the possibility.

So engaged was her mind that Mary hardly noticed the worsening of the headache she'd suffered all day. She picked her way across the mill dam fording place with just enough daylight left to avoid the slick icy patches and stepped safely onto the north bank of Cammock's Creek.

There was only a moment's warning—it had never happened so suddenly. Should she risk going back over the ford to the Shapleighs'? Or press on to the Booths', who'd bought the Mavericks' place?

Then the dreaded black explosion in her head reared up and struck.

Her beautiful green silk shoes—Mary hadn't worn them in such a long, long time, but she was now. The lush summer meadow down by the river looked lovely. Everything gleamed with brilliance. Her mother stood next to her, smiling, holding a little babe in her arms. *I must be dreaming.* Migwah too was there, smiling. Mary felt strangely at peace. Actually, she felt waves of joy. *Can this be real?* With a yelp, Greylock jumped up on her, his tail wagging nonstop. But it wasn't until Mary's grandmother reached out to embrace her that she finally understood.

❧

John Thompson stood near the door of his parents' parlour, feeling numb. His mother was dying—of that there was no question. From what Mr. Booth and his servants could tell, she had lain in the snow for hours, having fallen off a small precipice near their house. She had not regained consciousness, and it was now morning. John and his father had gotten the news at their camp in the dead of night and had rushed home as fast as they could.

"She must have had one of her spells," his aunts whispered. "'Twas Mr. Booth's hound that found her and set to baying. They say she was off the lane a ways into the woods."

John's younger brothers knelt by the bedstead. James held their mother's hand, his forehead on the counterpane and Alexander by his side. Willy and Robert sat nearby, fetched from their masters. Little Judith was in Aunt Sarah's arms.

"Ma-ma-ma," she said, impatiently reaching her tiny arms for her mother.

Grandfather White stood reading scripture. On the end of his long straight nose, a tear clung, quivering, until he wiped it away with his handkerchief.

There wasn't a dry eye in the room other than John's own. Their father sat at the foot of the bedstead, staring at the floor, face in his hands.

"She's gone," someone said.

Suddenly, John had to leave. He didn't know how he felt except that he didn't feel well. He couldn't breathe. He stumbled through the kitchen and out through the dooryard, the soft hiss of falling snow a deafening rush in his ears. Walking over to a tree, he leaned his forehead on his forearm against the trunk. He could not remember the last time he'd cried. In a rush of anger, he kicked at the tree with his boot.

"Good morning. Is that you, John Thompson?" rang a woman's voice.

John glanced around to see his great-aunt Rebekah standing behind him, a look of surprise upon her face. He turned back toward the tree.

"I've come to see your mother. Is she at home?"

He shook his head no, closing his eyes. He could barely speak. Pressure crushed his chest and his throat as he got the words out. "She's *dead*."

There was a stunned silence behind him.

"*Dead*?" his great-aunt said.

Still facing the tree, tears began to flow down John's cheeks.

A minute went by. The distant sound of a wail could be heard from the house.

"I was just going . . . going . . . to thank her," Rebekah stammered, her voice sounding lost. "She saved Elias's life yesterday."

John didn't know why the annoying woman continued to stand behind him. He wanted to be left alone. Couldn't she see?

Rebekah spoke again. "Your mother carried off now, as she was then . . ."

"*What?*" John demanded. He whirled around. Red-eyed and snuffling, he faced his great-aunt, knowing the grief in his face brutal to behold. He didn't care. "*What did you just say*?"

Rebekah looked away uneasily before her eyes swept back to meet his. "She didn't tell you? Years ago, after dark one evening, I witnessed a group of men force their way into your father's house and carry your mother away against her will. You were just a little boy. I was standing about where you are now, coming from your grandmother's to fetch a loom sley."

John couldn't believe what he was hearing. Inside the enormity of his grief, something dark and heavy moved aside. He'd never understood what had happened that night. He'd been so small. All he remembered was that his mother had screamed for him to stay upstairs and Greylock had been snarling.

"I told your mother what I saw—that I knew she was innocent. But there was nothing I could have done," she explained nervously. "I was afraid for my own life . . . I'm sorry." With that, Rebekah turned and began to walk away.

"*Why*?" John burst out angrily, taking several steps in her direction. "*Why did it happen*?"

Rebekah paused. She looked back over her shoulder and shook her head. "Your mother was a good healer, John. Too good, perhaps."

As the meaning of her words sank in, John watched Rebekah's cloaked figure walk away through the falling snow, which began to whirl thicker and thicker around him as he stood rooted to the spot.

"John?" came a sorrowful little voice from behind him.

He turned. James, whose young face held indescribable pain, stood behind him in the snow. Without hesitation, John took a step, opened his arms, and embraced his brother for the first time in his life. He lifted James off his feet, hugging him, while the tears flowed freely from both of them.

A September Evening

I parked my car along the side of a neighboring street, glad for a new moon and the reassuring cover of darkness. However, even at eleven o'clock at night, I found the house that now occupied the land lit like a city cathedral. I crossed the lawn, a velvety green during the day, hoping I wouldn't be seen. Truth being stranger than fiction, I dreaded having to explain my business to the homeowner or a police officer. The night felt cold, and I shivered.

"You already know where Mary's buried," the psychic had told me.

Having asked the divine for guidance, I was not disappointed. As I stepped onto the place where my eyes and heart have always been drawn in passing, a wave of energy radiated out of the ground. The energy encompassed me—cellular, undeniable, drawing my body magnetically. I knelt reverently and placed my hands upon the dew-wet grass. The love pouring out of the earth was *astounding.* I certainly did not expect this! I had thought that I would feel profound sadness. Could I be imagining it? I stepped away into comparative nothingness, and my heart could not wait to step back again onto such sacred ground. Above, thousands of silvery stars graced the sky, shimmering magically in witness.

I knew then and there, without the shadow of doubt, as much as I had ever known anything, that I had found Mary's grave—*my* grave. I had come full circle; a special gift indeed.

The End.

Postscript

After Mary's death, the children's aunt Hannah came to keep house. Mary's body was buried quickly and without ceremony in a secret grave in the dead of night, to be exhumed and buried privately when the ground thawed. Many believed her seizures were proof she was possessed by the devil, and William was afraid that her grave might be disturbed. Within a few days of her death, William burned all her writings. He wanted to release her memory and was also afraid of what the papers could reveal.

That spring, William saw a beautiful widow crossing the Cammock's Creek fording place and fell in love with her. He began to court her, gifting her his mare. They were married soon after. William moved his three youngest children down to his new wife's house in the Baylands on part of her brother's estate, where they began a new life together. Short it was to be, for on a sultry summer's night, after only a few weeks of marriage, William suffered a heart attack in bed with his new wife and died.

For a while, it looked like James, Alexander, and Judith would be provided for by their stepmother until a fever at the end of that summer claimed her life. Unfortunately, the woman's full-grown son, known as Black Joe—a one-eyed pirate of violent repute—seized control of her property, including what had been William's. The three younger Thompson children fled to their grandfather's and were taken under the wing of their aunt Hannah, who soon married a young man named Robert Allen. Their childhood home near Cold Harbor was left fairly empty, containing only four small children's blankets and some old wooden forms, what William had left behind when he married the widow, as was documented in a court record of William's remaining estate.

John Thompson, old enough to farm his father's plantation by 1677, married Sarah Woodman, the daughter of Mary's beloved, John Woodman, consummating what their parents could not. In

1708, John and James Thompson sold their father's old homestead to their cousin Francis Allen. In 1715, John Thompson conveyed his father's old fifty-acre grant beyond Cocheco Log Swamp to John Tuttle, an early settler whose family still farms and owns much land at Dover Point to this day. In 1716, John Thompson was of Berwick. He fathered seven children.

William Thompson Jr. was apprenticed to the blacksmith Richard Otis of Cocheco years before the treacherous Indian attack upon the Otis garrison and married Mary Lovering. He was wounded in the Indian Wars. He settled in Somersworth, New Hampshire, and had at least one child, William, who survived to adulthood.

Robert Thompson, apprenticed to a man of letters, Tobias Hanson of Dover, died young. He was strangled to death with his nightshirt when found asleep in bed with his girlfriend by her furious brother.

James Thompson became a tailor, married his cousin Elizabeth Frye, and fathered no fewer than thirteen children. He resided near his brother Alexander in Brixham, just past the northwest branch of the York River, eventually moving north with his family to New Meadows in Brunswick, Maine. His grandson was Brigadier General Samuel Thompson of the American Revolution.

Alexander Thompson, granted land in the Brixham area of Kittery in 1698, lived out his life there as a planter, marrying Hannah Curtis of York and fathering nine children. A historic house on Brixham Road that dates from the 1720s and is currently a bed-and-breakfast was likely Alexander's homestead, as there is an old Thompson burial ground up behind it. It is also likely that the foundation and hearth of this house are much older and contain part of Alexander's house.

There has been much speculation as to the disappearance of the youngest Thompson, Judith, to the extent that she might have been raised by the Allen family under a pseudonym. Unfortunately, according to my sources, she was run over by a horse cart when she was nine years old, chasing a piece of paper blowing in the wind. It may have been a blessing that she escaped the Indian attacks of 1692.

Major Richard Waldron, who founded the town of Cocheco—modern-day Dover, New Hampshire—was not so fortunate. In a 1689 revenge raid, the Indians held him down upon his dining room table, each canceling out their individual account with a slashed cut across his chest. Then they continued to torture him, cutting off his hands and other appendages before forcing him to fall upon his own sword.

Mary's father died some time after February 8, 1678 or 1679, possibly close to the following transcription date of October 11, 1681. Much of his original land holdings had already been divided among his daughters' individual families, documented by records as well as by a surviving map. At his death, he left all of his remaining goods, chattels, and land to his daughter Hannah Allen, her husband, and children for posterity. His final will follows at the end of this book.

Epilogue

I am five years old, swinging in my backyard on a sunny June day. My legs propel me higher and higher, the deep blue sky and big puffy white clouds are drawing me upward, and my spirit is soaring. Until I hear my kindergarten teacher's voice in my head saying, "We are no more significant than a tiny grain of sand in this vast universe." It was the lesson from a story she had read to us in class.

My spirit stopped mid-flight at such a thought. Out of curiosity, I tried it on. I allowed the swing to slow and contracted my awareness back down into my body, and smaller still, imagining myself as a tiny grain of sand lost in the universe. It did not feel good. Matter of fact, it felt so untrue and repressive that part of me got very angry. *No!* I silently cried. I knew differently—I had just experienced it.

I sent my awareness back up into those clouds and kept expanding it outward. It felt much better. Suddenly I was not just an insignificant grain of sand, but rather the opposite: *I was everything.* Tapping into this place, I could feel a direct connection to the *All.* The I AM presence we all share. I was every little grain of sand and everything else besides. I even knew what a random molecule of energy was doing on the other side of the universe, because I could feel it.

Our separation is an illusion. Every atom in the universe is part of us, part of the whole. It is time for humanity's negative expression to be brought out to face the light, to heal and transmute, and for us to move on into the future of our dreams and a new age.

Bring me my Bow of Burning gold:
Bring me my Arrows of desire:
Bring me my Spear: O clouds unfold!
Bring me my Chariot of fire.

~William Blake

Author's Note

This work of reimagined historical fiction is based upon a true story from the seventeenth-century Piscataqua. Most of my characters were real people, albeit fictionalized. I have used the surviving record and other written documentation to capture authentic elements of their personalities and lives. My impetus for telling Mary's story was not only to give Mary a voice and to heal her experience, but to also share the knowledge of all that I uncovered and to better understand Mary's life in the grand scheme of things. Mary White was my great-grandmother of eleven generations ago. All is forgiven. Collectively, we have been and done everything over our eons of existence. After three hundred and fifty years, I am likely related to most of my characters either by blood or through marriage. DNA analysis has also positively identified Eastern Woodland Indian in my genome, which my family records date from the time of the American revolution.

I want to thank all those who helped nourish this story from its beginnings. The Big House writers' dog and pony show, who have kept me enormously entertained and blissed with their talent. My friends and family—especially my children, Alexy and Max, who shared a lot of their mother growing up with her writing. They did have fun, helping to explore historic sites on foot and by canoe and enjoyed a seventeenth-century banquet at Plimouth Plantation. I want to thank all the gifted individuals whose insight helped illuminate Mary's life and piece together the truth, and for the support of my three illustrious writing guides, who mean the world to me. A big thank you to my editors, and to all who read my manuscript and gave feedback over the years, as well as the the helpful museum, historical society, and library staff both in Old England and New England. To my soulmate, Michael Nelson, a National Book Award for Poetry winner and children's author, who read Mary's story in its completed form and cried. Finally, to my father, for his limitless encouragement and support.

I hope you enjoy this glimpse of seventeenth-century New England through Mary's eyes. It is my hope that my readers will carry away with them the wisdom that Mary gleaned as well as a richer sense of the Piscataqua region and how it was at the time of our forebears' arrival. Interestingly enough, many of our struggles then in this early modern period are still being brought to the light of day and worked through in the present time.

To all Christian people to whom this present writing shall Come, & appeare: Know ye that I John White of Could Harbour on Kittery side in the County of Yorke now in the Massatusetts Jurisdiction, sendeth greeting; Know ye that I John White father unto Hannah Allen, wife of Robert Allen, for diverse good Causes & Considerations, besides my natural love which I bear to my natural Child Hannah Allen, do give, & for ever give unto Robert Allen and his wife, & his children which shee now hath, by Robert Allen only, more especially after his decease, & my daughter Hannah, I do design & bequeath what I give unto them, unto Francis Allen son unto Robert Allen after my decease.

I do freely give all my Estate to my son & daughter, during their lives, & after their decease. I do order as is above expressed, to my grandson Francis, or the next Eldest Child if it please God to take him away, that shall succeede him in ages, that is to say my house & land, & all my land & housing, which I now have in the Towne shipe of Kittery, & all my Cattle & kind of what nature souer, with all the Moveeables, within doores or with out, to bee for the soole & proper use of my son & daughter during their lives, after my death, only one heffer which I now have in being, to bee at my disposeing, before my death, & for all & every thing after my death (excepting the Heffer I do freely give unto my son & daughter Hannah Allen, & her heirs for ever as is above expressed) & for all other Children or Children's Children, this my deed of gift shall Cut them from demanding any thing from my son & daughter or recovering any part of that which was my Estate or now in my possession, that is my sons sons after my death, but they shall peaceably enjoy them, & their heirs forever, but dureing my natural life I will have my being in & upon the above expressed Estate, & after my death to bee theirs, how is above writing, in witness whereunto I have set my hand & seale this first of November one thousand six hundred seventy eight.

The marke of John White

The above written John White acknowledged the above written deede of Gyft with his hand & seale to it, to bee his act & deede this 8th day of Febru: 1678: before mee
John Wincoll Associate

A true Coppy of this Deede above written transcribed, & with originall Compared this 11th day October 1681: p Edw: Rishworth Re: Cor:

Made in the USA
Middletown, DE
09 May 2021

39264267R00215